T. W. Speight

The Grey Monk

Table of contents

CHAPTER I.
CHAPTER II.
CHAPTER III.
CHAPTER IV.
CHAPTER V.
CHAPTER VI.
CHAPTER VII.
CHAPTER VIII.
CHAPTER IX.
CHAPTER X.
CHAPTER XI.
CHAPTER XII.
CHAPTER XIII.
CHAPTER XIV.
CHAPTER XV.
CHAPTER XVI.
CHAPTER XVII.
CHAPTER XVIII.
CHAPTER XIX.
CHAPTER XX.
CHAPTER XXI.
CHAPTER XXII.
CHAPTER XXIII.
CHAPTER XXIV.
CHAPTER XXV.
CHAPTER XXVI.
CHAPTER XXVII.
CHAPTER XXVIII.
CHAPTER XXIX.
CHAPTER XXX.
CHAPTER XXXI.
CHAPTER XXXII.
CHAPTER XXXIII.
CHAPTER XXXIV.
CHAPTER XXXV.
CHAPTER XXXVI.
CHAPTER XXXVII.
CHAPTER XXXVIII.
CHAPTER XXXIX.
CHAPTER XL.
CHAPTER XLI.

CHAPTER XLII.
CHAPTER XLIII.
CHAPTER XLIV.
CHAPTER XLV.
CHAPTER XLVI.
CHAPTER XLVII.
CHAPTER XLVIII.
CHAPTER XLIX.
CHAPTER L.
CHAPTER LI.

CHAPTER I.

ALEC'S SENTENCE.

It was a wild and stormy October night. The big moon-faced clock in the entrance-hall, in its slow and solemn fashion, as of a horologe that felt the burden of its years, had just announced the hour of eleven.

In his study alone, busy among his coins and curios, sat Sir Gilbert Clare of Withington Chase, Hertfordshire, and Chase Ridings, Yorkshire, a handsome, well-preserved man, in years somewhere between fifty and sixty. He had a tall, thin, upright figure, strongly marked features of an aquiline type, a snow-white moustache, and an expression at once proud and imperious.

It would, indeed, have been difficult to find a prouder man than Sir Gilbert. He was proud of the long line of his ancestors, of the brave men and beautiful women who, from their faded frames in the picture gallery, seemed to smile approval on the latest representative of their race. He was proud of the unsullied name which had come down to him from them, on which no action of his had ever cast the shadow of a stain. He was proud of the position, which he accepted as his by right, in his native county; he was proud of his three sturdy boys, at this hour wrapped in the sleep of innocent childhood. But his pride was strictly locked up in his own bosom. No syllable ever escaped him which told of its existence. To the world at large, and even to the members of his own household, he was a man of a quick and irascible temper, of cold manners and unsympathetic ways.

Proud as Sir Gilbert had just cause for being, there was one point, and one that could in no wise be ignored, at which his pride was touched severely.

His eldest son and heir was a disappointment and a failure. He had fought against the knowledge as long as it had been possible for him to do so, but some months had now gone by since the bitter truth had forced itself upon him in a way he could no longer pretend to ignore. He had caused private inquiries to be made, the result of which had satisfied him that, from being simply a good-natured harum-scarum spendthrift, the young man was gradually degenerating into a betting man and a turf gambler of a type especially obnoxious to the fastidious baronet. He told himself that he would almost as soon have had his son become a common pickpocket.

It never entered his mind to suspect that the evidence of Alec's delinquencies which had been laid before him, and to obtain which he had paid a heavy price, might, to some extent, have been manufactured; that the shadows of the picture might have been purposely darkened in order that he might be supplied with that which he presumably looked for. He had accepted it in full and without question.

It had been Alec's misfortune to get mixed up with a fast set while at college, and he seemed never to have quite broken with them afterwards.
At the Chase he and his stepmother had not got on well together--for the present Lady Clare was the baronet's second wife--and when, shortly after coming of age, he announced his intention of making his home, for a time at least, with some of his mother's relatives in London, Sir Gilbert had offered no opposition to the arrangement, for he was wise enough to recognise that two such opposite dispositions as those of his present wife and his eldest son could not possibly agree.
Then it presently came to his ears that Alec had gone into bachelor quarters of his own, after which came a long course of extravagances and debts of various kinds, such as well-to-do fathers have had to put up with from spendthrift sons for more centuries than history can tell us of.
Twice he had paid Alec's debts and started him afresh with a clean slate; but on the second occasion he had given him plainly to understand that he must look for no further help in that line, but confine himself strictly to the fairly liberal allowance which had been settled on him when he came of age. Despite the determination thus expressed, no very long time had elapsed before a couple of tradesmen's accounts for considerable sums were received by the baronet, with a request for an early liquidation of the same--not, however, sent by Alec, but by the creditors themselves. Instead of returning the bills to their senders, as most parents would have done, with a curt disavowal of all liability, Sir Gilbert chose rather to confiscate his son's allowance to the amount of the debts in question.
From that time, now upwards of half a year ago, there had been no communication of any kind between father and son. Alec, however, was not left wholly without means, he having still an income of a hundred and eighty pounds a year, derivable from funded property left him by his mother.
Sir Gilbert had had an agreeable surprise in the course of the day with the evening of which we are now concerned, and yet it was a surprise not untinged with sadness.
His old friend Mr. Jopling, like himself an ardent numismatist and collector, had died a few weeks before, much to the baronet's regret. To-day there had reached him a tiny packet, forwarded by Mr. Jopling's executors, containing a couple of rare coins bequeathed him by his dead friend. One of them was a gold stater of Argos, with the head of Hera, the reverse being Diomedes carrying the palladium; while the other was a scarce fifty-shilling piece of Cromwell. Sir Gilbert had long envied his friend the possession of them, and now they were his own; therefore was the feeling with which he regarded them one of mingled pleasure and pain.
He had devoted the evening to a rearrangement of the contents of some of his cases and cabinets and to deciding upon a resting-place for his newly-acquired treasures.
It had been a labour of love. But, for all that, his thoughts every now and again would keep reverting from the pleasant task he had set himself to his eldest son;

for this was the latter's birthday, a fact which the father could not forget, although he would fain have kept it in the background of his memory. On just such a wild night twenty-four years before, had John Alexander Clare been born. With what bright hopes, with what glowing expectations he had been welcomed on the stage of life, Sir Gilbert alone could have told. A groan broke involuntarily from his lips when he pictured in thought the difference between then and now. His heart was very bitter against his son.

The night was creeping on apace.

In the great house everybody was in bed save the baronet, who was addicted to solitude and late hours. Outside, at recurring intervals, the wind blew in great stormy gusts, which anon died down to an inarticulate sobbing and wailing, as it might be of some lost spirit wandering round the old mansion, seeking ingress but finding none. There were voices in the wide-mouthed chimney; the rain lashed the windows furiously; by daybreak the trees would be nearly bare and all the woodways be covered by a sodden carpet of fallen leaves. Summer was dead indeed.

Suddenly, in a lull of the gale, Sir Gilbert was startled into the most vivid wakefulness by an unmistakable tapping at one of the two long windows which lighted the room. He listened in rigid silence till the tapping came again. Then he crossed to the window whence the sound had proceeded, and after having drawn back the curtains and unbarred and opened the shutters, he demanded in his sternest tones:

"Who is there?"

"It is I--Alec, your son," came the reply in a well-remembered voice.

Sir Gilbert drew a long breath and paused for a space of half-a-dozen seconds. Then he unhasped and flung wide the window, and John Alexander Clare, the scapegrace heir, rain-soaked and mud-bedraggled, stepped into the room.

His father closed the window after him, while Alec proceeded to relieve himself of his soft broad-brimmed hat and the long cloak which had enveloped him from head to foot.

Like his father, the heir of Withington Chase was tall and slender and as upright as a dart. He had the same aquiline, high-bred cast of features, but in his case there was lacking that expression of hauteur and domineering pride, which to a certain extent marred those of the elder man.

Sir Gilbert's eyes in colour were a cold bluish-grey, and, though not really small, had the appearance of being so owing to their being so deep set under his heavy brows and to his habit of contracting his lids when addressing himself to anyone. Alec's hazel eyes, inherited from his mother, were large, clear, and open as the day. The baronet's lips under his white moustache were thin and hard-set, and his rare smile was that of a cynic and a man who loved to find food for his sardonic humour in the faults and follies of his fellow-creatures. His son's mouth, if betraying a touch of that weakness which as often as not is the result of an overplus of good-nature, was yet an eminently pleasant one, while his smile was frankness itself. His cheeks were a little more sunken than they ought to have been at his age, and there were dark half-circles under his eyes, which seemed to hint at late hours and mornings that bring a headache. His hair, which he wore short and parted in the middle, was in colour a dark reddish-brown, as were also his short pointed beard and small moustache.

"And to what, sir, am I indebted for the honour of a visit at this untimely hour?" inquired Sir Gilbert in his most freezing accents, as his coldly critical eyes took in his son from head to foot.

Alec coloured for a moment and bit his lip, as if to keep down some rising emotion. Then, in a voice of studied calmness, he said, "Perhaps, sir, I may be permitted to take a seat; for, in point of fact, I am dead tired, and have much to say to you."

The baronet waved his son to a chair, and took another himself some distance away.

"I am here to-night, father, to make a confession."

"I presumed as much the moment I set eyes on you."

"I am afraid you will term it a very disgraceful confession."

"I have not much doubt on that point," responded the baronet grimly. "Disgrace and you seem to have gone hand in hand for a long time past."

"Folly, but not disgrace, father. At the worst----"

The baronet held up his hand. "I am not used to such hair-splitting distinctions. You may call it by what term you like, t, my way of thinking, it is nothing less than a disgrace when a young man permits himself to contract debts which he has no reasonable prospect--nay, which, in many cases, he has no intention of liquidating. But proceed, sir."

Apparently Alec found it no easy matter to proceed. The story he had to tell was, without doubt, a sufficiently discreditable one, and such as might well cause him to hesitate before he could summon up sufficient courage to enter on its recital. Put into the fewest possible words it came to this: he had lost heavily over a certain race, and had no means of meeting his liabilities. In three days' time, unless his father would come to his help, he would be posted as a defaulter, which, for a man in his position, meant outlawry and social extinction. He got through his confession somehow, speaking in hard, dry tones, almost as if he were relating an incident which referred to some stranger and in which he had no personal concern. He was leaning forward with his elbows on his knees, his fingers interlocked, and his eyes apparently intent on taking in the pattern of the carpet.

A harsh rasping laugh broke from Sir Gilbert.

"And are you really such an imbecile as to have come all the way to Withington, and on such a night as this, indulging yourself with the hope that I would as much as lift my little finger if by so doing I could avert the disgrace--the infamy--which you have wilfully accumulated on your worthless head? If you laid any such flattering unction to your soul, you can dismiss it at once. There is the window, sir; you can depart by the way you came."

Alec drew himself up, and for the first time looked his father straight in the face

with the old clear, unwavering look, which the latter remembered so well in him as a boy.
"You wrong me somewhat, sir," he said, with a bitter smile. "When I ventured to intrude upon you it was without the slightest expectation that, for my sake alone, you would move hand or foot to extricate me from the predicament in which my folly had landed me; but it seemed to me that you might, perhaps, be moved to do so by a consideration of a very different kind."
Sir Gilbert's heavy brows came together.
"I am certainly unaware of any such consideration as the one you speak of. But perhaps you will condescend to enlighten me."
"It has seemed to me, sir, that you might, for the sake of the family good name, do that which you refused to do to save the reputation of your eldest son."
An involuntary "Ah!" escaped the baronet. It was a view of the question which had not struck him before. For a minute or two he sat in frowning silence. Then he said:
"And are yours the lips that dare to put forward a plea for safeguarding that good name which you have so infamously chosen to imperil? Oh, this seems to me the vilest hypocrisy!"
Alec raised his hands with a deprecatory gesture, but did not attempt to vindicate himself by a word. Sir Gilbert rose and crossed to the window by which his son had entered. The shutters had not been replaced, and he stood gazing out into the night for what to Alec seemed a long time. The gale had temporarily abated, torn and jagged masses of cloud were hurrying across the sky as if hastening to some rendezvous, revealing translucent depths of moonlit space between their severed fringes.
"What is the sum of your liability in connection with this last most discreditable affair?" demanded Sir Gilbert, after a time, without turning his head.
"Six hundred pounds."
Again there was a space of silence.
Then the baronet said:
"If I consent to take this liability on my shoulders, it will not be for your sake--that I hope I have already made sufficiently clear--but to save the name of one of the oldest and most honoured families in the kingdom from being dragged through the mire. But not even for that will I do this thing without exacting certain terms from you in return."
"You have but to name your terms, sir, to secure for them an immediate acceptance."
He rose and crossed to the chimney-piece, and taking up a small ornament, examined it for a moment or two. Then, replacing it, he turned and confronted Sir Gilbert, who had now returned to his seat.
"Father," said Alec, and it was the first time he had uttered the word since his arrival, "although it may seem a hard thing for you to credit, I assure you most solemnly that I shall derive infinitely more pleasure from the fact that the honour of the Clares will suffer no stain through my folly, than from the

knowledge that my debt has been paid, and that I shall no longer have to fear being posted as a defaulter."

Then, after a momentary pause, he resumed:

"Without wishing in the least to try to extenuate my criminal folly in your eyes, which I am quite aware would be a useless effort, I may yet be allowed to remark that when I entered upon the transaction which has landed me in my present quagmire, I had every possible assurance a man can have in a matter into which the element of chance at all enters, that, instead of being a loser to the extent of six hundred pounds, I should be in pocket to the amount of three thousand. It was one of those things, which, at the time, seemed to me almost as sure as death. The commonest justice to myself compels me to say as much as that."

He had spoken slowly and quietly, giving its due emphasis to every word, but he might have been addressing himself to a graven image for any notice his father condescended to accord his words.

He now went back to his seat. Sir Gilbert had removed his chair, so that an oblong mahogany table now divided him and his son. Resting his arms on this and leaning forward a little, Alec said:

"And now, sir, will you be good enough to specify the terms which you propose to exact from me?

"My terms are these," replied Sir Gilbert, in the same tone that he might have used had he been laying down the conditions of a lease with his land-steward: "You will at once leave England, not to return to it without my express sanction. Further, should you choose to reside on the Continent, it must be in some place out of the ordinary lines of travel, where there will be little likelihood of your being seen or recognised by anyone who has known you in England. In return, I will relieve you of your liabilities of every kind whatsoever, and will, in addition, make you an allowance of two hundred and fifty pounds per annum, which shall be remitted to you quarterly through my solicitor, Mr. Page."

By the time Sir Gilbert had finished speaking, Alec's face had paled perceptibly. He lay back in his chair, and for a few seconds his eyes, wide open though they were, saw nothing of all that was around him. His heart beat painfully; he was as a man afflicted with vertigo.

That his father's conditions would be hard, he--knowing the man--had not doubted, but the reality dumfounded him.

Sir Gilbert was toying with his watch-guard, his eyes apparently fixed on a corner of the ceiling.

"Well, sir, have you nothing to say in answer to my proposition?" at length he asked, bringing his gaze back to his son's face. "Do you agree to my terms, or do you reject them?"

"I have no option but to agree to them. Beggars cannot be choosers." The bitterness at his heart made itself apparent in his words.

"Your last statement embodies a great truth, and one which you would do well to bear in mind for the rest of your life," said the baronet, with the nearest approach to a sneer he ever permitted himself. "It may, perhaps, be as well that I should recapitulate the terms of my proposition in order that there may be no after-mistake in the matter."

When he had done so, he said:

"Do you pledge me your word to carry out the conditions as laid down by me, in their entirety?"

"I pledge you my word to that effect."

Sir Gilbert rose and pushed back his chair.

"In that case, I need not detain you further. You know Page's address. Send him at once a complete list of your liabilities, with all needful particulars to enable him to settle the same. He will receive my instructions in the course of to-morrow to advance you a hundred pounds, or rather, to make you a present of them, as I neither know, nor care to know, how you are off for ready money. As soon as you have decided where to bestow your worthless self, you will write Page to that effect. And now I am not aware that I have anything more to add."

Alec had risen by this time and had picked up his hat and cloak. His eyes sought his father's eyes and met them. They stood confronting each other thus while one might have counted six slowly. The younger man's gaze was instinct with a grave questioning wistfulness. As plainly as speech could have done, it said:

"Father, have you no word of forgiveness for me before I go?"

But in Sir Gilbert's chilly blue-grey eyes was to be read no faintest response. Had his son been a stranger, whom he had never before set eyes on, he could not have regarded him with more apparent indifference. With a heavy sigh that seemed to choke back a sob, Alec turned, and crossing to the window by which he had entered, opened it. A moment he paused on the threshold, and threw a backward glance over his shoulder.

"Goodbye, father," he said in a voice that was scarcely above a whisper.

"Goodnight and goodbye," came the response in accents clear and unmoved.

An instant later and Alec was gone. Sir Gilbert waited till the noise of his son's footsteps on the gravel had died away. Then he crossed to the window and refastened the shutters, and drew again the heavy curtains. So departed from the home of his ancestors the heir of Withington Chase.

By this time the night was fair, but although the wind had spent much of its force, it still blew in fitful gusts. Having crossed the lawn and the flower-garden, Alec leaped the sunken fence which divided the latter from the park, and then turning sharply to the right, presently struck into a footpath, well known to him of old, which wound through the belt of timber that sheltered the Chase from the north and north-east winds. Having traversed this, he emerged into a wilder part of the grounds rarely trodden by anyone save an occasional poacher, or by that law-breaker's implacable foe, the gamekeeper, in the course of his nocturnal rounds.

Alec Clare was returning by the way he had come. He had quitted the London train at Westwood station, four miles away, where there was no one who knew him, rather than go on to Mapleford, the station nearest the Chase, where, even at that late hour, he could not have made sure of not being recognised: and he had his own reasons for wishing to keep his midnight visit a secret from everybody. His intention was to climb the wall at the far corner of the park where it abutted on a narrow lane which, at a distance of a quarter of a mile, opened on to the high road that led direct to Westwood station.

He was plunging forward through the rain-soaked bracken, feeling intolerably sore at heart, wroth with himself, his father and the world at large, but most of all with himself, and the prey to a dull heavy pain, which had its origin in the knowledge that he was leaving behind him the home of his birth, his mother's grave, and all the haunts that were inextricably interwoven with the memories of his boyhood, perhaps never to see them again--when suddenly from behind the bole of a huge elm a man stepped full in his path and barred the way.

Alec fell back a step or two with an involuntary exclamation, so startled was he, and next moment the man did the same. He was a big, burly fellow, dressed in velveteens and gaiters, and carrying a stout cudgel in his right hand.

"Why, lawks-a-me, if it ain't Master Alec!" he exclaimed with a gasp of astonishment; "and just as I'd made sure I was a going to cop one o' them confounded poachers. Well, wonders will never cease. I'm mortal glad to see you, sir, anyhow."

The speaker was Martin Rigg, Sir Gilbert's gamekeeper. Alec and he had been firm allies in days gone by. Many a night had the "young master" and the keeper gone the rounds together when the former was supposed to be sound asleep in bed. Many had been their escapades, even to the extent of doing a little night-poaching on their own account. All that Alec knew of woodcraft, of the "gentle art" and of the haunts and habits of birds and animals, he owed to Martin Rigg.

"Yes, it is I, Martin," replied the young man, now thoroughly roused from his abstraction. "If you took me for a poacher, I, at the first glance, took you for a ghost, or something equally as uncanny."

"For the Grey Monk, perhaps?" suggested the keeper, with a chuckle in his voice.

"You forget that the Grey Monk wears a cowl, and not even by starlight could your wide-awake be mistaken for that."

"Wide-awake or no wide-awake, sir, I've reason to believe that more than one timid servant lass has been ready to take her affidavy that she had seen the Grey Monk, when it's only been me that she's caught sight of in the dark, prowling among the trees, on the lookout for gins and snares."

"By the way," said Alec, but with the tone of one whose mind had far more serious things to occupy it, "has anything been seen of the family spectre of late?"

"No, sir--not of late. It's nigh on for three years since it was seen last, and then it was her ladyship who was nearly frightened out of her wits by it. She was coming downstairs at the time, and had reached the lowermost landing, when she saw the Grey Monk glide across the hall in the moonlight. She shrieked out, and they do say she nearly fainted. The best of it was that up to then she had always made light of the ghost, and said its appearances were nothing more than 'lucinations, whatever they may be. But she never said so after that night.

Sir Gilbert was awfully wild when he heard about it, and would fain have hushed it up; but it was too late. However, that's an old wife's tale by this time. As I said afore, sir, I'm mortal glad to see you."
"Not for one moment do I doubt you, old friend. All the same, I am sure you would like to know why I am here and where I am bound for at this hour of the night. Listen! there is the turret clock striking twelve. Well, I will tell you."
He waited till the clock had done striking; then resumed:
"I have just left my father. He and I have said goodbye to each other for a long time to come. I am on my way to Westwood station: you know the near cut. Forty-eight hours hence I shall have left England, to return I know not when."
"I am main sorry to hear that, Master Alec," remarked the keeper in a tone of real concern. In common with everybody connected with the Chase, and a good many people in no wise connected with it--for such things cannot be kept secret--he was cognisant of the breach between Sir Gilbert and his heir, and could form a pretty shrewd guess as to the origin of it.
"And I am no less sorry to have it to tell," replied Alec. "Now, when I tell you further that I don't want anyone to know of my present visit to the Chase, nor to hear from your lips that you have as much as set eyes on me, you will, I am sure, respect my wishes."
"O' course I will, sir. You may make yourself easy on that score. I *dreamt* as I saw you--that's all--and I don't tell my dreams to nobody."

CHAPTER II.

AN OLD FAMILY AND ITS HOME.

Withington Chase was a fine old Jacobean mansion, which had been added to from time to time as whim or necessity had dictated.

The walls of the original structure were composed of small red bricks, relieved at frequent intervals, as far as the main frontage was concerned, by fluted pilasters of white stone with Ionic capitals, which, when seen from a little distance, had all the effect of marble. However incongruous and out of keeping with the general scheme of the house the various additions which had been patched on to it during the course of the last two centuries might have seemed when they were crude and new, Time's chastening fingers had mellowed them to a certain degree of beauty, so that in these latter days the general effect was that of a harmonious and homogeneous whole.

Originally there had been a much older mansion, which, after having been partially destroyed by fire, had been razed to the ground, all of it save one sturdy fragment which, for some unknown reason, had been allowed to stand.

This relic of a state of things long vanished was an octagonal tower, about sixty feet in height, built of undressed blocks of grey stone, held together by a mortar as hard as themselves. The interior of the tower consisted of three small rooms, one above the other, with a leaded roof surmounted by a breast-high parapet. Each of the rooms was lighted by a couple of long narrow openings in the wall, which at one time might have been glazed, but were so no longer. Of these rooms the ground floor one alone was now put to any service, access to the others, owing to the rotten state of the woodwork, being deemed a risk not worth adventuring. The basement in question was used as a receptacle for gardeners' tools, and a general storage place for things horticultural, which had been allowed to accumulate there for years.

As already stated, the tower had formed a part of the older mansion of Withington Chase, although what the intention had been in building it, and to what special purposes it had been put, nobody nowadays seemed to know. There it was, however; and there--the elements being its only enemies--it was likely to remain for some centuries to come. It was about five or six hundred yards apart from the more modern mansion, the space between the two being occupied by the belt of timber before mentioned.

The main entrance to Withington Chase was approached by a broad carriage-drive, which swept with a graceful curve from the lodge some half a mile away. The park was well timbered, and contained a number of grand old trees said to have been planted before the present mansion was in existence. In front of the house, but intersected by the drive, was a spacious expanse of closely-shaven lawn, to the right of which was a small but choicely kept flower-garden, while on its left was a shrubbery of tall clipped hedges and thick clumps of evergreens, among the sheltered paths of which Sir Gilbert found it pleasant to take his constitutional when the weather was too cold and raw to allow of his walking elsewhere in the open air.

The master of Withington Chase was proud of his long descent, and that not without reason.

He could trace back his pedigree on the male side in unbroken sequence to the time of Henry IV. One head of the family had fought at Agincourt, another had distinguished himself at Malplaquet; while scions of the family, more than one could count on one's fingers, had fought and, in several cases, died for their king and country wherever the British flag had penetrated. Quite a number of Clares had been in Parliament from time to time, and if none of them had been noted for his eloquence, or had risen to office, they had all possessed the negative virtue of being staunch voters, men whose political opinions could be relied upon never to stray beyond the hard and fast lines laid down by their own party.

The present baronet had taken no share in public affairs, and had declined more than once to allow himself to be nominated for a seat in Parliament. An occasional appearance on the magisterial bench, which grew still more occasional with advancing years, just sufficed to remind his brother justices and the good folk of Mapleford, that Sir Gilbert Clare of Withington Chase had not yet been gathered to his ancestors in the family vault.

Sir Gilbert, at the age of five-and-twenty, had inherited an impoverished estate, and, by consequence, a diminished revenue.

His father had been a man of fashion and a gamester, under the Regency, and in the course of a few years of reckless expenditure had contrived to undo the work of several generations of thrifty progenitors. This was a state of things which the young baronet at once set himself to remedy. The town house and its contents were sold to the highest bidder; the Yorkshire property was let on lease to a wealthy manufacturer; while the Withington establishment was cut down to the lowest limits compatible with keeping up his station in the county.

Unfortunately for his worldly prospects--and he was the first to admit the fact later on--Sir Gilbert had married about a year prior to his father's death, and, little likely as one would have deemed him, with his cold temperament, to commit such an imprudence, had married for love. His bride had come of a good family, but beyond a trifling dowry of a few thousand pounds, had had nothing save a pretty face, and a piquant manner to recommend her. Such as she was, however, she had contrived to fascinate the haughty young heir of Withington Chase.

Alas! that it should have to be told, but in the course of a few brief years after marriage the pretty face had become a memory of the past, and the piquant manner had degenerated into the querulous repinings of a semi-invalid; for Lady Clare was one of those women who find in a naturally delicate constitution an ample excuse for shirking all the active duties of life, and for coddling themselves into a state of chronic invalidism, the chief features of which, in her case, seemed to be reclining the day through on a couch, and being waited on, hand and foot, by everyone about her.

Under these circumstances it was scarcely to be wondered at that, after a time, Sir Gilbert's home-life became intolerable to him. He was by nature of a restless disposition, with a strong inclination for travel and adventure, and by degrees his absences from the Chase grew longer, till at length it came to pass that he would be away for several months at a time.

It was during one of these absences that his wife died, greatly to his surprise and relief. She had so coddled herself up for years, and had made of herself such a hothouse plant, that a slight chill, too trivial in the first instance to seem worth notice, had sufficed to carry her off. She left behind her a son ten years old, the John Alexander Clare to whom we have already been introduced.

Whatever might have been Lady Clare's defects in other ways, she had passionately loved her child.

Unfortunately, however, not content with loving him, she had done her best to spoil him. This, Sir Gilbert's frequent absences had allowed her ample opportunities for doing. When he was at the Chase it was tacitly understood between mother and son that matters were on a different footing. At such times her ladyship curbed, in some measure, the display of her affection, and Alec left off bird-nesting and consorting with Martin Rigg, and attended assiduously at the rectory, where the Rev. Bruce Amor was doing his best to ground him in the humanities.

With his mother's death everything was changed for Alec.

Whether Sir Gilbert had all along been aware of the way in which his son was being spoiled, but had his own reasons for ignoring the fact, or whether some meddler had made it his business to enlighten him, the result was the same as far as the boy was concerned. In place of good, easy-going Mr. Amor, he was now put under the charge of a tutor whose reputation as a martinet had been his chief qualification in the eyes of the baronet. Mr. Duggan's instructions were to prepare the lad for a public school and in the meantime, as Sir Gilbert expressed it, to "break him in."

And now for Alec began an experience which was all the harder to bear by reason of what had gone before.

The new tutor was like a baleful shadow which dogged him wherever he went. From the time he rose till the time he went to bed he could never get rid of him for more than a few minutes at a time. It was a tyranny which at length became almost unbearable and went far towards breaking the lad's all but indomitable spirit.

One day, when he had been only a few weeks at the Chase, Mr. Duggan, with the view, perhaps, of keeping up his reputation as a martinet, chose, by way of punishment for some trifling fault, to administer a sound caning to his pupil. The lad took his punishment without a murmur, but half an hour later, he was missing; nor, when search came to be made, was he anywhere to be found.

Alec, however, was no great distance away.

Being nearly as active as a squirrel, he had climbed the bole of one of the big old trees in the park, and there, for two days and nights--the month being June--he lay perdu in his leafy shelter, being supplied with food meanwhile by Martin Rigg, who was the only person in the secret of his hiding-place. It was only his father's threat, conveyed to him by that faithful servitor, to send for Captain Darville's bloodhounds and so track him down, that induced him to give himself up.

For this freak he was sentenced to a week of bread-and-water in a darkened room. Even so, he was not left wholly forlorn, food and candles and books being surreptitiously conveyed to him from the servants' hall. But Mr. Duggan never laid hands on him again.

In due course this period of his life came to an end, and it was with something of the feeling of a captive released after a long imprisonment that he one day found himself on his way to Harrow, from which place, in the natural sequence of things, he proceeded to Cambridge.

All his life Alec had stood in awe of his father. It was a feeling which, to some extent, had been fostered by his mother. To both of them it had been as a load lifted off their lives when the baronet left home on one of his excursions, and both had looked forward with dread to his return. There had been no cordiality, no sympathy, no *rapprochement* in any proper sense of the word, between father and son.

That, however, had been owing to no fault on the boy's part, for Alec's was one of those bright, open dispositions which respond readily to whatever kindly influences may be brought to bear on them. But Sir Gilbert had no liking for children, or young people, and it was not in his nature to make any exception even in the case of his own son. He had kept himself aloof from him from the first, and with the lapse of years the silent, passive breach between the two, if such it could be termed, grew gradually wider and more impossible of being bridged over. Many an hour's heartache had the boy, more especially after his mother's death, but there was too large a tincture of family pride in his composition to allow of even an inkling of what he felt to be visible on the surface. More than once in after-life he said bitterly to himself: "If when I was young, my father had treated me as other fathers treat their sons, I should have been a different man from what I am now."

That might, or might not, have been the case.

It was while Alec was at Harrow that Sir Gilbert married again.

There was no question of sentiment mixed up with his second matrimonial venture, as there had been with his first. It was the simple fact of Miss Delmayne being possessed of a fortune of sixty thousand pounds in her own right that led him to propose to her.

On her part, the lady, who had seen thirty summers, had no illusions. She was perfectly aware for what reason she was being sought, but, all the same, it seemed to her that she would have been very foolish to let slip the chance of becoming Lady Clare, of Withington Chase.

She was a capable, managing woman, who allowed her husband to go and come and do just as he liked, without any repining or questioning on her part--a mode of procedure which just suited the baronet. On the other hand, she tolerated no interference in domestic matters, or the indoor management of the Chase. It may be accounted as a virtue in her that she was no more inclined for an extravagant style of living than was her husband. Still more did this become the case after her three sons were born; indeed, for the sake of their future she began after a time to develop a disposition which, in a person of her social position, might almost be termed penurious.

Lady Clare's special grievance, and it was one which debarred her from seeking the sympathy of others--the one thorn in her pillow--was the existence of her husband's eldest son.

In that particular, if in no other, it seemed to her that Providence had dealt hardly with her. No such person ought to have been born; or, if that could not have been avoided, his sojourn in this vale of tears should have been of the briefest. To her it seemed a monstrous thing that anyone other than her own darling Randolph should be the legal heir to his father's title and estates. More especially hard did it seem to her in view of the fact that a third of the dowry she had brought her husband had gone to clear off certain old mortgages contracted by the preceding baronet, and in so far, might be said to have benefited the estate in perpetuity.

Yet, in the face of this, Randolph, at his father's death, would only be entitled to a younger son's share of the baronet's savings--provided there should be any to divide--both the Hertfordshire and the Yorkshire estates being strictly entailed. Her ladyship felt that she had indeed just cause for repining.

She was coldly gracious to Alec, whenever that young man made his appearance at the Chase, which, as time went on, became less frequently than ever. He felt that he was not wanted at home, that he had now become less to his father even than he had been before, and he knew that his instincts did not deceive him when they told him that in her ladyship he had an enemy whom no efforts on his part would avail to conciliate.

It was as well, perhaps, for more reasons than one, that Lady Clare had no knowledge of the considerable sums disbursed by the baronet from time to time in liquidation of the debts contracted by his spendthrift heir. In those matters Mr. Page, the family solicitor, was the only person taken into Sir Gilbert's confidence.

It was a source of gratification to her ladyship to know that father and son lived on permanently bad terms with each other; and when, after that October night which saw the heir banished from home, her husband told her that Alec had gone abroad, and that they were not likely to be troubled with him or his affairs again for a long time to come, she sincerely rejoiced. Alec was wild and careless of his health, and reckless in many ways. There was no knowing what might come to pass. It no longer seemed to her the foolish daydream she had deemed it heretofore, that she might, perhaps, live to hear her son addressed as Sir Randolph Clare of Withington Chase.

It was well for her ladyship, as it is for all of us, that there was no invisible hand to draw aside the curtain of the future and reveal to her even a glimpse of what was to be.

Meanwhile, the real heir had unaccountably vanished from the haunts which had known him, and was as one dead to that little world in which he had been such a familiar figure. No word of him, or message of any kind reached his whilom associates. A vague rumour got spread about, originating no one seemed to know how or whence, that he had joined a certain exploring expedition which just then was being a good deal talked about; but it was a rumour which was never confirmed.

Men talked and wondered for a little while, and then presently he was forgotten.

CHAPTER III.

ALEC'S PROPOSITION.

With the inmates of Withington Chase two uneventful years glided imperceptibly away. Between Sir Gilbert and his wife the name of the proscribed heir was never mentioned; to all seeming he had vanished out of their lives as completely as if he had never existed. That his image still dwelt more or less in his father's thoughts was only in the natural order of things, but to faithful Mr. Page alone, from whom the baronet had few or no secrets, did Alec's name ever cross his lips, and to him no oftener than was unavoidable.

The lawyer had duly remitted his quarterly allowance to the young man, forwarding it now to one obscure continental town and now to another, in accordance with Alec's written request; but, beyond that, nothing whatever was known of him or his whereabouts.

Then one day the baronet received a letter from his son, dated from Catanzaro, a small out-of-the-way town in southern Italy.

In it the writer stated that he was utterly tired of the idle, purposeless life he had been leading for the past two years, and that if his father would agree to give him six thousand pounds down, he would emigrate to the United States and never trouble him for another shilling as long as he lived. But he would do more, much more, than that, should his father consent to his proposition. In that case he would agree to the cutting off of the entail and would sign whatever documents might be needful for the due carrying out of that design. Sir Gilbert sat staring at the letter after he had finished reading it like a man whose faculties had been paralysed by sheer amazement.

So absorbed was his attention that he was unconscious of the door behind him being opened and of the entry of his wife. Her footfalls made no noise on the thick carpet. She went up behind him and was on the point of placing a hand on his shoulder, when her gaze vas attracted to the letter which lay spread open on the writing-table in front of him.

Lady Clare was more than a score of years younger than her husband and her eyesight was still as keen as ever it had been. Half-a-dozen seconds sufficed her to take in the sense of Alec's letter, the handwriting of which she had at once recognised. A little gasp escaped her before she knew it. An instant later the baronet had started to his feet, and was confronting her with flaming eyes; involuntarily his hand closed over the letter.

"Madam, I am not in the habit of being startled in this way," he said, "nor do I like it."

"On the contrary, dear, it was you who startled me," she replied in her blandest

accents, with a hand pressed to her left side. "Of course I naturally supposed that you had heard the door opened and shut, and was on the point of addressing you when you started up as if you had been shot."
"Humph! I have had occasion before to-day to beg of you not to be quite so feline in your movements," he answered with something like a snarl. "Did you--did you read any portion of the letter that was on the table in front of me?"
"My dear Gilbert, what *do* you take me for! That there *was* a letter there, I am aware, but as for reading as much as a line of it----"
"There, there, that will do. Just ring the bell, will you, and then tell me what you want to see me about."
When the servant came in response to the summons, he said: "Tell Graves to bring the dog-cart round at once."
Ten minutes later saw Sir Gilbert on his way to Mapleford with his son's letter in his pocket. In such a contingency he felt that he could not do better than seek the advice of his valued counsellor.
Mr. Page, a tall, lanky, somewhat loose-jointed man, with a long thin face, a prominent nose and an expression that was a curious compound of hard common sense, shrewdness and good-nature, gave vent to a low whistle when he had come to the end of Alec's epistle.
"What an exceedingly foolish young man!" were his first words.
"Why so, pray--why so?" demanded the baronet with a lifting of his eyebrows.
"To offer to sell his birthright for a mess of pottage--for that is what he here proposes to do."
"Six thousand pounds is a large sum, Page."
"In itself it may perhaps seem so, but what is it in comparison with the reversion of Withington Chase and the other entailed property? Why, it's not equivalent to one year's rent-roll! A very foolish young man!"
"It is to be presumed that he knows his own business best," remarked the baronet drily. "Besides, you seem to forget the many hundreds of pounds--nay, I may say thousands--that I have had to disburse at different times by reason of his extravagance."
The lawyer shook his head.
"There's more under the surface, I feel convinced, than either you or I yet know of." Then, after a pause, during which he seemed lost in thought, he added, "I should not be in the least surprised if a woman were at the bottom of this business."
The baronet was startled.
"That is a possibility which did not suggest itself to me," he said. "It would, indeed, be just like Alec to finish up his career by contracting a low marriage." Then with a shrug he added: "But he can please himself about that when once the proposition embodied by him in his letter has been duly carried into effect."
"Then you really mean to accept his offer to cut off the entail?"
"I do. If I had any hesitation before, your last suggestion would have effectually disposed of it. I am certainly inclined to believe that you have hit upon the real

reason which underlies his offer. Well, I am glad he has sufficient sense and good-feeling left to betake himself to a country where there's not a creature who knows him. In that case a *mé*salliance* on his part will be a matter of very minor consequence. And now let us consider by what means we can most readily lay our hands on six thousand pounds."

A week later Sir Gilbert and Mr. Page set out for Italy.

It had never been the baronet's practice to take his wife into his confidence about matters which, from his point of view, did not concern her, consequently he had kept his own counsel as far as Alec's letter and its contents were concerned. It would be time enough to tell her after the all-important document should have been signed by which Alec renounced his birthright. He began to regard young Randolph, the present Lady Clare's eldest son, with very different eyes from those with which he had hitherto looked upon the boy. A few more days and *he* would be the heir of Withington. The pity of it was that the title could not descend to him as well as the estates. That was a point as to which the law was manifestly to blame.

Lady Clare betrayed not the slightest interest as to the nature of the business which was taking her husband and Mr. Page all the way to Italy. So well did she play her part that no faintest suspicion entered Sir Gilbert's mind that she had any knowledge of the existence of Alec's letter, much less of the nature of its contents. She judged, and rightly, that her husband would not have been at the trouble to go to Italy and take his lawyer with him, unless he had agreed to accept the terms proposed by his eldest son. After all, then, the one great grievance of her life would cease to exist, and her darling Randolph would become his father's heir, as he ought to have been all along! Only herself knew with what eager anxiety she awaited her husband's return. Surely, surely, he would not be so cruel as to keep the good news from her an hour after it should be his to tell! He could not fail to know how happy it would make her.

The theory propounded by Mr. Page as to the motive which lay at the foundation of Alec's letter to his father, was not very wide of the mark. Had it not been for a certain pair of brilliant black eyes, in all probability it would never have been written.

About six months before, in the course of his aimless wanderings Alec had found himself and his very limited luggage at Catanzaro, a small but romantically situated Calabrian town, a few miles inland from the Gulf of Squillace.

The place had pleased him and he had made up his mind to stay there awhile.

He had accordingly taken up his quarters at the principal *osteria* , kept by one Giuseppe Rispani. Alec lived very simply, and, of late, had learnt to confine his wants within narrow limits, so that his father's allowance, conjointly with his own income of one hundred and eighty pounds a year, amply sufficed for all his needs.

Rispani was a widower with one son, who had lately left home for England in the hope of bettering his fortunes, and one daughter, Giovanna by name, at that time a beautiful girl of nineteen.

Rispani's wife had been an Englishwoman, whom he had married for the sake of her little fortune of five hundred pounds, while she had married him for his *beaux yeaux* ; for in early life the Italian had been a very handsome man, with a soft tongue and a persuasive manner which poor Miss Verinder had found it impossible to resist.

The Signora Rispani, who at one time had been a governess, and, later on, companion to a lady of rank, was a woman of considerable education and refinement. She took great pains with the tuition and bringing up of her daughter, and to her mother Giovanna owed it that she was almost as familiar with the English tongue as the Italian.

Unfortunately the Signora died when Giovanna was about thirteen years old, just the age when a mother's care and watchfulness were most needed, for the girl's disposition, like her father's, was cold, calculating, and avaricious; and when the one person was gone whose untiring effort it had been to keep down the weeds of selfishness and greed of which her nature was so prolific--for the Signora had by no means been blind to her daughter's defects--it was not difficult to foretell what the result would be.

If Giuseppe Rispani had known anything of the doctrine of heredity, he might have pointed to his daughter as a living example of it as far as the reproduction in her of certain of his own most predominant qualities was concerned.

In appearance Giovanna was a true daughter of the sunny South.

Her figure was tall, with a certain stateliness of carriage that became her well. Her complexion was of the clearest and most transparent olive, her eyes and hair as black as midnight, while her features were almost classic in the regularity of their outlines. In any country in the world Giovanna Rispani would have been accounted a very beautiful young woman.

Vanna had not reached the age of nineteen without having had several suitors, eligible and otherwise, for her hand, but to one and all she had turned a deaf ear. Her father had in no wise tried to influence her choice, being, indeed, firmly persuaded in his own mind that it would have been futile to attempt to do so; but had merely laughed pleasantly as each baffled aspirant went his way, and remarked that Vanna, had plenty of time before her in which to make up her mind.

Alec Clare had not been many days an inmate of the *osteria* of the Golden Fig before it became clear to Vanna Rispani, that in the tall, handsome young Englishman, she had achieved another conquest.

Vanna had never made a practice of waiting on her father's guests, holding herself, indeed, somewhat haughtily aloof, but she condescended to wait on Alec. It was not his looks that attracted her, but the fact that in him she found some one who could talk to her in her mother's native tongue.

She was proud of her ability to speak English, but it was an acquisition which had been in some danger of becoming rusty from disuse; now, however, a day rarely passed without she and Alec having at least one long talk together. To him, too, who had lived for the last two years among what might be termed the byeways of life, it was an inexpressible pleasure to have lighted on some one with whom he could converse in his own tongue; for although by this time he could speak Italian almost as fluently as a native, his thoughts and self-communings were all couched in the language to which he had been born.

Giovanna was wholly free from self-consciousness and *mauvaise honte* ; she was as self-possessed as a woman twice her age; consequently there was a charming ease and naturalness in her intercourse with Alec, which he found increasingly fascinating as time went on.

It was surprising what a number of things they found to talk about, and how naturally one subject seemed to lead up to another. If sometimes Alec's talk went a little over the girl's head, if he now and then started a subject which for her was devoid of interest, she was careful not to betray the fact. She might be secretly bored, but her lips never lost their smile, nor her eyes their sparkle.

The heir of Withington Chase lingered on week after week in the little Italian town till a couple of months had gone by, without caring to ask himself why he did so.

At length the time came when he had neither the power nor the will to tear himself away. Self-deception was a species of weakness in which he had never indulged; he had always dealt frankly with himself, and he did so now. He was in love with the innkeeper's daughter, and he admitted it. More than once, in years gone by, his fancy had been taken captive, but in every case the day had come, and that after no long time, when he had snapped the silken thread that loosely held him, and had gone on his way again, heart whole and fancy free.

But it was no frail silken chain that held him now: he was a helpless captive bound hand and foot in Love's golden fetters.

When, however, he asked himself what prospect there was of his passion being reciprocated, he could but reply that he had no grounds whatever for answering the question in his own favour. That Vanna sought his society and that she derived a certain amount of pleasure from it, could not be doubted; but, on the other hand, every one of those signs was wanting which are supposed to foreshadow the dawn of love in a young girl's heart. She was as easy and unembarrassed in his company as in that of her father, which, of itself; seemed to indicate the absence of any special regard for him. And yet there were times when an inscrutable something glanced at him for a moment out of the depths of her magnificent eyes and kindled a sudden flame of hope in his heart, which, if it quickly died down again, left behind it a certain glow less evanescent than itself.

At length a time arrived when it became clear to Alec that matters between himself and Vanna could not go on much longer as they were. The state of uncertainty in which he lived was fast becoming intolerable to him. Not much longer could he keep silent. He would give words to the passion that was consuming him and win all or lose all by the result.

On more than one occasion in the course of their many talks together, Giovanna had so far opened her mind as to confide to Alec the longing which beset her to get away from the dull and narrow routine of her life in her native town. She wanted to see something of the world, to live a larger and freer existence in some country beyond the sea.

Probably it was owing to the influence of these talks that the inception of the scheme was due which, a few weeks later, Alec embodied in his letter to his father.

Should the latter prove willing to give him the sum he had specified, he would ask Giovanna to become his wife, and if she consented, he would seek with her a home in the New World, where his six thousand pounds would, he confidently hoped, prove the corner-stone from which to build up one of those colossal fortunes in comparison with which the revenues of Withington Chase would seem insignificant indeed. In any case, as he truthfully stated in his letter, he was heartily sick of the idle, purposeless existence he had been leading for a couple of years. For aught he knew to the contrary, his father might never revoke the promise extracted from him not to return to England till leave should be given him to do so.

Meanwhile his life was slowly rusting away.

CHAPTER IV.

AN OFFER AND ITS ACCEPTANCE.

Sir Gilbert Clare and Mr. Page reached Catanzaro in due course. They were met by Alec, who had been apprised by the lawyer of the time when they might be expected to arrive, and who had secured rooms for them at the Golden Fig, the *osteria* at which he himself had been a guest for so long a time.

Father and son greeted each other with a grave silent bow. Alec flushed to the roots of his hair as soon as he realized that it was Sir Gilbert's intention to treat him as a stranger; then as suddenly he turned pale. Next moment his pride came to his aid. He drew himself up, and turning courteously to Mr. Page, expressed to him his fear that he must have found the journey both tedious and fatiguing.

At dinner, which had been ordered by Alec beforehand, the two arrivals were waited upon by Rispani in person. This also was by arrangement with Alec, who, for some reason which he could not have defined to himself, was desirous that, for the time being, Giovanna should keep in the background.

It is to be borne in mind that Rispani had no suspicion, either then or afterwards, that the English "Milor" was Alec's father, or, indeed, any relation whatever of the young man. Ever since he had come abroad, young Clare had dropped his surname and had simply been known as "Mr. John Alexander," a cognomen which his Italian friends, to whom the English syllables seemed a concatenation of barbarous sounds, had not failed to naturalise into "Il Signor Alessandro."

Both Sir Gilbert and Mr. Page retired at an early hour.

The lawyer, who despite Alec's failings, had a very genuine liking for him, would fain have secured half an hour's private talk with the young man, but there was no possibility of such a thing till the baronet had sought his own room, and then Alec was nowhere to be found. He had gone for a long solitary walk, and there was no knowing when he would be back. The hour of ten next morning had already been named as that which was to see the important business entered upon which had brought the two Englishmen so far from home.

Mr. Page had not failed to come prepared with the legal document to which, in the presence of the requisite witnesses, the heir would be required to affix that signature which would leave him an heir no longer.

The lawyer had anticipated some difficulty in obtaining a couple of witnesses in that out-of-the-way spot with sufficient knowledge of English to comprehend what was required of them, but it proved to be a difficulty that was readily overcome with the help of Alec. In Giuseppe Rispani and a friend of his who at one time had filled the position of *courrier de place* , were found precisely the two people needed.

No sooner was breakfast over than word was sent to Alec that everything was in readiness. Then he and the witnesses proceeded upstairs to the *sala* which had been set aside for the use of the *forestieri* . A slight haughty inclination of the head was the sole greeting vouchsafed them by Sir Gilbert as they entered the room.

It may be here remarked that Alec had neither dined nor breakfasted with his father. Time had availed nothing to soften the latter's hostility towards his eldest son.

The baronet's chair was apart near the window. On a table in the middle of the room were pens and ink, together with a formidable looking document.

Mr. Page, having shaken hands with Alec, greeted the two Italians in his most urbane manner, and then motioned them to a couple of chairs on the opposite side of the table. Next he handed the paper to Alec, who sat down on the third chair while he glanced over its various clauses, the lawyer standing at his elbow while he did so. That done, without a moment's hesitation, Alec dipped a pen in the ink and wrote his name in full at the foot in bold flowing characters. He then made way for the witnesses, standing aside with folded arms. At Mr. Page's invitation, Rispani moved to the chair vacated by Alec and proceeded to scrawl his signature on the line indicated by the lawyer's finger. A like process was then gone through by the second Italian. Neither of them had the least notion as to the contents of the document to which they had appended their signatures. Mr. Page had taken care of that. A sheet of blotting-paper which he had applied to Alec's signature was left so as to cover three-fourths of the paper, while the sleeve of his coat, as he indicated the spot where each witness was to write his name, effectually hid the last of the three words, "John Alexander Clare."

He had not lost sight of the fact that in Catanzaro Alec was known only as the Signor Alessandro.

As soon as the Italians were gone Mr. Page sat down, and from the breast pocket of his coat produced a bulky packet of bank notes of various denominations, which, with the help of a moistened forefinger, he proceeded to count with methodical deliberation.

Having satisfied himself on a point about which he had felt perfectly sure beforehand, he pushed the notes across the table to Alec.

"There, sir," he said; "if you will be at the trouble of counting them, you will find that they amount in the aggregate to exactly six thousand pounds."

"I will take your word for that, Mr. Page," replied Alec, with a bitter smile as he crumpled up the notes and thrust them into his pocket.

By this a carriage, previously ordered, was at the door. The two gentlemen had arranged to post as far as Reggio. Sir Gilbert, who despite his husk of frigidity, was far from comfortable in his mind, and was especially desirous of getting away at the earliest possible moment, had already drawn on his gloves and taken possession of his dust-coat and umbrella. He now extended his rigid fingers to his son, whose hand instinctively closed over them, but without any consciousness of the slightest pressure in return.

"Goodbye," said the baronet. "You have my best wishes for your prosperity in the future. At any time it will gratify me to hear that you are doing well. Now, Mr. Page, if you are ready."
With that the fingers were withdrawn, and turning on his heel, he stalked solemnly out, leaving his son, who had said no word in reply, standing in the middle of the room.
Next moment Mr. Page was wringing Alec's hand.
"Goodbye, my dear boy, and may Heaven bless and prosper you," exclaimed the lawyer, with an unwonted tremor in his voice. "Never forget that in Cornelius Page you have a firm friend; and don't fail to advise me from time to time of your whereabouts."
Three minutes later, as one in a dream, Alec heard the crack of the driver's whip and the rattle of the carriage as it jolted over the narrow paved street. Then when the last sound had died away, his manhood suddenly broke down. Sinking into a chair, with his elbows resting on the table and his face covered with his hands, he let the tears drop silently between his fingers.
Now it so happened that there was one feature about the *osteria* of the Golden Fig, which, for various reasons, it is to be hoped is by no means common to similar houses of entertainment either in Italy or elsewhere.
The peculiarity in question was neither more nor less than a peephole, or place of espial, behind one corner of the elaborate plaster scroll-work of fruit and foliage which ran round the ceiling of the room in which the scene related above had taken place. This spy-hole was reached by means of a flight of steps shut up from ordinary view in what looked like a tall clothes closet in the adjoining chamber.
The house was an old one, and what purpose this secret place of observation had originally served it was now impossible to tell. Rispani had found it there when he took the house, and on more than one occasion had taken advantage of it to pry into the doings of his guests; but never to such good purpose as today, for from that coign of vantage he had been an unseen witness of the transfer of the roll of notes to Signor Alessandro.
Immediately after the departure of the Englishman Rispani sought his daughter.
"The Signor Alessandro loves thee--is it not so?" he said to her in Italian. There was something in his tone which convinced Vanna that he had a special motive in putting the question.
"His eyes have told me that he loves me, but his words never."
"Thou lovest him in return?"
"I like him--yes; better than I like any one. But as for loving him--no."
"Should he ask thee to wed him, what will thy answer be?"
"It will be time enough to decide that when he *has* asked me."
"He *will* ask thee--I feel sure of it--and thy answer must be yes--yes--yes!"
Vanna's dark orbs looked the surprise she felt.
"Listen," resumed Rispani, laying a hand on her arm and speaking into her ear. "One of the strangers who have just gone gave the Signor Alessandro bank-notes

to the value of six thousand pounds English money. These eyes saw him do it. Think! Six thousand pounds!"

Father and daughter looked meaningly at each other. In the eyes of both sparkled the same cold avaricious gleam. At that moment the likeness between them was almost startling.

Giuseppe Rispani had prophesied rightly. At the hour of sunset Alec Clare sought Giovanna and found her where she sat under the grape trellis in the far garden. Nowhere could there have been a spot more suitable for the purpose he had in view. Vanna might have had a prevision that he would look for her there.

Alec had dreaded lest, when the crucial moment should have come, his tongue would fail him and that he should find himself the prey of a silence, at once painful and absurd. But no such mishap befell him.

How the declaration brought itself about he could hardly have told afterwards; all he knew was that he found it surprisingly easy and simple to give utterance to what he wanted to say. But it may have been that Vanna smoothed the way for him after a fashion which, in his preoccupation, he was scarcely conscious of. In any case, he spoke with an ardour and a manly earnestness which did not fail to carry conviction to his listener's heart. It was impossible to doubt his sincerity.

Vanna had already been made love to by more than one impulsive Italian, but she now discovered that this Englishman, ordinarily so undemonstrative and phlegmatic, could, the occasion being given him, rise to a height of passionate fervour which transformed him for the time being into a veritable son of the sunny South. Taking both the girl's unresisting hands in his, and devouring her with his eyes, he ended with the words, "Giovanna, will you be mine?"

No faintest tinge of superadded emotion flushed the clear olive of Vanna's cheek, but the heavy fringes of her eyelids lifted and the midnight orbs behind them gave back Alec look for look.

Then the full ripe lips curved into a siren-like smile, the cool brown fingers softly returned her lover's clasp, and in a whisper came the words:

"I will be yours."

CHAPTER V.

AT ONE FELL BLOW.

We are under other skies and the time is again two years later. "Alec Clare, by all that's wonderful!"

The exclamation came from one of two men who, happening to be bent on getting into a street car at the same moment, found themselves unexpectedly face to face. It was followed next moment by a hearty hand-grip, and then the long-parted acquaintances--friends, in the best sense of the word, they could hardly have been termed--sat down side by side.

It was at Pineapple City, a thriving and intensely go-ahead township on the borders of Lake Michigan, that the meeting just recorded took place.

Denis Boyd and Alec Clare had been intimate at college, without being exactly chums. Their fathers had been friends of long standing, and it seemed only natural to the two young men that they should copy their sires' example. Boyd had read far more assiduously than the heir of Withington Chase had ever cared to do: his father was far from being a rich man and he was anxious about his degree. Their college career had come to an end at the same time, they had gone down together and had parted with mutual good wishes and an implied promise to meet again in town later on, since which time till now they had not set eyes on each other.

"And now tell me what fortune, good or bad, has landed you in this out-of-the-way spot," began Boyd. "Of course I assume that, like myself, you are merely a bird of passage."

"On the contrary, this place is my home. I am engaged in business here."

Denis Boyd gave vent to a low whistle.

"Strange how things turn out, is it not?" continued Alec. "But before I add to your surprise, suppose you make your own confession, and tell me how it comes to pass that you happen to be here."

Boyd laughed. "My confession--to accept your own term--will be of the briefest and baldest. You may, or may not, remember that I was destined for the Law, but shortly after you and I parted my father came to grief over a bank failure, and I was compelled to look out for some immediate means of earning a living. A situation in a commercial house in Liverpool offered itself, which I gladly accepted, and there I have been ever since, working my way up by slow but sure degrees. I am over in the States on a matter of business for my firm, which admits of my combining a little holiday-making with it. I reached here late last evening, got through my business a couple of hours ago, and am killing time while waiting to be picked up by a train going East in exactly half an hour and five minutes from now. But here we are at the depot. Won't you alight and keep me company for my remaining thirty-five minutes? My portmanteau is in the cloakroom, or whatever they call the place in this part of the world."

Accordingly they alighted and proceeded to stroll up and down the station platform.

While the other had been talking, Alec had had time to pull himself together and to decide how far he should, or should not, take Boyd into his confidence. For various reasons he would much have preferred not meeting him, but that was beyond help now; and, after all, Boyd was a gentleman and the least hint would suffice to seal his lips.

"I suppose," began Alec, with a little laugh, "that I am not the first fellow by many who has contrived to find himself at odds with his father, or whose father thought he had just cause to find fault with the error of his ways; at any rate, the pater and I came to the conclusion that we should be better apart for at least a few years to come. For a time I wandered about the Continent, leading a free-and-easy Bohemian sort of life. At length I grew tired of doing nothing, and having had a certain amount of capital placed at my command, which I was desirous of tripling, or quadrupling, as the case might be, I determined to try my fortune in the States. That was two years ago. The result, considering my utter lack of business knowledge, was only what might have been expected. I gained a certain amount of experience, it is true, but it was at the expense of half my capital. I was disheartened, but by no means despairing. Leaving the scene of my ill fortune, I came West. I had no particular object in halting even for an hour at Pineapple City, beyond being tired with a long railway journey and intolerably bored by a fellow traveller who persisted in clinging to me like a leech, and whom I was determined to get rid of at any cost. Well, I had not been here many hours before I made the acquaintance of an Englishman of the name of Travis, a gentleman by birth and education, who, like yourself, had lighted on evil days, and had been lured all this way from home in the hope of being able to make a living, and ultimately, perhaps, a competence. The profession he had set up in was that of a breeder and trainer of horses for riding and carriage purposes. It was a business which he believed to be capable of considerable extension, and, just then, he was looking out for a partner who was prepared to invest a certain number of dollars in the concern. The opportunity seemed to me one which I should have been foolish to let pass me, more especially as I happen to know something about horseflesh; and, not to bore you with details, I will merely add that, after due investigation, I became Frank Travis's partner. That happened two months ago."

"From what you have just told me," said Boyd, "I conclude that you have no present intention of returning to England."

"None whatever," answered Alec drily.

"And have you never regretted your self-imposed expatriation?"

Alec shook his head. "So far I have had no cause whatever for doing so."

At this juncture they were all but run down by a man who was coming full tilt out of the refreshment buffet. "Ah, Mr. Alexander, glad to see you," he exclaimed. "Have only time to say that the pair of chestnuts you and your partner sold me a fortnight ago have turned out perfect rippers--yes, sir, rippers. My wife--ah-ha!--hasn't once been out of temper with me since I bought 'em. By-bye." And with that he was gone.

Denis Boyd looked at Alec, and the latter read a certain question in his eyes.

"When I came out to the States I chose to drop my surname. I am known to everybody here simply as John Alexander," he said quietly. "And look here, Boyd," he added, "I shall be glad if, when you get back home, you will make no mention of having met me. I have certain reasons for asking this of you."

"My dear fellow, not a word more is needed," replied the other heartily. "You may rely upon my silence."

A minute or two before, Boyd had been on the point of asking Alec whether he was still a bachelor, but it now seemed to him that such a question might savour, if not exactly of impertinence, yet of a desire to pry into a matter which was really no concern of his. It was evident there were incidents in his friend's career which he did not wish to have touched on. He would leave his question unasked.

A few minutes later Boyd's train steamed into the station.

After having parted from his friend, Alec was tempted by the fineness of the evening to go for a solitary ramble into the outskirts of the town, which, in one direction, could almost claim to be termed picturesque. His encounter with Boyd had served to awaken in him thoughts and memories which had long been dormant, but which now for a little while claimed him as their own with a persistency that would not be denied. It was not so much the scenes of his college life that his meeting with Boyd had recalled to visionary existence, but still earlier scenes connected with his life at the Chase. Once more he was a boy by his mother's side, and felt her caressing hand smooth down his ruffled curls; once more he was pacing the dusky coverts with Martin Rigg, flushing now a covey of young partridges, and now some crusty old pheasant that evidently resented being disturbed; or else he was galloping through the park at a break-neck pace on his shaggy Shetland pony. And then, like some grim spectre, the image of his father came gliding in, and all the happy pictures vanished, as when the dark slide of a magic lantern is suddenly shut down.

He came back to the present and its more immediate interests with a sigh.

There were several circumstances in his life since they had last met, of which he had hinted nothing to Boyd, and he was grateful to his friend for having forborne to question him more closely, as many men in like circumstances would not have failed to do.

For instance, he, Alec, had breathed no syllable having reference to his marriage. That, indeed, was with him a subject about which he could bear to speak to no one, for long before this he had discovered, to his bitter cost, that his marriage was a failure, and that in asking Giovanna Rispani to become his wife he had committed one of the greatest mistakes which it is possible for a man to make. He and his wife had scarcely an interest in common. Giovanna had never really cared for him, but had married him for the sake of his money. To her limited experience, six thousand pounds had represented unbounded riches; for her it meant travel, and fine clothes, and sojourning at big hotels in such cities as Milan, or Paris, or London.

Bitter, very bitter was her disappointment when, after their arrival in America, her husband took up his abode in a third-rate town in one of the Eastern States, where he conceived that there was an opening for the profitable investment of a portion of his capital. At that time his dream was to make a fortune, whereas he had only succeeded in losing his money, and in helping to build up the fortunes of others. All Giovanna's foolish dreams had vanished like a wreath of mist at sunrise, and intensely did she resent the fact. There was nothing of the scold about her, nor had she any of those pettish, irritating ways, by means of which so many women make their discontent with their surroundings felt. She was a cold, proud, silent, disappointed woman, who withdrew into herself, and who manifested not the slightest interest in her husband, or any of his concerns. She hated the country to which he had brought her; the climate was atrocious; the people among whom she dwelt, and all their ways, were antipathetic to her; she grew homesick and pined for her own country and her own people. One child had been born of the marriage.

When Alec went West in further search of that fortune which seemed so chary of smiling on him, he left his wife and child behind. At that time he had still a little over two thousand pounds remaining of the six thousand he had received from Mr. Page. This balance had lately been reduced by the sum of fifteen hundred pounds, that being the price he had paid for the privilege of entering into partnership with Mr. Frank Travis.

Good fellow as the latter was, and much as he esteemed him, not even to him had Alec confided the fact that he was a married man. It was not that he had the slightest wish to make a secret of it, but simply from an innate disinclination to speak of his private affairs to any one. Once each week he wrote to Giovanna. In view of the relations now existing between them, he was not weak enough to encumber his letters with any superfluous terms of endearment, which would merely have caused her lip to curl with quiet scorn; his epistles were rather such as a sober business-like brother might have penned to an equally sober and business-like sister. He had kept her informed as to the progress of his negotiations with Travis, and when the matter between them was concluded he did not fail to tell her at what cost the partnership had been secured by him.

All this time he had been living at a boarding-house, but now that his business matters were finally arranged there was no reason why he should not at once look out for a permanent home to which he could remove his wife and child.

In the last letter he had written to Giovanna he had told her that he hoped another month at most would see them together again, by which time the house he had in his mind's eye, a newly built one, would be finished and ready for occupation. In his stroll this evening his footsteps naturally gravitated in the direction of the house in question. His choice of it had in part been determined by reason of its somewhat romantic situation. It was built on a considerable elevation, and from it the eye ranged over a wide extent of wooded undulating country, rising here and there into rocky eminences which owed everything to Nature and nothing to art. A flash of silver on the horizon revealed that the waters of Lake Michigan were no great distance away.

To the eyes of Alec there was something in this landscape that was almost Italian in character, and he flattered himself with the fancy that perchance it would please Giovanna and that she might find in it a charm that would serve in some measure to lessen her regrets for the country he had brought her from.

After he had reached the house and had ascertained what progress the workmen had made since his last visit, and had settled in his mind after what fashion he would like the garden and shrubbery laid out, he sauntered back towards the town. At the boarding-house he found his partner awaiting him. A business telegram had arrived in the course of the afternoon which necessitated that one or the other of them should set out next morning for Milwaukee, on the opposite shore of the lake. After talking matters over, it was decided that Alec should be the one to undertake the journey. It was now Tuesday, and the probability was that he would be back by Saturday evening at the latest.

Next forenoon Travis drove his partner as far as the steamboat wharf at Davisville and there shook hands with him and bade him goodbye. They had no prevision of what the next few days would bring forth.

As it fell out, Alec's business detained him longer than he had thought it would, necessitating, among other things, an up-country journey of two score miles to a place where no railway had yet penetrated. It was not till a late hour on Monday afternoon that he got back to the hotel at Milwaukee, where he had secured a room on his arrival there the previous Wednesday.

"A letter for you, Mr. Alexander," said the hotel clerk to him as he was passing through the hall. "Been here since Saturday."

As Alec took the letter he saw that the address was in his partner's writing. Anticipating nothing of greater moment than an ordinary business communication, he lingered to glance over the latest batch of telegrams, and proceeded leisurely to his own room before opening the envelope. But all his *sang-froid* vanished the moment his eye lighted on the contents, and in its stead a deadly fear gripped him by the heart. There were two enclosures, one a brief hurried scrawl from Travis, the other a black-edged missive from his wife. Of what fatal news was this last the messenger? Could it be that his child was dead? or--or was it merely that Vanna had had news from home of the death of some one there? It was the former dire possibility that had smitten him with an unspeakable dread.

He steadied himself sufficiently to read what his partner had to tell him before breaking the black-edged envelope.

"Dear Alexander" (wrote Travis), "the enclosed was brought here by a boarding-house messenger a few minutes ago. As it may be of importance that it should reach you with the least possible delay, and as you have wired me not to expect

you back before Tuesday, I mail it on at once.
"Sincerely yours,
"Frank Travis."

Then he tore open his wife's letter.

A single devouring glance at the first half dozen lines was enough. His child was dead!

He could read no further then. The lines danced and quivered before his eyes. The letter fluttered from his fingers. For a moment or two every drop of blood seemed drawn from his heart. He caught at a chair and sank into it. He was as one smitten by a blow from an invisible hand. The love his wife had repudiated and would have none of, had been lavished by him, secretly and undemonstratively, on his child. His affection for it had been of that deep intense kind which neither seeks nor finds for itself an adequate outlet in words. And now he was bereft of the one object that had made life still sweet to him, and henceforward naught was left him save the dust and ashes of existence!

Afternoon had darkened into evening, and night had come before he roused himself sufficiently to pick up his wife's letter and read it through to the end. By that time a lighted lamp had been brought him.

He now noticed for the first time that the letter bore a date a week old, but just then he could no more than vaguely wonder why and how it had been delayed. Giovanna had always been in the habit of beginning her epistles to her husband without troubling herself to employ any of those preliminary terms of affection or politeness which most writers make use of; and her present one was no exception to the rule.

"It has become my most painful task" (she began) "to have to inform you that our child died in the course of Friday night last, after only a few hours' illness. Everything was done for it that could be done, but in vain. The doctor whom I had summoned was present when the end came. The funeral took place to-day, Monday. I enclose you the certificate of burial.

"It seemed to me that it would have been useless, as well as foolish, to bring you upwards of seven hundred miles merely in order that you might be present at the interment. All was over. Your presence could have availed nothing.

"With the death of my babe the strongest link in the chain which bound me to you, is broken. Had it lived I should not have taken the step I have now determined upon: which is, to at once go back to my own home, in my own country--which I ought never to have left.

"Both you and I have long been aware of the terrible mistake we made in taking upon ourselves the obligations of matrimony. It is not too late, however (or so I think and believe), to undo in some measure at least the folly of which we were mutually guilty. There is one way, and one only, by means of which this can be

effected. It is for us to separate--it is for you to go your way, and I to go mine--and to be virtually dead to each other henceforward and for ever.
"I shall leave this place three hours hence on my way to New York, whence I shall take the steamer for Europe, but whether I shall proceed direct to Italy, or whether I shall first visit my mother's relatives in England, I have not yet decided. In any case, it would be useless for you to follow me. My mind is fully made up, and nothing would induce me to return to you.
"When you left this place three months ago you put into my hands a number of blank signed cheques which I was to fill up at my own discretion for whatever sums I might find myself in need of while you were away. By means of one of the cheques in question I have drawn out the remaining balance standing to your credit in the bank, amounting to a trifle over five hundred pounds. You are not the man to begrudge me this sum, I am sure, for you were ever generosity itself towards me.
"And now I have nothing more to add, except to bid you farewell, and to ask you to believe that you have, in all sincerity, the best wishes for your future happiness and prosperity of one who regrets that she cannot love you as such a man as you deserves to be loved.
"Giovanna.

"P.S. I have arranged for this letter not to be posted till a week after my departure, so that by the time you read these lines I shall be halfway on my road to Europe."

Alas, poor Alec! Wife and child lost to him at one fell blow! As regarded the latter, he could but bow his head in all humility, as it behoves all of us to do when our turn comes to be smitten, and breathe the words: "Thy will be done." But Vanna? Oh, the callousness, the cruelty that breathed through almost every line of her letter! He had wept for the loss of his child, and it had been an infinite relief to him to do so--but his eyes were dry now; he had no tears left for her. It seemed rather as if her desertion of him served, during those first bitter hours, to kindle in his heart a dull smouldering fire of resentment, which was none the less intense in that it betrayed nothing of itself on the surface. Go after her, indeed!--try, with endearments and protestations, to induce her to return! Not a single step would he stir in pursuit. He and she had done with each other for ever.
The miserable hours trod slowly in the footsteps of each other, and the night wore itself away somehow. He never undressed, or went to bed, but about

daybreak he flung himself on a couch, where he sank into a half slumber which lasted till the people of the house were astir and the world had woke up to another day.

He was glad when ten o'clock had come, at which hour he set foot on board *The Prairie Belle* on his way back to Pineapple City.

CHAPTER VI.

ALEC'S FATE.

Denis Boyd did not forget the promise he had given Alec Clare not to mention his encounter with the latter after his return to England. It did not, however, seem to him that there was any necessity to include his father in the embargo thus laid on his tongue. Accordingly when, a little later, Colonel Boyd went on a visit to his son, the latter, knowing that his father and Sir Gilbert were acquaintances of many years' standing, mentioned, as one of the minor incidents of his recent visit to the States, his meeting with young Clare, without any thought that the Colonel might have occasion to deem it worth his while to mention the circumstance again. As it fell out, however, a few weeks later, Colonel Boyd and Sir Gilbert found themselves together in the reading-room of the London club of which both were members. They had not met for some time, for of late years the baronet's visits to the metropolis had become few and far between. They greeted each other heartily, and agreed to lunch together.

In the course of the meal the Colonel said: "By the way, Clare, my lad and yours stumbled across each other quite by accident a little while ago in the States, where Denny had been sent on a matter of business for his firm."

"Ah, indeed," remarked the baronet as he set down the glass of wine he had been in the act of raising to his lips. "And how was Alec?"

"First-rate, for anything I was told to the contrary. They had only a very short time together, as I understood, and seeing that they were chums at college, they would have plenty of subjects to talk about."

"No doubt--no doubt. By-the-bye, did your boy say whereabouts in the States it was--in New York, or Boston, or Chicago--that he came across Alec?"

"Oh, it was in some quite outlandish place I believe; but I did not trouble to remember the name."

"I am rather anxious to ascertain Alec's address, and for this reason: his godmother, Mrs. Fleming, died lately and left him a legacy of two thousand pounds. The executors, being anxious to wind up the estate, have applied to me for his address, which I am unable to furnish them with. You see, Alec kicked over the traces pretty considerably some time ago, and he and I parted in a huff, since which he has not condescended to keep me *au courant* of his movements. Now, if your boy can supply me with his address, it will get me out of my difficulty with Mrs. Fleming's executors."

"I have no doubt Denny can furnish you with what you want. I will write to him by to-night's post, and advise you of the result the moment I hear from him."

Denis Boyd, in view of his promise to Alec Clare, could not help feeling annoyed at the turn the affair had taken; and yet, as he put it to himself, what harm could come of his furnishing Sir Gilbert with the information he asked for? Apparently the only purpose for which the baronet required his son's address was that he might thereby be enabled to inform him that a certain legacy was awaiting his instructions. Really, when he, Boyd, came to think of it, Alec ought to be very grateful to him, and doubtless would be were he made aware of the circumstances, for having had it in his power to do him such a capital turn.

His brief note to his father was to the effect that young Clare, who passed in the States under the name of "John Alexander," was at the time the writer met him, residing at Pineapple City, a town on the borders of Lake Michigan, in the State of the same name; and, further, that he was engaged in business there, his partner being an Englishman of the name of Travis.

This note was at once forwarded by Colonel Boyd to Sir Gilbert, who lost no time in taking it in person to Mr. Page.

As it happened, the lawyer about that time had occasion to send a confidential member of his staff to America, to make certain inquiries in the interests of one of his clients; so it was decided that, instead of trusting to the chances of a letter reaching Alec through the medium of the post, the clerk in question, Winch by name, should proceed as far as Pineapple City, seek out "Mr. John Alexander," and deliver into his hands the communication which would be entrusted to him for that purpose.

The letter referred to was written by Mr. Page, and was read and approved of by Sir Gilbert before being sealed up. It was nothing more than a briefly worded intimation to the effect that two thousand pounds, being the amount of the late Mrs. Fleming's legacy to her godson, was awaiting his disposal in the hands of the executors at such and such an address. But the baronet had no knowledge of the little private note from the same pen which the lawyer contrived to smuggle into the envelope. In it he reproached Alec for having allowed so long a time to pass without communicating with him, begging him at once to repair the omission, and assuring him that in the writer he had a friend who might always be relied upon to keep a watchful eye over his interests.

Mr. Winch started on his long journey in due course. He would attend, first of all, to that other business which was taking him across the Atlantic, and then make the best of his way to Pineapple City.

Mr. Winch was an undersized, podgy man, with a round full-moon sort of face and cold fish-like eyes of no hue in particular, to which a pair of spectacles lent a still more vacuous expression. He was clean shaven, always dressed in well-worn black, and, wet or fine, was never seen without a serviceable alpaca umbrella. He had been Mr. Page's confidential clerk for many years, and that gentleman esteemed him highly. Behind that Dutch-clock-like mask of a face was a complex-working brain which delighted in secrets and mysteries, and occasionally went so far as to imagine them where none existed. Although his employer had never told him so--for that was one of the few matters which the lawyer kept to himself--Mr. Winch had not the least doubt in his mind that the John Alexander to whom the letter of which he was the bearer was addressed and the heir of Withington Chase, who had set out on his travels upwards of four years ago and had never returned, were one and the same person. The name alone had been enough to furnish him with the first hint. He seemed to scent a most delightful mystery. Mr. Winch was jubilant, although, to look at him, nobody would have guessed it.

What, then, must have been his feelings--indeed, it is not too much to say that a tear blurred his spectacles--as on the morning of the twenty-first day after his departure from Liverpool he stood in the telegraph office at Pineapple City and wrote out the following cablegram, addressed to Mr. Page:

"J. A. killed. Steamboat explosion--September 18th. Am returning at once."

The mystery on which he had counted had all at once collapsed owing to the death of the person chiefly concerned.

It became Mr. Page's unenviable duty, on receipt of the above message, to convey the news to Sir Gilbert. Over what passed between the two on that occasion we need not linger.

On arriving at Liverpool, Mr. Winch telegraphed to his employer by which train he might be expected to reach Mapleford. It was as a consequence of this message that he found Sir Gilbert Clare seated in Mr. Page's private office when, after a preliminary tap at the door, he was bidden to enter.

"Glad to see you back, Winch, and looking so well," said Mr. Page heartily, as he shook hands with his subordinate. "Of course I know already from your advices the nature of the arrangements you were enabled to make in that matter of Lord Dovercourt, and I congratulate you on your success. Later on we will go through the details one by one. But, sit down. What I want you to do first of all is to furnish me with the whole of the particulars you have been able to obtain confirmatory of the cablegram by which you advised me of the death of Mr. John Alexander."

Mr. Winch seated himself opposite his employer at the big square writing-table in the centre of the room. Sir Gilbert sat with his back to them and facing the fire. Although he appeared to be immersed in *The Times* , and betrayed no more interest in what followed than any stranger might have done, the reason that had brought him there was perfectly transparent to Mr. Winch, who could not help saying to himself: "Surely to goodness, Mr. Page does not think me such an innocent as not to be able to see through Sir Gilbert's little plot!"

Much of what Mr. Winch had to relate will have already been anticipated by the reader. We need only take up his narrative at the point where Alec Clare, on the morning following the receipt of his wife's letter, stepped on board the *Prairie Belle* at Milwaukee, in the expectation of landing at Davisville about nine o'clock the same evening. But the *Prairie Belle* never reached Davisville. When about a dozen miles from that place, and soon after nightfall, one of her boilers exploded. The vessel parted amidships, and five minutes later all that was left of her sank in deep water. The accident happened only about half a mile from the shore, and a number of boats at once put out to the rescue of the survivors, of whom a considerable number were picked up, several of them, however, being so badly injured that they afterwards succumbed. Of those saved John Alexander was not one. The only inference which could be drawn, was that, either, like many among both passengers and crew, he had been killed outright by the explosion, and that his body had gone down with the ship, or else that, even though, perhaps unhurt, he had sunk before help could reach him from the shore. In any case, alive or dead, nothing was seen or heard of him after the explosion, which had happened just eight weeks prior to Mr. Winch's interview with Mr. Frank Travis.

"I presume," said Mr. Page, "it is a matter of absolute certainty that Mr. Alexander was really on board the ill-fated vessel at the time of the accident."

"That was a question I did not fail to put to Mr. Travis. In reply he told me that among the survivors was a person well acquainted with Mr. Alexander, who had been talking to him only a few minutes before the explosion."

"In that case, I am afraid there is no room left for doubt as to the poor fellow's fate. A sad end, truly, for any one to come to!--I think that will do for the present, Mr. Winch. We will go into other matters later on."

"By-the-way, sir, there is one point which I have not yet mentioned. It is this: When Mr. Alexander, some little time prior to his death, entered into partnership with Mr. Travis, he put the sum of fifteen hundred pounds into the business. That amount Mr. Travis desired me to say that he shall be prepared to refund to Mr. Alexander's heir-at-law after due substantiation of claim and reasonable notice having been given him."

"Hum! very honourable on the part of Mr. Travis. It is a matter, however, as to which there is no immediate hurry, and in regard to which I can take no steps without instructions."

As soon as Mr. Winch had closed the door behind him the baronet faced round.

"It is all true, then!" he exclaimed. "There seems no longer any room for hope."

"None whatever, I am afraid, Sir Gilbert."

"He was my son, Page--my firstborn! I cannot forget that whatever his faults--and they were many--may they lie lightly on his head!"

When, on his return home, the baronet broke the news to his wife, that lady, being a fairly good actress, had no difficulty in giving the needful lugubrious twist to her features, but when she strove to eliminate a tear, she was not so successful. "I am so sorry," she said softly, laying a plump hand for a moment on her husband's shoulder. "Sorry for his sake, poor fellow!--and sorry for yours. But you must strive not to give way, dear. You may rely upon it that it has been ordained for the best." To herself she said: "So, after all, the title as well as the estates will come to Randolph! That is only as it should be. I hate the thought of having to go into mourning, but I suppose there's no help for it."

Poor Lady Clare!

No long time elapsed before a marble tablet was placed *in situ* above the family pew in Withington Church--where there were many more tablets to keep it company--which recorded that it was to the memory of John Alexander Clare, "who was accidentally killed abroad" on such and such a date, "in the twenty-eighth year of his age."

"To think," said Mr. Winch as he one day read the inscription through his spectacles, "that there are only three people in England who know how that poor young man really came by his death, and that I am one of them! But what reason had he for dropping his surname and hiding his identity? Ah! those are mysteries which I'm afraid I shall never now have a chance of fathoming."

By Sir Gilbert's desire, no communication was ever entered into with Mr. Frank Travis. The baronet preferred to sacrifice the fifteen hundred pounds which Alec had invested in the business rather than reopen before the eyes of strangers a chapter of family history which, as he trusted, was now closed for ever.

CHAPTER VII.

TOO LATE.

Years nearly a score have come and gone since Mr. Winch brought home the news of the untimely demise of the whilom heir of Withington Chase.

Many have been the changes under the old roof-tree during that time. Sir Gilbert Clare, who is now entering on his seventy-fourth year, is both a widower and childless. Not only is the second Lady Clare dead, but her three sons have followed her to the tomb. Two of them have died of consumption when on the verge of manhood, while the youngest has been accidentally drowned.

Yes, a lonely, childless old man is Sir Gilbert, but still carrying himself bravely before the world, as if in defiance of all the blows a cruel fate has aimed at him, and still retaining a large measure of his old irritability of temper and imperiousness of manner. Would it be too much to wonder whether his heart is ever touched with compunction, or regret, when his eyes chance to rest on a certain tablet above the family pew--that pew now empty of all but himself--which professes to record the death of his firstborn? That, however, is one of those things known to himself alone.

The venue of our story now changes to St. Oswyth's, a town in the Midlands of some twelve to fifteen thousand inhabitants.

It was the fourteenth of May, and Ethel Thursby's nineteenth birthday. Nowhere was there a happier girl than she. Breakfast was just over, and she had come out into the garden to gather a posy of such flowers as were already in bloom for the drawing-room table. Earlier there had been congratulations and presents from her aunts. Miss Matilda had given her "such a love" of a gold watch and chain, while Miss Jane's gift had taken the shape of an inlaid writing-desk filled with stationery stamped with Ethel's monogram, so that really, as she told herself, it was quite a pity her correspondents were so few in number, and that she could not well write to any of them oftener than once a week. Nor had Tamsin forgotten her--dear, rugged, true-hearted Tamsin, who had been her aunt's maid, and hers too for that matter, for more years than she could remember. Ethel's present from her had been a silver thimble, having engraven on its rim the appropriate legend, "A stitch in time saves nine."

While busying herself with the gathering and arrangement of her flowers, Ethel's thoughts were engaged on two very diverse subjects. As she rose from the

breakfast-table this morning, her Aunt Matilda had said to her:
"My dear, I and my sister would like to see you in the drawing-room at twelve precisely, when we shall have something of importance to communicate to you."
That the girl should wonder to herself what the "something of importance" could be was but natural.
But just then she had neither time nor inclination to wonder overmuch, her thoughts being almost exclusively taken up by an altogether different matter. The communication which she hoped to be able to make to her aunts a few hours hence, far outweighed, in her estimation, anything they could possibly have to say to her. For had not Launce promised that to-day, on her birthday, to wit, he would take off the embargo of silence he had imposed upon her, and give her leave to inform her aunts of their engagement? It was a secret which had weighed upon her ever since, in response to his persistent entreaties, she had yielded a reluctant consent to an arrangement so totally opposed to her feelings and modes of thought. No one but herself could tell how happy she should feel when it was a secret no longer.

The Miss Thursbys had come to reside at St. Oswyth's when Ethel was about two years old. She was an orphan, and who, if not they, should take charge of the parentless girl and bring her up as their own? Even then they were spinsters of mature age, but beyond silvering their hair in some measure, the intervening years had changed them scarcely at all. They belonged to that happy class of persons, with equable tempers, untroubled by dyspepsia and uncorroded by pessimism, whom Time loves to touch with the gentlest of fingers. He does not overlook them entirely, but the furrows he traces on their placid brows are few and far between. And so they go on for years, growing older by gradations so gentle as to be scarcely perceptible; for, say as we will, the old scythe-man has his favourites.
The sisters, on coming to St. Oswyth's, had bought Vale View House--a substantial modern-built mansion, standing in its own pleasant grounds, but a world too big for the requirements of their unpretentious establishment. That, however, was nobody's business but their own.
There they had settled down, and there, in "quiet innocency," it was their hope to spend the remaining term of their lives.
They had a joint income, derivable in part from property left them by their father, and in part by their brother, of about eight hundred pounds a year. In addition to their faithful Tamsin, they kept a couple of maid-servants, a cook, a youth in buttons, and a man who combined the duties of gardener with those of groom to Flossie, the pony driven by them in their pretty little basket-carriage. They came of a Quaker stock, but their father had seceded when they were quite young. They still, however, retained much of the traditional simplicity of dress

and demeanour of their progenitors and "thee'd" and "thou'd" each other when they were alone, but rarely, or never, when in the company of others.
Be it known, further, that Miss Matilda and Miss Jane were twins, they having been born within half-an-hour of each other.
Owing, however, to some stupid mismanagement on the part of the nurse, they had got "mixed," so to speak, when only a few hours old, and it was not positively known which of them was the elder.
In this embarrassing state of affairs they had long ago--that is to say, from the date of their commencing to keep house together--come to a mutual arrangement by which they agreed to take it in turns, month and month about, to enact the part of elder sister, during which time the other deferred to her in every way, only, in her turn, to occupy the superior position and be deferred to throughout the following month.
It was an arrangement well understood among the circle of their friends and acquaintance, but, in order that there should be no mistake in the matter, each in turn, during the month she filled the *rô*le* of elder sister, wore round her neck, by way of distinguishing token, an old-fashioned gold chain from which was suspended an equally old-fashioned locket, which, when open, displayed on one side a miniature of their mother, and on the other a lock of their father's hair.
Thus it came to pass that whenever people visited at Vale View House, or whenever they were called upon by the sisters, they would nudge each other and whisper, "This is Miss Matilda's month," or Miss Jane's, according to which of them was wearing the chain and locket; and to that one they would have been considered by the sisters as lacking in good manners, had they failed to address her as " *Miss* Thursby," or to treat her with an added shade of deference as representing for the time being the head of the family.
By every one who knew them, both rich and poor (and to numbers of poor people they were very well known indeed) the ladies of Vale View were beloved and respected; although it might be that there were not wanting some would-be "superior" persons who smiled to themselves at certain old-fashioned ways and quaint simplicities of speech and manner which they were quite incapable of appreciating. But such people are to be met with everywhere. It was Mrs. Trippington-Fynes, a new-comer at St. Oswyth's, and regarded as quite an acquisition to the somewhat restricted circle of society in the little town, who, after having been introduced to the Misses Thursby and chatted with them awhile, remarked to Mrs. Sandilands, wife of the popular squire of that name:
"Do you know, my dear, I find them quite too deliciously archaic."
It was a phrase that was repeated and taken up, and for many a day afterwards the sisters were spoken of by one person or another as being "quite too deliciously archaic, don't you know."
But we have left Ethel all this time alone in the garden.
Following her with our eyes, while she pursues her dainty occupation, what do we see? A slender supple figure of medium height, every movement of which

betrays an easy unstudied grace with which training has evidently had nothing to do. A small head crowned with plaits and coils of glossy dark brown hair; eyes, too, of a brown so dark that unless you are privileged to gaze into them by sunlight, you would be almost ready to wager that they are absolutely black; large and luminous, with here and there a tiny fleck of ruddy light, they respond instantaneously to every fluctuating emotion of the loving, brave, reverent soul which looks out at you through them. The face, with its candid brow, its rather short straight nose and the soft curves of its chin, has the ineffable charm of purity, of equable pulses, of slow-breathing health both of mind and body; the whole expression is one of sweet, grave steadfastness.

To connect Ethel Thursby in one's thoughts with such feminine weaknesses as a fit of hysterics, or an attack of "nerves," would seem as preposterous as to assume that the man in the moon is afflicted after a similar fashion. This morning she is wearing a lavender-coloured frock of some soft clinging stuff which displays to perfection the charming contours of her figure. Her collarette and cuffs are of lace, woven by a crippled girl in a neighbouring village, whom Ethel counts as one among the number of her humble friends.

The sound of footsteps on the gravel of the carriage drive breaks up her reverie. She turns to behold Everard Lisle, and, as she does so, a smile of welcome illumines her face.

The young man in question was the son of the vicar of the parish church of St. Oswyth's, and had been intended for the medical profession, for which he had displayed much natural aptitude; but an illness, the result of overwork while a student in Paris, had left him with weakened eyesight.

Having been ordered to give up his studies for a long time to come, and to confine himself to some outdoor occupation, he had chosen to become the pupil and, later on, the assistant to an architect and land surveyor in St. Oswyth's; and so much did his new profession prove to his liking, and so well did it agree with his health, that at length he definitively decided to discard the one for which he had originally been intended.

Everard's father, the Rev. Harold Lisle, and Sir Gilbert Clare--at that time simply Mr. Clare--had been contemporaries at college, but strangers to each other previously to a certain afternoon, when it had been the good fortune of the former to save the life of the latter, who had been seized with cramp while bathing.

From that time they had never quite lost touch of each other, so that when Sir Gilbert, who always felt that he owed a debt of gratitude to his preserver, became in want of some one to fill the double post of amanuensis to himself--his eyesight having failed him considerably of late--and assistant to his land-steward, Mr. Kinaby, whose health was breaking up, he wrote to the Rev. Harold, offering the position in question to his son, of whose affairs he had some knowledge, by whom it was gladly accepted. Everard Lisle, who had now been a couple of months at Withington Chase, had come over to St. Oswyth's to-day for a special purpose, the nature of which will presently appear.

He had known Ethel Thursby for years, and had loved her as long as he had known her.
They had met frequently, sometimes at his own home, for now and then the ladies from Vale View took tea with his mother, and sometimes in general society. When he had first known her she had been still a schoolgirl, and he had told himself that he could afford to wait till she should be of an age to listen to what he had to say to her.
Then had come the break in his prospects consequent on his illness, after which he had had to begin the world afresh. Knowing that he would have to rely solely upon his own exertions--for his father's living was far from being a lucrative one and there were several fledgelings still under the parental roof--and that some years must necessarily elapse before he would be able to marry, with rare self-abnegation he determined neither by word nor sign to betray his love to the object of it till he should have some assured prospect of being able to ask her to share with him such a home as she was entitled to expect. To that prospect he had at length attained, and he was here to-day with the determination to tell her all that he had carefully hidden in his heart for so long a time. But delays are dangerous in love, as in so many other of the affairs of life, as Everard was presently destined to find to his cost. He was a well set-up resolute-looking young fellow, clear-eyed and clear-skinned, and groomed to perfection; in brief, as far as appearance was concerned, a typical young Briton of the latter half of the nineteenth century.
He was making directly for the house, but the moment he caught sight of Ethel his face flushed, a sudden sparkle leapt to his eyes, and he at once turned and made across the lawn towards her. In one hand he was carrying a bouquet of choice orchids covered up in tissue paper.
Ethel, seeing him thus unexpectedly, supposed, naturally enough, that he had come to spend a brief holiday at home, not troubling herself to remember that only a couple of months had gone by since he had taken up the duties of his new position.
"This is a surprise," she said smilingly as she gave him her hand. "I quite thought you were a hundred miles away at the least. That's about the distance, is it not, to--to--I forget its name--the place where you are now living?"
They turned together and strolled slowly along.
"That is about the distance," he smilingly replied. "Duty ought, perhaps, to have kept me at Withington Chase, but inclination has brought me to St. Oswyth's. I did not forget that this is your birthday, Miss Ethel; as a proof of which I venture to offer you these few flowers. Will you deign to accept them with the giver's best wishes for your health and happiness." As he spoke he stripped the paper off the bouquet and offered it for Ethel's acceptance.
She took it without a shadow of hesitation, first coming to a stand and placing on the lawn the basket in which she had been gathering her own flowers. "Oh, how lovely--how exquisitely lovely!" she exclaimed with unfeigned admiration. Flowers such as those were a revelation to her. "It was very very kind of you, Mr.

Lisle, to remember my birthday in such a charming fashion. My aunts will be as delighted as I am. Of course you will come in and see them now that you are here."

Even now there was no dawn of suspicion in her heart as to the real purport of his visit. Everard's courage sank a little, but he had come all the way from the Chase to seek his opportunity, and now that he had found it he was not the man to let it slip through his fingers.

"One moment, if you please," he pleaded. "There is something that I wish particularly to say to you."

"Yes?" she said interrogatively, turning her gaze full upon him, with the slightest inflection of surprise in her voice.

Then, all at once, she saw that in his eyes which revealed to her what it was he was about to say to her, and before the clear intense flame of love which glowed in their depths, her own eyes sank abashed and dismayed. To her it came, indeed, as a revelation. For a moment or two all the pulses of her being seemed to stand still. She said to herself, "I am dreaming--presently I shall awake." Everard took her hand and she did not know it. From her unresisting fingers he withdrew the bouquet and placed it on the basket at her feet. It was only when he began to speak that she came to herself. Between the spot where they were standing and the house a large clump of evergreens intervened. From none of the windows could they be overlooked.

Everard, reading in her face some portion of that which was passing through her mind, gave her a few moments in which to recover herself; before saying more. Then, not without misgivings, he resumed:

"It was more, far more, than merely to congratulate you on your birthday and offer you a few flowers that brought me here to-day. It was to tell you that I love you--that I have loved you in secret for years--it was to ask you to be my wife."

A faintly-breathed "Oh!" fluttered from Ethel's lips. She withdrew her fingers from his clasp gently but firmly. Everard's heart sank still lower, but he went bravely on:

"Many a time before to-day," he continued, "have I been tempted to speak to you, to tell you what I am telling you now, but it was a temptation to which I would not yield. I was a poor man with no prospects worth speaking of; and I would not seek to entangle you in an engagement which might have to last for years. But, after long waiting, Fortune's wheel has turned for me, and now----"

He ceased abruptly at the touch of her hand on his sleeve. Her large dark eyes--and at that moment they looked to him larger and darker than they had ever looked before--were gazing into his beseechingly.

"Not a word more--not one, please, Mr. Lisle," she entreated. "Oh, I am so sorry that you have told me this!"

"Is my telling it you, then, of no avail?" he demanded, a little hoarsely.

"Of none whatever," she replied with a slow shake of her head.

His eyes scanned her face searchingly and read there but too surely that his sentence was irrevocable. His chest rose and fell a few times. Not all at once

could he command himself.
"So be it," he said at length. "We must all bow to the inevitable. Mine has been the mistake, and mine must be the penalty. I will not urge you by a word more, because I feel how useless it would be to do so. Nor will I longer intrude upon your time. We shall always, I trust, meet as friends in time to come."
"It would grieve me to think otherwise." Then, as she held out her hand: "Always as friends, Mr. Lisle, come what may."
With one hand he lifted his hat and with the other he raised her fingers to his lips.
"I am so sorry," again broke involuntarily from Ethel.
"The sorrow and the regret are for me," answered Everard with a dim smile as, after touching her fingers with his lips, he released them with a sort of gentle reluctance. "For you I trust there are in store many, many returns of to-day, each and all of them crowned with happiness."
Half-a-minute later she was alone.
"Everard Lisle loves me!" she murmured to herself as he disappeared round a bend of the drive. "How strange it seems! And yet, now that he has told me, I can call to mind a dozen little things, any one of which would have revealed his secret to me had I not been so blind. How cruel he must have thought me! how abrupt! And yet what other answer was it possible for me to give him? None whatever."
It may seem strange, nay, perhaps, almost incredible, to that class of young women who are in the habit of regarding three-fourths of the eligible bachelors whom they encounter here and there in society in the light of potential lovers, that Ethel Thursby had never so regarded Everard Lisle. But so it was. She had liked him, she now told herself, far better than she had liked any other of the young men whom she was in the habit of occasionally meeting; but liking is not love, and besides, Launce Keymer had already whispered certain words in her ear.
Perhaps--perhaps, if Everard Lisle had been the first to speak, who could have told what might have happened? Was there some faint premonition in her heart, as this question put itself to her, that he to whom she had given her love might, peradventure, prove less worthy of the gift than Everard would have done?
"No--no!" she told herself almost passionately. "Dear Launce is everything--yes, everything--that any girl could wish for in the man she loves."
Then she began to cry a little, being all the while indignant with herself because her tears would come in her own despite. Then with a start she bethought herself that she had to meet her aunts in the drawing-room at noon, and eleven had struck long ago. She dried her eyes and took up her flowers. More than once, as she walked towards the house, her face was hidden in the bouquet Everard had brought her. What would have been his thoughts had he been there to see?

CHAPTER VIII.

THE EBONY CASKET.

AT five minutes to twelve the two Miss Thursbys, who prided themselves on their punctuality, entered the drawing-room together, or rather, to speak more correctly Miss Matilda entered first, with Miss Jane close on her footsteps, this happening to be the former's month for enacting the part of elder sister, as a consequence of which she wore what might be termed the "chain of office" with its pendant locket. That something out of the common was on foot could not be doubted, seeing that at that early hour of the day the sisters were already attired in their puce-coloured lutestring gowns, and were wearing their "company caps" and best lace mittens--a conjunction rarely, if ever, witnessed except when some special visitors were expected at Vale View.

Earlier in the day--before breakfast, indeed--they had told each other sadly and for the last time, as if their courage needed stimulating by reiterated assurances, that a certain revelation must no longer be delayed. It had been Matthew's--their dead brother's--wish that Ethel should be told on her nineteenth birthday, and with them his wishes had always been law. And yet it was a grievous thing to have to do. It seemed to them that after to-day "the child," as they still continued to call Ethel between themselves, could never regard them with quite the same eyes as heretofore. Very downcast they looked as they sat there on the ottoman, side by side, waiting for the timepiece to chime the hour of noon.

They were tall fair women, thin without being in the least degree angular; with blue eyes, rather long straight noses, and a slight droop at the corners of the mouth, which, when they were not engaged in conversation, lent them an habitually pensive air, although, in reality, they could be sprightly enough on occasion. When younger they had been noted for their lovely pink-and-white complexions, and their cheeks still retained the delicate ivory clearness of an arum lily. If one had been asked to sum up in the fewest possible words the predominant expression of the twin sisters--so strangely alike and yet not without discernible points of difference--one would have said that it was a mixture in equal parts of sweetness and goodness, and, in so saying, one would not have been far wrong. How it had come to pass that two such women--or neither of them--had never married, was one of those delicate problems which no mere bystander is justified in trying to solve. That they themselves could have told the reason why, had they chosen to do so, is scarcely to be doubted.

On the centre table stood a quaintly carved ebony casket, clamped with silver and having a silver plate let into the lid, on which, in Old English characters, was engraved the monogram, "M. T." Tamsin had brought it in and placed it there a few minutes before the entrance of the sisters.

Scarcely had the timepiece chimed the last stroke of twelve when the door opened and Ethel entered the room. Miss Matilda rose and, crossing to her, embraced her tenderly, an example which was at once followed by Miss Jane. This ceremonious greeting, taken in conjunction with her aunts' "robes of state," and the presence of the ebony casket, which she had never seen opened, but which, as long as she could remember, had been known to her as the depository of Uncle Matthew's papers, all sufficed to convince the girl that some momentous occasion was at hand. Her cheeks paled perceptibly and her limbs began to tremble. Then she drew in her breath, called herself a coward, and asked herself what she had to fear. A moment or two she stood, and then she seated herself in the pretty fancy-chair which she called her own. It had been her Aunt Jane's gift on her sixteenth birthday.

"My dear child," began Miss Matilda--and then she was compelled to pause for a few seconds before she could continue--"My dear child," she repeated, "your Aunt Jane and I have asked you to meet us in order that we may reveal to you certain circumstances connected with your early history of which you have heretofore been kept purposely in ignorance, but which it was the desire of our dear brother should be made known to you on your nineteenth birthday. That day has now arrived, and we are here in order to carry out our brother's wishes."

Miss Matilda paused again, and glanced at her sister, who responded by an encouraging nod, as much as to say, "Very nicely put, indeed." Miss Matilda resumed:

"My dear Ethel, you have been brought up to call my sister and me by the title of Aunt--and very sweet, as coming from your lips, it has sounded in our ears--and to the world at large you have passed as our niece. But the time has now come when the truth must no longer be withheld from you. My child, you are *not* our niece, nor any relative whatsoever. It grieves me to the heart to have to tell you this."

Here the spinster's voice quavered and broke; she turned away her face. Miss Jane was biting her underlip in an effort to keep down her emotion; one of her hands stole out and clasped a hand of her sister.

A low, inarticulate cry broke from Ethel. It was the cry of one not merely wounded, but stunned. She half rose from her chair and then sat down again and stared from one to the other, her eyes saying for her that which her lips were powerless to utter. Then all in a moment her tongue was loosened as if a cord had been cut. An instant later she was on her knees in front of the sisters, pressing a hand of each "Then, if you are not my aunts, whose child am I?" she cried aloud.

It was a quarter of an hour later. The sisters had mingled their tears with Ethel's. They had petted and made much of her till some measure of composure had come back to her. She knew that she had not yet been told all there was to tell; there was more to follow; but no second shock could equal the first. The worst was known to her; it could matter little---or so just then it seemed to her--what still remained to be told.

Presently Miss Matilda resumed her interrupted narrative.

"Many years ago--between nineteen and twenty, in point of fact--my brother Matthew, by the death of a half-cousin who had made his home in the United States, came in for a considerable legacy in the shape of landed property in that country. As a consequence, Matthew deemed it necessary that he should go out there in order to look after his interests, and he kindly offered to take my sister and me with him for a holiday. To this day Jane and I look back to that journey as the one great event of our lives. We remained in the States about three months, during which time we saw much, both of the country and the people. In the hope that the longer sea voyage would prove beneficial to my brother's health, we came back by a sailing vessel named *The Pandora* , instead of by steamer, as on our outward journey. It was in the course of our return voyage that certain events happened in connection with you, my dear child, having an important bearing on your future; an account of which, later on, and when he felt that his time in this world was growing short, my brother embodied in the form of a written statement, which was placed by him in his ebony casket and the same given into the custody of myself and sister a few hours before he breathed his last. It is that statement which I shall now proceed to place in your hands and which it has become your duty to open and read."

As she finished speaking, Miss Matilda rose and having selected one of the keys which hung from her chatelaine, proceeded to unlock and open the casket, which proved to be full of legal-looking documents--deeds, securities and what not. From underneath these she presently drew forth an oblong envelope which she handed to Ethel. It was fastened on one side with a large red seal and on the other was endorsed, "To my adopted Niece. To be opened by her on her nineteenth birthday, or sooner should my sisters deem it advisable.--M. T."

Ethel's hands trembled in spite of her. She looked at Miss Matilda with a pitiful smile. "Will not you open it and read it for me, dear aunt--if"--with a little sigh--"I may still be allowed to call you by that name?"

"My child, it is *your* place, nay, your duty, to open it and read what you will find written therein;" adding, with a touch of that old-fashioned phraseology which became her so well: "And I have never yet found my Ethel unresponsive to the call of duty."

Ethel said no more, but at once broke the seal and drew forth the enclosure, which consisted of a double sheet of letter paper closely covered with writing in a bold, masculine hand. The sisters, sitting bolt upright, one mittened hand laid across the other, looked on in silence. Having laid aside the envelope and straightened out the enclosure, Ethel said to Miss Matilda: "Do you wish me to

read it aloud?"
"My dear, that is entirely a matter for your own judgment. My sister and I are already cognisant of the contents, our brother having permitted us to peruse the paper previously to sealing it up."
"Still, I think I should prefer to read it aloud."
"As you please, my love."
A faint wintry smile lighted up the faces of the sisters. It was perhaps because they were so sad at heart that they smiled. It is a way their sex sometimes have.
Without further preface Ethel began to read:--

"My Dear Child,--When these lines meet your eye the hand that penned them will be dust.
"Having reason to feel assured that my remaining span of life will be a brief one, I have deemed it best, in your interests, and with a view to any contingencies which may arise in the future, to draw up a clear and succinct statement of the circumstances which first served to bring you under the notice of my sisters and myself, and led to our taking charge of you, temporarily, as we thought at the time, and ultimately to your adoption by us.
"In the autumn of the year 18-- my sisters and I, after a brief sojourn in the United States, took passage on our return voyage from New York to London by the clipper ship *Pandora* . There were not more than a score of passengers in addition to ourselves, but among them was a certain Mrs. Montmorenci-Vane, with her child, a baby about six months old. Her nursemaid, according to her account, having deserted her within an hour or two of her coming on board, she engaged a young woman from among the steerage passengers to look after her child during the voyage. Unfortunately, when the voyage was about half accomplished, Mrs. Montmorenci-Vane fell overboard one dark night and was lost. There was no one on the Pandora who knew anything about her; she was a complete stranger to every one. In this state of affairs, my sisters, who had their maid Tamsin with them, took upon themselves the care of the drowned woman's babe for the rest of the voyage, in the expectation that some one would meet the ship on its arrival--some relative or friend--into whose hands they could transfer it.
"In point of fact, when the *Pandora* reached the London Dock it was met by a thin, shabbily-dressed, consumptive-looking man, who had come to inquire for his sister, one Martha Griggs. There was no such person on board, but, by means of a photograph, he recognised his sister in the Mrs. Montmorenci-Vane, who had fallen overboard. Never did I see a man more utterly dumfounded than he. His sister had been unmarried. Only a few months before she had gone out to the States as maid to a wealthy lady, who, a little later, had died there. She had written to her brother that she was coming home by the *Pandora* , and had

asked him to meet the ship. But as to why she had chosen to call herself Mrs. Montmorenci-Vane, why she had gone to the extravagance of paying for a cabin passage, and whence she had obtained the child she passed off on board as her own, he professed himself as being utterly unable to comprehend. That the man's wonder and amazement were genuine it was impossible to doubt.

"He was a poor man, he averred, with a family of his own, and he would have nothing to do with his sister's child, which, according to his account, was not hers at all. For anything he cared, it might go to the workhouse. He went away like a dazed man, with a promise that he would call on me the next morning; but he failed to do so, and I have never set eyes on him from that day to this.

"That the child thus strangely thrown on our hands should be committed to the tender mercies of the workhouse was not to be thought of. For the time being it was put out to nurse, where my sisters were satisfied that it would be well cared for. When, a couple of years later, they went to reside permanently at St. Oswyth's, they took the child with them, they having decided to adopt it; and, in order that the tongue of idle rumour and scandal might have no cause to wag, at my persuasion they consented to the innocent ruse of passing the girl off to the world as their niece.

"I need scarcely add that you, my dear Ethel, are the child in question.

"In these few lines are summed up the whole of the facts bearing upon your early history which are known to my sisters and myself. I may, however, be allowed to record my firm belief that the person who called herself Mrs. Montmorenci-Vane was not your mother. That, after this length of time, the mystery of your birth and parentage will ever be cleared up, seems to me exceedingly doubtful; but even should such prove to be the case, who shall venture to say that the knowledge has not been withheld from you for some wise purpose. That, should you be spared, you will grow up to be a comfort and a blessing to those who have made their home your home, and that you will return them love for love, I feel fully assured.

"Matthew Thursby."

CHAPTER IX.

ETHEL AND TAMSIN.

When Ethel had read Matthew Thursby's letter to the last word she quietly refolded the paper and laid it on the table. The sisters were watching her every movement intently. She wished they would speak--that they would say something--anything. But it seemed as if they were waiting for her to break the silence. Her eyes turned from one to the other. In their faces she read nothing save love and compassion. Then, with a sob in her throat, she spoke.

"And I--the child of a stranger--a nobody's child, owe everything to you! But for you I might have starved, or found my only home in the workhouse! Oh! how can I ever love you half enough? But now I have learnt this, I feel that I have no longer a right to call this place my home. I must go out into the world and earn my living. I must strive to----"

"Ethel!" exclaimed an austere voice, that of Miss Matilda.

There was an inflection in it which the girl had not heard for years--not since some juvenile peccadillo had momentarily excited the spinster's ire. "Nothing which has occurred this morning justifies you in adopting such a tone towards my sister and myself. You seem to forget that what comes as news to you has been known to us from the first. Why, then, should you assume that the mere fact of your having learnt certain things to-day for the first time should have the effect of abrogating arrangements which have been in existence for a longer period than you can remember?" Miss Matilda's style in her more didactic moments was unconsciously modelled to some extent on that of her favourite authors, the English essayists of the eighteenth century.

"Forgive me for speaking as I did," pleaded Ethel, with eyes that were blinded with tears. "But, indeed, I am so overcome by what you have told me, and what I have just read, that I know not either what to say or what to do."

"There is nothing for you to do--nothing whatever," said Miss Matilda, still with a touch of peremptoriness.

"And perhaps, my dear, if you were to say as little as possible just now, it might be as well," interposed Miss Jane for the first time. Then turning to her sister, she added: "The poor child needs a little time to recover herself."

"There I agree with you, and I think the best thing she can do is to go and lie down for an hour." Then to Ethel, with a sudden softening of the voice, she said: "Child, child, cannot you understand that, despite all you have learnt to-day, nothing is to be changed--that you are still to be our niece, and we are still to be your aunts, and that everything is to go on precisely as before? Vale View will continue to be your home, as it has been for as long as you can remember, and you must never again hint at such a thing as going out into the world to earn your living, unless you wish your aunts to believe that you have ceased to care for them."

"And," added Miss Jane, with one of her sweetest smiles, "that you are tired of living under the same roof with two humdrum old women."

What reply Ethel would have made will never be known, because at this juncture there came a tap at the door, which was followed by the appearance of Charlotte, the parlourmaid, carrying a salver with a card on it. "If you please, ma'am," said the girl, "I've shown the lady into the morning-room."

"Tell Mrs. Lucas Dexter that I and my sister will be with her almost immediately," answered Miss Matilda, after a glance at the card.

As the girl left the room by one door, Ethel stole softly out by another.

The sisters looked at each other. It was a look which said, as plainly as words could have done, "How very fortunate that we happen to be wearing our puce lutestrings and our best caps this afternoon!"

The Hon. Mrs. Lucas Dexter was one of the great ladies of the neighbourhood, and had never condescended to call at Vale View but twice before, on both of which occasions she had contrived to extract a small cheque from the sisters. Indeed, it was a peculiarity of hers never to call upon anyone who was not quite in her own set, or whose position in the social scale, which in small provincial centres is marked by so many gradations, was admittedly below her own, without making them pay for the privilege in the shape of a subscription to one or other of the benevolent schemes in which she professed to be interested. Those among the small gentry of St. Oswyth's, and such of the professional people as were tolerably well-to-do, would have been pleased to have the Hon. Mrs. Lucas Dexter call upon them twice as often as she did, and would have looked upon the two or three guineas of which each of her visits depleted them as money well laid out, in so far as it had been the means of securing her presence for a quarter of an hour in their drawing-rooms. But there were others, to whom every guinea was an object, who would have been glad if she had passed them by altogether, and who groaned in spirit, while smiling a sickly smile, when the inevitable tablets and pencil were produced, and Mrs. Dexter, fixing her victim through her *pince-nez* , said, with that stand-and-deliver air which few people were found bold enough to resist: "And pray, what sum shall I have the pleasure of putting down opposite *your* name?"

Although Miss Matilda had advised Ethel to go and lie down awhile, the latter had no inclination for anything of the sort. Instead, she went in search of Tamsin, and found her in her own room, an apartment situated between the dressing-rooms of the sisters, and having a door which opened into each of them. Tamsin had been on board the *Pandora* , when Ethel's supposed mother had lost her life, and had a knowledge of all the events connected with that far-off time. Ethel could talk to her and question her, as she could not talk to or question her "aunts," and there were half-a-score things she was burning to hear about.

Tamsin was sitting in her favourite spot, on the broad, low, cushioned window-seat of her room. She was crooning to herself one of the quaint hymns she had learnt at her mother's knee half a century before. She had a short, rather dumpy figure, and very homely features. Her eyes were at once shrewd and good-humoured, and she had a very pleasant smile. Her still plentiful grey hair was crowned by a plain net cap, with goffered frills, bound over the crown of the head with a broad black ribbon. In age she was some three or four years older than her mistresses, whose service she had entered soon after they left school, and with whom she had remained ever since. Tamsin was famed for her skill as a needlewoman, and this afternoon she was engaged on some fine sewing, which it was her pride to be still able to see to do without the aid of spectacles.

Ethel burst into the room, and before Tamsin knew what had happened, she found herself being violently hugged.

"I know all!" exclaimed the girl. Next moment she corrected herself. "No, not quite all, but much--a great deal. I have just been reading Uncle Matthew's letter, written a little while before he died, with directions that it should be opened by me on my nineteenth birthday. And to think that you--you dear, but artful old thing--have known all these years everything there is in the letter, and yet have never breathed the least hint that I was somebody altogether different from the Ethel Thursby I have always believed myself to be!"

"The secret was not mine, dearie," replied Tamsin, as she pulled her cap into shape. "What would my mistresses have thought, if by as much as a single word, I had betrayed their trust in me? No, no, it was far better for you in every way, that you should be told nothing about these things till you were grown up. You would only have kept on bothering your child's brain to no good purpose."

"But, oh! Tamsin, to think that my aunts are not my aunts, and that I have no more right to bear their name than the veriest beggar that walks the streets!" There was that in her voice which told the elder woman that her tears were very close to the surface.

"Listen, honey," said Tamsin, as she stroked the girl's brown hair fondly. And thereupon, only in different words, and homelier phraseology, she proceeded to state the case to almost the same effect that it had been stated by Miss Matilda already. The mere fact that a certain piece of information, hitherto, for wise reasons, kept from her, had been told her to-day, did not and could not in the remotest degree affect the relations which had existed for so long a time between herself and her supposed aunts. They had chosen to adopt her as their niece when she was an infant, and such she would continue to be to them so long as it should please Providence to leave unsevered the thread of their earthly existence. She, Ethel, must strive to forget that Miss Matilda and Miss Jane were not her aunts in reality, and must continue to regard them in precisely the same light that she had always done.

Ethel sat awhile in silence after Tamsin had finished speaking. Then she said: "Just now it all seems so strange and incredible to me, that I find it almost as hard to believe as I should one of the fairy tales I used to read when a girl. In time, no doubt, I shall get used to it, so that it will seem as if I must have known of it all along; but that will not be to-day, nor to-morrow." A sigh broke from her. She sat staring out of the window without seeing anything of that which her eyes rested upon.

Presently she resumed: "But now that I have been told so much, I want to know more. There are several questions, Tamsin, which I do not care to ask my aunts, but which I don't in the least mind asking you."

Tamsin screwed up her mouth, but said nothing. It altogether depended on the nature of the girl's questions whether they would be answered by her or no.

"First of all," resumed Ethel, "Uncle Matthew, in his letter, states it as his belief that the--the person who passed me off on board ship as being her child was not in reality my mother, but he omits to give any reason for such a belief. You were there. Can you tell me what his reasons were, or what was your own belief in the matter?"

Tamsin's needle stopped in the middle of a stitch. She did not reply at once, but seemed to be considering within herself in what terms she should answer the question.

"My belief was the same as Mr. Matthew's," at length she replied. "Mrs. Vane had not been two days on board before I said to myself, 'It's very strange to me if that woman is that child's mother.' It was not merely that she didn't seem to care about you, and was never so pleased as when you were out of her sight, but from a score of different things, each a trifle in itself, that I so judged her."

"Was she--was she a lady?"

Tamsin shook her head. "She was not what *I* should call a lady, and I think I know a real lady when I see one as well as most people. She was not at all bad-looking, but as full of vanity as a peacock. Even at breakfast-time she always appeared in a silk or satin gown, with a lot of jewellery about her, which is not what ladies are in the habit of doing. Then, she used to make little slips in her talk, so that one could form a pretty good guess that her bringing up had been nothing particular. Her greatest delight was to flirt and carry on with the unmarried gentlemen on board, who used to encourage her in every way they could think of; just to make fun of her afterwards among themselves. But, with all her faults, hers was a dreadful fate--poor thing! To be laughing and giggling one minute, and playing off; as she supposed, one admirer against another, and the next to be overboard in the great black waste of waters! One wild despairing shriek came borne to our ears, and then all was silence. Oh, it was terrible!"

There was a long pause, and then Tamsin said: "I suppose, dearie, that Mr. Matthew in his letter told you about a certain person coming to the ship and inquiring for his sister, and of his recognising her in a photograph of Mrs. Vane which was shown him?"

Ethel nodded assent.

"And you would also be told how the man in question stated that his sister had gone out as lady's-maid only a little while before, that she was unmarried, and that it was impossible you should be her child?"

"Uncle Matthew's letter told me all that."

"Then, do you think, yourself, that any further evidence is needed to prove that, whoever else's daughter you may be, you are not the child of the woman who called herself Mrs. Montmorenci-Vane?"

"I suppose it must be as you say," replied Ethel. "So that the mystery of my birth remains as much a mystery as ever, and, after all these years, there is very little likelihood of its ever being solved."

"And if it has been kept from you, you may rely upon it that it has been for the best. How can you tell from what unhappiness, from what unknown dangers, you may have been saved? Instead of encouraging vain dreams about a past which is locked up from you, try to reckon up by how many blessings you are surrounded. Think what a happy girl you are, or ought to be, in comparison with what you might have been, and----"

"Oh, you dear old Tamsin, don't for one moment get it into your head that I am anything but grateful and thankful from the bottom of my heart for--for--oh, for everything!"

She had flung her arms round Tamsin's neck, and she now cried softly on her shoulder for a minute or two.

Presently she looked up with an April smile. "What a weak, foolish girl you must think me," she said. "But I have shed my last tear now for ever so long to come. I feel as if there's not another left for anybody. So, now tell me this: If nobody knows whose child I am, nor where I came from, how is it known that to-day is my nineteenth birthday?"

"That is very easily answered. It was on the 14th of November that Mrs. Vane brought you on board the *Pandora* . She told more than one person that you were just six months old, so that, if she spoke the truth, you were born sometime about the 14th of May in the same year, and that was the date which Mr. Matthew afterwards decided should be kept as your birthday."

"So that, besides so many other things, I owe my birthdays to Uncle Matthew. And what happy days they have always been! How I wish he had lived to see the child grow up on whose head he showered so many kindnesses! And now, Tamsin, the next thing I want to know is, who it was that gave me the name of Ethel."

"It was the name Mrs. Vane called you by, so, of course, there was no thought of changing it later on; but whether it was your real name, or only one the poor woman had taken a fancy to call you by, she alone could have told us. But see, there goes Mrs. Lucas Dexter's carriage! You had better run away now, honey. The bell will be almost sure to ring for me in a minute or two."

It is still the same day. The early dinner is over, and Ethel is again strolling by herself in the grounds. She feels that she wants to be alone. As yet, she can scarcely realise the news her birthday has brought her. As yet, it all seems so strange and incomprehensible. It is as if an earthquake had shaken the foundations of her life, leaving nothing stable or steadfast around her. Her aunts have said that everything is to go on as before, that not a word is to be said to any one. But one exception there must be--she must tell her lover--she must have no secrets from him. Perhaps, when he learns that she is a waif, a child of unknown parentage, and without a home other than that which charity has afforded her, he will---- But no; not even in her inmost thoughts will she so far wrong him as to deem him capable of that.

There is a hillock in the grounds, from the summit of which, a stretch of high road leading to the town is visible. More than once she climbs it to look out for her lover. At length she discerns him in the distance and her heart begins to flutter like a frightened bird in its cage. Presently she takes out her handkerchief, and waves it as a signal to him. He sees it and waves his hat in return. Then she runs down the hillock, and so times herself that at the moment he opens the side door, which admits people on foot to the grounds of Vale View, she is there to meet him.

CHAPTER X.

LAUNCE KEYMER.

Launce Keymer was a good-looking young fellow, with an insinuating manner and a plausible tongue. Being possessed of so many advantages, it was scarcely to be wondered at that he was extremely popular among the marriageable young ladies of St. Oswyth's and its neighbourhood. He was the son of a local brewer, and assisted his father in the business. He had been spoiled and indulged while young, and, as an only son, had been allowed a free rein in his extravagances. But, with a second family growing up, and an expensive wife half his own age, the elder Keymer found it a difficult matter nowadays to meet Launce's frequent demands on his purse. In short, the only thing left for the latter to do--and it was a point as to which both father and son were in thorough accord--was to marry a girl with money.

Now, it so happened that Keymer *pè*re* had a cousin, who was a clerk in the office of Mr. Linaway, the chief lawyer in St. Oswyth's--a man with a large family and a very limited income, whom the brewer had more than once been able to help, at little or no cost to himself. This cousin, Tuttle by name, not ungrateful for past favours, and with an eye, perhaps, to any which the future might have in store for him, and having some reason to believe that Launce was looking out for a wife with a fortune, determined to do the brewer what he termed "a good turn," in confiding to him a certain professional secret which he had learnt by accident, and of which he was supposed to be wholly ignorant.

"The very man I've been wanting to see for the last week or more," said Tuttle to the elder Keymer, next time they met. "Rather a curious thing happened to me about ten days ago, which I want to tell you about. I'll turn and walk part of the way with you, if you don't mind. Well, you must know that one forenoon I had occasion to visit the strong room which opens out of the governor's private office, in order to obtain some title-deeds which were wanted, but which I was not at once able to find, owing to their having been misplaced. While thus engaged, the governor rang his bell for Mr. Dix, the managing clerk. I suppose the old boy, who is beginning to break up, and whose memory fails him strangely at times, had quite forgotten that I was there within hearing. But be that as it may, he proceeded to give Dix instructions for the drawing up of a couple of wills, the particulars of which he was to keep strictly to himself. The wills in question were those of the two Miss Thursbys of Vale View House. The governor talks in a low voice, and mumbles a good deal, so that I was not able to catch all he said; but I picked up enough to satisfy myself that, with the exception of a few hundreds, to be distributed amongst various charities, an annuity to an old servant, and a few minor legacies, the whole of the property of both sisters is bequeathed to the young lady known as Miss Ethel Thursby--their niece, I believe she is. Of course, I can only make a rough guess as to the value of the property in question, which seems to consist chiefly of securities of various kinds; but there's no doubt in my mind that, if realised, it would mount up to a respectable number of thousands. That being the case, Cousin Bob, it might be worth your boy's while to make up to the heiress, who is, I believe, a very pretty girl into the bargain. But not a word to a soul of what I've just told you, unless you want me to lose my berth and be ruined for life."

The hint thus afforded was too precious not to be followed up and acted upon.

Launce Keymer had already been introduced to Ethel, he having met her on two or three occasions at garden parties and other gatherings of young people. He had admired her for the time being, as he admired every pretty girl he met, and had thought no more about her. Truth to tell, Ethel was not the kind of girl to attract more than a passing glance of admiration from the brewer's son. She was too quietly dignified and "stand-offish"; she was lacking in dash and "go"; she was one of those girls whom he felt instinctively it would be unwise to talk slang to; there was something about her which, when in her company, compelled him to be upon his best behaviour; he never felt quite what he termed "at home" with her; as a consequence of which, while always smilingly polite to her, he had rather shunned than sought her society.

When the brewer had told his son that he must either change his mode of life, or marry a girl with money, the latter had pertinently asked: "Where am I to find her?" That there was an overplus of marriageable young women at St. Oswyth's, as there is in all small provincial towns, was a melancholy fact which could not be gainsaid, nor that many of them were nice girls, carefully brought up, well educated, and in every way fitted to make a reasonable man happy; but, alas! they were one and all comparatively poor. Several of them had small dowries, and would inherit something considerable at the death of their parents; but 'tis ill waiting for dead men's shoes, and Launce Keymer's needs were those of the immediate future. Meantime, while waiting for the coming heiress, he flirted to his heart's content, but, so far as was known, contrived to steer clear of any serious entanglement.

And now, lo and behold! the heiress was here--had been here, at his elbow all the time, without his having had the least suspicion of the fact.

No long time was allowed to elapse after the interview between Mr. Keymer and his cousin before Launce began to seize every opportunity that came in his way to pay assiduous court to the heiress of Vale View. There was a good deal of quiet gaiety in St. Oswyth's that winter and spring, and they met on a number of occasions. It is not needful that we should linger over what came to pass. Launce, with a cleverness which, in a better cause, would have done him credit, did his best to adapt himself to what he called Ethel's "Quaker-like ways," toning himself down, so to speak, when in her presence, content to feel his way gradually, and not to startle her by too premature a declaration of his love, or what he wished her to regard as such. As already stated, he was both handsome and plausible. Ethel had never had such attentions paid her by any one else, and, almost before she knew what had befallen her, her heart had capitulated. When he had, as he conceived, sufficiently paved the way, Launce seized an opportunity to press his suit with well-simulated ardour, and succeeded in winning from the shrinking girl a half-reluctant consent, which, as soon as the glamour of his presence was removed, sent her to her chamber, there to shed tears which had in them a sting of poignant regret.

But she had passed her word, and she was too loyal to attempt to recall it. As the days went on, she strove to persuade herself that she had not made a mistake, but that she really did love Launce, and it may be that she gradually succeeded in hoodwinking herself into such a belief. Yet at times there was a strange aching void in her heart which puzzled and frightened her. She had always understood that when people were in love it was for them a season of unalloyed happiness; but she, alas! was far from happy.

And then there was that hateful promise which Launce had extracted from her, not to speak of their engagement to any one till he should give her leave to do so. It was only for a few weeks, he told her, probably a month at the most, that he asked her to keep unbroken silence. Private reasons of an imperative nature compelled him to ask this favour at her hands. She had yielded to his importunity, but none the less did she realise how disloyal it was on her part to have a secret--and such a secret--locked up from her aunts.

The fact was that Launce Keymer, unknown to his father, or any one at St. Oswyth's, had for some time past been making love to a pretty nursery governess at Dulminster, the county town, a dozen miles away, to which place he ran over by train on a couple of evenings in each week. Furthermore, he had been infatuated enough--and he now reviled himself in bitter terms for his folly--to write her a number of compromising letters, such as if produced in an action for breach of promise would infallibly land him in heavy damages. He knew that Hetty Blair had more than one correspondent in St. Oswyth's, and that, if the news of his engagement with Ethel Thursby were once made public, it could scarcely fail to reach her ears. Not that he would have minded that in the least, if Hetty had only burnt or otherwise destroyed those fatal letters. But, as he was well aware, she had done nothing of the kind. He had seen them with his own eyes, tied round with white ribbon, where they lay in the girl's old-fashioned workbox which stood on the top of the bureau in her mother's little parlour, and his object was to get them back into his own hands before his engagement to Ethel got noised abroad. That once accomplished, he felt that he could afford to snap his fingers at Miss Hetty Blair.

It may seem strange that such a cool, calculating, mercenary fellow as Launce Keymer should so far have run counter to all the principles by which it was his ambition to regulate his life as to permit himself to fall in love with a young person who was compelled to work for her daily bread. But it was just one of those things which occasionally come to pass, as if to upset all one's preconceived notions of what we poor mortals think ought to happen, and to prove by what contradictory impulses hearts the most calculating and unemotional are sometimes swayed, as by a force they are powerless to resist.

Hetty Blair was a pretty brunette, with sparkling black eyes, full ripe lips, and a vivacious, not to say saucy, manner. She was genuinely in love with Keymer, and jealously miserable, although she strove to hide the fact from her lover, because for five evenings out of seven she saw nothing of him, and had no assurance that he was not making love to some one else at St. Oswyth's--which was precisely what he was doing.

Miss Blair, who at this time was filling the post of day-governess to the two young children of a major on half-pay, had her home with her mother in a little cottage in a suburb of Dulminster. Keymer was in the habit of visiting Hetty twice a week, on Wednesdays, when the girl's pupils were allowed a half-holiday, and on Saturdays, when business with the young brewer was over at an early hour; consequently, when he made an unexpected appearance at the cottage on a certain Thursday afternoon, when he was fully aware that Hetty was from home, Mrs. Blair could not refrain from expressing her surprise. His explanation was, that having to come to Dulminster on business for his father, he could not resist the temptation of arranging a little surprise for Hetty. Accordingly, he had brought her a bouquet of hothouse flowers, and one of those delicious Madeira cakes of which she was so fond, and if Mrs. Blair would so far oblige him as to step upstairs, where she kept her little cellaret, and bring down one of those half dozen of choice bottles of port he had once sent her, he should feel that his little surprise was complete.

Mrs. Blair did not object in the least. She had a weakness for port, as Launce, who was a great favourite with her, was quite aware. Accordingly she trotted slowly upstairs, for she was somewhat infirm, leaving Keymer alone, smoking his cigar in the little parlour, and he was still occupied in the same harmless fashion when she returned, ten minutes later. But in the interim he had contrived either to pick or force the lock of Hetty's workbox and obtain possession of his letters. Presently he took his leave. His father, he explained, would expect him back by six o'clock at the latest; but of course he should see Hetty as usual on Saturday.

It was on the day prior to Ethel Thursby's birthday that Launce Keymer regained possession of his letters.

CHAPTER XI.

HOPES AND FEARS.

Launce Keymer was radiant as he opened the side door which admitted him to the grounds of Vale View. He had got back those compromising letters, which had been the bugbear of his life ever since he had won Ethel's promise to become his wife. Hetty Blair might rave and storm to her heart's content, as no doubt she would do, for she was a girl with a temper of her own, but it was no longer in her power to harm him, and beyond that he cared not at all. There was nothing now to hinder him from pressing forward his suit with Ethel, and it should be owing to no lukewarmness on his part if they were not married before the end of summer. Of course he was quite aware that the wills which the spinsters had caused to be drawn up in favour of their niece made no provision for her in the event of her marriage, and would only benefit her after the demise of one or both of them. But he had seen and heard enough of the Miss Thursbys to imbue him with a feeling of all but absolute certainty that they would not fail, on her marriage, to liberally dower the girl who was destined ultimately to succeed to the whole of their property--always provided that she married in accordance with their wishes, and he had far too good an opinion of himself to fear that his suit would meet with any discouragement at their hands. In any case, the risk of his wedding a dowerless wife was one which, in Ethel's case, Keymer was fully prepared to face; indeed, to him it seemed an almost infinitesimal one.

Master Launce gave a well-feigned start of joyful surprise when, on opening the green door, he found Ethel waiting for him just inside it, although he had quite expected to find her there. An instant later she was imprisoned in his arms, while half-a-dozen passionate kisses were imprinted in quick succession on her flaming face. One cool kiss on a coyly proffered cheek was the utmost she had ever conceded her lover before. Never had he ventured to put his arms around her till to-day. When he released her she stood panting and indignant, and half inclined to cry. But Launce only looked at her with laughing eyes.

"I could not have helped it, darling, had it been to save my life," he said. "For one thing, it is your birthday, and surely on such an occasion a lover's kisses are the sweetest congratulations he can offer. And then, again, I am the bearer of good news. The need no longer exists for keeping our engagement a secret. I am here this afternoon to seek an interview with your aunts, and I trust that by the time we are a couple of days older all the world of St. Oswyth's will know that you and I are betrothed."

Ethel did not reply; she had not yet recovered her equanimity. They had turned, and were now sauntering slowly across the lawn. Launce's promise to at once seek an interview with her aunts had served to lift a weight off her heart, and yet she was conscious of a certain shrinking, not untinged with regret, now that the time had come when the secret of her engagement would be a secret no longer. It seemed to her as if the act of telling her aunts would serve to bind her irrevocably to a promise which till now she had felt in some vague sort of way she could have broken had she willed to do so. Now, however, that power would be lost to her for ever. For better for worse, she had accepted this man for her life partner, and she must abide by the result. She told herself that she ought to be very, very glad, and yet, somehow, there was no glow of gladness at her heart.

"I am given to understand," resumed Launce presently, "that nowadays young ladies are in the habit of looking for something on their birthdays much more substantial than mere kisses and good wishes. So, as I have no desire to be behind other people in such matters, I venture to offer this little trinket for your acceptance, in the hope that it may sometimes serve to remind you of the giver."

While speaking he had drawn from his pocket a pretty bracelet of novel design, having on it the letter 'E' formed with small diamonds and emeralds. Mr. Keymer senior had groaned in spirit while drawing the cheque to pay for it, but, for all that, he looked upon it as money well laid out. Taking Ethel's left hand in his, Launce proceeded to fix the bracelet round her wrist. Then raising his hat for a moment, he touched her fingers with his lips as respectfully as if she had been a princess. It was an effect which had been duly planned beforehand, as had also the apparently spontaneous embrace on which he had audaciously ventured at the moment of seeing her.

"It is exceedingly pretty, and you are very kind," murmured Ethel, as she let her eyes dwell for a moment on his. But, for all that, she felt as if the bracelet were a manacle.

"And now," resumed Launce, "the sooner I get over my formidable interview with your aunts, the better it will be for all concerned."

His words served like a shock to bring back to Ethel's mind all that had happened to her since the morning, which the events of the last few minutes had served temporarily to banish, and to remind her of the painful duty she had still to perform. There was no way of escape. To have married Launce without having first made known to him as much of the story of her early life as was known to herself, would have been disloyal both to herself and him, and that was a possibility which did not find a moment's lodgment in her thoughts. All the same, the task she had set herself was none the less a hard one to fulfil.

But there was no time for hesitation. Already Launce had come to a halt. In another moment he would have turned and bent his steps towards the house. She laid a detaining hand on his sleeve. "Before you see my aunts," she said in a slightly tremulous voice, "I have something of much importance to reveal to you--something of which I myself had no knowledge till this morning."

He turned on her a quick startled look. There was something in the way she had spoken which convinced him that it was no ordinary young lady's secret--such as the confession of some prior girlish romance--that was about to be told him. It was quite out of the question that this pure-eyed, candid-browed, fair young creature could have anything to reveal which could in any way affect his suit for her hand. It might be that her conscience--and that she had a very tender conscience he did not doubt--troubled her about some trivial sin of omission, or commission, as to which she felt that she must take him into her confidence, but at which he, a man, could well afford to smile, and never give to it as much as a second thought.

The look of startled surprise merged into one of his brightest smiles. He pressed her hand as if to give her confidence. "Whatever may be the nature of what you have to tell me," he said, "you are at least assured beforehand of my sympathy, should you deem it worthy of acceptance."

She cast on him a grateful look. "Here is my favourite walk," she said. "Let us turn into it. It is the most secluded spot in the grounds, and, as a rule, the gardener and I have it all to ourselves."

It seemed as if she were pitifully desirous of delaying her revelation till the last possible moment. Now, however, she drew in her breath and took the plunge which could no longer be avoided. In brief but clear terms she proceeded to narrate to her astonished listener the details of that romantic episode of which she had been the baby heroine. She told him all as it had been told to her; she kept nothing back. Keymer listened with growing uneasiness. He had drawn one of her hands within his arm, and, as they strolled along, turning and retracing their steps from one end of the walk to the other, he pressed it gently to his side from time to time, as if to assure her that the sympathy he had promised her was hers in fullest measure.

There was a little space of silence after she had come to an end. He was turning over in his mind all that she had just told him, piecing together the different facts, and making of the narrative a connected whole. Had he formulated aloud the conclusion he presently arrived at, he would have stated it thus: "The old maids have all along been aware that the girl was no relative of theirs, and yet, with this knowledge clearly in their minds, they have chosen to make her their heiress; consequently, the simple fact of their having told her about certain things, which had previously been kept from her of set purpose, will in no way serve to alter the disposition of their property. She will still remain their heiress, and the world at large will not know otherwise than that she is their niece. Nothing will be changed."

Launce's brain worked nimbly on occasions of emergency, and the silence had not lasted more than half a minute before he flashed on Ethel one of his most seductive smiles. "Darling," he said, in tones the tenderest at his command, "what you have now told me will only serve, if that be possible, to make you dearer to me than you were before. I assure you that I appreciate to the full the confidence thus placed in me. It proves what you may perhaps think stood in no need of proof--that you have a genuine regard for me, and unless that warmer sentiment which I trust in your case is not wholly absent be based on regard and--and on some measure of esteem, it can only be likened to one of those shallow-rooted plants which the first tempest infallibly uproots."

Launce had an excellent memory, and his last sentence had been conveyed bodily from a novel he had lately been reading. "It is just the sort of trashy aphorism that Ethel would appreciate," he had said to himself, and he had resolved to retain it in his mind till a suitable occasion should arise for making use of it. After a scarcely perceptible pause, he resumed:

"I am afraid you wronged me somewhat in your thoughts in making your confession, if I may be allowed to call it so, seem such a measure of necessity. As if any love worthy of the name could be affected, or lessened, by the fact of your being the child of unknown parents, and owing all you possess to the kindness of others in no way bound to you by the ties of kindred! I trust, for the honour of my sex, there are not many men with whom such considerations would have more weight than a grain of sand."

He spoke with so much earnestness and with such a tone of conviction, that it was impossible for Ethel not to be impressed by his words. She glanced up into his face. He was certainly very good-looking, especially just now when his features were lighted up with what seemed to her like the glow of a chivalrous and high-souled passion. She told herself that he had never been so dear to her as at that moment. She felt that she *almost* loved him.

"It was not because I distrusted your affection that I told you what I did," she said gently, "but as a simple matter of right and justice, in view of the relations that exist between us."

"In any case, we may now regard it as an incident that is over and done with. For my part, I see no need for either you or I ever to refer to it again. And now, perhaps, I may be allowed to go in search of your aunts and explain to them the errand which has brought me here."

"Yes, you have my permission to go now," answered Ethel, with a smile that was born of a blush.

They turned in the direction of the house, parting at a point where the path divided in two. Keymer took the road to the right, which would bring him out close to the main entrance of Vale View. Ethel took the one to the left, and entered the house by way of the conservatory, going straight to her own room, where she remained alone, lost in a tangled maze of thoughts in which the past, the present, and the future were inextricably mixed up, till Tamsin knocked at her door, an hour later, and brought her word that her aunts would like to see her in the drawing-room.

"And there's been a young man shut up with them for sixty minutes by the clock," added the elder woman as she glanced shrewdly at the girl. "I fancy it's young Mr. Keymer, the brewer's son. I hope he's not here on your account, honey. I had a good look at him when I took him in a cup of tea half an hour ago. (It's Charlotte's afternoon off, so I did the waiting myself.) He's fair enough to look upon, but, oh I my dearie, he's far too smooth-spoken for me--butter itself would hardly melt in his mouth: and why does he glance at you sideways out of the corners of his eyes when he thinks you're not looking? A man not to be trusted, for all his pleasant tongue. Have heed to an old woman's instinct, honey, and don't you have anything to do with him."

Ethel was too flustered to reply. She gave Tamsin a look which the latter was unable to interpret, and then ran quickly downstairs. She paused at the drawing-room door and pressed her hand to her side for a few seconds. Her heart was pulsating at railway speed. Tamsin's words rang in her ears. "A man not to be trusted." But she had trusted him and would trust him to the end! She drew herself up proudly, turned the handle of the door and went in.

It is to be borne in mind that the ladies of Vale View were already acquainted with young Keymer, they having met him at various social gatherings during the course of the last year or two. His good looks and *debonnair* manner had not failed to prepossess them in his favour, as they did nearly every one with whom he was brought in contact.

There was a small fire in the grate, for the spring evenings were still chilly, and Launce was standing by it with one elbow resting on the chimney-piece. Ethel's eyes sought his face for a moment as she entered the room. One glance at it was enough to tell her that he had won the day.

Miss Matilda rose from her chair and met Ethel halfway across the room. Taking the girl's head between her hands, she drew it forward and imprinted a tender kiss on the pure young brow.

"My love, we congratulate you," she said simply, but her voice trembled, and the smile that accompanied her words was closely allied to tears.

"Can you ever forgive me for having kept it secret from you for four whole weeks?" demanded Ethel tremulously.

"My dear," replied Miss Matilda, with a touch of stateliness, "Mr. Keymer has already been good enough to explain that it was only by his express desire you consented to do so. He had his reasons. Not a word more is needed."

CHAPTER XII.

A RECREANT LOVER.

The day was two hours older.

Launce Keymer had not required much pressing to induce him to accept the invitation of the ladies of Vale View to join them over their early supper. The sisters had been used to early hours in their youth, and as they did not account themselves as being in any respect fashionable folk, they had seen no reason to alter their ways now they were growing old. In the dining-room the lamps were lighted and the curtains drawn. The circular table was laid out with immaculate napery and gleaming silver, with a china centre bowl heaped with some of the flowers Ethel had gathered earlier in the day, supplemented by other blooms from the conservatory. Charlotte, deftest of waiting-maids, in her neat black dress and snowy cuffs and apron, had an eye to the wants of each and all.

Keymer was in the brightest of spirits, and did not allow the talk to flag for a moment. The sisters had not laughed so much for a long time as they did over his description of a voyage in bad weather from Boulogne to Folkestone. He was a capital mimic, and the way in which he hit off the idiosyncrasies of sundry of those on board was genuinely diverting, without any trace of the vulgarity to which such a subject so readily lends itself; for Launce Keymer was clever enough to know where to draw the line in accordance with the class of company in which he happened to find himself. As for Charlotte, she was several times compelled to turn her back on the table, and even then was unable wholly to suppress the giggle with which she could not help greeting some of Mr. Keymer's sallies.

If Ethel did not laugh much, a smile was rarely long absent from her lips, while there was a sparkle in her eyes and a flush on her cheeks such as, to those who knew her well, might almost have seemed due to a touch of fever. But, if such were the case, they had their origin in a fever of the mind rather than of the body. Was she happy? She could not have told. Had the question put itself to her, she would have thrust it aside, and have resolutely refused to answer it. Self-analysis was about the last thing she would have cared to enter upon just then; indeed, she was far too healthy-minded to indulge much at any time in introspective moods and fancies. So many surprising things had happened to her in the course of the day, that she might well be excused for feeling as if she had not yet recovered her mental equilibrium. She ate scarcely anything, and to her that scene at the supper-table was almost as unreal as some phantasmagoria, conjured up by an overwrought brain. What she needed was a long night's sleep to calm her overheated pulses, and restore the delicate balance of her nervous system which a crowd of circumstances had for the moment sufficed to disturb.

Supper was just over, but the ladies had not yet risen from the table, when Fanny, the under-housemaid, entered the room with a letter which had arrived by the evening post. The letter was addressed to "The Misses Thursby," but, as a matter of course, she took it direct to Miss Matilda, as she would have taken it to Miss Jane had it not arrived till a fortnight later. Miss Matilda examined the address and postmark through her *pince-nez* , which she did not wear habitually, but only when reading or writing.

"It bears the London postmark," she remarked to her sister, across the table; "but the writing of the address is strange to me." Then turning to Launce, with a smile and a little bow, she said: "Have I your permission, Mr. Keymer?"

"Most certainly, my dear madam," he replied, with a grave inclination of the head. Then, while Miss Matilda was occupied with the opening and reading of her letter, he said to himself, glancing from one sister to the other: "What a couple of queer old frumps they are! They are awfully nice and good, though, far too good, not to say goody-goody, for the like of me. If I were compelled to be shut up here, I should be bored to death in a week. I suppose this place will be Ethel's, when they have gone over to the majority. Well, by that time, what's Ethel's will be mine, and it strikes me I could make myself pretty comfortable at Vale View, with a thousand, or twelve hundred a year. No, on second thoughts, I could never bear to settle down here. I should let the place and----but what's up with the old damsel? She looks as if she might be going to have a fit."

And, indeed, Miss Matilda's face, as she read the letter, had gradually faded to a dull, ashen hue.

"What is it, Mattie, dear?" demanded Miss Jane, with a gasp. It was a proof how much she was moved that she should have addressed her sister before company by the familiar name of her girlhood.

"Oh, aunty, what has happened?" broke in Ethel.

For answer Miss Matilda pushed the letter across the table to her sister. "Perhaps you had better read it for yourself," she said. Then turning to Charlotte, she added: "You can leave the room till I ring."

Miss Jane, with fingers that trembled slightly, brought her *pince-nez* into requisition and did as her sister had bidden her. "What does it mean?" she asked when she had read it through; but there was a frightened look in her eyes which seemed to indicate that, in part at least, she guessed.

"It means ruin, sister--nothing less than ruin," replied Miss Matilda in her most solemn tones, "should what is here stated prove on further investigation to be the fact."

At the word "ruin" Keymer's marrow seemed to freeze. If the sisters were ruined, where, then, would be the fortune which Ethel was to have inherited as their heiress?

For a while no one spoke. What, indeed, was there to say? The shock was of a kind which words could do nothing to mitigate, and at no time were the sisters in the habit of giving vent to their feelings in futile exclamations. They were of the

women who suffer mostly in silence.
Presently, Miss Matilda, reading in the look with which Keymer was regarding her what seemed like a note of interrogation, said to herself: "It is due to him that he should be told the particulars of our loss; for is he not now almost like one of ourselves?" With that she handed him the letter. "Oblige me by reading this, Mr. Keymer," she said. "Your doing so will save me the necessity of a long explanation."
He took the letter in silence.
Well might Miss Matilda turn pale when she read it. Briefly stated, the information it conveyed (afterwards supplemented by her for Keymer's further enlightenment) was to the following purport: The London solicitor through whom, and through whose father before him, nearly all the monetary affairs of the sisters had been managed since the time when they were quite young women, had recently died. Although Mr. Tidson's cheque for the interest due on account of the various investments he was supposed to have made on their behalf had come to hand with the utmost regularity, the securities which should have represented the investments in question were not now to be found, and there was only too much reason to fear that the dead man had surreptitiously disposed of them from time to time and applied the proceeds to his own use. The letter concluded with an intimation that the sisters should hear further from the writer in the course of a few days.
As Launce Keymer, a little later, walked homeward through the dewy night, the word *ruin* rang in his ears like a knell. Ethel Thursby (or whatever her right name was, or ought to be) was a charming girl, no one more so--although, perhaps, a trifle too demure and puritanical for his taste--and, as heiress to the spinsters, he would gladly have made her his wife. But to marry her without a shilling to call her own, either now or in time to come, was an altogether different affair.
Launce lost no time on the morrow in laying the case before his father. That astute person, having heard him quietly to the end, said: "What a very fortunate thing it is that this news has come to hand now, instead of later on. Of course the affair must not be allowed to proceed any further till we have ascertained for a fact whether the old maids are, or are not, ruined. After all, it is just possible that the missing securities may turn up and nobody be a penny the poorer. By the way, has the girl any letters written by you in her possession?"
"Not a single line."
"So much the better. Now, what you must do is to disappear from the scene for awhile. You can run down to Cornwall and stay with your uncle for a week or two."
"But," urged Launce, "I can't, with any show of decency, leave home without either calling on, or writing to Ethel, and giving some more or less plausible excuse for my absence."
"You must neither call nor write," said his father. "You had better start by the three o'clock train this afternoon, and have your right wrist bound up as if the result of a sprain. I will make all needful excuses for you."

Launce Keymer was one of that numerous class of young men who can do with an unlimited quantity of holidays, and his father's suggestion seemed to him in every way an admirable one. Accordingly, the three o'clock train carried him away in due course, with his wrist bound up in accordance with his father's directions; but by the time St. Oswyth's had been left half-a-dozen miles behind, the bandage was unrolled and flung out of the carriage window.

In the course of the same afternoon a note, addressed to "Miss Thursby," was delivered at Vale View. In it Mr. Keymer senior begged to inform that lady, that, in consequence of his son having been called away by telegram owing to the serious illness of a near relative, he--Launce--would not be able to dine at Vale View that day, as promised. His son would himself have written had he not unfortunately happened to sprain his wrist so severely that it would be impossible for him to hold a pen for some time to come.

The note made no mention of Ethel, purposely leaving it an open question whether, before quitting home, Launce had, or had not, confided to his father the fact of his engagement.

Later in the day Mr. Keymer senior made it his business to call on his cousin, the lawyer's clerk. To him he said: "I have reason to believe that the Miss Thursbys of Vale View have lost the greater part, if not the whole, of their fortune. What I want you to do is, to keep your eyes and ears open and pick up whatever scraps of information may come in your way tending to prove either the truth or falsity of the rumour which has reached me."

The brewer argued with himself that if the news conveyed by the letter which Launce had read should prove to be correct, the sisters would go to his cousin's employer, as their local man of business, and seek his advice in the matter--which, some few days later, was precisely what they did.

CHAPTER XIII.

CAPTAIN VERINDER AND HIS VISITOR.

While the events bearing on the life-story of Ethel Thursby, as narrated in the last few chapters, were duly working themselves out, certain other events destined to exercise an important influence on her future, the chief factors in which were two people of whose very existence she was unaware, were in process of evolution.

It was eleven o'clock on a bright May morning, and Captain Verinder, who had only lately risen and had but just finished his breakfast, which this morning had consisted of nothing more substantial than a tumbler of rum and milk, was engaged in a rueful examination of the pockets of the suit of clothes he had been wearing the previous evening.

"Not a stiver more," he said, with a grimace, as he tossed his waistcoat across the room; and with that he turned and counted for the second time the little pile of silver and coppers which he had previously extracted from his pockets and placed on the chimney-piece. "Seven shillings and elevenpence-ha'penny, all told," he muttered; "and there's seventeen days yet to be got through before the end of the month."

It was not the first time by many that he had found himself "cornered," but the process became none the pleasanter through repetition.

He turned away with a shrug, and began to charge his meerschaum with the strong tobacco he was in the habit of smoking.

"When we find ourselves in a hole of our own digging, or in a scrape, the result of our own folly, we have a way of telling ourselves that the truest philosophy is to grin and bear it. Of course there's nothing else to be done, but it's only cold pudding at the best." He spoke aloud as he had a way of doing when alone. "Verinder, my dear boy, if there was ever any man who sold himself cheap, you were that one last night. Let us hope you will take the lesson to heart, and not carry your nose quite so high in the air in time to come."

Having lighted his pipe, he drew his shabby dressing-gown about him and seated himself in a somewhat dilapidated easy-chair by his open window in Tilney Street, Soho--a narrow thoroughfare of tall, old-fashioned houses that had seen better days.

For anything beyond a small assured income of eighty pounds a year, Captain Verinder had to trust to the exercise of his wits. At this time he was a man of sixty, rather below the medium height, but still slim and upright for his years, and with something that might be termed semi-military in his appearance and carriage. The mental exercise in question took the form of billiards. Although far from being a fine player, his natural aptitude for the game had been cultivated by long practice, till he had attained a degree of proficiency at it which he found to answer his purpose very well indeed. That purpose was neither more nor less than to haunt the public rooms within a wide radius of his lodgings, on the lookout for those simpletons with more money than sense, of whom there is an unfailing supply in big cities, who can only be convinced at the expense of their pocket that in the art of billiard-playing they have not yet got beyond their apprenticeship. The Captain regarded it as a very poor week indeed at the end of which he did not find himself in pocket to the extent of fifty shillings, or three pounds--or rather, would have found himself that sum in pocket but for his ineradicable propensity for treating himself and others to innumerable "drinks" and cigars. When perfectly sober, he was one of the stingiest of mortals, but after his third glass he began to thaw, and, a little later, the veriest stranger would have been welcome to share his last shilling. It is a by no means uncommon trait.

On the evening of the day prior to the one with which we are now concerned, the Captain, in the course of his rounds, had encountered a sheep-faced, but gentlemanly-looking young fellow, in whom he thought he saw an easy prey.

What, then, was his rage and amazement when at the end of the evening the Captain's eyes opened to the fact that it was a case of the biter being bitten, and that the sheep-faced provincial, instead of being the greenhorn he looked, was, in reality, a graduate in the same school as himself.

Small wonder, then, was it that his thoughts this morning were bitter, when, after emptying his pockets, he realised that the absurdly inadequate sum of seven and elevenpence-halfpenny was all that was left him to exist on till the next quarterly payment of his income should fall due, which would not be till between a fortnight and three weeks hence.

He was still smoking moodily when he heard his landlady's shuffling footsteps on the stairs, and, a moment later, her head was protruded into the room. "If you please, Captain, here's a lady asking for you," said Mrs. Rapp, a Londoner born and bred.

"A lady asking for me? Impossible!" exclaimed the Captain as he started to his feet.

"Not at all impossible, Uncle Augustus," said a full rich voice, and thereupon, following close upon the heels of Mrs. Rapp, there advanced into the room a tall and stately female figure, attired in black. Pausing in the middle of the floor, she raised the veil which had hitherto partially shrouded her features.

The captain stared for a moment or two, and then from his lips broke the one word, "Giovanna!"

"Yes, it is I--your niece Giovanna--come all the way from Italy to see you."

Mrs. Rapp discreetly withdrew.

Notwithstanding her years, which now numbered not far short of forty, Giovanna was still a very handsome woman, with a large and generous style of beauty which would have made her a striking figure anywhere. Although she called the Captain uncle, there was no blood relationship between the two, her mother having been merely Augustus Verinder's stepsister by a previous marriage. They had never met but once before, when the Captain had spent a month at the *osteria* of Giuseppe Rispani, Giovanna being at that time a girl of sixteen. Ever since her desertion of her husband in America she had passed as a widow--la Signora Alessandro. She had not been without offers of marriage meanwhile, but had not seen her way to accept any of them. As to whether her husband was alive or dead, she had no knowledge.

Giuseppe Rispani had recently died, and Vanna, having realised the small fortune bequeathed her by him, had now come to England, which she had long wished to visit.

In the course of the confidential talk that ensued between Vanna and her uncle she was induced by the latter to relate to him all about her marriage, the details of which were quite new to him.

She began by telling him of the arrival of the young Englishman, Mr. Alexander, at Catanzaro; of his long stay at the *osteria* of the Golden Fig; of the coming of two other Englishmen, one of whom proved to be the father of Mr. Alexander, and of their departure next day. Then she proceeded to recount how the young Englishman proposed to her, how she accepted him, and how she did not learn till her marriage-day that her husband's full name was John Alexander Clare. She made no mention of her father's discovery by means of the peephole in the ceiling, but simply said, "I knew before my marriage that my husband's father, on the occasion of his visit, had given him six thousand pounds in English money." Then she went on to tell of the departure of her husband and herself for America, of the death of their child; and of their subsequent separation, which she made out to have been a matter of mutual arrangement; and wound up by saying, "From that day to this I have heard no tidings of my husband."

"Neither, I'll wager, have you ever made any effort to find out who the father was that could afford to give his son six thousand pounds in order to get rid of him," remarked the Captain when she had come to the end of her narrative.

"No. What business was it of mine?" demanded Vanna with a stare.

"Ah, that's just the point which you have never thought it worth your while to test. Yet, who can say that it might not have proved to be very much your business indeed?"

Then to himself he added: "This seems to me a little matter which may be worth inquiring into. But, good gracious! to think that there should be such imbeciles in the world as this niece of mine!"

CHAPTER XIV.

THE CAPTAIN TAKES A LITTLE JOURNEY.

The more Captain Verinder turned over in his mind the chief points of the story told him by his niece, the more convinced he became that it was indeed, as he had remarked to himself at the time, a matter worth inquiring into.

The Captain, when once he had made up his mind to any particular course of action, was not a man to let the grass grow under his feet. His first proceeding was to seek out a certain billiard-room acquaintance of the name of Tring--a man who had got through two fortunes in his time and was now reduced to earning a scanty livelihood by literary hackwork at the British Museum. Having given him the particulars of the information he required, the Captain met him by appointment a couple of days later.

"The only person I can find," said Tring, "of the name specified by you that seems likely to answer to your requirements, is a certain Sir Gilbert Clare, of Withington Chase, Hertfordshire, the representative of one of the oldest titles in the kingdom."

Captain Verinder, having taken a note of the name and address in his pocket-book and paid the other for his trouble, went his way. His next step, the following morning, was to call on Giovanna with a request for the loan of ten pounds.

"'Tis not for myself I ask it," he said with one of the grandiloquent airs in which he sometimes indulged. "It will be expended to the last farthing in your service, my dear. I refrain from saying more at present, save that in the course of a few days I hope to be the bearer of news that will--well, that will astonish you very considerably."

Vanna raised no objection to lending her uncle the amount he asked for, although by this time she had seen enough of him to feel pretty sure that she would never see a shilling of it back.

In the course of the following day Captain Verinder booked himself by train to Mapleford, which station he had ascertained to be the nearest to the point he was bound for. His object was to try to discover whether the John Alexander Clare whom his niece had married so many years before was in any way related to, or connected with, Sir Gilbert Clare of Withington Chase.

The Captain having located himself at the best hotel, and partaken of a dinner such as had been altogether beyond his means for a long time past, proceeded

to take a quiet stroll about the little town, which, however, had nothing of interest to offer for his inspection. Later on he found his way into the coffee-room of the hotel, which place, as he had expected it would, drew to itself in the course of the evening a round dozen or more of the better class of tradespeople and others, all of whom, it was evident, were in the habit of frequently meeting there. Here he found no difficulty in ascertaining everything about Sir Gilbert that it concerned him to know. Thus, he learnt that Sir Gilbert's son by his first marriage had left England, after a quarrel with his father, more than twenty years before, and that, a few years later, news had come to hand that he had lost his life through some accident abroad, only, nobody seemed to know either the nature of the accident in question, or where it had happened. Further, the Captain learnt that the second Lady Clare and her three sons were all dead, and that Sir Gilbert, a broken, childless old man of seventy-four, was living at the Chase in a seclusion that was rarely broken by any visitor from the outside world.
It was on a Friday that the Captain went down to Mapleford, and the following Monday saw him back in town. He had stayed in the country over Sunday in order that he might be present at morning service at the church, just beyond the precincts of the Chase, which Sir Gilbert made a point of attending, and where several generations of his progenitors were buried.
The Captain wanted to see for himself what kind of man Sir Gilbert was. The latter arrived in due course, alone and on foot, and from the place where he sat Verinder had an unimpeded view of him. When service was over the Captain took a stroll round the church, pausing to look at every monument and to read every inscription commemorative of dead and gone members of the Clare family. One inscription, and one only, had any special interest for him. It was that which recorded the death of "John Alexander Clare, eldest son of Sir Gilbert Clare, who was accidentally killed abroad" on such and such a date. "I would wager a hundred pound note to a fiver--if I had one," said the Captain with emphasis, "that this tablet refers to Vanna's husband and to no one else. It's altogether out of the question that there should have been two John Alexander Clares living at the same time. And to think that the young man has been dead for seventeen years and that his widow has known nothing about it? What a fortunate thing it is for her that she has got a man of the world like me at her back! From this day forward her interests and mine are identical."
A jubilant man was Captain Verinder when he went back to London next day.
About midday on Tuesday he called on Giovanna at the boarding-house--one largely frequented by foreigners--at which she had located herself for the time being. That the news of which he was the bearer was a great surprise to her hardly needs to be stated. It was both a surprise and a shock, for although she had never really cared for Alec as a wife should care for her husband, and had left him of her own accord and under most cruel circumstances, through all the years which had intervened since then his image had been often in her thoughts, but it was as a man still living and in the prime of life that he had dwelt in her memory. Consequently, to be told suddenly that he had met with a violent death

seventeen years before, which pointed to a time almost immediately after her desertion of him, was enough to thrill her through every fibre of her being.

Well, whatever uncertainty she might heretofore have felt with regard to her husband's fate had no longer any room for existence. She had been a widow all these years without knowing it.

Before long the Captain went on to speak of Sir Gilbert, and to detail all that he had heard in reference to him. He had always been rather clever as an amateur sketcher, and could catch a likeness better than most people, and he now took pencil and paper and with a few bold strokes drew an outline portrait of the baronet. Pushing it across the table to Vanna, he said: "Does that in any way resemble the English *milor* who travelled all the way to Catanzaro to see the Mr. John Alexander who became your husband a little later?"

"Yes, that is the man," said Vanna quietly when she had examined the sketch.

"Ah; I thought as much," remarked her uncle drily.

"And now that you have found out all this about Sir Gilbert Clare, in what way does it, or can it, affect me?" queried Vanna presently.

The Captain regarded her with a pitying smile, as he might a child who had asked him some utterly preposterous question.

"Cannot you see that the fact of your father-in-law being a rich and childless man may be made--I say *made* --to affect your fortunes very materially--very materially indeed? That is," he added a moment after, "if you only know how to put the knowledge thus acquired to a practical use."

Giovanna shook her head. It was evident that she could not in the least comprehend what her uncle was driving at.

The Captain's shoulders went up nearly to his ears. "What a very fortunate thing it is, my dear, that at such an important crisis of your life you have by your side a thorough man of the world like myself--and one so completely devoted to your interests! Were you my own child I could not entertain a greater regard and affection for you than I do."

Vanna sat grandly unmoved, her statuesque features betraying no slightest trace of emotion.

"As cold as a marble goddess," muttered the Captain under his breath as he produced his cigar case, for he was a man who regarded smoking as one of the necessaries of existence.

For a little space he smoked in silence; then all at once he said, as if it were an echo of some thought he had been revolving in his mind: "What a pity, what an enormous pity it is, that your child did not live till now!"

A sudden spasm, gone almost as soon as it had come, contracted the muscles of Vanna's face; her teeth bit hard into her underlip; but never a word answered she.

"Come," said the Captain a few minutes later; "put on your things and let us go for a stroll in the Park. It's a lovely afternoon, and there will be no end of swells in the Row."

Nothing loth was Giovanna to comply. As yet she had seen hardly anything of

London, and what she had seen had not impressed her over favourably. It had been one of the dreams of her life to see Hyde Park in the height of the season, and now her dream was about to be fulfilled. In ten minutes she was ready to set out.

The Captain chartered a hansom--it was the first time his niece had been in one--telling the driver to take his time and go by way of Regent Street and Piccadilly. Here at length was London as Vanna had imagined it to be.

As the Captain had prophesied, the Row was crowded. They strolled about for a while in the warm sunshine, and then found a couple of chairs whence they could take in the varied features of the passing show at their leisure. A proud man was Captain Verinder that day. In all that gay and fashionable throng there were not, in his opinion, more than three or four women who in point of looks were fit to be matched with the one by his side--that is to say (to compare one thing with another), if a rose may be considered to be in the perfection of its beauty when it is fully blown, and not when it is merely a blushing bud of undeveloped possibilities. Although nearing her fortieth birthday, Giovanna--unlike the majority of her countrywomen, who age early--was remarkably young-looking for her years. But then she was English on her mother's side, and that may have had something to do with the matter. She was wearing a charming half-mourning costume, with bonnet to match, which she had bought since her arrival in London. Many were the glances of admiration of which she was the recipient, many the heads that were turned for a second look at her tall figure, so stately and yet so graceful, with her pale classic features, clear-cut as some antique gem, as she threaded her way through the crowd with the proud composed air of one "to the manner born." Well might Captain Verinder feel proud of his charge.

"Do you see that *blasé** -looking man driving that pair of splendid chestnuts?" he said to Vanna a few minutes after they had sat down. "He is Lord Elvaston, one of the greatest *roué**s about town. He used to know me well enough before he came into his fortune a score of years ago, when he was not above borrowing a five-pound note from anybody who would lend him one. Now, of course, he passes me as if he had never set eyes on me in his life. But such is the way of the world, more especially of the world of fashion."

Then a few minutes later, "Note that painted woman in the too palpable wig being driven slowly past in her yellow chariot. That is Lady Anne Baxendale. Her father was only a country rector on three hundred a year. The rectory grounds adjoined those of the house where I was born. Your mother, when a girl, and little Nan Cotsmore were great friends. I've seen them play skipping-rope by the hour together."

But Verinder had another motive in view in thus introducing his niece to one of the most striking spectacles which the metropolis has to offer for the delectation of the strangers within its gates. He wanted to excite in her bosom a feeling which should be compounded in about equal measure of envy and discontent--envy of those who, although, for the passing hour, she seemed as one of themselves, were yet as far removed from her by their wealth and position as if she and they were inhabitants of two totally different spheres (which, indeed, in one sense, they were); and discontent with the humble and prosaic surroundings of her own obscure existence. If he had read Giovanna aright, it seemed to him that it ought not to be a difficult matter to foment within her the very undesirable sentiments in question.

"Are you sorry, my dear, that I brought you here this afternoon?" he asked, after a longer pause than common.

"Sorry! oh no, how could I be? It is a beautiful sight. Nay, it is more than beautiful, it is magnificent. This is London as I used to dream of it."

"But never, I'll wager, with any thought that it might possibly one day become a reality to you."

"A reality, you mean, as far as it can become such to one who, like myself, is a mere looker-on."

"When I spoke of its becoming a reality to you, I did not mean merely as a spectator, but as an actor in the show--a recognised actor in it and acknowledged as one of themselves by the 'smartest' people here."

Giovanna turned two deep wondering eyes on the Captain.

"You talk in riddles, Uncle," she said quietly.

"You seem to forget, my dear--or rather, perhaps, I ought to say that you fail sufficiently to realise in your thoughts--the position which is, or ought to be, yours by right of your marriage with the late John Alexander Clare. You are the widow of the heir of Withington Chase, the daughter-in-law of a wealthy baronet of ancient family. As such, your proper position is there--there, as one of the glittering throng passing and repassing before our eyes. You ought to be riding in your own brougham or barouche, with your own coachman and footman. You ought to be wearing the family diamonds--who has so much right to them as you?--and where is there another woman who would show them off to better advantage? You ought to have your own little establishment in town, with your own servants--say, a flat of six or seven rooms somewhere in Belgravia, where you could invite your old uncle to come and see you as often as you might feel inclined for his company. I repeat, that all these things ought of right to be yours."

Giovanna's nostrils dilated, a hard cold glitter came into her eyes, her bosom began to rise and fall more quickly than it was wont to do; there was a chord in her somewhat lymphatic nature which responded to her uncle's words. Her own diamonds, her own carriage, her own establishment in London, and, above all, to be transformed from a nobody into a Somebody, and to have the great world of rank and fashion recognise her as one of themselves! Oh, it was too much! The vision was too dazzling. A low cry, half of pain, half of pleasure, broke from her. The Captain was watching her out of a corner of his eye. But presently a chill struck her and her face blanched a little. Turning to Verinder, she said:

"But you seem to have forgotten, Uncle, that Sir Gilbert Clare does not so much as know of my existence--nay, the chances are that he was not even aware that

his son was ever married."
"But I mean him to be made aware both of one fact and the other before he is very much older," responded the Captain with a sinister smile. "Ah! a spot or two of rain. We had better be moving." Then, as they rose: "There is only one course open to us, Vanna *mia* ," he whispered meaningly, "and that is, to *find* Sir Gilbert an heir."

CHAPTER XV.

CONSPIRATORS THREE.

When Captain Verinder enunciated the startling statement with which the last chapter concludes, he had already conceived a certain scheme in his brain, which, in the course of next day, he took the first steps towards reducing to practice, but without saying a word to his niece of his intentions.

Many years before, Giovanna's only brother, Luigi Rispani, had come to London by way of advancing his fortunes. He was energetic and persevering, with a gift for languages, and after a time he obtained the post of foreign correspondent in a city house of business. A little later he married a country-woman of his own, and then, after a few years, both he and his wife died, leaving one son behind them who was named after his father. This son was now about twenty years old, a dark-eyed, good-looking, quick-witted young fellow, but having within him the germs of certain scampish propensities, which, up till now, had only been able to develop themselves after a weak and tentative fashion. Luigi earned his living in part as drawing-master to a number of cheap suburban boarding-schools, and in part, when his other duties were over for the day, by acting as check-taker at one of the West End theatres.

The Captain and the elder Rispani had been on fairly intimate terms, and after the latter's death he had never altogether lost sight of the lad. Sometimes, when he had been more than usually lucky at billiards, he would look up young Luigi and treat him to a dinner of four or five courses at some foreign restaurant in the neighbourhood of Leicester Square, and at parting press a couple of half-crowns into his unreluctant palm. Verinder, who by long habit had become a tolerably shrewd reader of character, had long ago summed up in his mind the most salient characteristics of Luigi Rispani, and he now said to himself, with a pleasant sense of elation: "Here is the very tool I need ready to my hand. If I were to search London round I could not find one that would suit my purpose better."

This evening he sought out Luigi at the theatre where the young man was engaged, and after shaking hands with him, said: "I wish to see you most particularly. Come to my den after you have finished here and I will tell you what I want you for."

Luigi went straight from the theatre to his uncle's rooms. (As long as he could remember he had been used to calling the Captain "uncle"). The ghostly light of dawn was in the eastern sky before the two separated. The nature of the business discussed by them will be made clear by a conversation which took place next day between the Captain and his niece.

"You have not forgotten our talk in the Park the day before yesterday?" said the former.
"There was much in it which I am not likely readily to forget. All the same, you said certain things which, the more I think of them, the more extravagant and incapable of ever being realised they seem to me."
"That is just what I am here to-day to endeavour to disprove," remarked the Captain in his dryest tones. "You don't object to my smoking, I know. Thanks."
As soon as he had selected and lighted a cigar, he resumed:
"You already know my views as to the position which, in my opinion, you ought to occupy as daughter-in-law to Sir Gilbert Clare of Withington Chase. That you have an undoubted claim on the old baronet I think very few people would be found to dispute, and the question we have now to consider is the most desirable mode of urging that claim upon his notice in order that the utmost possible advantage may accrue to you therefrom. As you justly remarked the other day, the probability is that Sir Gilbert was never made aware of his son's marriage, and, consequently, cannot have the remotest suspicion that the young man left a widow to mourn his loss. Now, from all I heard of the baronet when I was in the country last week, I take him to be a hardfisted, penurious curmudgeon, who, to judge from his style of living, must be laying by several thousands a year--though, why he should care to do so, goodness only knows, seeing that he has nobody he cares about to leave his savings to--the next heir being a half-cousin with whom he has been at outs for the last thirty years. Now, it seems to me, taking into account the kind of man he is, that if you were to introduce yourself to his notice merely on the ground of being the widow of his son--who died nearly twenty years ago--and a person of whom probably he has never heard before, he might perhaps, without wholly ignoring your claim upon him, not merely satisfy his conscience, but persuade himself into the belief that he was acting a most generous part by you, if he were to allow you a paltry hundred, or, at the most, a couple of hundred pounds a year as long as he lives. But, Giovanna, my dear, it is more--much more--than that that I want to help you to secure for yourself. I want to see you in the position which would have been yours at your husband's death had you married John Alexander Clare with his father's full knowledge and consent. In that case you would undoubtedly have had a jointure of not less than seven or eight hundred a year, and I want us two to try whether we cannot see our way to secure something like an equivalent settlement for you, even after all this length of time."
Vanna was staring straight before her with an introspective expression in her midnight orbs. When the silence had lasted some time, she said very quietly:
"You are working out some scheme in your brain, Uncle, I feel sure of it; you have something more to tell me--something to propose. Is it not so?"
He considered the ash of his cigar for a moment or two, then, lifting his eyes to her face, he said:
"What a pity--what a very great pity it is that your boy did not live to be here to-day!"

As before, when he spoke of the loss of her child, an indescribable expression flitted across Giovanna's face.
"That is precisely what you said the other day," she remarked, coldly. "Where is the use of referring a second time to a misfortune which happened so long ago?"
"Because I cannot help contrasting your position to-day with what it would have been could you but have taken your boy by the hand, and have said to Sir Gilbert: 'You lost your son and heir long years ago: but to-day I bring you a grandson to take his place. Here is the new heir of Withington Chase.' In that case, how the old man would have welcomed you!--nothing would have seemed too good for you, so overjoyed would he have been. The position which ought to have been yours from the first would then be accorded you, and you would take your place in society as the daughter-in-law of Sir Gilbert Clare, and the mother of the next heir. And then, a little later, my Vanna, you would marry again. Oh, yes, you would! Marry money--and perhaps a title to boot. Why not? You are one of the handsomest women in London, or else I don't know a handsome woman when I see one!"
Vanna rose abruptly from her chair, and then sat down again. For once she was profoundly moved.
"Oh, Uncle, this is the merest folly!" she cried. "Why talk of impossibilities? Let us keep to realities. I thought you had something to propose--something, perhaps, that would----"
"So I have, my dear; so I have something to propose," responded the Captain, with a chuckle. "What I said to you the other day was, 'There is only one course open to us, and that is to find Sir Gilbert an heir.'"
"Well?" demanded Vanna with wide-open eyes. "I failed to understand your meaning then and I am not a bit the wiser now."
"Listen then. Although, owing to circumstances to which I need not further refer, we are not in a position to go before Sir Gilbert and produce the real heir, is that any reason why we should not find a substitute who would answer both his purpose and ours just as well as the genuine article?" His cunning eyes were watching her eagerly.
Vanna's face expressed a growing wonder, but it was a wonder largely compounded of bewilderment.
" *Ecoutez* ," resumed her uncle. "Let us assume for the moment that you agree with me what a very desirable thing it would be to provide Sir Gilbert with an heir, even though it would, of necessity, have to be a fictitious one. Being, then, so far in accord, naturally the first question would be, 'But where are we to find the heir in question--or rather, someone by whom he could be personated?' To which I should reply that I am prepared at any moment to lay my finger on the one person out of all the hundreds and thousands of people in this big city best suited to our purpose. That person is none other than your own nephew (whom I believe you have never yet set eyes on), the son of your only brother, Luigi Rispani."
Sheer amazement kept Giovanna silent.

"I have already seen Luigi and sounded him in the matter," resumed the Captain. "He fully agrees with me that the idea is a most admirable one, and one which, if carried out in all its details with that care and foresight which I should not fail to bestow on it, could not prove otherwise than brilliantly successful. In short, Luigi places himself unreservedly in my hands. So now, my dear Vanna, it only remains for you to follow your nephew's excellent example."

It is not needful that we should recount in detail what further passed between uncle and niece either at this or subsequent interviews. Enough to say that when once she had been talked over into giving her consent, and had thoroughly mastered the details of the scheme as proposed to be carried out by her uncle, she entered fully into the affair, and seemed to have thrown whatever moral scruples might at one time have feebly held her back completely to the winds. But before all this came about Luigi Rispani and his aunt had been brought together. Although English blood on the female side ran in the veins of both, they might have been pure Italians for anything in their looks which proclaimed the contrary. In point of fact, there was a very marked family likeness between the two, so much so, indeed, that the Captain could not help saying to himself with a chuckle, "Nobody seeing them together, would take them for other than mother and son."

At length all the details of the scheme were so far elaborated and agreed upon by our three conspirators that Verinder felt the time had come for him to make his first important move, which was, to seek an interview with Sir Gilbert Clare, or, as he preferred to express it, to "beard the lion in his den."

CHAPTER XVI.

HOW SIR GILBERT RECEIVED THE NEWS.

It is to be hoped that the reader has not quite forgotten the existence of Everard Lisle.

After Ethel Thursby's refusal of him on her eighteenth birthday he went back with a sad heart to his duties at Withington Chase. There he had rooms in the house of Mr. Kinaby, the land steward, an old red brick house situated a little way outside the precincts of the park. Mr. Kinaby's health had been failing for some time, and Everard was gradually taking over the greater part of his duties. Every morning he went to the Chase to see to Sir Gilbert's correspondence and take his instructions in reference to the estate and other matters. But he had still other duties to attend to. In addition to being a numismatist of some note and a collector of curios, Sir Gilbert of late years had developed into an antiquarian and archæ*ologist, and for some time past had been engaged in putting together the framework of what he intended ultimately to elaborate into an exhaustive history of the "hundred" of the county in which the Chase was situated, as natives of which his ancestors for three centuries back had played more or less conspicuous parts. In furtherance of this labour of love, for such it was to him, he found Everard very useful in the way of hunting up authorities, making extracts and transcribing his notes into a calligraphy which it would be possible for a compositor to set up--when, at some as yet unknown date, the great work should be sufficiently advanced to be sent to press--without having to tear his hair in the process.

Sir Gilbert, whom advancing years had tended to render more of a recluse than ever, had gradually, and by a process of which he himself was scarcely conscious, begun to entertain a great liking (in his frigid, undemonstrative way) for this frank-eyed, clear-headed, straightforward young man, in whom he could detect no faintest trace of sycophancy, and who knew so well how to retain the full measure of his own self-respect without in any way grating against the *amour-propre* of his employer. Lisle had evolved a happy faculty of managing the lonely cantankerous old man, for whom he often felt a profound pity, as no one before had ever succeeded in managing him. Thus it had come to pass that a week never went by without Everard being asked to dine once, and frequently oftener, at the Chase. On these occasions, when dinner was over, the old man and the young one would wind up the evening by playing a few sober games of chess or backgammon, at both of which Sir Gilbert was an adept. By the time the turret clock struck ten, Everard would be strolling back through the park in the direction of his rooms, with no company save a cigar and his own thoughts. At such seasons, with the fresh night air blowing about him, with the stars raining down sweet influences upon him, and with the huge ghost-like trees to sentinel him on his way, whither ought a young man's thoughts to wing their flight save to the one fair being, fairer to him than all the world beside, who holds captive his heart, a willing prisoner!

But, in Everard's case, she who still held his heart captive did so all unwittingly. She had rejected his proffered love and all was at an end between them. He could never hope to win her for his wife, but that seemed to him no reason, however little such a course might recommend itself to his cooler judgment, why he should not go on loving her just as he had done all along, In any case, he did go on loving her, nor did it seem possible to him that a time should ever come when he could do otherwise. He knew that in all human probability the day was not far distant when he should hear the news of her marriage with another, and he tried to school himself by anticipation, so that when the shock should come, he might be enabled to bear it with manly equanimity.

On a certain morning, as Sir Gilbert Clare and Everard Lisle were engaged together in the library at Withington Chase, a servant entered carrying a highly-glazed card on a salver. "I have shown the gentleman into the morning-room, sir," said the man as he presented the card.

Sir Gilbert took it and adjusted his *pince-nez* . "Captain Verinder," he read aloud. "Have no recollection of anyone of that name. Um-um. I suppose I must go and see what he wants me for." Then, to the man, "Tell Captain Verinder I will be with him immediately."

The Captain had come down from town by an early train and had made his way on foot from the railway station to the Chase. He had not seen anything of the old mansion on the occasion of his previous visit, and as he drew near, approaching it by way of the drive, he could not help being much impressed, not merely by its size and the noble simplicity of its faç*ade, but by the old-time air of stately, if somewhat faded, dignity which seemed as integral a part of it as the ivy which clung round its gables and chimneys, or the patches of many-coloured lichen with which time had encrusted its high-pitched roof. Nor was this impression lessened when, in response to his summons, a servant in livery opened wide the great double doors, and having taken his card, ushered him through the big echoing hall, hung with trophies of war and the chase, into a charming room furnished in the Empire style--although, to be sure, the gilding was tarnished and the coverings of chairs and lounges considerably the worse for wear--which looked out through its long windows on a gay parterre of flowers, and was shut in with a sort of sweet privacy by a semi-circular hedge of laurel and box. And here Sir Gilbert found his visitor some three minutes later.

The Captain, it may be remembered, had only seen the baronet once before, on that Sunday morning when he took account of him in his high-backed pew at church. Now that he beheld him close at hand, he could not help saying to himself, "What a grand wreck of a man!--and what a splendid fellow he must have been in his prime!" And indeed, although Sir Gilbert's one-time height of six feet two inches was now slightly curtailed owing to the burden of his years, he still towered above most people with whom he came in contact, as though he were descended from some heroic race of old, while his shaggy brows, his white drooping moustache, his high thin nose and his eyes still luminous with a sort of untamed fire, lent to his aspect a something of leonine majesty.

"Captain Verinder, I presume," said Sir Gilbert as he advanced, holding the other's card between his thumb and forefinger. The Captain bowed. "You have--a--um--the advantage of me, sir. But pray be seated." His keen critical eyes were taking Verinder in from head to foot as he spoke. It was a scrutiny which, despite his coolness and his habitual indifference to the opinion of others, somewhat disconcerted the latter.

"I have taken the liberty of intruding upon you, Sir Gilbert," he began, as he drew forward a chair and gave a little preliminary cough behind his hand, "in order that I may have an opportunity of laying before you certain information which has only quite recently come into my possession, but which, I feel sure, when you have been made aware of it, you will agree with me is of the greatest possible importance."

Sir Gilbert opened his eyes a little wider than usual. "Pray proceed, sir," he said stiffly.

"The information to which I refer bears especially on certain incidents in the life of your late son and heir, Mr. John Alexander Clare."

On the instant Sir Gilbert's figure became as rigid as a ramrod. His lips opened and then shut again without a sound.

"Unless my information is at fault," resumed the Captain, "the last occasion on which you and your son met was when, accompanied by another gentleman, you stopped for a few hours at Catanzaro in Calabria, at which place Mr. Clare was then residing."

Sir Gilbert contented himself with bowing a grave assent. His face just then was a puzzle.

"Shortly afterwards Mr. Clare emigrated to the United States, and there, between two and three years later, he unfortunately met with his death through an accident." Here the Captain paused and looked questionably at Sir Gilbert.

"Your information, Mr.--er--Captain Verinder, is quite correct as far as it goes," said the latter as if in response to the look. "Still, I fail to see in what way--er--in short----"

"Why I, a stranger, have had the impertinence to come here and talk to you about matters which, as you doubtless think, can be no possible concern of mine," interposed Verinder coolly. "That is the precise point, Sir Gilbert, as to which I now propose to enlighten you."

Drawing his chair a few inches closer to that of Sir Gilbert he resumed:

"I have merely recapitulated certain facts already known to you in order that I might thereby be enabled to lead up to certain other facts which, as I have every reason to believe, have never been brought under your cognisance."

He paused for a moment as if to allow his next words to gather force thereby.

"Sir, is it within your knowledge that when your son left Italy for America he took with him--a wife?"

At these words Sir Gilbert's jaw dropped, a curious glaze came over his eyes and his fingers began to twitch spasmodically. The Captain sprang to his feet; he was on the point of ringing for help, but a gesture on the part of the baronet restrained him.

"I shall be better in a minute or two," he said in a hoarse whisper. Verinder crossed to the window. Two or three minutes passed, then a hollow changed voice said: "What proof have you that your most strange statement is true?"

"The most convincing of all proofs, Sir Gilbert--a living one. Your son's wife--or widow, as I ought rather to term her--is in London at this moment."

"Alive?--and I have known nothing of her existence all these years! It is incredible, sir--incredible. I am being made the victim of some vile conspiracy."

"Conspiracy, indeed! Nothing of the kind, sir, I give you my word--the word of an officer and a gentleman--hem! I condescend to overlook your words, Sir Gilbert, in consideration of the singularity of the circumstances, otherwise----"

The rest of the sentence was drowned in a cough. He said no more, but twisted one end of his moustache viciously, and scowled at the chandelier.

"It is incredible," Sir Gilbert kept murmuring under his breath without heeding Verinder. The latter waited patiently. One half his tale, and that the more amazing half, had yet to be told. At length Sir Gilbert seemed to pull himself together. Turning on his visitor a face which seemed even more sternly set than usual, he said: "Assuming for the moment, sir, the accuracy of what you have just told me--which, mind you, at present I am by no means prepared to admit--will you be good enough to inform me who and what the--the person was with whom my son was so foolishly weak as to contract a secret marriage."

It was a question for which the Captain had prepared himself, and he answered it on the moment.

"The lady in question was born in Italy, her father being a native of that country, and her mother an Englishwoman. Signor Rispani was a scion of an impoverished patrician family which can boast of I know not how many quarterings with other families as noble as itself."

This latter statement, it may be remarked, was a deliberate invention on the Captain's part. He had calculated that it would not be without its effect on the baronet, as also that the latter, in all probability, had never heard the name of Rispani, or, if he had heard it during his brief sojourn at Catanzaro, that he had long ago forgotten it.

"Um--um. And the young woman's mother--what of her? You say she was an Englishwoman."

"Her mother, Sir Gilbert Clare, was my sister," replied the Captain as he laid his hand over the region of his heart and bent his head, while his look said as plainly as words, "After that statement, it would be nothing less than an impertinence on your part to inquire further."

Sir Gilbert bowed with his most courtly air. "Thank you very much, Captain

Verinder," he said. Then, after stroking his chin for a few seconds, he went on: "May I ask, sir, whether your visit here to-day is with the knowledge and sanction of your niece--that is to say of the--the lady whom you allege to be the widow of my son?"

"Had my visit not been undertaken at her express desire, it would not have taken place at all."

"Um. Then will it be thought presumptuous on my part to ask by what particular motive your niece is actuated in asking you, after a silence which has lasted nearly a score of years, to bring under my notice certain facts hitherto, I admit, unknown to me, but which, for anything which has yet been advanced to the contrary, might just as well have been left in the oblivion to which, apparently, they have for so long a time been consigned."

There was a veiled insolence in this request, or so it seemed to Verinder, which sent an angry flush mounting to the very roots of his dyed hair. It was only by a supreme effort that he succeeded in keeping back the retort that rose to his lips. Not till he had drawn several breaths did he trust himself to reply. Then he said:

"Should you condescend, Sir Gilbert, to grant my niece an interview, you will find her amply prepared to furnish you with such an explanation of her long silence as, I venture to think, you will find it impossible to cavil at. But the one great reason which has induced her, at what may be called the eleventh hour, to rake certain facts out of oblivion, as you have so expressively termed it, and bring them before you, is, because it seems to her an imperative duty that you should no longer be left in ignorance of the existence of your grandson--of the son of your son, the late John Alexander Clare."

"What is that you say?" almost shrieked Sir Gilbert. "A grandson! the child of my son Alec--and alive!"

"Very much alive, Sir Gilbert, if you will allow me to say so," returned the Captain, with something between a grin and a sneer. "And as fine, and handsome, and clever a young man as you would find in a day's march."

Sir Gilbert lay back in his chair, his chin drooping on his breast and his eyes closed. His face was of a ghastly pallor, his lips moved inaudibly. In the shock of Verinder's news he had forgotten the man's presence. An invisible hand had snatched him away. He was there in body but for the time his spirit was otherwhere.

The Captain was biting his nails and regarding him furtively. "How will he take it?" he asked himself. "I have a presentiment that my little scheme will result in a brilliant success. For all Sir Gilbert looks as strong as some gnarled old monarch of the woods, who can say whether he's sound at the core? Looks are deceptive things, and at his age he might go off at a day's notice--nay, without any notice at all. It was nothing less than a stroke of genius to represent Vanna's father as belonging to the old Italian nobility. It touched him in a weak spot. Vanna must on no account forget that she is no longer an innkeeper's daughter, but a person of much greater consequence. Well, I will give her credit for one thing; as far as looks and bearing go, she might be a princess born, or the daughter of a duke.

Ah! who comes now?"
The question was elicited by a discreet tap at the door, which was followed, an instant later, by the entrance of a servant.
"If you please, Sir Gilbert," said the man, "Lady Nelthorpe has called and would like to see you. Her ladyship wished me to say that she won't detain you more than five minutes."
The sound of the man's voice served to break Sir Gilbert's waking trance. He opened his eyes, gave a little start, and grasping an arm of his chair with either hand, he drew himself into an upright position. Next moment he was himself again.
"Repeat your message," he said to the man in his usual curt, imperious tones; and when that had been done, he said: "Tell her ladyship that I will be with her in three minutes," adding, *sotto voce* , "Plague take the woman! she never calls on me except when she wants to cozen me out of a cheque for one or other of her preposterous projects."
Then his eyes turned to Verinder, who had drawn his chair somewhat aside on the entrance of the servant, and as he did so, the expression of his face changed. "Pardon me," he said, "if for the moment I had forgotten your presence. I am getting into years," he added with a faint sigh, "and at times--only at times, mind you--my memory fails me somewhat. The news you have brought me, Captain--er--er--Dear me, how annoying!"
"Verinder," suggested the other.
"To be sure, to be sure. The news you have brought me, Captain Verinder, is of such a surprising kind that I may be pardoned if I find myself unable all at once to realise it as something within the bounds of possibility. It--it seems like an incident culled from some romance." Here he rose to his feet. There was a strange yearning look in his eyes as he turned and faced the Captain. "Do you mean to assure me, sir, on your word as a man of honour," he said in a voice the deep impressiveness of which was not without a touch of pathos, "that you are prepared to produce before me a young man whom you will vouch for as being the offspring of my son John Alexander Clare."
Laying a hand over his heart, the Captain, who had also risen, said with grave solemnity: "On my word of honour, Sir Gilbert Clare, that is what I am prepared to do. Your grandson shall be produced before you whensoever and wheresoever may be most convenient to you."
Sir Gilbert took a turn or two in silence. Many memories were at work within him. "No, I will not see the young man just yet. Bring his mother first and let me see and question her. There are several points that will have to be cleared up to my satisfaction before--before---- But I need say no more at present."
"Will you be good enough, Sir Gilbert, to name a time for your interview with my niece?"
"To-morrow at eleven, if that will suit you and her." Then he added under his breath: "Ah, if my faithful, shrewd old Page were only here to help me to investigate this business! The longer I live the more I miss him."

CHAPTER XVII.

SIR GILBERT AND GIOVANNA.

Punctually at eleven o'clock next forenoon Captain Verinder, accompanied by his niece, alighted from the fly which had conveyed them from the railway station, at the foot of the flight of semi-circular steps leading to the portico which sheltered the main entrance to the mansion of Withington Chase.

So elated had the Captain been by the result of his interview with Sir Gilbert, that, after detailing to his niece on his return all that had passed between them, he had insisted that she, he and Luigi should all dine together in a private room at a certain popular restaurant (of course at Vanna's expense), when he did not fail to toast Sir Gilbert in a bumper of Clicquot. "Here's to your grandsire, my boy," he said to Luigi as he drained his glass; then, having refilled it, he added: "And here's to the coming lord of Withington Chase, and may he never forget all that his old uncle has done for him!"

A little later he remarked: "I don't think it will be long, my boy, before you come into your inheritance. The old man's breaking up, that's plainly to be seen. I shouldn't be surprised if the next winter tries him severely. He coughed several times during our interview, and a very hollow cough it was."

"And when he is dead and gone, shall I be Sir Luigi Clare?" asked the young man.

"Sir Luigi Clare!" echoed the Captain. "There's a point, now, which I had completely overlooked, while flattering myself that I had forgotten nothing. You will come into the title of course on Sir Gilbert's death. But Sir Luigi Clare will never do. It's altogether too outlandish. We must re-christen you, and that at once."

"Why not make English of the name by turning Luigi into Lewis?" demanded Giovanna.

"The very thing!" replied the Captain. "Which goes to prove that two heads are better than one--especially, my dear, when one of them happens to belong to your sex. Now I come to think, among other inscriptions in the little church at the Chase was one to the memory of a certain Colonel Lewis Clare who fell in some battle or other a long time ago. Now, what more natural," he went on with a meaning look at Luigi, "than that your *father* , instead of naming you after himself, should have preferred to call you after his brave ancestor? Yes, Lewis Clare will do very well indeed--Sir Lewis that will be later on."

Although Giovanna's only visible betrayal of the fact was by a touch of unwonted pallor in her cheeks, she was the prey of a dozen conflicting emotions as the doors of Withington Chase were flung wide and she and her uncle crossed the threshold. "And this was my husband's home when a boy," was her first thought as her gaze wandered round the entrance hall. "How little I suspected such a thing! There must have been some powerful motive at work to cause him to quit such a roof and to change his name and marry an innkeeper's daughter and seek a new home thousands of miles away. What was that motive, I wonder?"

"Will you come this way, please," said the trained voice of the man in livery a second later, and with that they were presently shown into the same morning-room into which the Captain had been ushered the day before.

"And now, my dear, the crucial moment is at hand," said the Captain to Vanna as soon as they were alone. "I hope you have forgotten none of the points in which I have so carefully coached you up."

"I don't think there is much fear of that. I never forget anything which it is essential that I should remember."

"One last caution, however. Take your time in answering Sir Gilbert's questions, and, above all things, don't get flurried."

"Did you ever know me to get flurried, Uncle Verinder?"

"No, 'pon my word, I don't think I ever did. But then I have known you such a very short while."

At this juncture the door opened and Sir Gilbert entered the room.

The Captain and Vanna both rose as he came slowly forward, his eyes fixed scrutinisingly on his daughter-in-law. Her stately presence and the classic beauty of her features impressed him at the first glance, and therewith came a sudden *bouleversement* of all his preconceived notions of what she would be like. On the spot he acknowledged to himself that he had done her an injustice in his thoughts. After favouring Verinder with a curt nod of recognition, he went up to Giovanna and held out his hand with an air of old-fashioned courtesy.

"Am I to presume, madam, that I see before me the widow of my late son, John Alexander Clare?"

"That was my husband's full name, Sir Gilbert--the name he was married in--although, for reasons of his own, he chose to be known to the world simply as Mr. John Alexander."

"To be sure--to be sure." The rich full contralto of her voice sounded pleasantly in his ears. "That was a fact well-known to me at the time. But pray be seated." A wave of his hand included Verinder in the invitation.

He had dropped Giovanna's hand, and there had been a sudden change in his tone as he spoke the last words. The fact was that he had caught the Captain smiling and rubbing one hand within the other with an air of supreme satisfaction, although the other had certainly not intended that he should do anything of the kind, and therewith he had chilled under a sudden breath of suspicion. "What, after all, if I am being victimised by a couple of schemers!" he said to himself. "And yet that any woman with such a face as that should lend

herself---- No, no--I cannot believe it."
Both the others could see that some change had come over him, but were at a loss to guess the cause of it.
"And where was it, madam, if I may be allowed to ask, that you first made the acquaintance of my son?"
"At Catanzaro, Sir Gilbert."
"So--so. Alec's long stay in that, to me, detestable hole of a place is now explained." This was said half to himself. "And where, madam, were you and my son united in the bonds of matrimony?"
"We were married at Malta, at the English church there."
"Ah, then you are a Protestant!"
Giovanna gravely inclined her head. "My father was a Roman Catholic, but my mother was an Englishwoman and a Protestant. My only brother was brought up in the faith of his father, I in that of my mother."
"So much the better--so much the better," ejaculated Sir Gilbert, quite unaware that the words were spoken aloud.
It was a fact that Giovanna had been married at the English church at Valetta, but a prior ceremony had been gone through at Catanzaro, at which a Romish priest had been the celebrant, for Giuseppe Rispani was too good a Catholic, or had the reputation of being one, not to insist upon his daughter being married in accordance with the rites and ceremonies of his own church. That being done, he had raised no objection to accompanying the young couple as far as Malta (to him, indeed, it was a pleasure trip with all expenses paid), there to give away the bride when the ceremony was gone through for the second time. After that Rispani had bidden his daughter goodbye and gone back home, first, however, borrowing a couple of hundred pounds from his English son-in-law in order, as he averred, that he might have the means of carrying out certain much needed alterations and improvements in the *osteria* of the Golden Fig. It is to be feared, however, that the amount in question never got any further than his own pocket.
After the departure of Rispani the newly-wedded couple had made the best of their way to the United States.
To return.
"In that case, madam," resumed the baronet after a brief pause, "you have doubtless been at pains to preserve your marriage certificate."
Giovanna had preserved it, had, in fact, brought it with her this morning. She now produced it, a creased and faded-looking document, from the satchel suspended from her waist-belt, opened it and handed it to Sir Gilbert; who, having adjusted his *pince-nez* and drawn his chair up to the centre table, smoothed out the certificate upon it and proceeded to read it slowly and carefully from beginning to end, his lips shaping each word silently as he spoke it to himself. It purported to be, and was a duly certified copy of the entry in the register of the Protestant church at Valetta of the marriage solemnised on the date specified between John Alexander Clare and Giovanna Rispani. It would

have been idle to dispute its genuineness, even had there been any inclination, which was far from being the case, on Sir Gilbert's part to do so.

"Madam, the document seems to me in every respect satisfactory," he said gravely as he refolded it and handed it back to Giovanna with a bow.

In return she put into his hands a framed photograph of herself and her husband, taken within a few days of their marriage. "Possibly, Sir Gilbert, this may not be without some interest for you," she said in her quiet, measured tones.

The old man took the photograph and carried it to the window. Scarcely was his back turned before the Captain flashed a look at Vanna which said, "Everything, so far, going on first-rate."

One, two, three minutes were ticked off by the clock on the chimney-piece before Sir Gilbert came back to his chair. His hand trembled a little as he returned the photograph to Giovanna. "Yes, that is Alec to the life," he said. "Poor boy! poor boy!" A deep sigh broke from him as he resumed his seat.

For a little space no one spoke.

It was Sir Gilbert who broke the silence. "Unless I am misinformed, madam, you and your husband found your way to the United States no long time after your marriage?"

"We did, Sir Gilbert. And here a little point occurs to me about which it may be as well to enlighten you. Up to the morning of our marriage I had never known my husband by any other name than John Alexander. The only explanation proffered by him after the ceremony was over was, that he had deemed it best, for certain private reasons, to temporarily drop his surname. As to the nature of his reasons, he never enlightened me, and, indeed, so little curious was I to learn them that, as far as I now remember, the subject was never again broached between us, and after our arrival in America we were known simply as Mr. and Mrs. Alexander."

"Quite right, quite right," said Sir Gilbert. "My son, for family reasons, chose, right up to the time of his death, to keep his surname in abeyance. Well, and what happened after your arrival in the States?"

"We settled in a place called Barrytown in one of the Eastern States, where John (I always called my husband John, Sir Gilbert) thought he saw an opening for the profitable investment of his capital. But he had had no training, and in all business relations was little better than a child compared with the shrewd Yankees in whose midst he had chosen to locate himself. The result was what might have been expected. Instead of making money, at the end of two years he found himself about four thousand pounds poorer than when he had started in business."

"That was burning his fingers with a vengeance," interpolated the Captain, who had so far maintained a diplomatic silence.

Sir Gilbert glared at him for an instant and then turned his shoulder a couple of inches more towards him. "Proceed, madam, pray proceed," he said blandly to Giovanna.

"By that time our child was born and my health had given way. The doctors told John that the climate of the Eastern States was too inclement for me, and that if I stayed there another winter he would risk losing me. Thereupon he decided to break up our home and go further inland in search at once of a climate that would be likely to agree with me, and of an opening for what was left of his capital which promised better results than his first venture had brought him. Meanwhile I was to go back to Italy, of course taking my child with me, and strive to recruit my health in my native air. As soon as he found himself prospering and had settled where our new home was to be, he would send for me, or fetch me to join him. Well, sir, we parted, my husband seeing me on board ship at New York, little thinking that we should never see each other again. Two letters from him reached me after my arrival at home, in the second of which he told me that he was going to penetrate still further west, or south, I forget which. After that came a silence which has remained unbroken till the present day."

As Giovanna ended, her head sank forward a little and, as if involuntarily, the fingers of her right hand sought and pressed the golden hoop which still graced the third finger of her left hand.

The Captain had been on thorns for the last few minutes for fear lest she should trip, or contradict herself over some point of the narrative which he had so carefully elaborated for her. Now he began to breathe more freely. They were by no means out of the wood yet, but everything had gone so smoothly up till now that it was surely not unreasonable to hope their good fortune would attend them to the end.

"And you never made any effort to trace your husband?" said Sir Gilbert after a pause.

"Sir Gilbert!" exclaimed Giovanna in a tone of genuine amazement. "Please to consider the circumstances of the case. Month after month went by, and every morning on opening my eyes, my first words were, 'Surely I shall have a letter to-day.' But none came. Not till a year had gone by did I give up all hope. Whether my husband was alive or dead, I knew not. What was I to do? America is a big country, and even if I had gone back to New York, I altogether fail to see how it would have been possible for me to trace him after the lapse of so long a time."

"You are quite right, madam. My question was a foolish one. When the year had gone by, what then? Did you never make any attempt to seek out your husband's relatives?"

"Never, Sir Gilbert. It was a matter I did not feel myself at liberty to pry into. Seeing that my husband had never spoken to me about his friends and connections, a certain pride--shall I call it?--withheld me from trying to penetrate a secret which he had not seen fit to share with me."

"At length, however, you saw cause to think differently."

"I was about to explain, Sir Gilbert," said Giovanna with a touch of hauteur which became her well. "Time went on till my son was twelve years old, and then my father died (I had lost my mother many years before), after which event I determined to come to England, where my only brother had been some time settled. I wanted my son to become acquainted with his father's country, and to train him up to become as much like an Englishman as possible. Besides, as time went on it became requisite that he should do something for his living, the whole of my income not amounting to more than a hundred pounds of English money a year. Not to weary you, Gilbert, I will merely add that my son is now, and has been for some time past, earning his living in London as a drawing-master."

"As a drawing-master?" ejaculated Sir Gilbert as if to himself.

"It was quite by accident that my uncle here discovered that my late husband was your eldest son, Sir Gilbert; but after the discovery had been made it became a matter of anxious thought with us whether we should, or should not, proceed any further in the affair. At length we decided that, as a matter of simple justice to you, we were bound to acquaint you with the fact that you had a grandson living of whose existence you had heretofore been unaware, leaving it for you to make whatever use of the knowledge you might deem best."

" *Brava! bravissima!* " ejaculated the Captain under his breath as Giovanna came to an end. "I could not have done it better myself. Not a hitch nor a slip anywhere. What will the old boy do now?"

What the "old boy" did was to take a few silent turns about the room with his hands behind his back, his eyes bent on the carpet, and his head sunk between his shoulders. It was his invariable practice when mentally puzzled or perturbed.

"Madam," he said at length, coming to a halt and planting himself on the hearthrug with his back towards the grate, "nothing could have been more straightforward, or perspicacious than the narrative with which you have just favoured me, and I have no hesitation in saying that to me it seems to bear the stamp of absolute truth. Singularly enough, it happens that I am in a position to enlighten you and set your mind at rest for ever as to the fate of your husband. Poor Alec was killed by the explosion of a steamboat at a date which, I doubt not, will prove on investigation to have been within a few months of the parting between you and him. No wonder, my dear lady, that you looked in vain for any more letters from him."

"Oh, Sir Gilbert," ejaculated Giovanna, "what an awful fate was his! My poor John! My poor husband!"

She covered her face with her hands and bent her head over the end of the couch on which she was seated. Sir Gilbert turned his back and took up first one ornament off the mantel-piece and then another. The Captain tried to look sympathetic, but failed signally. No long time passed before Giovanna sat up and quietly wiped her eyes. Sir Gilbert had felt sure that she was not the kind of woman to make a scene, or go into hysterics, and he secretly commended her good sense. He now turned and cleared his voice. During the last minute or two he had made up his mind to a certain course.

"My dear madam," he began, "I trust you will do me the favour of bringing your son to the Chase to-morrow forenoon and introducing him to me." He was careful not to say "my grandson."

Giovanna's heart went up with a bound. "I will do so with the greatest pleasure, Sir Gilbert," she replied in her usual composed tones, but her cheeks flushed a little and a sudden light leapt to her eyes.

"There remains one point, however," resumed Sir Gilbert, "about which it may be as well to say a few words, so that, in time to come, no misapprehension in the matter may exist on the part of anyone concerned." Again he cleared his voice. "When my son left England it was by my request. He was deeply involved in debt--not for the first or second time--and he applied to me, as he had done before, to extricate him from his difficulties. This I agreed to do on condition that he would go abroad and stay there till he should have my permission to return. He agreed to the condition and went. At the end of two years he wrote me to the effect that he was desirous of emigrating and pushing his fortunes in the United States, and that if I would pay over to him the sum of six thousand pounds he would sanction the cutting off of the family entail. It was an offer which, after consideration, I decided to accept. I had three other sons then living, and from what I knew of Alec it seemed clear to me that after my death he would simply make ducks and drakes of the property. Accordingly, I went out to Catanzaro, taking my lawyer with me. The six thousand pounds was paid over to my son, and in return he signed certain documents, by the provisions of which he cut himself off from all succession to the family estates. Now, I have only spoken of this fact at so much length because I wish it to be clearly understood that no right of succession to the Clare estates any longer exists, and that it is open to me to will every acre of land and every shilling of which I may die possessed, to whomsoever I may choose to constitute my heirs."

CHAPTER XVIII.

THE FALSE HEIR.

Sir Gilbert Clare's deliberate announcement, evidently not made without a purpose, that the family estates were no longer entailed, was one which carried dismay to the heart of Captain Verinder. His face fell on the instant, and for a little while the ruddy colour faded out of his cheeks. Although aware that the baronet's eyes were glancing keenly from him to Giovanna, and then back, he could not for the life of him help showing that the blow had struck home.

Sir Gilbert smiled grimly to himself.

"As I thought, this fellow is at the bottom of the business," he murmured, but this time not aloud. "It is he who has found me out and induced his niece to lay her case before me, evidently in the expectation of being able to feather his nest out of her, or me, or both of us. Well, we shall see. As regards his niece, I am more than ever inclined to believe in her. The story she told me was remarkably clear and straightforward. But *festina lente* must still be my motto."

Then he rose. "And now, my dear madam," he said, addressing himself pointedly to Giovanna and wholly ignoring the Captain, "I must ask you to excuse me till to-morrow, when I shall expect to see you here, accompanied by your son, at the same hour as to-day. I would not have quitted you so abruptly but that I have a couple of my tenant farmers waiting all this time to see me about some repairs. But you must not leave the Chase without partaking of some refreshment. Pardon me if I insist. I cannot sit down with you myself, I am sorry to say, for I am under the strictest dietetic regimen. They are terrible tyrants, these doctors. Till to-morrow at eleven, then."

Therewith he shook hands cordially with Giovanna, but the Captain he merely favoured with a curt nod, as it might be a nod of dismissal to one of his dependents; and, indeed, he had already made up his mind that he had seen quite enough of Captain Verinder.

Presently a servant appeared with a liberally appointed luncheon tray, at sight of which the Captain brightened visibly, for he was one of those men to whom the good things of the table never appeal in vain.

It was not till they were jogging back to the station in their fly, which had been kept waiting for them, that Giovanna said: "I am not sure that I quite got at the meaning of Sir Gilbert's speech about what he called the entail. Does it mean that---- But perhaps you had better tell me what it does mean."

The Captain drew down the corners of his mouth. "Oh, there's no possible mistake about his meaning. It seems that your husband was so unspeakably foolish as, in return for the sum of six thousand pound, to deprive himself and his heirs of what otherwise would have been their undoubted birthright. Thus the estate of Withington Chase, and other estates into the bargain, for anything I know to the contrary, instead of descending through the law of entail to Sir Gilbert's grandson (whom we hope to have the pleasure of introducing to him to-morrow), have, as the result of that act, become the baronet's sole and personal property, to sell, or give away, or do what the dickens he likes with. I wish with all my heart that John Alexander Clare had been at the bottom of the Red Sea before putting his hand to any such iniquitous document."

"Then, if Sir Gilbert chooses to adopt Luigi as his grandson it does not follow that he will come into the property?"

"It certainly does not follow that he will; but neither does it follow that he won't. Everything hinges on how Sir Gilbert takes to him. If Luigi plays his cards skilfully, there's no reason why he should not come in for everything when the old gentleman dies. On the other hand, if he plays them badly, he may be left without a shilling."

"And the title?" queried Giovanna.

"Oh, the title can't be cut off as the entail has been. That descends to the next heir, whoever he may be, and nothing can deprive him of it. But where would be the good of the title, I should like to know, without the means to keep it up? It would be a white elephant--worse than useless. Everything depends on Luigi."

"He seems to me a rather clever young man."

"Oh yes, he's clever enough in his way," said the Captain with a short laugh. "The question is whether he's not a little bit too clever. There lies our danger."

This was rather beyond Giovanna; but, as their fly drew up next minute at the station, nothing more was said; and as there were several other passengers in the compartment by which they travelled up to town, all further private conversation was deferred till they reached Giovanna's rooms, where they found Luigi impatiently awaiting their arrival.

The young Italian was a rank coward both morally and physically, and when told that he would have to face Sir Gilbert Clare on the morrow in his assumed *rô*le* of grandson to the baronet, his cheeks blanched and a nervous trembling took possession of him, which was not allayed till the Captain had administered to him a tolerably stiff dose of brandy.

As already stated, Luigi was a fairly good-looking young man. He was tall and slender, with a pale olive complexion and clear cut features of an almost purely Greek type. His eyes were large, black and expressive, and the knowledge of how to make the most of them had come to him by intuition, as it does to the majority of his race. Jet black, soft and silky were his hair and moustache. He was very proud of his long tapering hands, and his carefully trimmed nails. Some of his friends said they were the hands of an artist, others, less complimentary, averred that he had the digits of a pickpocket. Both statements went beyond the mark, as the generality of extreme statements do, for although Luigi Rispani was a fairly clever drawing-master, he was entirely lacking in the creative faculty, and although he had no moral scruples whatever in lending himself to a scheme for defrauding Sir Gilbert Clare, nothing less than hard compulsion--a twinge of starvation, for instance--would have induced him to insert his hand into another man's pocket and abstract therefrom a watch or purse. In the opinion of some people a transaction of the latter kind would have been much more venial than the one to which he had given his assent, but such was not Luigi Rispani's way of thinking, and such is not the way of thinking of thousands of others.

Our three conspirators did not separate till a late hour, for, on the strength of his coming good fortune, Luigi had already thrown up his post at the theatre. As a matter of course, the Captain was spokesman-in-chief. He it was who thought out every detail and strove to foresee and provide against every contingency which might unexpectedly crop up at the morrow's interview. The others had little to do beyond listening and assenting and trying to fix in their memory, so that they might be available at the right moment, the different points enumerated by him.

In matters of business Captain Verinder was punctuality itself, and our little party of three pulled up at the door of Withington Chase as the turret clock was striking eleven. Having been ushered into the morning room as before, they were left to themselves for a few minutes. Then the footman reappeared with a request that "the lady and the young gentleman" would be good enough to follow him. Before quitting the room he rather ostentatiously placed a couple of newspapers on the centre table.

Captain Verinder was left alone; he realised the fact unpleasantly. Starting to his feet, he began to pace the room with anything but placid strides. His face turned a purplish red, he shook his clenched hands at an imaginary foe, and anathematised Sir Gilbert in tones not loud but deep. He was quite aware that the baronet had conceived an unaccountable dislike for him, but he had not thought it would take a form of such active hostility as had now evinced itself. It was more than a slight--it was an insult--as he fumingly told himself: but all the same, it was one which he was not in a position to resent.

After all, as he assured himself when he had in some measure calmed down, it was really a matter of little moment, even if Sir Gilbert should continue to ignore him; he might feel sore at the time, but he would soon get over that. The great point was that the scheme he had so carefully elaborated was on the high road to success; the rest, as far as he was concerned, was a trifling matter indeed. Let but Luigi and Vanna attain to the positions he had designated them for, and henceforth with him--Augustus Verinder--all would go well. Farewell, then, to his existence of semi-genteel pauperism, and to his long struggle against a fate which had so persistently turned a cold shoulder to him, and would have none of his wooing! For the rest of his days he would be able to live as a gentleman ought to live.

On leaving the morning-room, Giovanna and Luigi were conducted to the library, where they found Sir Gilbert awaiting them. The baronet received them with that frigid ceremoniousness to which Giovanna was becoming accustomed by this time, but which did not tend to put Luigi more at his ease. But the mere fact of Sir Gilbert betraying no outward signs of perturbation afforded no gauge by which to measure the depth of the emotions at work below. All his life it had been natural to him to mask his feelings, and at his age it was not to be expected that he should alter. In reality, he was profoundly moved--a fact which increased, rather than diminished, the ingrained austerity of his manner, and deepened the vertical line between his shaggy eyebrows.

"Madam, I wish you a very good day," he said, as he took Giovanna's hand for a moment and bent over it. "You are punctuality itself--a commendable virtue in your sex! but one, unless they are somewhat belied, more honoured by them in the breach than the observance."

Sir Gilbert's banter, on the very rare occasions on which he condescended to indulge in it, was of a somewhat ponderous and old-fashioned kind. Not that he was in any bantering mood to-day--far from it; his only object was, by means of it, the more effectually to conceal the inward tremor which had seized him now the moment had come which was to give him a grandson to take the place of the son whom he had banished long years before.

For the moment Giovanna found nothing to say in reply. For the first time she seemed to realise the enormity of the fraud to which she had lent herself, and the shame of it. But it was too late to go back even had she been willing to do so--which was doubtful: for it is no uncommon experience for a person to recognise to the full the blackness of any wrong-doing in which he or she may be engaged, and yet not to falter, or swerve for a moment from the line of action they have laid down for themselves.

"And this, madam, is the grandson whom you have brought from the kingdom of Nowhere to make me a present of," continued Sir Gilbert as he faced Luigi.

"This, sir, is your grandson, Lewis Clare," replied Giovanna in quiet measured tones.

"Lewis Clare!--why Lewis?" demanded the old man, turning quickly on her.

"It was the name his father chose for him. Was there not--pardon the question--a certain Colonel Lewis Clare, who lived a great number of years ago and who fell in battle?"

The baronet nodded.

"It was after him that my husband named the boy," added Giovanna, her black eyes looking Sir Gilbert unflinchingly in the face.

"He might have done worse--he might have done very much worse. It is a name to be proud of, madam."

Then he again faced Luigi, eyeing him critically and keenly.

"So, sir, I am given to understand that you have been brought up in England, consequently I presume that you speak the English language as well as I do."

"Scarcely that, I am afraid, sir," answered Luigi with a glint of his white teeth; "although I pride myself on being more of an Englishman than an Italian."

"Then you belie your looks," muttered the old man as he turned abruptly away. He was bitterly disappointed. His secret hope had been to find another Alec, in any case as far as looks were concerned; for of late years the memory of his eldest son (through a reactionary process by no means uncommon when one whom we have treated ill or unjustly is lost to us for ever) had become very dear to him. But in this olive-skinned, black-eyed stripling, with his facile smile and gleaming teeth, he could trace no single trait or feature which served to recall his dead son. Voice, looks, manner, all were radically different; there was no shadow of resemblance anywhere.

"Still, he is my grandson, and for Alec's sake----" he murmured brokenly under his breath. "It would be altogether unjust to blame the boy, or to treat him in any way differently for what, after all, is no fault of his."

He had turned to the table and was making a pretence of searching among the papers and books with which it was encumbered for something which he apparently failed to find. Behind his back Giovanna and Luigi exchanged glances of perplexity and dismay. Drawing himself up with a sort of half-shake, as if trying to free himself from some harassing thought, and with a sigh meant for himself alone, Sir Gilbert again faced round.

"Pardon my remissness," he said with a little gesture of annoyance, on perceiving that both his visitors were still standing, "but it is not every day that one is presented with a grandson. Pray be seated," he added, and not till they had complied did he find a chair for himself.

He was evidently nonplussed what to say or do next. Although his disappointment was so extreme, and although he felt drawn towards Luigi by no frailest thread of affinity or kinship, he was sternly determined in his own mind that the fullest justice should be done to him, and that his position as the heir of Withington Chase should receive the amplest recognition both at his hands and those of the world at large. Perhaps--and who could say to the contrary?--liking would come in time. Perhaps, although it seemed hard to believe, the boy might gradually win his way to his grandfather's heart and become unspeakably dear to him.

"Your mother, young sir, tells me that for some time past you have been earning your living as a drawing-master," resumed Sir Gilbert when the silence had become painful to all three. He could not, just yet, bring himself to address his grandson after any more familiar or affectionate style.

"That is so, sir, and a very poor living I made of it."

"Ah--ha!" interjected Sir Gilbert, but whether by way of expressing approval, or disapproval, his hearers could not tell.

"You see, sir, there are so many drawing-masters not merely with more experience than I, but with more natural ability to begin with."

"Come now, that is well said, and becoming in a young fellow of your age: although, on the other hand, it is not perhaps advisable--more especially nowadays when everybody seems to make a point of blowing his or her special trumpet as loudly as possible--to underestimate yourself or treat yourself too diffidently. But tell me now, what you can do, or what you think you could do if the opportunity were afforded you. You have tastes, gifts, qualifications of some kind, I suppose?"

"If so, sir, they and I have hardly made acquaintance as yet. Both money and leisure have been such scarce commodities with me, and I have had to work so hard for my living that I suppose I hardly know myself as I really am, or perhaps I ought to say, as I should have been had the circumstances of my life been different."

"There is good sense in what you say. Your modesty becomes you."

Thanks to the Captain's coaching, it was evident that Luigi had already succeeded in creating a favourable impression.

"You have had no opportunity of learning to ride, or shoot, I suppose?" queried Sir Gilbert.

"None whatever, sir."

"Um--that's a pity! What about the classics? Have you any knowledge of Latin, or Greek?"

Luigi shook his head.

"Not the slightest, sir. Of course I know Italian as well as I know English, or better. French, too, I speak with some degree of fluency; but beyond that I am afraid you will find me nothing better than a rank duffer."

Sir Gilbert pricked up his ears.

"I hope you are not addicted to the use of slang, sir, as your last phrase would seem to imply," he said severely. "To me there are few things more detestable. Pray let me never hear any more of it."

Luigi was wise enough to refrain from replying. He simply coloured up and did his best to look ashamed.

Presently the baronet rose. It was a signal to which the others at once responded.

"To-day is Thursday," he said. "Come to me again at noon on Monday next. I have much to think of, many things to consider, but by that time I shall probably have arrived at some decision with regard to certain matters which materially concern all now present. Till then, goodbye."

As he held Giovanna's hand for a moment he said, "I am not aware there is any necessity for Captain Verinder's presence here again. Um--um--it is immensely kind of him to have interested himself as he has, but I should be sorry to put him to any further trouble in the affair." With his right hand grasping that of Luigi, he placed his left in kindly fashion on the young man's shoulder. "You and I, in all probability, will be much better acquainted by-and-by. In any case, I think I may safely say that the fault will rest with you if we are not."

No faintest suspicion clouded Sir Gilbert's mind that he was clasping the hand of an impostor.

CHAPTER XIX.

LUIGI ACKNOWLEDGED.

As on the previous day, luncheon was provided for the baronet's visitors, and, as before, they partook of it without his presence.

Giovanna, in her clear simple way, related to her uncle all that had passed--all except that last speech of Sir Gilbert, which she left to be told later on.

The Captain rubbed his hands gleefully.

"All has gone well so far, very well indeed," he said; "and now that the worst is over--by which I mean now that Luigi has been introduced to the old man and accepted by him as his grandson, as, from what you tell me, seems undoubtedly to be the case--now that the most difficult part of our task has been successfully accomplished, I don't mind saying that I shall sleep more soundly to-night than I have for the last week or more."

"It seems to me that Sir Gilbert favoured me with a precious cool reception," said Luigi, in an aggrieved tone; "in fact it was enough to freeze one. And those eyes of his seemed to go right through me; I was never so nervous in my life. I wouldn't go through such a quarter of an hour again for a good deal."

"There will be no call for you to do so," replied the Captain. "As I said before, you have gone through the worst. You know now the kind of man he is, and must act accordingly. If you only knew how"--adding, to himself, "and were not so self-opinionated and conceited"--"you might lead Sir Gilbert anywhere with your little finger. In the case of such a man, you have only to fall in with his humours, or make believe to fall in with them, and you may do anything in reason with him."

"If I had but your head on my shoulders, uncle!" exclaimed Luigi, with a smile that had a spice of mockery in it.

"Or my brains in your numbskull," retorted the Captain. "Oh, the chance--the golden chance that is now yours! One can but hope that you will know how to make the best of it."

It seemed to Giovanna that the time had now come for making her uncle acquainted with what Sir Gilbert had said about him. The Captain pulled a wry face for a moment, and then broke into one of his short harsh laughs.

"What a cantankerous old shaver he is!" he exclaimed. "I was sure from the first that he had taken a dislike to me." Then laying a hand on his niece's arm, he added in a voice which had become suddenly grave: "It matters not a grain of salt in what light Sir Gilbert chooses to regard me, so long as you and Luigi--especially the boy--contrive to keep in his good graces. That is the only thing of any real consequence."

For the next few days Sir Gilbert felt thoroughly unsettled and out of sorts. His ordinary avocations seemed to have lost all interest for him; he was unable to fix his attention on anything outside the special current of his thoughts for more than a few minutes at a time. He shut himself up in his own room, a small apartment which opened out of the library, and even Everard Lisle was only admitted to the briefest possible audience each forenoon. His mental attitude at this time was a puzzle to himself. A wonderful thing had come to pass. One which, had an inkling of it been permitted him beforehand, he should have assured himself could not fail to fill his few remaining days with a happiness undreamt of, and almost too deep to find expression in words. A gift, the most precious of any he could have asked for (seeing that we cannot bring back our lost ones from the tomb), had been vouchsafed to him, yet, strange to say, he felt little or none of that elation which would have seemed the natural outcome of such a state of affairs. Why was this, and to what cause was it attributable? He tried to look forward to the presence of his newly-found grandson as to something that would crown his life with a blessing, and to mentally picture their daily life together in time to come, but he derived no pleasure from the process; neither did the future, now that he looked at it with fresh eyes, as it were, take to itself any added brightness from the fact that a son of his son would succeed him when the time should have come for him to pass into the Silent Land.

"Is it that my heart is dead?" he sadly asked himself, "or is it because I am so old and have gone through so much, that only the ghost of either joy or sorrow will ever keep me company again? Or is it," he went on, "because in this youth who has so suddenly intruded himself into my life I can discern nothing that serves to recall his father to memory, nor any likeness, however vague, to any of my pictured ancestors in the long gallery--who are his ancestors also--that I seem in no way drawn towards him? I cannot tell why it is so. I only know that it is."

In one respect, however, he derived a certain amount of mordant satisfaction from the knowledge that he would now be followed by an heir in the direct line of descent. His detested kinsman, Colonel Eustace Clare, who, he felt sure, never missed a day without hoping it would bring the tidings of his death, would now, at what might be termed the eleventh hour, be baulked of his chance of succession to the title, even as the cutting off of the entail in years gone by had deprived him of all prospect of ever succeeding to the estates.

Monday at noon brought Giovanna and Luigi again to the Chase. Verinder had kept them company as far as Mapleford station, where they all alighted. It had been arranged that he should await, either their return, or the receipt of some message from them, at the railway hotel, it being impossible to say how long Sir Gilbert might choose to detain them. The Captain's impatience would not admit of his quietly awaiting their return in London.

If Sir Gilbert received his guests without any particular display of cordiality he yet greeted them with a grave and kindly courtesy which went far towards putting them at their ease. For the time the more brusque and imperious traits of his character failed to assert themselves: indeed, no stranger seeing him on this occasion only, would have as much as suspected their existence. To-day he kept the others company at luncheon, although all he partook of was a biscuit and a glass of Madeira. By special invitation Everard Lisle made a fourth at table.

When once Sir Gilbert had made up his mind to acknowledge Giovanna as his daughter-in-law, and Luigi as his grandson, he was not a man to stick at half measures. The acknowledgment should be full and complete, and Everard Lisle was the person he chose to whom first to communicate his intentions, with which purpose in view he invited him to dine at the Chase on Sunday. It was as they sat together after dinner that Sir Gilbert broke his news.

"For the present I shall have the boy to live with me," he said. "I want us to become better acquainted. My daughter-in-law, if she chooses to do so, can take up her residence at Maylings, the family dower-house, although not used as such in my time, which has stood empty since old Miss Hopkins's death three years ago. Of course the news that my grandson and his mother have been received and acknowledged by me will very soon get noised abroad, and as you are likely, owing to your being at the Chase so much, to be appealed to on the point by a number of people, I want you to be in a position to confirm the accuracy of the report and to give it the stamp of verity. That all sorts of ridiculous stories will get about, originating in the fact of my grandson's and daughter-in-law's existence not having been made public till now, I do not doubt, but with any, or all, such inventions you need have nothing to do. We have simply to deal with the two or three plain facts of the case."

Thus it fell out that Everard Lisle was already prepared for the meeting on Monday. The baronet introduced him simply as "My secretary, Mr. Lisle."

As Luigi did not proffer his hand, Everard contented himself by bowing slightly. But Sir Gilbert did not fail to notice the omission.

"Where is your hand, sir?" he demanded of his pseudo grandson with a drawing together of his shaggy brows. "Let me tell you that, young as Mr. Lisle is, I hold him in the highest esteem and regard."

Luigi smilingly hastened to repair his oversight. He was quick-witted enough in some things. "A favourite, evidently," he said to himself with an almost imperceptible shrug. "I suppose it will be to my interest to keep in with this fellow for the present, but when it comes to my turn he shall very soon be presented with the order of his going."

It seemed to Lisle that the best thing he could do would be to draw young Clare into talk over luncheon and leave Sir Gilbert and Mrs. Clare to get on together as best they could. Luigi responded readily enough to Everard's advances, all he asked just then being to be left alone by his "grandfather," whom he still regarded with secret fear and trembling, the enormity of the fraud of which he had been guilty impressing itself far more unpleasantly on his consciousness when in the presence of the baronet than at any other time. Both the young men were careful to confine their talk to the merest generalities. Both of them were on their guard, neither of them could tell yet what his future relations towards the other might develop into.

As for the baronet, he proceeded to mount one of his antiquarian hobbies (it may have been of set purpose, and in order to save both Giovanna and himself the awkwardness of having to make talk about nothing in particular) and ambled on, apparently to the content of both himself and his listener. Nothing more was required of Mrs. Clare than to look interested and to interject an occasional "Yes," or "No," or "Indeed," at the proper moment, all of which she did to perfection, although three-fourths of Sir Gilbert's monologue was clearly beyond her comprehension.

When luncheon was over, the baronet, turning to Everard, said: "Mr. Lisle, I want you to be good enough to conduct Mrs. Clare and my grandson over the house and grounds, and to show them everything worth seeing. Mrs. Burton will place herself at your disposal as far as the house is concerned, and you can impound Shotover to show you over the gardens, and so forth. For myself, I am sorry that the infirmities of age should have so far prevailed over me as to preclude me from undertaking a task which otherwise would have been one of unmixed pleasure. You will find me in the library when you have finished your peregrination: but there is no need whatever for you to hurry yourselves."

CHAPTER XX.

SIR GILBERT'S DECISION.

The Mrs. Burton referred to by Sir Gilbert was housekeeper at the Chase, having held that position since the death of the second Lady Clare. She was a widow, middle-aged, thin, prim, and as upright as a dart, and was still able to pride herself on the slimness of her figure. Her manners pertained to what might be termed the severely genteel school. She was careful to impress upon everyone with whom she was brought into contact that she was "a lady by birth," but it was a statement which she evidently intended people to accept unfortified by any particulars of her parentage and early history, with regard to which, indeed, it was noticed that she was studiously reticent. Her peculiarities notwithstanding, she made an excellent housekeeper, and the baronet valued her accordingly.

It had not been often in the course of her uneventful existence that anyone had succeeded in more than faintly stirring the chilly shallows of Mrs. Burton's gentility, but this morning she had been more nearly startled out of her propriety than had happened to her since her advent at Withington Chase.

Sir Gilbert had sent for her immediately after breakfast, and without a word of preface, and with no more apparent concern than if he were giving his orders about dinner, had said:

"Mrs. Burton, I am expecting two people to luncheon to-day whom you have never yet seen, and probably never as much as heard of. They are my daughter-in-law and my grandson. After luncheon I should like them to be shown by you over the house. Mr. Lisle will accompany them in my place. So if you will kindly hold yourself in readiness and meanwhile give orders for the shutters of the unused rooms to be thrown open, and for an article or two of furniture here and there to be uncovered, I shall feel obliged."

Mrs. Burton had issued the requisite orders and had then shut herself up in her room to think over the astounding news which had just been told her, while endeavouring to regain her much-disturbed equanimity. She was one of those women who seem to have a special faculty for ferreting out every particular, or incident of consequence in the career of anyone in whom they are interested, and she had flattered herself that there was no fact of any moment in the life of Sir Gilbert with which she was not already acquainted. To-day, however, he had proved to her how egregiously she had been mistaken. A daughter-in-law and a grandson, and she, Felicia Burton, not to have known of their existence! She felt as if Sir Gilbert had put a grievous personal affront upon her.

But she was her usual prim, precise, close-lipped self when in her dress of black satin, a heavy gold chain round her neck, her faded hair crowned with a tasteful lace cap, and carrying a bunch of highly polished keys, she proceeded to show the little party over what might be termed the state apartments of the old mansion, not one of which had been entered by Sir Gilbert since his second wife's death. From room to room they went in leisurely fashion--the large drawing-room, the small ditto, "my lady's boudoir," the state dining-room, and so on, taking each in turn; and then upstairs, where a couple of the "best bedrooms" invited inspection--each and all being denuded of carpets and curtains, and of everything except its own special suite of furniture. Still, no great exercise of the imagination was needed to picture what those spacious and stately apartments must at one time have looked like, nor what they might very easily be made to look like again. Last of all they came to the picture-gallery, where the housekeeper, with an elaborate courtesy and a thin acid smile, took her leave.

"What a rummy old card!" was Luigi's outspoken comment almost before her back was turned.

"Lewis, how can you speak of her in that way?" exclaimed Giovanna. "To me she has something of the air of a broken-down duchess."

"As if you had ever seen a broken-down duchess, mother!" retorted the young man flippantly.

"Mrs. Burton is a lady by birth--at least, so she gives everyone to understand," remarked Everard drily. "And now, Mr. Clare, here we are among the painted effigies of your ancestors. I have already made the acquaintance of most of them, as far as it is possible for a man still in the flesh to do so. Would you like me to introduce you to any of them?"

"N--no, I think not. Fact is, I don't care a rap about the whole boiling of 'em."

"Idiot!" hissed Giovanna in his ear. Then turning to Everard with a smile, she said: "I am afraid my son is falling into an absurd habit--sadly too common among the young men of to-day--of depreciating things which they really understand and care about, although they won't admit it. One day I must show you some of Lewis's drawings and water-colours. He has done nothing in oils as yet, I believe. I fancy they will rather surprise you."

"What rubbish you talk, mother!" exclaimed Luigi.

"By the way," continued Mrs. Clare without heeding him, "if among these portraits there is one of my son's namesake, the Colonel Lewis Clare who was killed in battle, I should certainly like to have it pointed out to me."

Luigi yawned openly.

"I am sorry not to be able to gratify your wish," responded Lisle. "No portrait of Colonel Clare is known to be in existence."

From the gallery they made their way by a side door into the grounds, where Shotover, the gardener, was awaiting them.

Among other things at the Chase which had suffered from neglect since Lady Clare's death, owing to Sir Gilbert's penurious style of living, were the gardens and glass-houses, for whereas Shotover had formerly had four able-bodied assistants under him, himself and a youth had now to attend to everything. As a consequence, many things had to be left undone, or only half done, much to the old fellow's disgust: To-day, however, a whisper had reached him that the young gentleman whom he was presently to show over the grounds was none other than his master's grandson and heir--although where he had so suddenly sprung from nobody seemed to know--and he determined to turn the opportunity to account in the way of pointing out the difference between past and present as far as his department was concerned, in the hope that his doing so might be the means before long of bringing about a more desirable state of affairs.

It was by no means displeasing to Luigi to be addressed by Shotover in such deferential terms, and to be appealed to almost as if he were already master of everything he saw around him. In return he put on a very gracious and affable demeanour, which secretly tickled Lisle even while it annoyed him, and agreed with Shotover that matters were in a very bad way indeed, and that he would not fail to bear in mind all that he had seen and heard while they had been together. He had already decided in his own mind upon several alterations and improvements originating in certain hints skilfully thrown out by the old man.

But all his new-found sense of self-importance vanished the moment he found himself back in Sir Gilbert's presence. He could not have told himself why it should be so, but the fact was that under the baronet's keen and penetrating gaze he seemed to shrink and wither, to have, as it were, every rag of self-deception stripped off him and made to recognise himself for the sorry scamp and swindler that he was. Small wonder that he felt he would rather be anywhere than in the company of his "grandfather." Had he had to deal with almost any other kind of man he would have tried to curry favour by fawning and flattery, but something told him that in the present case such a course would be about the worst he could adopt. He tried to console himself with the hope that when he should have seen more of Sir Gilbert, and so have become more accustomed to his presence, this very disagreeable feeling would gradually wear itself away.

Lisle having some outdoor business to attend to left the others at the door of the library and went his way. Mrs. Clare's stately beauty had not failed to impress him. He had found her somewhat reserved, and, while listening with apparent interest to all he had to say, originating few remarks of her own. He had, however, judged this reticence to be natural to her and not merely put on as a cloak for the occasion; and, in so thinking, he was not very wide of the mark, for at no time had Giovanna been a talkative woman, and now that she found herself in a sphere so new and strange it seemed to her that, for the present at all events, her wisest course was to listen to everyone and say as little as possible in return, and by so doing afford others no opportunity of gauging the depths of her ignorance.

Lisle found himself somewhat at sea when it came to a question of summing up Luigi. Sir Gilbert had furnished him with no information as to how and where the young man had been brought up, and, in lack of some such data, he felt as if he were floundering in the dark. Lewis Clare spoke English with the ease and fluency of one to the manner born, even to the point, judging from certain of his remarks, of being an adept in slang. That he was not a gentleman in himself was certain, and it was equally certain that he lacked the indefinable *cachet* of one who has been in the habit of mixing in good society. Yet it would be perhaps scarcely correct to call, him vulgar, using the term in its commoner acceptation. "None the less, he's a conceited, ignorant young puppy," concluded Lisle, "and the chances are that, with a free hand given him, he will develop by-and-by into something still more objectionable. Where has he sprung from, I wonder? and for what reason, has he been kept in the background all these years? Can it have been that Sir Gilbert himself had no knowledge till lately of the existence of such a descendant?"

But these were vain questions, as Everard Lisle was well aware.

"And now," said Sir Gilbert after he had put a few questions, chiefly to Giovanna, on her and Luigi's return from their round--"and now the time has come for me to enlighten you with regard to my intentions--that is to say, as far as they have reference to the present state of affairs. In what way I may see fit in time to come to change, modify, or even to wholly cancel the arrangements I now propose to make it is of course impossible for me even to conjecture. As for you, young sir," turning to Luigi, "you will, for the present, take up your quarters here. There are certain acquirements to which you have hitherto had no opportunity of devoting yourself, but without at least a smattering of which no gentleman's education can be considered complete. You are not too old to learn, and I shall look to you to do your utmost, under proper tuition and surveillance, to remedy the defects in question. I shall, of course, make you a certain money allowance, the amount of which I have not yet determined, but I tell you at once that although it will, in my opinion, be amply sufficient to meet the unavoidable *menus frais* of a person in your position, it will not admit of your launching into any extravagances or unnecessary expenses. And now one word of caution. See to it that on no account you allow yourself to become involved in debt. That is one of the few things I should find it difficult to overlook."

Poor Luigi felt as if his heart were on the point of sinking into his boots.

Without waiting for a word in reply the baronet turned to Giovanna.

"What I have to propose, my dear madam, for your acceptance as the widow of my eldest son, is an allowance of four hundred pounds per annum to be paid you quarterly in advance. I am also in a position to place at your service, of course rent-free, a certain house known as Maylings, which belongs to me and is at the present time unoccupied. It is old-fashioned, but roomy and comfortable, and stands in its own plot of ground at the north-east corner of the park. Should you decide upon occupying it, I shall at once issue instructions to have it fitted up out of the spare furniture at the Chase. What say you, madam, what say you?"

It is not needful to record what Giovanna said. It was brief, but to the purpose. The baronet, who hated wordiness, although a little given to indulge in it himself on occasion, was evidently well pleased at the way she expressed herself. It was a matter of course that she should accept Maylings as her future home, although with certain unspoken reservations which, however, concerned no one but herself.

Luigi and she stayed to dinner, the hour for which at the Chase was the primitive one of five. Before leaving it was arranged that they should return on the Thursday following, Luigi to remain *en permanence* , and Giovanna to make the Chase her home till Maylings should be ready to receive her. Sir Gilbert did not fail to present her with a cheque for her first quarter's allowance. To Luigi he gave one for fifty pounds, together with a note to his tailor, in order that the young man might be enabled to furnish himself with an outfit such as became the grandson of Sir Gilbert Clare and the heir of Withington Chase. His last words as he held Luigi's hand for a moment at parting were----

"My boy, as you behave to me, so will you find that I shall behave to you."

CHAPTER XXI.

AFFAIRS AT ST. OSWYTH'S.

Leaving Giovanna and Luigi to establish themselves in their new home and accustom themselves, so far as they may be able, to that changed condition of life to which the success of Captain Verinder's nefarious scheme has elevated them, we will hie back awhile to St. Oswyth's and ascertain how fortune has been dealing with our friends in that pleasant little town since we parted from them last.

When Mrs. Lisle, in one of her letters, informed her son that, owing to the loss of the greater part of their fortune the Miss Thursbys had been compelled to give up Vale View House and remove to an inexpensive cottage in the suburbs, she stated no more than the simple fact. Through the rascality of their agent, whose misdeeds had not been brought to light till he was beyond the reach of earthly reckoning, the sisters had lost the greater part of their property past all hope of recovery. All they had left was a somewhat fluctuating income, derivable from railway stock, which brought them in about two hundred a year. To this would be added the rental derivable from Vale View, which was their own property, as soon as a tenant should be found for it; for the present, however, it was standing empty. A matter of something over a hundred pounds had accrued to them from the sale of their surplus furniture and such other things as they no longer had a use for. More than all, they had felt the parting from Flossie, their gentle, steady-going old pony, but they had the consolation of knowing that in Mrs. Rudd it had found a mistress who would treat it with no less kindness than they had done.

It had been generally supposed among their friends and acquaintances, in view of their simple and unostentatious mode of life, that the sisters must have a few snug thousands--the result of their savings through a long course of years--put away somewhere: but such a supposition was wholly at variance with fact. In the belief that their income was as safe as the Bank of England, the sisters had never deemed it necessary to put by any portion of it, but had disbursed every shilling of whatever surplus was left in secret charity.

It was a matter of course that Tamsin should cling to them in their fallen fortunes, and accompany them to their new home. For the future she, and a young maid-servant, would be the only domestics whom they would be able to keep. But Tamsin, although heretofore her position had merely been that of maid to the sisters, had had the advantage of a sound bringing-up at home, and in days gone by had often lamented that sundry of her domestic acquirements had no scope for their exercise. Now, however, she would be able to prove both her skill as a cook and her deftness as parlourmaid, and all the housewifely gifts on which she secretly prided herself would have an opportunity of being brought into play. At length she felt that she was in her proper element.

As for the sisters, their sudden reverse of fortune was powerless to sour them or change them in any way. They remained just the same sweet and gracious ladies they had always been; and if such a thing were possible, they were beloved and respected more than ever by all who had the happiness of counting them among their friends. Their chief regret arose from the fact that they were no longer in a position to dispense their charities on the same scale as before.

The cottage to which they had removed--known as Rose Mount--made a pleasant little home, and its seven or eight rooms were amply sufficient for their changed needs. It stood on a sunny slope fronting the south, where flowers of a score different kinds--especially the one from which the cottage took its name--grew and blossomed to perfection. The thick hedge of evergreens which divided it from the highroad imparted to it that air of privacy and seclusion which the sisters loved.

With Ethel, meanwhile, affairs had by no means been at a standstill.

Day succeeded day till they had merged into weeks after Launce Keymer's sudden departure from St. Oswyth's, and still Ethel looked in vain for a letter or a message of some kind from him. She had no knowledge of his whereabouts, and however extreme her desire might be to communicate with him, she felt that only as a last resource could she prevail upon herself to ask for information from her lover's father. For one thing, she was by no means sure that Launce had broken the news of their engagement to Mr. Keymer senior. There had certainly been nothing in the note which the brewer wrote to Miss Thursby to indicate that such was the case. She was powerless to move.

Her aunts, even while in the midst of their own more personal anxieties, did not fail to sympathise with her over a state of affairs which was as much a puzzle to them as it was to her. Equally with Ethel, they felt that it was out of the question that they should ask the elder Mr. Keymer for an explanation of his son's silence, more especially now that their drop from affluence to comparative penury was a fact known to everybody. Could it be possible, they asked each other, that the fact in question had any bearing on Launce Keymer's mysterious silence? Had he merely engaged himself to Ethel in the expectation that, as her aunts' heiress, he would secure a rich wife for himself? and now, when he found his expectations dashed to the ground, was he so incredibly base as to want to break faith with her? These were questions which, although the sisters could not help putting, they shrank from any endeavour to find an answer to them. It was a hard matter at all times for them to think ill of anyone, and they recoiled especially from doing so in the present case. Not for the world would they have whispered a word to Ethel which would have seemed to cast the faintest shadow of suspicion on her lover's truth and constancy.

As the reader will have already surmised, the news that the ladies of Vale View had undoubtedly lost the greater part of their money was not long in being conveyed to the elder Keymer by his cousin, Mr. Tuttle, clerk to Mr. Linaway the lawyer, the latter, as it may be remembered, having been employed by the sisters to draw up their wills and look after their business matters generally. To Mr. Linaway they had gone the day following the receipt of the letter which Launce Keymer had been allowed to read on that memorable evening when he was received at Vale View as Ethel's acknowledged lover.

Keymer senior had at once communicated with his son, and as they were both agreed that the affair, as between the latter and Ethel, must at once be nipped in the bud, it had been deemed advisable that Launce should stay where he was for the present. As far as was known, the sisters had not spoken of the engagement to anyone, and by-and-by he would be able to come back and brazen out the affair with impunity.

But there was one person who had by no means forgiven Launce Keymer's treachery towards her, and had made up her mind to be revenged upon him in one way or another. The person in question was Miss Hetty Blair, the pretty governess at Dulminster, whose workbox Keymer had rifled of the letters he himself had written her.

On discovering her loss Hetty had at once leaped to the very natural conclusion that her whilom lover had deserted her, and repossessed himself of his letters in consequence of his having forsaken her for someone else. The question that at once put itself to her was, as to the means by which it would be possible to find out who that someone was. Jealousy, and a determination to be revenged on her perfidious lover, worked very powerfully within her. She was by no means the kind of young woman to sit down helplessly under so foul a wrong and content herself with bemoaning her fate and shedding an infinitude of tears. She had really loved Keymer, and the blow he had aimed at her was such as she could neither forgive nor forget, and not till she should have succeeded in returning it with interest would she rest satisfied.

Her first step, despite her mother's protests, was to quit Dulminster and take lodgings in St. Oswyth's in a back street within a stone's throw of Keymer's home. She was not long ascertaining that Launce had left the town only a couple of days after his theft of the letters, but that no one, unless it were his father, knew either where he had gone, or the business which had taken him away. Neither did all Hetty's inquiries, perseveringly as she conducted them, tend to enlighten her on the one point about which she was more anxious than any other. If Launce were engaged to any young lady at St. Oswyth's, no one there seemed to know of it. That at various times he had flirted more or less desperately with half a score of damsels was not open to dispute; but there matters had ended, and not even the whisper of an engagement reached Hetty from anywhere.

In such a state of affairs it was only natural that she should ask herself whether Keymer, unknown to his friends and acquaintances, might not have left home on purpose to marry someone at a distance, and might not, at that very time, be on his bridal tour. It was a tormenting thought, and one of which Hetty could by no means disabuse her mind.

Anyone less persevering or less determined to leave no stone unturned in the task she had set herself would have gone back home disheartened, and have done her utmost to forget that anyone so unspeakably mean as Launce Keymer had proved himself to be should ever have beguiled her into loving him. But Miss Hetty was made of different stuff. She knew that Keymer could not stay away for ever. It might be months, perhaps even a year, before he returned. But that he would return she felt little doubt, and should he then bring with him a wife--well, in that case, let him look to himself! Meanwhile she would stay on where she was.

It was as well for the success of her purpose that she decided to do so. Among others whose acquaintance she had succeeded in making since her arrival at St. Oswyth's was the nursery governess at Mr. Keymer's (for the brewer's youngest child by his second marriage was as yet but seven years old), who, like herself, belonged to Dulminster, a fact which Hetty put forward as a sort of bond to draw them together. The result was that they met frequently when Miss Doris Lane was out with her youthful charge, and had many confidential gossips together in which, however, Hetty's part was more that of listener than talker. Thus by degrees she learnt more about Launce and his "carryings on" than she had ever known before, and it was by no means a flattering portrait which the governess sketched for her. Still, all this in no way served to advance the object Hetty had in view, seeing that Doris, no more than others, was in a position to point to any young lady as being Launce Keymer's *fiancé*e* , although in their talks together Hetty recurred again and again to that particular topic.

At length Doris said one day with a touch of impatience:

"Why are you for ever asking me whether I am sure Mr. Launce is not engaged to somebody? It's enough to make one fancy that you are fishing for him yourself."

Then Hetty took a sudden resolution. From what she had seen of Doris she thought she might be trusted, and in any case the time had come when it seemed better to risk telling her secret, if by so doing anything could be gained, rather than go on from day to day in utter ignorance of that which she was burning to discover.

"It is not because I am fishing for Launce Keymer," she said, "but because till a few weeks ago he was my promised husband, and because it ended in his treating me like the scoundrel he is, that I want to know whether he has flung me aside in order that he may engage himself to someone else."

Doris gasped and opened her eyes to their widest extent, and for a few moments could find nothing to say.

Then presently Hetty went on to tell of the loss of her letters and the means by which it had been accomplished. This sent Doris's indignation up to boiling-point, which thereupon proceeded to vent itself in certain expressions which, as referring to himself, Launce Keymer would scarcely have cared to listen to.

Miss Lane's sympathy and outspoken indignation were sweet to Hetty, who had often longed for a confidant to whom she could open her mind. "And yet now I've told her, she can help me no more than she could before," she said to herself

with a sigh. But in so saying she was mistaken, as was presently to be proved.
A sudden thought seemed to strike Doris.
"How stupid I must be," she said, "not to have recollected before (though, mind you, even now I don't know that it's a matter of any consequence), that Mary Deane, the housemaid, when she was brushing and arranging some clothes which Mr. Launce had left behind him, found the photo of a young lady in one of the pockets of his overcoat. Mary dropped it in my room as she was dusting, and then told me all about it, and went and put it back where she had found it. Now do you think----"
Here Doris stopped and looked inquiringly at Hetty.
"It does not matter what I think," replied the latter, "but you will be doing me a very great service indeed if you can obtain possession of the likeness and entrust it to me for one day. The next it shall be given back to you safe and sound. Will you do this for me?"
Doris would have done more than that had more been required of her, so worked upon had her feelings been by the tale told her by the other. At their next meeting the likeness was produced and handed over to Hetty.
"It's a sweet face, don't you think?" asked Doris, as Hetty stood gazing at the photograph with bent brows.
"It's a beautiful face," she replied, "and if Launce Keymer gave me up because he had the chance of winning this girl for his wife, I can hardly wonder at it. But he need not have robbed me of my letters."
She bit her lip in an effort to keep back the tears which had sprung to her eyes.
On turning the portrait over she saw that it bore the name of a local photographer. This was so far fortunate for the purpose she had in view, although had it borne a London or even a Paris address she would have carried out her scheme in exactly the same way.
Turning to Doris she said:
"I will leave you now and meet you again in half an hour, when I will give you back the likeness."
In the course of the afternoon of next day Miss Blair knocked at the door of Rose Mount and asked to see Miss Ethel Thursby. She had experienced no difficulty in obtaining the latter's name and address from the photographer who had taken the likeness. Hetty having been shown into the tiny drawing-room by Tamsin, was presently joined by Ethel, who could not help wondering as to the nature of the business which had caused her to be sought out by a perfect stranger.
Her visitor did not leave her long in doubt.
"My name is Hetty Blair," she began, "my home is at Dulminster, and I earn my living as a daily governess. And now, Miss Thursby, will you please to pardon the question I am about to ask you, which is: Do you happen to be acquainted with a person of the name of Mr. Launce Keymer?"
On the instant a lovely flush suffused Ethel's cheeks, which was not mitigated by the fact that Miss Blair was looking at her with parted lips and eagerly anxious eyes. She felt indignant with herself at having been surprised into a display of so

much emotion and perhaps a little indignant with her questioner. She had not failed to notice that Miss Blair employed the word "person" in her mention of Keymer.

"The gentleman you speak of is my friend," she replied with a touch of hauteur, "although I am at a loss to know in what way that fact concerns you, or why----"

"I have presumed to come here and question you about him. That you will learn presently. Mr. Launce Keymer being, as you say, your friend, did he ever take you so far into his confidence as to tell you that he had engaged himself by a solemn promise to marry someone else?"

The colour vanished from Ethel's face, leaving it of a deathlike pallor. There was a little space of silence which to both the girls was fraught with pain. Then Ethel said faintly:

"No, Mr. Keymer never told me that."

"I thought not," answered Hetty, quietly. "Miss Thursby, I am the someone--I, humble Hetty Blair, nursery governess, whom Launce Keymer promised to make his wife."

"I cannot believe it," came from Ethel, but her words lacked the accent of conviction.

"It *is* hard to believe, is it not, that any man should be such a villain? But, for all that, it's the simple truth, as I can prove in a way which even you will find it impossible to dispute. If you will allow me, I will sit down, for the truth is I shake like an aspen."

"Pray pardon my forgetfulness," said Ethel, and with that she seated herself on a sofa a little distance away.

"I think he must have been fond of me at one time, or he would never have written me the letters he did," resumed Hetty presently. Ethel's eyes were fixed intently on her. She sat leaning a little forward, her hands with tightly interlocked fingers resting on her lap. At the word "letters" she could not repress a start.

"Though I began to suspect latterly," continued Hetty, "that he was no longer quite as fond of me as he used to be, I did not doubt his love, and, least of all, did I think he would behave to me as only a scoundrel could behave. I had a number of letters from him at different times--eight in all. He used to go over to Dulminster twice a week to see me. He knew where I kept the letters--in a little workbox which stood on the sideboard in my mother's parlour where we used to sit together. Well, one afternoon, when he knew I was from home, he came to the house, and having sent my mother out on an errand, while she was gone, he broke open my workbox and stole my letters--that is to say, his letters to me; and from that day to this I have never set eyes on him, nor heard from him in any way. And the man who did that was Mr. Launce Keymer."

Ethel sat as one bereft of speech. It was as if the tides of her physical life had been arrested in full flow and sent surging back to overwhelm heart and brain alike, only to be released a few moments later and let go madly on their way. As yet but one coherent thought could frame itself in her mind: "And this is the man whose promised wife I am!"

Then she became conscious that Hetty was speaking again.
"I told you just now, Miss Thursby, that I had eight letters in all from him, but there were only six in the workbox when he rifled it. The remaining two were in a drawer in my bedroom. I have brought them with me to-day for you to read if you would like to do so."
"Not for worlds!" gasped Ethel.
"You are quite welcome to do so. You would then see for yourself how he used to write of me as his 'darling Hetty,' and his 'sweet little wife that is to be.' What wretches some men are, to be sure!"
Ethel found herself automatically counting her heart beats--"one, two--one, two--one, two." She was faint and dizzy.
Hetty was regarding her with eyes that were blurred with tears.
After a little, Ethel's dizziness passed. Bending her gaze on Hetty, she said:
"But what induced you to seek *me* out--that is to say, me rather than anyone else--and tell me all this about Mr. Keymer?"
"It was because I found out by accident that he was in the habit of carrying your likeness about with him, and I knew he was not the kind of man to do that unless----"
Ethel held up her hand. "That is enough," she said softly.

CHAPTER XXII.

FATHER AND SON.

"He is unworthy of either your love or mine," were Ethel's parting words to Hetty as they stood together in the porch at Rose Mount. With that she drew the other to her and kissed her, and then Hetty went her way with a full heart.

Next day she went back home to Dulminster and recommenced the round of her daily duties, to all outward seeming as if nothing had happened to her. But for her the romance of life was over. In the darkened chamber of her heart she mourned alone over the corpse of her dead love. Some day, in all probability, she would marry; for although her lover had proved false to her, she had no intention of fading into an old maid with no prospect before her beyond that of teaching one generation of children after another. She looked forward to having a home of her own, and a husband to work for her; but, for all that, she did not fail to tell herself that although she would never marry anyone whom she did not like, and even love after a fashion, yet that she could never care for another as she had cared for the man whose vows had been written in water. With the memory of him was associated all the glamour and romance of her young life, which, once gone, can return never more.

On the morning of the day following that of Hetty Blair's call at Rose Mount, Mr. Keymer senior found among his letters one superscribed to his son. Its only postmark was that of St. Oswyth's. The brewer turned it over more than once, and re-read the address with growing curiosity. "Quite a young lady's hand; my first wife used to write almost exactly like it," he muttered. "It must be from *her* --nay, I'm sure it is. In that case I shall be perfectly justified in opening it. The little affair as between Miss Ethel Thursby and my son is one which concerns me as much as, if not more than, it does Launce himself."

Without more ado he took his penknife, slit open the envelope, and extracted the enclosure. "Ah, as I thought. Dated from Rose Mount, that little white cottage on the Shackleford Road where I am told the spinsters have gone to reside since their come-down in the world; and signed 'Ethel Thursby.' I rather expected the young lady would have written long before now. Reproaching him for his silence and all that sort of thing, I don't doubt. Well, well, poor girl, one can't wonder at it. I wish, for all our sakes, that matters had turned out differently. But Providence orders things after its own fashion, and we can but submit."

With that he lay back in his chair and settled his spectacles on his nose. His face was a study as he read.

"If--remembering what passed between you and me only a few hours before you left St. Oswyth's--I were to begin by stating that during the weeks which followed your departure I did not look and expect to hear from you, nor fail to wonder at your unaccountable silence, I should be asserting that which was not the fact.

"I *did* look and expect to hear from you, and was wholly at a loss to understand why I failed to do so. Now, I am no longer at a loss. The motive by which you have all along been actuated has at length been made clear to me. The scales have been plucked from before my eyes.

"From what I now know of you, it is impossible for me any longer to doubt that when you asked me to become your wife, it was not because you cared for me for myself, but because you looked forward to my one day becoming the heiress of my dear aunts. When, however, on the evening of my birthday, you gathered from a certain letter which you were allowed to read that my aunts had lost the greater part of their fortune, you at once made up your mind to snap the chain by which you had bound yourself to me such a little while before. The readiest way of effecting this, as it seemed to you, was to abruptly quit St. Oswyth's a few hours later without informing me of the place for which you were bound, and to maintain an unbroken silence from that time forward.

"I congratulate you on the success which has crowned your efforts.

"But there remains another point connected with the affair about which it is due to myself that I should say something, although it is one the particulars of which you doubtless hoped could by no possibility reach me.

"When you first induced me to promise to become your wife you begged of me to keep our engagement a secret from everyone till you should give me leave to speak of it. It was a request to which I weakly acceded, although I was made very unhappy thereby. Not that I had the faintest notion of the base advantage which you proposed to take of my silence. But I am ignorant no longer. You were afraid that if the fact of our engagement were made public it might reach the ears of one to whom you were already bound by a solemn promise of marriage. It was not that you cared in the least about your promise; your fear was lest certain compromising letters written by you from time to time might be brought up in judgment against you, and not till an opportunity should offer itself for you to regain possession of them were you willing that your engagement to me should become known.

"The wished-for opportunity came at last, and you, who doubtless would be highly indignant if anyone were to speak of you as other than a gentleman and a man of honour--you condescended to break open and rifle the workbox of her into whose ear, only a few hours before, you had been whispering false vows of love and constancy! But you had your reward; you got back your letters; you had no longer anything to fear, or so you flattered yourself. You hurried back to me and told me smilingly that the need for keeping our engagement a secret no longer existed. I have taken the trouble of writing to you at so much length in order to prove to you that the full measure of your baseness is known to me.

How utterly mean and despicable you have become in my eyes, in what utter loathing and contempt I hold you, I leave you to imagine for yourself--and you could scarcely imagine anything that exceeds the reality.
"Ethel Thursby."

The hot colour mounted to Mr. Keymer's face as he read the concluding lines of Ethel's epistle. He had always regarded himself as a man of honour and of the strictest integrity in his dealings with others, as one careful never to overpass that thin line which in but too many instances is all that divides trade morality from that other commodity, often hardly to be distinguished from it, of which the law takes cognisance; but there was that in some of Miss Thursby's phrases which stung him to the quick, not merely on Launce's account, but on his own. When, acting on the information imparted to him that the Miss Thursbys had willed all they possessed to their niece, he had urged his son to endeavour to secure the heiress for his wife; and when, on its being subsequently shown that she was an heiress no longer, he had given a helping hand in the rupture of the engagement--it had seemed to him that he had only acted as any sensible man of the world, who had his son's welfare at heart, would have acted. All at once, however, a fresh and entirely different light had been thrown on his action in the affair, and, for the first time, he seemed to see it in its true colours and to recognise it for the despicable and dishonourable piece of business it really was. The brewer was not used to blushing for himself, or his actions, and the sensation was by no means a pleasant one.

But before long all such unpleasant personal considerations became, to a great extent, merged in a feeling of annoyed wonder, originating in certain statements in the letter which seemed clearly to implicate his son in some more or less discreditable transactions with some other female, of which he, his father, knew absolutely nothing. Of what folly had Launce been guilty?

Without more ado he at once despatched a brief telegram to his son, who was still sojourning with his uncle in Cornwall: "Return by first train without fail."

Indeed, now that Miss Thursby had rejected Launce of her own accord, there was no valid reason why he should not at once come back home. The engagement had never been made public; neither Miss Thursby nor her aunts would, for their own sakes, care to speak of it, and the whole episode might be regarded as over and done with by all concerned. In so far Miss Thursby's stinging epistle had served to put an end to a state of affairs the climax of which, in any case, could hardly have been devoid of unpleasant features of some kind.

Launce Keymer did not reach home till the afternoon of next day He had been away on a fishing expedition when the telegram arrived and, as a consequence, had missed the last through train to London. He had not found the journey a pleasant one, his father's curt telegram having served to utterly unnerve him.

What had happened to cause him to be so peremptorily summoned?

Launce took a cab at the station and drove straight to his father's office. The brewer was alone.

"Anything the matter, dad? All well at home, I hope?" queried Launce as he extended a hand which his father made believe not to see.

"There's a great deal the matter; more, perhaps, than you will find it easy to explain away," responded the brewer gruffly. "Take that chair and read this." As he spoke he took Ethel's letter from under a paperweight at his elbow and tossed it across the table to his son.

Launce read it to the end without a word. When he had done, he refolded it slowly, and then lifted his eyes and looked at his father, who was grimly watching him.

"Well, sir, what have you to say for yourself?" demanded the latter.

"Nothing much, except to confess that I have made a precious idiot of myself," replied Launce with an uneasy laugh. "Now that matters have come to this pass, I need scarcely say that any questions you may choose to put to me shall be answered truthfully and to the best of my ability."

And so by degrees, and by way of answers to his father's interrogatories, the story of Hetty Blair was told.

"Your conduct has indeed been that of an idiot--no milder term is applicable to it," remarked the brewer when he had brought his string of questions to an end. "That you have been headstrong and extravagant, I have long known--known it to my cost--but that you should have displayed such an utter lack of common sense in your dealings with this governessing girl, is what I should have found it impossible to believe had not facts, coupled with your own confession, proved to me how utterly mistaken I was. I have lost every atom of confidence in you, and from to-day----"

"It does not follow, because a man has made an egregious ass of himself once, that he must necessarily do so a second time," broke in Launce, a little sullenly. "Indeed, after the lesson I have just had read me, it would be absurd to suppose that I should ever commit myself in a similar way again."

"Not in the same way, perhaps, but in some other way equally as reprehensible. It is only wise men who profit by experience. Fools never learn. In which of the two categories do you assume to class yourself?"

Launce bit his lip, but refrained from replying.

Launce Keymer had scarcely been twenty-four hours at home before the nursemaid, Doris King, who was under promise to do so, had intimated the fact by letter to Miss Hetty Blair. Other notes followed, in which Hetty was informed that her former lover was going about just as he had been in the habit of doing before he left home, as gay, as smiling, and apparently as free from care as ever he had been. And so, indeed, he was, for Launce never dreamt that Hetty either could or would trouble him further. When all was said and done, he looked upon it that he had escaped handsomely out of both his entanglements, and as the particulars in neither case had come to the knowledge of the little world in which he habitually lived and moved, it seemed to him that he was perfectly at liberty to revert to that pleasant, social, *dé*gagé** mode of life to which all his inclinations tended, and of which unlimited and irresponsible flirtation formed an essential factor.

Ethel Thursby had said to Hetty: "The service you have done me is greater than you know. Not only have you shown me the kind of man Launce Keymer is, but you have opened my eyes to something else. When he asked me to become his wife it was in the belief that I should one day inherit my aunts' money, but within a few hours of his discovery that they had lost nearly all they were worth and that, consequently, there was no prospect of my inheriting anything, he left home suddenly and without coming to bid me goodbye, and from then till now no word of any kind has reached me from him. The reason of his silence is now made plain to me. He intends me to understand by it that he wishes our engagement to be considered as at an end--and so, indeed, from this hour it is."

These words recurred to Hetty again and again, and the oftener she thought them over the more clearly she saw that, instead of having, as she had hoped and intended, inflicted on her former lover an injury from which he would not readily recover, she had unwittingly rendered him an essential service by causing Miss Thursby of her own accord to break off an engagement towards the rupture of which he himself had already taken the first steps. The reflection was a mortifying one, and Hetty ground her sharp white teeth in impotent anger as often as it forced itself upon her. Then, one day, she bethought herself that two of Launce Keymer's letters were still in her possession, which, as breathing a more ardent attachment and being studded with more terms of endearment, she had chosen from the others to place under her pillow at night and help to bring her happy dreams. "If I have failed to make him suffer in the way I intended," she said to herself; "that is all the more reason why I should make him suffer in some other way."

Hetty had flirted with more than one would-be lover before Launce Keymer appeared on the scene and carried all before him. The one she had been most inclined to favour was a young solicitor's clerk, Ambrose Lydd by name. A week seldom went by without their passing each other in the street, and in the glances he cast on her Hetty read clearly enough that he was still no less infatuated with her than he had ever been. To him she now wrote a brief note, asking him to call upon her at her home the first evening he should find himself disengaged.

Three days later Mr. Keymer senior was waited upon by Ambrose Lydd, whose employer had granted him a few hours' leave of absence. The brewer, who was always affable and easy of access to possible customers, having glanced at his visitor's card, which showed him nothing but the other's name, requested him to be seated, and then looked blandly and inquiringly at him; but scarcely had the young solicitor's clerk opened his lips before Mr. Keymer's expression changed in a most remarkable degree.

"I am here to-day, Mr. Keymer, as representing the interests of a certain young lady, by name Miss Hetty Blair. It is a name, sir, that probably is not wholly strange to you."

The brewer considered before answering. He was unable to see that anything would be gained by his denial of any knowledge of the name, while, on the other hand, there was a possibility that his doing so might lead to his detection in a fib, which would be decidedly unpleasant. Besides, he was anxious to learn what lay in the background.

"Really, sir, it is too much to expect that I should charge my memory with every name that may be casually mentioned in my presence," was his cautious reply. "But, assuming that I may at some time or other have heard the name, what then?"

"Merely this, sir: that the lady in question, who resides at Dulminster, was, till some six or seven weeks ago, engaged to be married to your son, Mr. Launce Keymer, a fact of which you are possibly aware."

"I am most certainly unaware of anything of the kind, for the very good reason that no such engagement as you speak of ever existed." There was an angry sparkle in his eyes, but his tone was as dry and deliberate as ever. "That there may have been some silly harmless flirtation between the two, of a kind common enough among young people, I am willing to admit; but nothing more than that."

"It was very much more than a harmless flirtation, Mr. Keymer, as your son, were he here, would scarcely have the effrontery to deny. It was a formal engagement, duly sanctioned by Miss Blair's mother, at whose house your son was a frequent visitor, and by whom he was looked upon as her daughter's future husband."

"If some old woman chooses to make an ass of herself, that's no concern of mine. I repeat, that the affair, as between my son and Miss Blair, was nothing more than a silly flirtation."

"If that were the case, Mr. Keymer, why should your son have been so terribly anxious to get back certain letters addressed by him to Miss Blair, that he resorted to the extreme step of breaking open her workbox, an act which, had the lady been of a vindictive disposition, might have landed him in a very serious predicament indeed?"

The brewer shrugged his shoulders. "That is a question for my son to answer. And let me tell you, sir, that I am not in the habit of discussing his, or anybody's affairs with strangers; which reminds me that I am still in the dark as to the nature of the business which brought you here."

"Very few words will serve to enlighten you. When your son robbed Miss Blair of her letters he was doubtless under the impression that he had regained possession of all that he had ever written to her. Such, however, was not the case. Miss Blair still retains two letters, both of them couched in language with which it would be impossible to find fault on the score of its ambiguity; in point of fact, they breathe a most fervent devotion, and abound with terms of endearment such as none but accepted lovers are privileged to make use of. Now, sir, there can be little doubt that if Miss Blair chose to enter an action for breach of promise against your son, the letters in question would of themselves go far towards securing her a verdict with heavy damages. But, while determined that the wrong which has been inflicted on her shall not go unpunished, she has no wish to proceed to extremities, unless driven thereto. What, therefore, she has empowered me to do, is to offer to give up the two letters in return for a cheque, signed by you, for three hundred guineas."

"What!" shrieked the brewer, as he sprang to his feet, a patch of purple mantling in either cheek. "Three hundred guineas for a couple of worthless scrawls! What do you take me for? Get out of my office this instant and never let me set eyes on your ugly face again."

Ambrose Lydd did not offer to stir.

"I beg to remark, Mr. Keymer, that I am usually considered to be rather good-looking," he said with a quaint smile; "but in moments of excitement I am aware that we are liable to say things which we afterwards see reason to regret. But to come back to business. The letters in question, sir, if read in open court, as they undoubtedly will be if my client's very reasonable offer is met by a refusal, will prove to be anything rather than worthless scrawls. I have brought copies of them with me for your perusal. Here they are, sir; read them through carefully, after which, I venture to assert that your opinion as to their worthlessness will be considerably modified."

Speaking thus, the solicitor's clerk produced the copies he had brought with him, and rising, laid them on the brewer's blotting-pad.

Without a word more Mr. Keymer went back to his chair, his face still corrugated with a frown. He was annoyed with himself at having been surprised into a display of temper. Ambrose Lydd watched him keenly while he read the copies, but his features betrayed nothing. When he had come to the end of the second letter, looking Lydd steadily in the face, he said: "Sir, I find that my son is a more egregious ass than I believed him to be. Leave these documents with me, and let me have your address. You shall hear from me in the course of the week."

A few days later Miss Hetty Blair had the satisfaction of opening an account with the Dulminster Banking Company, who placed to her credit a cheque for three hundred guineas which bore the signature of Robert Keymer.

CHAPTER XXIII.

ETHEL'S CONFESSION.

It scarcely needs to be stated that Ethel Thursby's letter to Launce Keymer was written with the full knowledge and sanction of her aunts. When the particulars of her interview with Hetty Blair were told them, they could but hold up their hands in horrified amazement. Their worst fears, never even hinted at to Ethel, had been more than realised; there could no longer be any doubt as to the nature of the motives by which Keymer had been influenced. His treatment of Ethel had been bad enough, but his treatment of Hetty Blair revealed a depth of depravity which caused the gentle hearts of the sisters at once to shiver with affright and glow with thankfulness when they called to mind their darling's narrow escape from being united for life to such a man.

"I little thought I should live to see the day when I could truthfully say, 'I am glad our money has been taken from us,'" remarked Miss Matilda. "But, here and now, I can say it. To the loss of our money we owe it that Ethel is not by this time Mr. Launce Keymer's wife. It was one of those blessings in disguise at which we are prone to cavil because we fail at the time to recognise them for what they really are."

"But we ought not to forget what we owe to Miss Blair in the matter," suggested Miss Jane with that touch of deference due from her as second sister for the time being. "Her revelation would of itself have more than supplied cause enough for breaking off the match."

"Truly so, sister, if it had reached our ears in time; but we have no proof that it would have done so. Had Mr. Keymer not left home, he would probably have found means to defeat her object, and, in addition, would most likely have pressed for the marriage to take place as early as possible."

"In any case, we can never be sufficiently thankful that matters have fallen out as they have. I declare my nerves are all a-tingle at the thought of what Ethel has escaped."

"And I have dropped my stitch six times since she told us--a thing which never happened to me before."

"I was brought up in the belief that when men were bad--of course I mean very bad indeed--their wicked qualities rarely failed to make themselves apparent in their looks, or their manner, or--or in some other way, so that people of even ordinary discernment could be on their guard against them and not credit them with virtues they could lay no claim to. But Mr. Keymer had always such a pleasant, smiling, indeed, I might almost say fascinating way with him, that it seems difficult to connect him in one's thoughts with the actions of which we are now assured he was guilty."

Miss Jane spoke a little plaintively, like one who had lost another of the few illusions which advancing years had left her.

"I am afraid, sister," answered Miss Matilda, "that this notion of bad people having, as it were, the trade-mark of their evil natures stamped upon them for everybody to see, like many other of the traditions which one picks up in childhood, fails utterly when put to the proof. Mr. Keymer had certainly very pleasant manners and could make himself most agreeable. Yet we have it on Shakespeare's authority that a man 'may smile, and smile, and yet be a villain.'"

Ethel had not been present while the foregoing conversation took place. After imparting to her aunts everything told her by Miss Blair, she had gone to her own room to write the letter which, a little later, was received and opened by Mr. Keymer in his son's absence.

She now came back with the letter open in her hand, and going up to Miss Matilda, said: "Here is what I have written, dear aunt. Please to read it and tell me whether it is quite what you would like me to say."

Miss Matilda took the letter in silence, and when she had read it passed it on to her sister. Miss Jane having read it, also in silence, returned it to her sister, who then cleared her voice and drew herself up a little more stiffly.

"My dear child," she said to Ethel, "after a careful perusal of your epistle, I fail to see the slightest necessity for adding to it, or altering it by so much as a single word. It is severe, but not unduly so considering the circumstances which have given rise to it, and you seem to me to have nowhere overstepped that impalpable boundary which, be the nature of her communication whatever it may, no gentlewoman who respects herself can afford to ignore."

Here Miss Matilda paused and looked inquiringly at Miss Jane. "I am in full accord, sister, with all that you have said," remarked the latter in reply to the look. "Considering the peculiar difficulties with which the dear girl had to contend, it seems to me that she has expressed herself quite admirably."

"Quite admirably," echoed Miss Matilda. "Lucidity without verbosity should be the characteristic of all epistolary communications, and I am pleased to find that in this instance, as in so many others, our dear niece has not failed to profit by our teaching." Then to Ethel she said: "You had better post the letter yourself, dear, and then no eyes but your own will have cognisance of the address."

This Ethel deferred doing till later in the day, when another errand would take her into the town. For the present she laid the letter aside and quietly resumed the sewing on which she had been engaged when Miss Blair knocked at the door. She was a shade paler than common, but perfectly composed, as, indeed, she had been when telling the sisters Hetty's news. They now glanced at her and then at each other.

Not for the world would either of the sisters have been willing that their dear girl should imagine their hearts did not bleed for her in her trouble, and yet they felt that her very quietude imposed upon them a certain restraint in the expression of the sympathy they were longing to give vent to. Miss Jane, who was the more romantic of the two and still retained a vivid recollection of several of the heroines of the Rosa Matilda school of fiction on which her fancy had been nourished when a young woman scarcely out of her teens, would have held it to be no more than appropriate if, at the close of her interview with Miss Blair, Ethel had rushed into the sitting-room, her hair unbound and disordered and a frenzied glare in her eyes, and after a few incoherent exclamations, had either swooned right away, or gone off into violent hysterics. All Miss Jane's heroines had been addicted either to swooning or hysterics at the tragic crises of their lives, and that Ethel had failed to follow so proper an example was just a trifle disappointing.

To Miss Matilda it seemed that the sooner Ethel was encouraged to open her heart and seek from others that sympathy which, when we know it to be genuine, rarely fails to carry with it some measure of comfort, the better it would be for her. "And yet," she added to herself by way of afterthought, "it is not expected of the patient that he should probe his own wounds; it rests with others to do that. Just as likely as not, the dear girl wonders and feels hurt because neither my sister nor I by as much as a word have led her on to unbosom herself to us. She is evidently waiting for me to speak, and yet how to begin, or what to say, I know not."

She let her hands drop on her lap with a faint sigh. Her thimble fell unheeded on the floor. She was sitting by one of the two open windows and her gaze strayed out into the sunlit garden, while there came into her face a look of such perplexity and distress that Ethel, glancing up from her seat by the other window and seeing it, felt a sudden gush of pity and remorse.

Dropping her work, she rose and crossing quickly to the other window, drew a footstool close up to her aunt and sat down on it. Then taking one of Miss Matilda's still pretty hands, she held it closely.

"Dear aunt," she said, "I know that both you and Aunt Jane must think me a strange, cold, heartless girl because I seem so little affected by what has been told me to-day. And yet I feel it, although not perhaps in the way you think I ought to do. That, however, I cannot help. I am very much afraid that I shall shock you when I assure you that the breaking off of my engagement to Mr. Keymer comes as a positive relief to me. But you have taught me that the truth should never be hidden, and that is the truth. Now that I look back, it seems to me as if I could never have really cared for him as I have heard and read of other girls caring for those to whom they were engaged. Almost from the first moment of giving him my promise something whispered to me that I had made a mistake. I would have recalled it if I could, but I was too much of a coward to do so. I told myself that I was fickle and inconstant and did not know my own mind, and that love would grow and increase as time went on. Whether it would or no, I cannot tell. I was certainly pained by Mr. Keymer's unaccountable silence. None of us like to feel ourselves neglected, and that was how I felt. And yet, while looking every day for a letter, my heart always gave a little bound when the postman, on his last round, failed to bring me one, and I knew that I was safe till the morrow.

For all along a consciousness was working within me against which I vainly strove, that should a letter come, pressing that an early date might be fixed for my marriage, I should shrink from the prospect with something akin to terror, and what would then have happened I cannot tell. Now the necessity is one that will never have to be faced."

She paused and again pressed Miss Matilda's hand to her cheek.

"And now, dear aunt," she resumed, "you will perhaps understand better than ever before what a strange, inconsistent creature I am, brimful of contradictions which sway me this way and that and make me a puzzle to myself. Well, I have had my--my love experience, if I may call it so." An involuntary sigh fluttered from her lips. "And, dear aunts--both of you," she went on after an almost imperceptible pause, "I pray you to believe me when I say that it has left no wound behind it which time will not quickly heal. From to-day I shall be once more your own Ethel and no one shall ever come between us again."

It was one of those sweet, high-flown promises which young people make with every intention of keeping them, but which, five times out six, after-events laugh to scorn.

Ethel rose without a word more, and having pressed a tender kiss on Miss Matilda's faded cheek, would have gone, but the spinster detained her.

"My dear child," she said, "my sister and I cannot but feel gratified at your having chosen to open your heart to us in the way you have; but, indeed, it was not likely that the Ethel we have known and loved from childhood should be otherwise than open and straightforward as the day. As long as you live you will have cause to feel thankful that you have escaped becoming the wife of Mr. Launce Keymer, whose name from this hour shall be banished from our lips. And now, dear one, run away and keep your flowers company for half-an-hour before tea is brought in. The day has been a most trying one for you and the fresh air will do you good."

Before leaving the room Ethel crossed to Miss Jane and kissed her as she had her sister. "Heaven bless you, sweet one!" said the spinster fervently. Then, in a low voice, she added: "When I was as young as you are now *I* loved some one who deserted me for another. At the time I thought my heart would have broken--but it did not."

Ethel quitted the room like one walking in her sleep.

Aunt Jane, a love-lorn maiden of eighteen! It was a picture which so took her imagination that for the time she forgot all about herself and her own affairs. No thought that perhaps in years gone by, before she, Ethel, was born, Cupid might have winged one of his shafts at the heart of either of her aunts had ever entered her mind, or that they might have loved, and rejoiced, and suffered in the way so many of their sex are fated to do. To her, her aunts had always been the same sweet, faded, but wholly lovable middle-aged ladies they were to-day. Of late years the silver threads among their hair, and the fine lines marked by Time's etching needle on their placid expanse of brow and around the corners of their eyes might have become a little more observable; but that was all. And to think that behind Aunt Jane's calm exterior, and a soft serenity of manner which was like that of some gracious autumnal day, lay hidden the embers--long since extinct, it was true--of one of those too common love episodes (tragedies they might in many instances be termed) which culminate on one side in vows foresworn, and on the other in a heartache so extreme that till the soft hand of time brings some relief, death itself seems the only possible cure! Aunt Jane had gone through all this. How strange and wonderful it seemed!

On her way upstairs she had paused at the landing window, scarcely knowing that she did so, so deep in thought was she, and there Tamsin, coming out of one of the upper rooms, presently found her.

"Youth and daydreams go together," said the old woman. "Age has no daydreams, and all its pictures belong to the long ago."

Ethel, who had heard no footsteps, started at the sound of her voice.

"But I was not daydreaming--quite the contrary," she returned. "I was thinking about something which was told me a few minutes ago--something the like of which I had never imagined." Then, with a low sigh, she added: "Day-dreams and I have parted company for a long, long time to come, maybe for ever."

"What wicked words are those from one who is in love and engaged to be married! Fie upon you, child!"

"But I am not in love, indeed I am not, Tamsin! Nor have I ever been; I only fancied I was; but my eyes have been opened. And I am no longer engaged to be married."

"Sakes alive! dearie! What has happened?"

"A great deal has happened--much that seems almost too incredible for belief. All is over between Mr. Keymer and me. I have heard that about him to-day which at once puts an end to our engagement--and I have already written to tell him so."

"Now, Heaven be praised for that!" ejaculated Tamsin fervently. "You know I never liked him, and that I mistrusted him from the first moment I set eyes on him. Glad I am that all is over between you! It was not my place to speak when I knew you had given him your promise, but times and again I said sadly to myself, 'Surely, surely my rosebud was never intended for such a man as Mr. Launce Keymer!' Not once, but twenty times have I prayed on my bended knees that something might happen to stop your marriage. And now you tell me that my prayer has been answered. Oh, child, child! not for years has my old heart been gladdened as you have gladdened it this day."

Next moment Ethel's arms were round Tamsin's neck, and she was crying softly on her shoulder. Her full heart could hold no more.

CHAPTER XXIV.

TAMSIN SPEAKS HER MIND.

And so the days and weeks went by, and by general consent Launce Keymer's name was never mentioned at Rose Mount.

It was not owing to any lack of invitations that Ethel scarcely went anywhere that summer, but simply because of late she had lost all desire to do so. It is true that the Lovibonds and the Delaports and one or two other families at whose houses she had heretofore been a welcome visitor, nowadays saw fit to omit her name from the lists of those invited to their garden-parties and other festivities, but the major part of her friends were guilty of no such forgetfulness. To them her changed fortunes (for she could no longer be regarded as the heiress she once had been) made no apparent difference, and it was entirely her own fault that they saw so little of her.

But although Ethel chose to go scarcely anywhere, she was not without friends of her own age who came to seek her out in her self-imposed solitude and retail to her the very latest items of local gossip, consisting, as is usual in such cases, of a pretty equal admixture of fact and fiction. Thus it was that she came to learn of the violent quarrel which had taken place between Mr. Launce Keymer and his father, and of how the latter had cut down his son's allowance of three hundred a year to a pound a week. As a matter of course, a dozen different versions were afloat as to the origin of the quarrel, but, in reality, the facts of the case seemed to be known to no one except the two people concerned. Almost immediately afterwards Launce had left the town, and among all his intimates there was not one who professed to know where he had gone, or what had become of him.

All this was recounted to Ethel as a piece of news which would be likely to interest her as one who had known Launce Keymer and had met him several times in society in the course of the previous summer and winter. There was no faintest suspicion in the narrator's mind, so carefully had the secret of Ethel's brief engagement been kept, that for the latter her news might have an interest very different from any that she imagined.

When Ethel assured Miss Matilda that the wound from which she was suffering was one which time would quickly heal, she stated no more than she felt to be the fact. Between her and the man whose wife she had promised to become, everything was at an end; and although the relief was great--greater perhaps than she was aware of--she yet felt as if there was a void in her inner life which had never been there before. Her heart was empty. The doors of the temple were shut and the flame of the altar, which, truth to tell, had been of the frailest and feeblest, had been blown suddenly out. But Ethel turned away from

brooding over the past and set her face resolutely towards the future.
And so the summer wore on until the crown of it was turned and autumn was drawing on apace. It was Tamsin, whose eyes were ever keen where her darling was concerned, who was the first to notice that the wild-rose tints of Ethel's cheeks were paling to the delicate ivory of the lily. She watched her closely for several days without saying a word to anyone. At length she made up her mind to speak. It was Miss Jane's month, and to her she went.
"The child will just end by moping herself into a decline," said the sturdy dame after a few preliminary remarks. "Look at her cheeks--not a morsel of colour left in 'em, but just as if it had all been washed out. And then, her appetite! I've watched her at meal-times, and she hardly eats more than enough to keep a canary alive. And when did she sing last, pray, without being asked--she that used to be as merry as a thrush about the house and needed no asking at all? And her laugh that used to do one's heart good to hear--that's dead and buried. Whoever hears it nowadays?"
"But what is to be done, Tamsin?" pleaded Miss Jane, thoroughly frightened by the picture the old woman had drawn. "Where is a remedy to be found?"
"That is hardly for me to say, Miss Jane. But if Miss Ethel were a niece of mine, I'm pretty clear what I would do."
"And what would that be, Tamsin? You know that my sister and I are always pleased to listen to your suggestions."
"I should take her right away to the seaside, or to some place where she's never been before. It's change the girl wants. At her age they all need it. It's only when folk get elderly that they grow loth to leave their own chimney-corner. Young birds always want to try their wings; and to young folk it always seems as if there must be something better on the far side of the hill than on the side their eyes are used to."
"But the expense," faltered Miss Jane. "My sister and I have very little money by us, and our next dividends will not be due till the new year. And at the seaside one is robbed so terribly--at least, that is what *we* term it--although *they* , no doubt, call it by a different name."
Tamsin was running her fingers along the bottom of her apron in a sort of diffident way altogether unusual with her. "If it's only a question of expense, Miss Jane, that can soon be got over," she said. "As it happens, I've a matter of sixty pounds put away in the savings bank, not a penny of which will ever be the least bit of use to me--having neither chick nor child to leave it to. Take it, Miss Jane; it has been saved up out of the wages paid me by you and your sister. Take it and give the poor child the holiday she needs so sorely."
Rarely had Jane Thursby looked more distressed and perturbed than she did just then, and yet in her cheeks there was a delicate flush which for the passing moment made her seem almost a girl again. "How dare you, Tamsin, even to hint at such a thing!" she exclaimed in a voice which she vainly strove to render severe.
Then her lips began to tremble and a moisture shone in her eyes. Turning

suddenly and laying a hand on each of Tamsin's shoulders, she said with a quaver in her voice: "You foolish but generous-hearted creature, cannot you see--cannot you understand how impossible it is that my sister and I should accept any such offer?"

"No, Miss Jane, with all deference to you, I can neither see nor understand why it should be so. The money was yours to begin with, and if you don't have it before, it will come back to you when I'm dead and gone. I arranged that with Lawyer Tullock half a year agone. It's only a trifle, I know, but it's enough to pay for a month or two at the seaside; and to what better use could it be put, I should like to know, than in helping to bring back the roses to Miss Ethel's cheeks. So do you and Miss Matilda just put your pride in your pocket and take it with an old woman's blessing!"

"Oh no, we cannot, we cannot--God bless you all the same!" cried Miss Jane. "Of course I shall at once consult my sister, but I feel quite sure that in such a matter her sentiments will thoroughly coincide with my own."

Two vivid spots of red flamed out in Tamsin's cheeks. "And can you and Miss Matilda reconcile it to your consciences to sit down with folded hands and watch the poor child grow thinner and paler with every day that breaks, when the means by which health and strength might be given back to her are within your reach?" demanded the old woman in accents such as Miss Jane had never before heard from her lips. "Can you doubt the child was lent you so as to bring a sunshine into your lives which, but for her, you would never have known? And can you doubt that one day an account will be demanded of you by the Lender? When that day comes, what will your answer be?"

Without a word more Tamsin turned on her heel and flinging her apron up to her face, a sure sign that she was deeply moved, walked slowly out of the room, leaving Miss Jane like one petrified.

Miss Matilda happened to be from home at the time, but she had not been five minutes in the house before her sister was pouring into her ears an account of the morning's interview.

"Nothing could justify Tamsin in speaking to you as she did," said Miss Matilda with a highly offended air, when Miss Jane had come to an end. "It was most reprehensible on her part. She knows that she is privileged and she presumes on the fact. I agree with you that it is quite out of the question that we should accept her offer."

"But what if the dear girl is really pining and losing her appetite, as Tamsin states?" queried Miss Jane.

"Even in that case, it is impossible that we should make use of her money. Some other way must be found. But let us first satisfy ourselves that Tamsin is not alarming herself and us unnecessarily."

Accordingly for the next two days the sisters kept silent but unobtrusive watch over Ethel, a fact wholly unsuspected by her.

On the forenoon of the third day, Ethel being out of earshot in the garden, said Miss Jane to her sister: "I am greatly afraid that Tamsin was fully justified in what she said to me about the dear girl. Her appetite has certainly failed her, she moves languidly about the house, and has lost all, or nearly all, that sunny vivacity and liveliness of disposition which used to be one of her greatest charms. We must have been very blind, sister, not to have noticed all this for ourselves."

"It certainly seems strange that we failed to do so," returned Miss Matilda. "But the change in her has been so gradual as to be all but imperceptible, especially to us who are in the habit of seeing her from hour to hour every day of our lives. And besides"--with a sigh--"we have had so many things of late to engage our attention and occupy our thoughts. Still, I admit that it ought not to have been left for Tamsin to see and point out the change."

"Now that we have satisfied ourselves that there is a change, the question remains, what steps ought we, or can we, take in order to remedy it?"

"Tamsin's offer is not to be thought of. On that point my mind is made up. We must devise some other plan. Let us think."

Whenever Miss Matilda made use of this formula her sister knew that it was intended to apply to the speaker alone, for it was tacitly admitted between the sisters that Miss Matilda was the stronger-minded of the two, and that in all matters of doubt or difficulty her decision should be accepted as final. And Miss Jane was quite content that it should be so. Her knowledge of her own deficiencies awoke no slightest feeling of bitterness in her breast; rather indeed, was she proud of having a sister whose powers of mind and force of character were so superior to her own.

So now, during the silence that ensued, she cheerfully left it to her sister to mentally evolve a way out of the difficulty in which they found themselves, never for a moment doubting that she would succeed in doing so.

Ten minutes might have gone by when Miss Matilda, looking up from her work and pausing with her needle in mid-air, said: "I see one way, and only one, out of our difficulty."

"Yes?" remarked her sister tentatively.

"And that is to obtain a loan of fifty pounds on the security of our mother's jewellery (which is good, but old-fashioned), and the silver tea and coffee service given us by Uncle Henry on our twenty-first birthday."

"O Mattie, what a desecration!" exclaimed Miss Jane, her underlip beginning to quiver as it always did when she was much moved. "Desecration! I fail to understand you, sister."

"In having to pawn dear mamma's jewels."

"No such idea entered my mind. What I said was, that we should endeavour to obtain a loan on them in conjunction with the service. It seemed to me that Mr. Daykin, the banker, who has known us ever since we came to St. Oswyth's, would perhaps not object to advance the sum I have named on my frankly explaining to him the purpose for which we require it."

"That of course would make all the difference. And certainly Mr. Daykin has always treated us very nicely; besides which, he looks the personification of

benevolence."
"So did that elderly man who called at Vale View last year with a forged letter of introduction and obtained twenty pounds from us, and yet turned out to be nothing but a common impostor. I merely recall the fact as a proof that it is not safe to rely upon looks alone as an index of character. But that has nothing to do with Mr. Daykin, whom I believe to be a thoroughly good and kind-hearted man."
"Still, it will not be a pleasant errand on which to go to him."
"That cannot be helped. In this life duty and inclination by no means always go hand in hand."
"When do you purpose calling on him?"
"Some time in the course of to-morrow."
"Of course I shall accompany you."
"Thank you all the same, sister, but I think I should prefer to go alone. Five minutes will suffice for all I have to say to Mr. Daykin, and less than that for his answer. I shall take the jewels with me and one or two pieces of the service, just enough to enable him to estimate the value of the whole."
Miss Jane felt inwardly relieved at the thought of not having to face the banker on such an errand, while reproaching herself for not insisting that it was her bounden duty to accompany her sister.

CHAPTER XXV.

LADY PELL.

As soon as luncheon was over next day Miss Matilda prepared to set out on her self-imposed errand. Miss Jane had again offered to go with her and her offer had again been declined. A parcel had been made of the jewellery and one or two pieces of plate, which Tamsin would carry for her mistress as far as the door of Mr. Daykin's bank, but neither she nor Ethel was aware of what the contents consisted.

Miss Matilda, with rather a sad heart it must be confessed, was in the act of putting on her outdoor things when from the window of her room she saw a pair-horse brougham draw up at the garden-gate, from the box of which a powdered footman presently alighted, and after speaking to someone inside the carriage, opened the gate and entered the tiny demesne. A few seconds later the cottage resounded with a rat-a-tat loud enough to have awakened the seven sleepers. The door was opened by Tamsin, while Miss Matilda ceased her preparations pending the explanation of an incident so strange and unusual.

Presently Miss Jane in person burst into the room in what for her was a state of unwonted excitement.

"Lady Pell--here's her card--is desirous of an interview with one, or both of the Misses Thursby on a matter of business, and the footman is waiting at the door for an answer," she exclaimed in a breath. "I never heard her name before--did you, sister? and what can the business be she wants to see us about?"

"That is a question I am no more able to answer than you are," responded Miss Matilda, who was not so readily flustered as Miss Jane; "but a few minutes will doubtless serve to enlighten us. Will you send word by the man that both of us are at home and shall be pleased to see her ladyship. I will follow you downstairs in a couple of minutes."

When, three minutes later, Lady Pell entered the little sitting-room the sisters saw before them a woman considerably taller than either of themselves; thin, but not unusually so, and carrying herself with an uprightness that would have done credit to a grenadier. In age she might be anything between sixty and seventy. She had Roman features of a pronounced type which time had served to accentuate, so that it was now difficult to realise that she had ever been accounted handsome. There had always been a certain masculine element about her, more seeming, perhaps, than real, which was not lessened by a faint suspicion of a moustache which, in certain lights, could be seen to shade her upper lip. She was richly but soberly dressed, as became a person who in her day had filled the distinguished position of London's Lady Mayoress.

"My card will have told you who I am," she began, addressing herself smilingly to Miss Matilda, who was wearing the heavy gold chain which marked her as occupying for the time the position of elder sister. "For the present I am staying with my friends at Foljambe Court, and my business here is to see you with reference to Vale View House, which is to let, and which, I am told, is your property. I was directed in the first instance to a house agent's in the town, but I prefer to deal with principals whenever I find it possible to do so."

All this was spoken rapidly in the clear staccato tones of one who was in the habit of making herself heard in whatsoever company she might be.

"Will you not be seated?" It was Miss Matilda's soft voice, in marked contrast to Lady Pell's, which preferred the request.

Lady Pell sat down on the nearest chair, while the sisters seated themselves side by side on the sofa opposite her.

"It's not for myself that I'm looking for a house," she resumed, "but for my stepdaughter, Mrs. Loftus, who has been ordered by her physician to exchange the air of London for seven or eight months of the year for that of the country. I had a glimpse of Vale View--there's not much of it can be seen from the road--when I was out driving the other day, and it seemed to me just the kind of place Amelia is in want of. By the way, I have not yet inquired as to the rent--a point," she smilingly added, "which is usually regarded as one of paramount importance."

"The rent is one hundred guineas a year," answered Miss Matilda.

"Hum. I fancy that is rather more than Amelia thought of giving. Still, I don't suppose a few guineas more or less would be allowed to stand in her way if the place suited her in other respects. I should like to go thoroughly over it, so as to be in a position to send her a full report. I presume there is no objection to my doing so."

"None whatever, Lady Pell. The keys shall be placed at your disposal whenever you please."

"There's no time like the time present. I've nothing to do this afternoon and I'll go at once. By-the-bye, is there anyone that knows the place who can go with me?"

The sisters looked at each other in perplexity.

On the spur of the moment they could not think of anyone. Why, oh why, had she not gone to the house agent and done her business through him!

Lady Pell was looking from one to the other with an amused smile. She had heard a good deal from one of her friends about the twins and their little peculiarities. "Who is that very pretty girl I saw busy in the garden just now?" she asked.

"That is our niece," responded Miss Jane, speaking for the first time.

"Then perhaps she will condescend to act as my cicerone."

The faces of the sisters lighted up.

"You could not have a more efficient one," responded Miss Matilda.

"I have a weakness for young and pretty faces," resumed Lady Pell, "due perhaps to the fact that it is so long since I was young myself and that at no time was I ever otherwise than plain-looking."

Ethel was at once summoned, introduced to Lady Pell, and told what was required of her. In a very short time the two were being driven in the brougham in the direction of Vale View, calling on their way at the house agent's to obtain possession of the keys.

When they got back to Rose Mount, afternoon tea had just been brought in, whereupon Miss Matilda begged of her ladyship to join them, which she frankly did. But long before this she and Ethel had become on excellent terms with each other, for, unlike the sisters, who had been rather overawed by their visitor's authoritative manner and high-pitched voice, the girl had hardly been ten minutes in Lady Pell's company before, as by a sort of instinct, she seemed to divine the existence of the really fine qualities out of which her character was built up. Lady Pell recognised this and was proportionally gratified, and from that moment she laid herself out to draw Ethel to her by a bond which should prove a source of interest and pleasure to both.

By the time tea was over the sisters had discovered that their first and not altogether flattering estimate of Lady Pell was a quite erroneous one. They too felt drawn towards her although in a lesser degree, just as Ethel had been. Behind a magisterial and somewhat repellent exterior, which to many people caused her to seem a somewhat formidable personage, lay a transparent sincerity of purpose and a hatred of pretence or cant of any kind, which had an attraction for, and gradually endeared her to, those of a like disposition to her own. Then too, she was a well-informed person, with singularly clear and observant faculties, who, when she chose, could be very good company, and on the present occasion she did so choose. She had not failed to notice that the sisters had been repelled, and perhaps somewhat cowed, by her slightly aggressive manner at their opening interview, and she now set herself to reverse the mental verdict which they had evidently passed upon her.

Most people of Lady Pell's position and standing in society would have seen in the sisters only a couple of impoverished old maids whose good opinion could be of no possible consequence to anybody. But her ladyship had a way of looking at people and things from other than a mere surface and conventional point of view. From the first the sisters attracted her, and she made up her mind then and there that she would see more of them. Speaking of them next day to her hostess at Foljambe Court she said: "They are a couple of gems--that is the only word I can think of which conveys my impression of them--and I shall feel proud to be reckoned among the number of their friends."

Lady Pell's first words to Miss Matilda after the return of herself and Ethel from their inspection of Vale View, were: "Well, Miss Thursby, your niece and I have done what I call a very fair afternoon's work, and if she is not tired, I must confess that I am. We have been into every nook and corner of the house--upstairs, downstairs, and in my lady's chamber--and a pretty tramp we found it--that is to say, I did, for I am by no means so active as I once was. Then we extended our survey to the offices and outhouses, the coach-house and stable and, lastly, to the grounds. Now, as I am one of those people who dislike to lock up their opinions, especially when, as in the present instance, the opinion happens to be a favourable one, I will at once admit that I am greatly pleased with the house and its surroundings. It seems to me the very place to suit my stepdaughter. I will write her by to-night's post, asking her to run down and look over it for herself, so that you may shortly expect to see me here again."

This was good news for the sisters. The letting of Vale View meant a very desirable addition to their limited means.

Following upon this, as already recounted, came afternoon tea, over which her ladyship kept them all alive by her vivacious and somewhat quizzical account of her presentation at court, and of sundry other experiences during the term of her late husband's year of office as Lord Mayor.

Her last words to Ethel before going were: "Take notice, my dear, that I shall call for you at three o'clock to-morrow to take you for a drive. You are looking a little bit peaky, and a long country drive will do you good."

"What excellent company her ladyship is!" said Miss Matilda to her sister as they stood and watched the brougham drive away.

"I cannot remember when I laughed so much in so short a time as I have this afternoon."

"And she is so good-natured with it all. Besides, it is quite evident that she is as quick to see and quiz her own little peculiarities as she is those of others."

"I wonder whether she will quiz you and me to her friends, when she gets back to Foljambe Court."

"I think it very likely," responded Miss Matilda drily. "But that she will not do it ill-naturedly we may be sure."

It was the same evening. The sisters had retired each to her own chamber, and Miss Jane was in the act of arranging her hair for the night, when Miss Matilda, in dressing-gown and slippers, appeared suddenly before her.

"Sister," she said, "what a pair of numskulls you and I must be to imagine that our only way of raising the sum of fifty pounds was by obtaining it on the loan of our jewellery and plate!"

"And what other way is there?" demanded Miss Jane with a stare. "A way that would have occurred to anyone but two ignorant women who know nothing about business affairs. We can, I feel sure, and that without the least difficulty, obtain an advance, not merely of fifty pounds, but of several times that amount, if required, on the security of the title-deeds of Vale View (our joint freehold property), which are at present in the custody of Mr. Linaway."

"Oh, Mattie, how clever of you to have thought of such a thing! And what a relief it will be not to have mamma's jewels go out of our own keeping even for a single day!"

Miss Matilda nodded assent. "I don't mind confessing now," she said, "that last night I scarcely slept a wink for thinking of my coming interview with Mr. Daykin. That I shall sleep soundly to-night I do not doubt."

Lady Pell was as good as her word. She called next afternoon in an open carriage and carried off Ethel for a ten-miles drive. A couple of days later she was at Rose Mount again, this time accompanied by her stepdaughter, Mrs. Loftus. They had called for the keys of Vale View. On their return the sisters had the gratification of being told that Mrs. Loftus had agreed to take the house, and would enter upon its tenancy almost immediately.

If, after the conclusion of the business between them, the sisters imagined that, in all likelihood, they should see no more of Lady Pell, they were mistaken. As long as she should remain at Foljambe Court she evidently intended not to lose sight of them. Seldom did she let more than a couple of days go by without calling at Rose Mount, and at least twice a week she insisted on taking Ethel for an afternoon drive. They all grew to like her more than at one time they would have thought it possible that they should like anyone after so brief an acquaintance.

Meanwhile no further steps were taken in the matter of the loan. Thanks to Lady Pell, Ethel was already looking brighter and better, and when the former confided to the sisters that her visit would not terminate till the middle of September, Miss Matilda said to Miss Jane when they were alone: "We shall lose nothing by delaying our holiday till after Lady Pell's departure. A decided improvement is already discernible in the dear girl's health; besides which, all the seaside resorts will be much less crowded, and, consequently, far pleasanter during the latter half of September than they are now."

But all these dispositions came to naught one afternoon when Lady Pell's visit had still about a week to run. She was sitting with the sisters, Ethel being out of the room, when she startled them as they had rarely been startled by saying apropos to nothing that had gone before: "My dear friends, if I may be permitted to call you so, I want you to do me a very great favour, which is neither more nor less than to allow me to run off with your niece for a couple of months at the very least."

The sisters gazed at each other in consternation. Neither of them spoke: they could not.

"The fact is," resumed Lady Pell, "that my companion, Miss Beilby, whom you have heard me speak of as being away just now on account of her health, instead of recovering, as I had hoped she presently would do, has unfortunately taken a turn for the worse, and goodness only knows when she will be well enough to come back to me. While at Foljambe Court I don't much miss her, but as soon as I leave there I shall want someone to replace her for the time being. Now, that I have taken a great fancy to your niece you must by this time be well aware, and I think that if she were to come to me for a couple of months, or longer if you can spare her, the change could scarcely fail to prove beneficial to her, while, at the same time, you would be conferring on me a great personal favour. On leaving here I purpose going direct to a sunny châ*teau in France, the home of a very dear friend of mine, there to stay for some time. Is it asking too much that you should allow your niece to be my *compagnon de voyage?*"

As far as the reader is concerned, it will be enough to state that when, about a week later, Lady Pell left Foljambe Court and St. Oswyth's, she took Ethel with her.
Now, it may be here remarked, Lady Pell was first cousin to Sir Gilbert Clare.

CHAPTER XXVI.

GIOVANNA AT MAYLINGS.

While the events last recorded were working themselves out at St. Oswyth's, affairs at Withington Chase had not been at a standstill.

Luigi Rispani, now known to the world under his assumed name of Lewis Clare, had taken up his quarters at the Chase in his position as Sir Gilbert's grandson, while Giovanna, otherwise Mrs. Care, his supposed mother, was duly installed at Maylings, the house which the Baronet had had specially fitted up for her occupancy.

Plain to the verge of ugliness as far as its architectural pretensions were concerned, but roomy and homelike indoors, Maylings, which dated from the era of the Second George, was far too large a domicile for the limited requirements of Mrs. Clare; so much so, indeed, that Sir Gilbert contented himself with having about half its number of rooms furnished and made habitable. Its situation was somewhat lonely, there being no other house within a quarter of a mile of it. It stood back from the high road, fronting a huge clump of evergreens and a small carriage sweep, but from the drawing-room windows in the rear of the house one looked into a charming old-fashioned flower-garden. To Giovanna it all seemed very lonely and very dull.

One other thing, however, Sir Gilbert did which filled her with unfeigned pleasure, and that was to make her a present of a horse and brougham. And within a few days there arrived a grand piano, of which Giovanna at once determined to avail herself to the utmost. She had been gifted by nature with a full rich contralto voice, together with a large measure of that musical talent which seems inherent in the children of the Sunny South; but her life hitherto had afforded her no opportunity of cultivating either one or the other. Now, however, her opportunity had come, and the very first time Captain Verinder came to see her, she requested him to find her a competent teacher, male or female, she did not care which. Thus it presently came to pass that Signor Sampi, a grey-haired but clever musician, journeyed twice a week to Maylings, and in the cultivation of her long-neglected gifts Giovanna found a new pleasure in life.

Not for many a long year had such a sensation been known among the good folk of Mapleford and its neighbourhood as that with which Sir Gilbert Clare had provided them, and they did not fail to appreciate it to the full.

Giovanna had not been settled at Maylings more than a couple of days, before one carriage after another of the local gentry began to include it in their round of afternoon calls, and she found herself the recipient of quite a shower of visiting cards. Then presently Giovanna found herself under the necessity of returning at least a portion of the calls. She was a firm believer in first impressions, and for some of her callers she had conceived an immediate dislike which caused her silently to determine to see as little of them as possible in time to come. That, of course, is not the code of English society, which teaches us to smile our sweetest on those whom we dislike the most. But Giovanna had always been in the habit of giving way to her impulses, and she still had much to learn.

Sir Gilbert had felt from the first that it would not do for his daughter-in-law to live entirely alone. She must have some one of suitable age and character to fill the post of companion to her, whose services should be remunerated out of his own pocket. Accordingly he made it his business to call upon Mrs. Merton, the vicar's wife, and enlist her services in his behalf. It did not take that lady long to find precisely the kind of person Sir Gilbert wanted, in a certain Mrs. Tew, the widow of a minor canon, who, owing to some unfortunate speculations on her late husband's part, had found herself at his death but just removed beyond the verge of penury. Mrs. Tew was a lively, well-preserved little lady of fifty-five, who had seen something of the world in her youth, was tolerably well read, and contrived to keep herself fairly *au courant* with the chief topics of the day. She had not been long in her new position before she discovered that one of her principal duties would be to "make talk," both when people called upon Mrs. Clare, and when the latter returned their visits. No task could have been found more congenial to the canon's widow. She had always cherished the opinion that she was gifted with considerable conversational powers, although it was one which her late husband, who was of a morose, brooding disposition, had not encouraged her to reduce to practice, either in public or private. Now, however, that an opportunity was afforded her of compensating herself for the repression of years, she did not fail to avail herself of it. And as the little lady had a really pleasant manner, and never seemed at a loss for either ideas or words, and as no slightest tincture of malice ever tipped her tongue, everyone with whom she was brought into contact had a good word to say about her.

At no time had Giovanna been a loquacious woman, and it was not likely that she would willingly allow the people among whom she now mixed to discover how terribly ignorant she was about many of the subjects on which they talked so glibly. She had naturally good manners, and had been well trained by her English mother as long as that mother had lived, besides which she had excellent taste in dress, all of which told in her favour. But, when it became a question of something beyond manners and dress, Giovanna knew that, for her own credit's sake, her part in the social comedy must to all intents and purposes be a silent one. Her place was to listen to everybody with smiling courtesy, and to look as if she felt an intelligent interest in all that was talked about, but to say as little as possible in return; and, above all, unless driven into a corner, never to originate any proposition of her own.

It was precisely here that she found Mrs. Tew so invaluable. That lady proved herself a person of infinite tact and resource. Whenever there seemed a risk of

Mrs. Clare being drawn into a conversation about matters concerning which, as the canon's widow surmised, she was probably more or less ignorant, she, Mrs. Tew, came boldly to her rescue, and by means of some apposite remark or pertinent question, addressed directly to some other person in the company, contrived, to attract the current of talk to herself, or else to deflect it into some less dangerous channel.

Giovanna was sufficiently clear-sighted to see through Mrs. Tew's object, and was proportionately grateful; not being like some of her sex, who would have been more than annoyed at finding that their paid dependent had taken upon herself to gauge their ignorance, and had had the impertinence to assume that their educational acquirements were not on a par with those of the people with whom, for anything the said dependent was supposed to know to the contrary, they had been in the habit of mixing from youth upward. But whatever her faults in other directions might be, Giovanna had no false pride about her, and was not afflicted with any deficiency of common-sense.

Then again, the canon's widow had the tact never to bore Giovanna with too much, either of her talk or her company, when they two were at home together. The widow had her own cosy sitting-room, and there, when her presence was not required elsewhere, what between needlework and novel-reading, she never found the time hang heavy on her hands. The late canon had objected to novels on principle as being a species of mental pabulum beneath the consideration of reasonable beings, as well as entailing results which in many cases were positively harmful, and as long as he lived his wife had meekly acquiesced in his dictum. Now, however, that she was her own mistress, she proceeded to indemnify her starved imagination for its long abstinence. Fortunately there was a very tolerable library in Mapleford, which for her proved an inexhaustible mine of intellectual treasures. It mattered not that numbers of the works on its shelves dated back a quarter of a century or more, to her they were as new, fresh, and wonderful--perhaps more so--as if they had borne yesterday's imprimatur. And how she revelled in the love stories, dear little lady that she was! Hers had been a repressed and unsatisfied existence, and now when she sat, often till long after the rest of the household was abed, deep in some sweet tale of love and constancy, of partings and comings together again, she would feel for a little while as if she were again a girl in her teens with all life's possibilities still before her. Then, when she had read the last line of the last chapter, she would shut the book with a sigh and remove her spectacles, and murmur under her breath, "What would dear Stephen say if he knew how I had been occupying my time? I am afraid he would think me greatly to blame." For all that, undeterred by any qualms of conscience, she would begin a fresh novel next day with an unappeased appetite.

While Sir Gilbert had been at the pains to provide his daughter-in-law with a suitable companion, he doubtless expected, if the matter ever crossed his mind, that she would provide her own maid. But Giovanna, who all her life had been used to wait on herself, would have been quite satisfied to go on doing the same for ever had not Captain Verinder impressed upon her that, for a person in her position, a maid was an absolute necessity. Further than that, he undertook to supply her with the necessity in question, which he did in the person of Lucille Fretin, the daughter of one of his many more or less impecunious foreign acquaintances. It was quite understood between Lucille and the Captain that she should keep both her eyes and ears open, so as to be in a position to furnish him with a minute account of everything that went on under the roof at Maylings, together with any scraps of gossip, or information which might reach her anent the Chase and its inmates.

Captain Verinder, in view of the unaccountable dislike which Sir Gilbert Clare had conceived for him, kept strictly within the limits of the line of conduct which he had laid down for himself. The Chase itself he never went near, but on one evening in each week, when he knew that Giovanna was not dining with the Baronet, he ran down by the train which reached Mapleford at seven o'clock, driving from the station to Maylings in a fly, and walking back in time to catch the last up train.

When Giovanna, before her arrival at Maylings, put into her uncle's hands the cheque given her by Sir Gilbert, with a request that he would get it cashed for her, he made up his mind that ten pounds out of the hundred should find their way into his own pocket, as representing his modest commission on the very clever stroke of business which he had just succeeded in bringing to so fortunate a termination. He would give her further to understand that he should look forward to being allowed a similar sum out of each quarterly cheque of which his niece would henceforward be the recipient. But when, without a word or a hint on his part, Giovanna put into his hands, not ten, but twenty pounds of the hundred, he determined to wait and see what the next quarter would do for him; for it seemed not unlikely that he might benefit more by trusting to her generosity than by putting forward anything in the shape of a definite claim on his own account.

Certainly, forty, or even eighty pounds a year was not a very magnificent sum: still, it would make an acceptable addition to his limited income; besides which, he looked forward to squeezing a further allowance out of Luigi. Of course, when in the not distant future, as he trusted, Luigi should have become Sir Lewis Clare, with a rent-roll of something like eight thousand a year (for there was little doubt, unless he should make a consummate ass of himself meanwhile, that his grandfather would constitute him his heir), then indeed matters would assume a very different aspect so far as he, Augustus Verinder, was concerned. Meanwhile it was the day of small things and he must content himself as best he could to play a waiting game.

CHAPTER XXVII.

"MR. LEWIS CLARE."

Twice in each week, on Sunday and Wednesday, Giovanna dined at the Chase. It was a standing invitation which included Mrs. Tew, while Everard Lisle made a frequent fifth at the table. Luigi was there as a matter of course.

With his acknowledgment of his grandson and his daughter-in-law a fresh element had been imported into Sir Gilbert's life; but settled habits had too strong a hold upon him, and the groove in which he habitually moved had been trodden by him for too many years to allow of much deviation on his part, even under circumstances so exceptional as those the evolution of which we have thus far followed.

The fact of Luigi being now domiciled at the Chase in no way influenced or affected the position of Everard Lisle. Seeing that his grandson could neither play chess nor backgammon, Sir Gilbert was still as much dependent on Lisle as before for his after-dinner game, which seemed to have now become one of the settled institutions of his life.

If between Everard and Luigi there was no particular show of cordiality, as there certainly was not, there was at least a veneer of friendliness which, as is so often the case, served as a very fair substitute for the real article. Indeed, Lisle on his part had no desire to be on other than friendly terms with his employer's grandson; but Luigi would gladly have given a helping hand, could he have seen his way to do so, in causing the other to be sent about his business; or have taken steps to poison his grandfather's mind against him, had he not felt that the game was too dangerous a one to be entered upon while his own footing at the Chase had about it such elements of instability. That he was secretly jealous of Everard's influence over Sir Gilbert and of the latter's undisguised liking for him, hardly needs to be recorded; but he had wit enough to allow nothing of it to be seen on the surface; besides which, both his time and his thoughts were just then occupied with matters which concerned him far more nearly.

As may, or may not, be borne in mind by the reader, Sir Gilbert, at a certain memorable interview, intimated that, in his opinion, it was not too late for Luigi to apply himself to the acquisition of certain of those accomplishments which he, the Baronet, held to be essential to the education of a gentleman. Thus it came to pass that Luigi had not been more than a week at the Chase before he found himself put into the hands of the Rev. Eldred Merton, the vicar of St. Michael's, who had been known in his time as a successful "coach," with a view of having at least a smattering of classical lore instilled into him.

Then for Luigi began a period of purgatory, such as in his after-life he never looked back to without a shudder. He was utterly devoid of linguistic gifts, in any case as far as the dead languages were concerned, and before long he became the despair of his tutor; who, however, would not acknowledge himself beaten, for one reason, perhaps, because, being a married man with a numerous family, Sir Gilbert's guineas were very acceptable to him. So, four mornings in each week saw Luigi at the vicarage, and when his two hours' lesson had come to an end, it would have been hard to say whether pupil or tutor was the more rejoiced of the two.

But there was another series of lessons which Luigi was compelled by his grandfather to undergo, and which to him were a source of torture almost as keen, although different in kind, as that caused him by his classical studies. The lessons in question were those necessitated by the art of learning to ride. As it happened, Luigi had never been on horseback in his life, nor would he ever of his own free will have aspired to that "bad eminence." Both morally and physically he was an arrant coward, and, from his point of view, everyone who bestrode a horse ran a certain amount of risk to life and limb, which, for his part, he would very gladly have eschewed had it been in his power to do so. But his grandfather's orders were imperative, and there was nothing for him but to obey with the best grace possible. So, there being no such thing as a riding-school at Mapleford, Mr. Marsh from the livery-stables came over to the Chase on three afternoons in each week "in order to put the young squire through his paces," as he termed it. Never, as later on he openly avowed, had he had a pupil who made such slow progress and did him so little credit. "He's a regular funker, that's what he is," he would tell his wife in confidence. "He has no more pluck than a chicken. Not a bit like his father used to be at his age. Why, before Master Alec was eighteen, there was hardly a fence or a gate in the county that he hadn't topped. This chap will never top one as long as he lives."

Truth to tell, Luigi never succeeded in getting the better of the nervousness which invariably assailed him the moment he found himself astride a horse's back. After he had taken his twentieth lesson his timidity was as extreme as when he took his first. He was a coward by nature, and it was impossible for him to be anything else.

Being the kind of young man he was, that he should be terribly bored by the limitations of his life at the Chase goes without saying. To begin with, he hated the country. He missed his London acquaintances and the free-and-easy life to which he had been used in the metropolis. Then again, as the days and weeks went by, he never quite succeeded in feeling at his ease when in the presence of Sir Gilbert, nor even of demeaning himself as if he were. When they were together, it seemed as though he were unable to rid himself of a vivid sense of the guilty part he was playing, such as rarely troubled his easy-going conscience at other times. His manner was timid and nervous; indeed, whenever the Baronet betrayed an extra touch of irritability, it might almost be termed servile. He had somewhat the air of a cur who is conscious that the lash may come down on him at any moment.

But, by-and-by, when he perceived that it was possible to do so without much risk of detection, he began, on two or three afternoons a week, to find his way to the *King's Head* at Mapleford (being always careful to get back to the Chase in time for dinner), where was a billiard-room which was frequented by all the fast young men of the little town. There Luigi felt himself thoroughly at home; there his only happy hours were spent. He could handle a cue with some degree of proficiency, and, as the grandson of Sir Gilbert Clare and the prospective owner of Withington Chase, he took a certain social precedence over the other frequenters of the room. For the first time in his life he found himself flattered and made much of, and the sensation was an eminently agreeable one. But such company cannot be indulged in without a certain amount of expense, and it was a necessity of the position which had been so ungrudgingly accorded him that Luigi should spend his money with an air of careless liberality which was far from being native to him. Thus it fell out that what remained of the baronet's fifty pounds, after Captain Verinder had borrowed five of it, and he had equipped himself with a limited supply of those articles which the latter assured him were absolutely indispensable to his new position, began, when once he had taken to frequenting the *King's Head* , to melt away in a quite alarming fashion. As a consequence, he was presently compelled to apply to Giovanna for a loan of ten pounds, which, however, she refused to let him have till he had given her his solemn promise to repay her out of Sir Gilbert's next cheque.

At this time Luigi saw very little of Captain Verinder, or rather, the latter saw very little of him, although he more than once sent word through Giovanna that if it were not convenient for his nephew to meet him at Maylings, he had but to name his own time and place and the Captain would not fail to be there. But Luigi was never without an excuse of some kind for not making an appointment, and, indeed, exhibited a quite unaccountable reluctance to indulge in the pleasure of a *tê*te-a-tê*te* with his uncle. What he told himself was, that he was his own master now, at least as far as Verinder was concerned, and wasn't going to let himself be "preached at" by anybody: and that the Captain would preach at him, as he termed it, whenever they should come together, he felt fully assured. Besides, he had already discovered that his respected relative was possessed of a quite abnormal faculty for borrowing money, and having himself such a limited supply of that commodity, he was affectionately unwilling to subject his uncle to the pain of a refusal.

"Ungrateful hound!" exclaimed the Captain one day in a rage to Giovanna. "Does he dream, after all I have done for him, that he is at liberty to cast me off like an old glove? I will teach him a different lesson from that before he is much older."

CHAPTER XXVIII.

THE PROGRESS OF EVENTS.

Among other letters which Sir Gilbert Clare found on his breakfast-table on a certain September morning, was one which caused him to wrinkle his forehead and arch his shaggy eyebrows in a way by no means usual with him. Before laying it down he read it carefully through a second time, and then, unheedful of his other correspondence, and of the small china teapot at his elbow which was always brought in by Trant, the butler, the moment his master made his appearance, he lapsed into one of those fits of absent-mindedness which, in his case, were becoming more frequent with advancing years.

Luigi, from the opposite side of the table, was watching him with furtive eyes, and wondering whether it would be possible to obtain a sly glance over the letter which had had such an unusual effect upon his "grandfather."

Could he have had his wish, he would have read as follows:

"The Shrublands, Tuesday.

"My Dear Gilbert.--Please turn to the signature before reading further and satisfy yourself that it is really I who am writing to you after all this long time; for indeed, cousin, it must be nearly, if not quite, a score of years since we met last (it was shortly after my marriage, I remember), and no communication of any kind has passed between us in the interim.

"As you may perhaps recollect, I was always afflicted with a restless and roving disposition, and since poor dear Sir Thomas's death (now eight years ago) I have felt no disposition to permanently settle anywhere, but have preferred to live a wandering, Bedouin kind of life, pitching my tent here, there, or anywhere, but never for very long at a time. It is a species of existence which, although it is lacking in those elements of stability so precious to the majority of my home-clinging, hearth-loving sex, has yet about it certain elements of variety and entertainment which, in my estimation, more than serve to counterbalance its shortcomings.

"Finding myself here at the Shrublands in fulfilment of a promise of long-standing, and within half-a-dozen miles of your place, it has seemed to me (old memories even now not being quite dormant within me) that I could not do otherwise than make you aware of my propinquity and, further, intimate that if you can 'put me up' for a couple of nights--no longer--(together with my companion and maid), I shall be pleased to find myself once more under a roof which is associated in my mind with so many pleasant memories of the days that are no more.

"Your affectionate cousin,

"Louisa Pell."

Between Sir Gilbert and Lady Pell, when they were young people, there had been a something which, if it could not in strictness be termed a romantic episode, yet had in it the possibilities of one, and, had the fates proved propitious, would probably have eventuated in a way which would have changed the current of both their lives.

It was during the lifetime of Sir Gilbert's father and mother that Louisa Grayson, a tall, dashing, somewhat hoydenish girl of eighteen, was invited on a long visit to Withington Chase. Mr. Gilbert Clare, as he was then, who had just returned from a journey in Central America, had felt himself drawn towards his high-spirited, bright-eyed cousin, who, although few people would have called her handsome, was possessed of some singularly attractive qualities; while she, on her side, fell frankly in love with him. But it was not to be. Miss Grayson was summoned home by the dangerous illness of a relative, and her cousin let her go without putting to her the one definite question which her heart was hungering to be asked; after which quite a number of years passed before they met again. On his part, at least, it could have been nothing more than a passing fancy, seeing that within a twelvemonth of their parting, Sir Gilbert had seen, fallen in love with, and married his first wife. Whether in Lady Pell's case it had proved to be more than a passing fancy was a question which she alone could have answered.

"I shall be very glad to see Louisa, very glad indeed," murmured Sir Gilbert under his breath when he had read her letter for the second time, "and I take it as a favour on her part that she has offered to come to the Chase. Of course at our time of life--although I don't forget that she is a number of years younger than I--she cannot be so foolish as to imagine---- No, no; I will give her credit for more sense than that. She is no longer a flighty romantic schoolgirl; indeed, I remember that when I saw her last, she impressed me as having developed into quite a woman of the world. Still, a widow---- Um--um."

With that, as already related, he lapsed into one of his musing fits, which lasted till the entrance of Trant, who coughed and gazed reproachfully at his master on finding that he had not yet poured out his first cup of tea.

The first thing the Baronet did on retiring to his study after breakfast was to reply to Lady Pell's letter.

"My Dear Louisa," he wrote,--"Come to the Chase by all means--you ought to have come years ago--and stay as long as it suits you--the longer the better. You may rely upon receiving the heartiest of welcomes from
"Your affectionate cousin,
"Gilbert Clare."

This missive he at once despatched by a mounted groom to the Shrublands.
Now, in the course of the forenoon of the day preceding the arrival of Lady Pell's note, Giovanna had driven over from Maylings and had asked to see Sir Gilbert. The proceeding was such an unusual one on her part that it was not without a spice of anxiety that he joined her in the morning-room. But she at once reassured him that, as far as he was concerned, nothing serious was the matter.
"I have this morning received a letter from home," began Giovanna, "that is to say, from Catanzaro," she added by way of correcting herself, "which informs me that my grandmother (my father's mother), who is over ninety years of age, is dangerously ill and has expressed a strong desire to see me. Under the circumstances, Sir Gilbert, you will probably agree with me that it is my duty to hasten to her side. It will doubtless be the last opportunity I shall have of seeing her, but I did not care to set out on so long a journey without first taking your opinion in the matter."
"That was very thoughtful of you, my dear madam, very thoughtful indeed," replied the Baronet with a gratified air. "It is clearly your duty to lose no time in carrying out your venerable relative's wish. Is it your desire that your son should accompany you?"
"Oh dear, no, Sir Gilbert," replied Mrs. Clare hastily. "In cases where there is sickness in a house I have always found that young men are only in the way. They are not merely uncomfortable themselves but a source of discomfort to others."
"Very possibly you are right, madam. But my idea in mentioning your son was that he would be in a position to act as your travelling escort."
"But I am quite used to travelling alone, I assure you, Sir Gilbert, and am not in the least timid. For instance, when I returned from America I was quite alone."
"Possibly so, madam, possibly so," returned the Baronet stiffly. "That is a matter which pertains to the past and with which I have nothing to do. But it seemed to me that, in the position you now occupy as my daughter-in-law, you ought not to----"
"Pardon me, Sir Gilbert," interposed Giovanna in her smoothest tones, the

blunder of which she had been guilty dawning on her with a rush, "my remark had reference to an escort of the male sex only. It was far from my intention to travel alone. As a matter of course my maid will accompany me."
The Baronet's brow cleared in some measure. "Um--um. I had not thought about your maid. Of course--of course. But what, now, if Mrs. Tew were also to keep you company? In such a case expense need be no consideration."
"It is very kind of you to say so, sir. My first thought was to ask Mrs. Tew to share my journey, but then I called to mind that she is no longer so young as she has been, and that she is far from strong; and as it is my intention to get through to Catanzaro without stopping anywhere longer than may be necessitated by the change from one train or vehicle to another, I would not willingly run the risk of her breaking down by the way."
"Probably you are right, madam; the affair had not struck me in that light. As you say, at Mrs. Tew's time of life such a long and hurried journey might overtask her strength."
Speaking thus, he crossed to a side table where were pen and ink, and having extracted his cheque book from his breast pocket, he proceeded with the deliberation of old age to fill up a cheque for thirty guineas. Giovanna rose as he recrossed the room. She understood that the interview was at an end.
"Here is something towards defraying the expenses of your journey," he said as he pressed the cheque into her hand. "I trust that you will find your aged relative much improved by the time you reach her and that she may be spared to you for several years to come. Should you wish to see Lewis before setting out, as I presume you will, you will find him at the vicarage, which you will drive past on your way home. We shall miss you greatly and shall hope to see you again as speedily as may be. And, by the way, will you inform Mrs. Tew, with my compliments, that during your unavoidable absence we shall expect her at the Chase as usual."
Sir Gilbert escorted Giovanna to the door, where her brougham was waiting. As they shook hands and bade each other adieu no slightest prevision was in the mind of either that, as far as this world was concerned, it was their final farewell. For, like so many of us, they were the slaves of events, already in process of evolution, of which they had no cognisance and in the bringing about of which they had no share. They never met again.
Giovanna did not fail to deliver Sir Gilbert's message to Mrs. Tew, adding, "And of course the brougham will be wholly at your disposal while I am away."
Tears came into the little lady's eyes. "Both you and Sir Gilbert are most kind," she said, "and I am at a loss how to thank you sufficiently."
There had been no thought or intention on Giovanna's part of taking either Mrs. Tew or Lucille with her to Italy, and although, the moment her oversight was made patent to her, she hastened to assure Sir Gilbert that she had all along meant her maid to accompany her, the statement had merely emanated from her on the spur of the moment as being the only way in which she could extricate herself from the difficulty. Putting aside the additional expense to

which she would have been put, which she felt she could ill afford, there existed other and more cogent reasons why neither Lucille nor anyone else who knew her as Sir Gilbert Clare's daughter-in-law should accompany her to Catanzaro. For one thing, certain of her relatives on her father's side were little removed above the rank of peasants, while none of them were of a kind that would have reflected credit on her new position. Further, to none of them, for certain prudential reasons, had the secret of that position been divulged. Nobody at Catanzaro, when she should reappear among them, would know her as other than the daughter of the late Giuseppe Rispani, landlord of the *Golden Fig* , who, because she had the misfortune to have an Englishwoman for her mother, had chosen to take up her abode in that mother's native country. It was plainly imperative that on no account must Lucille be allowed to keep her company on her journey; but, for all that, after what she had told Sir Gilbert, it would not do to leave the girl behind at Maylings.

The letter from Catanzaro had, in the first instance, been addressed to Captain Verinder's lodgings, and had been reposted by him to Vanna, who now telegraphed to her uncle that she should leave Mapleford by a certain train, and requested him to meet her at the London terminus, which he accordingly did. Taking him out of earshot of her maid, Vanna in very few words put him in possession of the facts of the case. He quite agreed with her that her journey must be undertaken alone. So presently the girl was given half-a-sovereign and told that she could go back to her parents; in other words, take a holiday till she should hear from Captain Verinder, and that meanwhile her wages would go on as usual. It was an arrangement which suited Lucille to a nicety. Then Captain Verinder escorted his niece from one terminus to the other, and a little later saw her off by the Continental night mail.

But there were certain features in connection with Giovanna's proposed visit to Catanzaro which she had not deemed it advisable to reveal to anyone. The fact was that old Signora Rispani was quite a wealthy person for one in her station of life, and Vanna, who had always been her favourite granddaughter, was drawn to her death-bed more by the hope of inheriting, if not the whole, then a very considerable portion of her money, than by any real affection which she entertained for the old lady. In telling Sir Gilbert that her grandmother had expressed a strong desire to see her she had stated more than she was warranted in doing. In reality it was the signora's medical attendant who, in accordance with an arrangement Giovanna had made with him before coming to England, had informed her by letter of her grandmother's critical condition. It will be enough to state here that the signora held out for several weeks after her granddaughter's arrival, so that it was not till towards the middle of October that Mrs. Clare, richer by some hundreds of pounds than she had been on her arrival, once more set her face Englandwards, with a devout hope in her heart that she should never be under the necessity of setting eyes on Catanzaro or any of its inhabitants again.

But many strange things had happened while she had been away.

CHAPTER XXIX.

ARRIVALS AT THE CHASE.

It was in the course of the afternoon of the second day after the departure of Mrs. Clare that Lady Pell, accompanied by Miss Ethel Thursby, arrived at Withington Chase (her maid, in company with the luggage, would follow later on). They had been driven over from the Shrublands in Mrs. Forester's landau. Sir Gilbert was waiting in the entrance-hall to receive them. As Lady Pell advanced he went forward with outstretched hand.

"Welcome, Louisa, thrice welcome to the Chase!" he said in his most cordial tones. "It is indeed an immense pleasure to me to see you again after so long a time." With that he drew her closer, and stooping a little--for tall though her ladyship was, he was considerably the taller of the two--imprinted a cousinly salute on her cheek, which might once have been round, but was so no longer.

Sir Gilbert had never kissed her but once previously, when she was a girl of eighteen, and only a few hours before her mother's illness had summoned her away at a moment's notice. It was a kiss which had given birth in her heart to many delicious hopes, never destined to be fulfilled, and it still lived in her memory like the faint vague fragrance exhaled from a *pot-pourri* . But to-day her cousin's second kiss, so wholly unexpected, recalled in all its pain and all its sweetness that incident of long ago. For a moment or two her heart throbbed so that she could not speak. Then, with a little shiver, she came back to the present.

"It is very kind of you, cousin, to say such pretty things to me," she replied, with a curious little tremor in her voice and a dim wistful smile. Then, more composedly: "But, indeed, I must ask you to believe me, when I assure you that I am as pleased to find myself again at the dear old Chase as you can possibly be to see me here. And now you must allow me to introduce to you Miss Ethel Thursby, a very dear young friend of mine, who is good enough to keep an old woman company, and put up with her vagaries while her regular companion is incapacitated by illness." Then turning to Ethel: "Child, this is my kinsman, Sir Gilbert Clare, of whom you have many times heard me speak."

"It is a happiness to me to welcome Miss Thursby under my roof, not merely for my cousin's sake, but also for her own," said the Baronet, with simple old-fashioned courtesy as he took Ethel's timidly offered hand in his. Next moment a thrill went through him from head to foot, which even extended to his fingertips and was perceptible to Ethel, while a strangely startled look leapt into his eyes. It was as if a ghost from out the dead past had suddenly confronted him. Then he passed his hand across his eyes as if to sweep away the vision, murmuring under his breath as he did so: "No--no; I must indeed be getting into my dotage even to imagine such a thing."

He turned away with a stifled sigh. Lady Pell had observed nothing. She was gazing round the old entrance-hall, all the features of which had that half-strange, half-familiar air which inanimate things have a way of putting on when we have not seen them for a long time, more particularly when they happen to have formed the framework of some unforgettable episode in our private history.

Presently Mrs. Burton, the housekeeper, conducted the ladies to their rooms, and nothing more was seen of them till after the second dinner gong had sounded. It may be here recorded that when Ethel accompanied Lady Pell on her visit to Withington Chase, she was wholly unaware that Everard Lisle was living within half a mile of it, and that there was rarely more than one day out of the seven on which he did not spend some hours there. If the place had ever been mentioned in her hearing as that where Everard was now located, it had escaped her memory--which by no means implies that Everard himself was forgotten.

To-day, however, Lisle had not been asked to dine at the Chase, for one reason, because Mr. Kinaby, the steward, whose health had improved during the last few days, was desirous of his help in going through certain accounts and other matters connected with his stewardship.

On entering the drawing-room the two ladies found both the Baronet and Luigi there.

"Louisa," said Sir Gilbert, "allow me to introduce to you my grandson, Lewis Clare, the only son of my late eldest son, John Alexander Clare, whom I think you met once or twice when he was a youth. Lewis--my cousin, Lady Pell." Then, a few seconds later, when her ladyship and the young man had shaken hands: "Miss Thursby--my grandson."

The young people contented themselves with a simple bow, after which they each drew back a little way. Then said Sir Gilbert aside to her ladyship: "Of course you have heard that only quite recently was I made aware of the existence of my grandson."

"It would have been impossible for me not to have heard of it. It is the talk of the county--in everybody's mouth."

"And more than one pretty version of the affair has got into circulation, I do not doubt. Some people have more imagination than they are aware of. Give them but the merest thread of fact, and they will weave out of it a tissue of romance which does credit to their inventive powers, if to nothing else."

"But is not that your own fault in some measure? The central fact of the affair, that you had found your long-lost grandson and had installed him at the Chase, was one which you had evidently no wish to conceal, even had it been in your power to do so. Why, then---- But, really, I have no right to question you in the matter."

"Don't say that. Why, then, you were about to add, throw any cloak of concealment round the subordinate facts of the case? I will tell you why, my dear Louisa. Simply because, although I have chosen to acknowledge my grandson and to instal him in that position which the world--very mistakenly--regards as his by inalienable right, it by no means follows that there are not circumstances connected with the antecedents and personal history both of himself and his mother which I have no intention, if I can anyhow avoid it, of allowing to become public property. You, however, are in an altogether different position; from you I desire to have no concealments in the affair, and after dinner I will tell you all there is to tell."

It was with a curious mixture of sulkiness and gratification that Luigi took Miss Thursby in to dinner. His sulkiness arose from the fact that in the company of this beautiful girl he felt strangely bashful and out of his element; for once he was possessed by a vivid consciousness of being the very inferior creature that he really was, and it was one of those unsought conclusions which we prefer not to have forced upon us. His gratification arose from the fact that for the first time in his life he found himself in a position to treat a being in every other way so much above him, not merely as his social equal but as his inferior; for one of the parlour-maids who was deeply smitten with Luigi's good looks, and acted as a sort of house spy for him, had already whispered in his ear that the extremely pretty girl whom Lady Pell had brought with her was nothing more than her ladyship's companion.

Only a paid companion, and, as such, one who ought to feel herself honoured by whatever attentions the grandson of Sir Gilbert Clare might choose to pay her (for by this time Luigi had got into the way of taking himself and his position quite seriously), and yet, try as he might, he could not feel himself at home in her company. He felt altogether different when in the society of Miss Jennings, the barmaid at the *King's Head* , who, in her way, was a very pretty girl, and also a good girl. When with Miss J., as she was generally called by the young men of the billiard-room, he never felt in the slightest degree bashful, or ill at ease, and certainly never at a loss for words. Why, they two would go on "chaffing" each other for half an hour at a stretch when Miss J. happened to be in the humour and to have no other customers to claim her attention. And yet for all that, although he could not have told himself why, in his secret heart he did not wish Miss Thursby to be a bit different from what she was, for she was a revelation to him.

What on earth was he to talk to her about? he asked himself. His grandfather and Lady Pell were immersed in their recollections, and to go on sitting by Miss Thursby like a dummy was fast becoming intolerable. Evidently he must make a plunge of some kind.

"I suppose--er--that you and Lady Pell have knocked about a good deal together," at length he ventured to observe. Then seeing Ethel's look of surprise, he added hastily: "I mean that you have been great travellers, you know. I heard her ladyship say just now that something--er--put her in mind of--of something else she had seen abroad."

"I have only had the pleasure of knowing Lady Pell for about a couple of months," answered Ethel. "I believe she has been a considerable traveller in her time; indeed, she was to have gone to France this autumn had not sickness broken out in the house of the friend whom she was about to visit." It was a relief to Luigi to find that Miss Thursby was not a travelled person, as, in that case, she might have chosen to talk about things of which he knew next to nothing, and so have made his ignorance more patent than was desirable.

"I suppose, now, that you are pretty well acquainted with London," was his next remark. He was beginning to feel more at his ease.

Ethel shook her head. "My knowledge of London is very limited indeed. I spent a fortnight there once with my aunts, but that is the only time I have been there. I was brought up in a small provincial town, and know very little of the world beyond its narrow limits."

"I hope Lady Pell intends making a long stay at the Chase," he presently ventured to remark, "as, in that case, we shall also have the pleasure of *your* society, Miss Thursby. It's precious dull here, I can tell you. My grandfather goes nowhere, and only by rare chance does a visitor find his way to the Chase. Of course one can get through the day pretty well, but the evenings are awful. Most nights grandad has his secretary fellow to play chess, or backgammon with him, and there's poor me left without a soul to talk to. It's something cruel, I can assure you."

There was quite a pathetic note in Luigi's voice as he spoke the last words. Having once begun to touch on the subject of his own imaginary grievances, he could be fluent enough.

"But no doubt you have resources within yourself, Mr. Clare, sufficient to cause the time not to hang too heavily on your hands. Books and music, for instance, and--and probably other things."

"I don't know so much about that, Miss Thursby. I'm not much of a reading man, not built that way, don't you know. And one can't be everlastingly jingling by oneself on the piano; besides, Sir Gilbert wouldn't stand it when he's deep in a game of chess. No; what I do is to get through an awful amount of yawning, mixed with a little bit of drawing, for which--the drawing, not the yawning--there are people who say I have something of a gift. All the same it's inf--uncommonly slow work, Miss Thursby, I give you my word."

"Is it asking too much to be allowed to see your drawings, Mr. Clare?" queried Ethel. "Not that I have the slightest pretension to set myself up as a critic," she made haste to add, "being all but destitute of technical knowledge, and only able to appreciate a work of art of any kind in so far as it satisfies my conceptions of the beautiful, or appeals to my sense of humour, or pathos, or teaches me something which I feel it is good for me that I should know."

Luigi felt that the conversation was getting a little beyond him, so he contented himself with saying: "Oh, my sketches are quite at your service, you know; but I give you my word that you will find them awful rubbish."

After dinner, the evening was so sunny and pleasant, that Sir Gilbert caused a couple of lounging chairs to be placed on the terrace, where he and Lady Pell stationed themselves, ostensibly to watch the sunset, but in reality that they might enjoy a *tê*te-à*-tê*te* without any risk of being overheard by the young

people. At dinner their talk had mostly concerned itself with reminiscences of people whom they had known when they were forty years younger.
Meanwhile, Ethel, with Luigi standing by her, his hands deep in his pockets, was going through the latter's portfolio of drawings.
"And now," said Lady Pell presently, settling herself in her chair with a comfortable conviction that she was about to listen to a most interesting recital, "and now, cousin Gilbert, for your chapter of family romance. I confess that I am dying to hear the genuine version of the affair."
For a couple of minutes or so Sir Gilbert lay back with closed eyes, as if endeavouring to concentrate his thoughts on the task he had set himself to go through with. Then, in a low voice, slowly and hesitatingly at first, he began to tell that story with which the reader is already familiar. With some of its earlier incidents Lady Pell was acquainted; for instance, she knew that Alec Clare had left home in consequence of having quarrelled with his father about money matters, that, later on, he had settled in the United States, and there, some few years afterwards, had come to an untimely end. But the rest of Sir Gilbert's narrative, from the incident of the cutting off of the entail to his daughter-in-law's presentation of herself at the Chase, and his ultimate acknowledgment of his grandson, had for Lady Pell all the charm of novelty. She knew how much Sir Gilbert disliked being interrupted, and she listened to him in silence, but she causedand three minutes him to feel that it was the silence of one who was deeply interested in all he had to tell her. Neither was she in a hurry to speak when at length he had come to an end.
Her first words were: "Thank you, cousin Gilbert." Then, after a momentary pause: "I appreciate to the full the confidence you have seen fit to repose in me, and I need scarcely tell you it will be as sacred with me as if it had been poured into the ear of a father confessor. Certainly your narrative is a most extraordinary one; but one has only to read 'The Romance of the Peerage' to discover that still stranger things, and all duly authenticated, are associated with the private histories of some of our oldest families. Still, with all due deference, I must say that in this Italian-looking grandson of yours, I am unable to find a single trait which helps to recall his father to my memory, if, indeed, poor Alec was his father."
Sir Gilbert gave vent to a little angry snort.
"Do you mean to imply, Louisa, that----"
Lady Pell laid a hand on his sleeve.
"I mean to imply nothing. I only hope that you sifted the evidence most thoroughly before bringing yourself to accept this young man as your dead son's offspring."
"What do you take me for, Louisa? There was no flaw in the evidence--none whatever."
Lady Pell tapped her teeth with her fan. "Do you know, Gilbert," she said, "that I felt quite grieved when one day in the *Times* obituary I came across a notice of the death of Mr. Page, your old adviser, whom I remember quite well. What a

pity it is he did not live a few years longer."
The old man's shaggy brows came together for a moment, but that was the only notice he took.
"And this daughter-in-law of yours has gone back to Italy," continued her ladyship presently. "I should very much like to have seen her."
"You have only to extend your visit at the Chase in order to do so. I presume that Mrs. Clare will not be gone more than a month at the most."
Lady Pell shook her head. "I am only awaiting a letter from Madame de Bellecour in order to----"
At this juncture Luigi stepped out through the long window, and crossing to his grandfather, said: "Have you any objection, sir, to Miss Thursby playing the piano? If it will annoy you in the slightest degree, of course----"
"Not at all--not at all," broke in Sir Gilbert a little brusquely. "Let her play by all means. Why should it annoy me, eh?"
"Not a bit like poor Alec--not one little bit," remarked Lady Pell as if to herself; but, for a man of his years, Sir Gilbert's hearing was extraordinarily keen, and her words reached him.
His first impulse was to indulge in a little explosion, his second was to think better of it. After all, his cousin was merely enunciating a truth of which no one could be more unpleasantly conscious than he was; still, it is not always agreeable to have truths which we cannot deny, but would fain ignore, stated thus bluntly by another.
"And is it the boy's fault, Louisa, that he resembles in no way his father?" asked Sir Gilbert presently, but without any trace of irritability. "Which of us can help our looks?"
Lady Pell felt a touch of compunction. Without intending it, she had pricked her kinsman in a sore place. "Of course the young man is in no way to blame," she replied, "and it would be nonsense to impute any such meaning to my words. I could not help saying what I did because for hundreds of years back there has not been a Clare in the direct line whose features did not bear the unmistakable Clare stamp. If you dispute what I say, your own portrait gallery will suffice to convince you that I am right. But, as you are well aware, you can't dispute my dictum. Why, as far as features and expression go, you yourself are as like the Maurice Clare who fell at Marston Moor as one pea is like another. Still, as you justly observe, your grandson can in no way be held answerable for the misfortune of his looks, and if in other respects he fulfils your expectations, there's not a word more to be said."
There was a little space of silence; then, with a half sigh, Sir Gilbert said: "Between you and me, Louisa, that is just where the shoe pinches. Unfortunately, Lewis does *not* fulfil my expectations--far from it. But then, as I sometimes put it to myself, considering the way he was brought up, am I not asking more of him than I have any right to expect?"
"That certainly is a point of view which should not be lost sight of," responded her ladyship. "But what is it in particular that you complain of in him?"

"Oh, I am not complaining--nothing of the kind. I should not feel myself justified in doing so. It is simply that I am disappointed." Then placing a hand lightly on her arm, he added: "My great fear is that I shall never succeed in making a gentleman of him."
"That would indeed be a misfortune. He would be the first Clare against whom such an allegation could be brought."
"Knowing, as I did," resumed Sir Gilbert, "(for, as far as I am aware, his mother hid nothing from me), the defects under which he laboured as regards his education and upbringing, I determined to have them remedied as far as it might be possible to do at this late time of day. Accordingly I arranged with the vicar of St. Michael's, an old Cambridge man, to do what he could in the way of introducing Lewis to some, at least, of the great writers of antiquity. Of course I knew it was too late to do much unless the boy took kindly to the vicar's teaching. I also engaged a man to give him riding lessons. Well, I waited till several weeks had gone by without making any inquiry as to the progress he was making. I did not want it to seem as if I were in anyway hurrying the boy. The other day, however, I made it my business to call both on the vicar and on Marsh, the livery-stable keeper. From both I heard the same story, reluctantly told, of incompetence and hopeless failure. 'He'll never look anything but a figure of fun on horseback, sir; he's no more nerve than a mouse,'--was Marsh's uncompromising verdict; and from the vicar I had no better a report. 'I am grieved to say that it is simply a waste of time and money to endeavour to impart even a smattering of classical knowledge to Mr. Clare,' was what he had to say to me."
"That must be excessively disheartening for you," remarked her ladyship in her most sympathetic tones.
"Disheartening indeed, Louisa; still, all that might be overlooked and forgiven him in consideration of his bringing up, but unfortunately he seems to have contracted a number of low tastes, and to be addicted to a class of company which cannot but tend to degrade him still further. Some men's weaknesses and shortcomings are accidents of their lives and are more or less curable, others seem as if they had been bred in the system and cannot be eradicated. I greatly fear that my grandson's failings belong to the latter category."
"It grieves me greatly that you should have cause to say this of one who ought to be the comfort and stay of your declining years."
"The necessity is indeed a grievous one; but it is a relief to have someone to unburden my mind to. It was not till the evening of the day before yesterday that sundry of Lewis's shortcomings were brought under my notice, of which I had hitherto been purposely kept in ignorance. It appears that Trant, my butler, has a nephew who is billiard marker at the *King's Head* hotel in Mapleford. The two had not seen each other for some months till they met the other day. Then the young man revealed to his uncle certain facts which the latter deemed it his duty at once to lay before me. It seems that on two or three afternoons in each week, presumably when his lessons are over at the vicarage, where he generally stays

for luncheon, Lewis finds his way to the billiard room in question, which at that hour of the day is frequented by a number of idle and fast young men, where he poses as the grandson of Sir Gilbert Clare, and the great man of the company, treating all who care to drink at his expense, in other words, everybody who happens to be there. Nor is that all. One revelation led to another, and a little questioning on my part elicited the fact that, for some weeks past, Lewis has been in the habit, after he was supposed to have retired for the night, of stealing out of the house by one of the back entrances and making his way to the saddle-room, where he and Snell, a groom whom I took into my service about a year ago (for I keep a couple of horses still, although I make very little use of them), are in the habit of hobnobbing together over short pipes and whisky till long after midnight. Needless to say, Snell was packed off at a moment's notice, although I hold that he was by far the less blameworthy of the two."

"This is dreadful. Have you spoken to your grandson?"

"Not yet--not yet," answered Sir Gilbert a little wearily, "I have, perhaps weakly, delayed doing so. It is not merely a question of what I ought to say to him; that is a very simple matter--but of what I ought to do, in short, of what steps it behoves me to take in order to break him of his wretched propensities at once and for ever. That he will make me all sorts of fine promises I do not doubt, but can I trust his promises? I am afraid not. At the time he may fully intend to keep them, but the moment temptation comes in his way they will be powerless to restrain him. Of late I have made it my business to study him. He puzzled me at first, but after Trant's revelation--well, well!" He was silent and sat rubbing one hand slowly and softly within the other, a look of perplexity and distress clouding his grand old features. Then after a pause he added with an unwonted quaver in his voice: "He is my grandson and I cannot cast him adrift. To do so now, to relegate him to the position from which I raised him, would merely be to put a premium on his ruin."

To this Lady Pell apparently found nothing to reply.

For the last few minutes, the sound of music had reached them from the drawing-room, but now came a burst of song, so clear, so sweet, so penetrating, that they both listened, spell-bound. Not a word passed between them till the song had come to an end. Then Sir Gilbert said: "I have not enjoyed anything so much for a long time. Miss Thursby is not only possessed of an exquisite organ, but she has been taught how to use it to the best advantage. She sings with taste, *brio* and expression. In her, Louisa, you have evidently secured a treasure."

"She's a dear, good girl--which is far better than having an exquisite organ, as you term it--and if she were my own daughter could scarcely love her more than I do."

"The sun has set, and the evening is growing chilly; suppose we go indoors. Miss Thursby must sing to us again."

Miss Thursby was only too pleased to find that her song had afforded Sir Gilbert so much pleasure, and, at his request, she sang again and again, Luigi standing by her meanwhile and turning over her music. A spell was upon him, under the

influence of which he felt as if he scarcely knew himself. Emotions and feelings were at work within him to which he had heretofore been a stranger. He caught flying gleams of something higher and better than existence had yet revealed to him. He thought of "Miss J." and scorned himself for his fatuity.
Outside on the terrace it was grey dusk. The long windows were still wide open. A single lamp had been lighted in the drawing-room, which shone on the two figures at the piano. In the semi-obscurity which shrouded the rest of the room, sat Sir Gilbert and Lady Pell, dim figures faintly outlined. Miss Thursby, at Sir Gilbert's request, was singing "Robin Adair." She had just begun the second verse when all in the room were startled by three or four piercing shrieks following quickly on each other, and evidently proceeding from someone on the terrace. Ethel stopped singing on the moment and sprang to her feet, as did Lady Pell. Sir Gilbert, with surprising agility for a man of his years, made a dash for the open window, followed more leisurely by Luigi. But scarcely had the Baronet set foot on the terrace before a female figure almost literally stumbled into his arms. So taken aback was he that he could only splutter out: "What! what! Who are you? What's amiss?"
At the sound of his voice the girl--who was none other than Bessie Ogden, the under-housemaid--started back as if she had been shot, and although she was shaking in every limb and the pallor of her face was discernible through the dusk, she contrived to bob a little curtsey. "Oh, sir," she said, "I humbly beg your pardon. I had no idea it was you I run against, but I was so frightened that I quite lost my head."
"But what was it that frightened you?" demanded Sir Gilbert, who had recognised the girl, a little impatiently.
Then Bessie, half crying and still trembling from the shock she had undergone, contrived to tell her tale. It had been her "afternoon out," and in coming back she had taken a short cut across the terrace (which she had no business to do), and when opposite the drawing-room windows had been confronted by a tall, dark, hooded figure, which had appeared suddenly from behind a clump of evergreens, and, a few seconds later, had vanished as mysteriously as it had come.
By this time Trant and Mrs. Burton, followed by the rest of the servants, had appeared on the scene, drawn thither by Bessie's shrieks.
Sir Gilbert gave vent to an impatient snort. "Here, Mrs. Burton," he said in a tone of grave displeasure, "take this idiot away and give her a good talking to. If I hear any more of this nonsense she shall be sent about her business at a moment's notice."
Lady Pell, Ethel, and Luigi were standing together just outside the window.
"It is the Grey Brother whom the girl believes she has seen."
"And who is the Grey Brother, Lady Pell, if I may take the liberty of asking?" queried Luigi.
Lady Pell bit her lip. She had spoken aloud without intending to do so. "The Grey Brother, Mr. Clare, is the family spectre," she said behind her fan. "But not a

word of this before your grandfather, unless you wish to have your head snapped off."

CHAPTER XXX.

AN UNEXPECTED MEETING.

It was evident that Sir Gilbert Clare was very much put out by the scene just enacted on the terrace. As soon as the last of the servants had gone back indoors he re-entered the drawing-room, where Trant now proceeded to light the centre lamp and the candles in the girandoles, and resumed his seat by Lady Pell. Luigi and Ethel, at the opposite end of the long room, were engaged in turning over a book of foreign photographs. He was always glad to put as wide a space as possible between his "grandfather" and himself, and she had tact enough to be aware that after so untoward an interruption, the baronet might not be in the humour for any more music.

"Now, who," said Sir Gilbert, "can have put the notion into that silly girl's head about the so-called Grey Brother? (Of course *you* know the family legend, Louisa.) She has only been about half-a-year in my service, and, if I remember aright, she came to us all the way from Sussex."

"But she did not mention the Grey Brother by name, did she?" queried her ladyship. "As I understood her, what she said was, that when opposite the drawing-room windows she was confronted by a tall, dark, hooded figure--nothing more specific than that."

"And what could such a description refer to, pray, except to the Grey Brother? I suppose that in the servants' hall such legends die hard, and that any story, or incident which savours of the supernatural, is handed down from one generation of domestics to another. If we could get to the bottom of the affair, I have no doubt we should find that this Sussex girl has had the legend recounted to her by somebody, and that it so impressed her imagination that the first time she finds herself alone in the grounds in the dusk of evening, she is prepared to distort every queer-looking shrub or bush into a semblance of the family apparition, and, indeed, would feel herself rather aggrieved than otherwise should it fail to appear to her. You may rely upon it, that girl Ogden will be the heroine of the servants' hall for half a year to come."

"Still, it seems clear to me that she saw *something* . I never witnessed a more genuine case of fright. But of course the question is what that something was."

"Had there been a moon, I should have said that what frightened her was nothing more substantial than her own shadow. In all likelihood it was a poacher, or a tramp, or some other vagabond who was prowling about where he had no business to be. And that reminds me of something."

He rose and rang the bell, and then to Trant, who responded to the summons, he said: "Send for Bostock, and bid him and his man keep a sharp lookout to-night. I have reason to suppose that there are one or more bad characters lurking about the grounds."

Bostock was the keeper who, some years before, had succeeded Martin Rigg, the latter having been permanently disabled in a poaching affray. Martin Rigg, it may be remembered, was the last to bid God-speed to Alec Clare on that night when Sir Gilbert pronounced sentence of banishment on his eldest son.

"I presume from what you said just now," remarked Lady Pell when Trant had come and gone, "that of late years you have not been troubled by any of these visitations, or appearances, or whatever is the proper term for them?"

"Not for twenty years, or more, so that I felt myself justified in hoping that the Grey Brother had died a natural death and been buried out of sight for ever. Now I come to think, it was a little while before Alec left home--um--um--for the last time that we were bothered and annoyed with quite a series of appearances, or what were said to be such."

"Ah, poor Alec--poor boy--what a fate was his!" exclaimed her ladyship with a sigh. "The apparition has never manifested itself to you, Cousin Gilbert?"

"Certainly not," replied Sir Gilbert with emphasis. "Nor to my father before me. My mother *fancied* that she caught a glimpse of the figure on several occasions, not outside the house where it is generally said to be seen, but indoors, in the picture-gallery, or on the stairs, or elsewhere; but she was an excitable woman--excitable in more ways than one--and my father always pooh-poohed her statements of what she professed to have seen as so many hallucinations, although, as a matter of course, he wholly failed in converting her to his own point of view."

Next morning, on coming down to breakfast, Lady Pell found by her plate a black-bordered letter bearing a French postmark. At sight of it she exclaimed: "Then the poor child is dead! What a pity! And he was the only grandson."

Sir Gilbert, who was already seated at table, glanced inquiringly at her.

"I think I told you," she said in answer to the look, "that it was originally my intention, after leaving the Shrublands, to have gone direct to France, there to stay till well on for Christmas with a very old friend of mine, indeed, the only one of my school companions whose friendship I have retained till now. On the eve of starting I received a letter from Julie in which she asked me, in consequence of her grandson's illness, to put off my visit till I should hear from her again. It was merely a feverish cold, she wrote, and not the slightest danger was apprehended. But this black-bordered missive, even before I open it, tells me but too surely what has happened."

She said no more, but opened the letter. Tears were in her eyes when she laid it down a couple of minutes later. For awhile the meal progressed in silence.

Sir Gilbert was the first to speak. "Am I right, Louisa, in supposing that, owing to your friend's loss, your visit to France will have to be postponed indefinitely?" he asked.

"Postponed till spring undoubtedly. Madame de Bellecour presses me to go after a week or two, but at such a time I should feel myself little better than an

intruder."
"In that case there can be no valid reason why you should not prolong your visit at the Chase, and give to us the time you originally intended to devote to your friend in France."
Lady Pell in the act of helping herself to sugar considered for a few moments. Then she said: "Thank you for your offer, Cousin Gilbert. I will think it over and let you know my decision later on."
After breakfast Lady Pell went to her room to write some letters. At such times, as Ethel was aware, she preferred to be alone. So, it being one of those lovely autumn mornings which are among the choicest of the year, Ethel put on her hat and quitted the house with the intention of exploring the grounds, and making herself better acquainted with the Chase and its surroundings.
What the uppermost subject in her thoughts was as she went sauntering along, careless whether she took this path or the other, she was never afterwards able to remember. All she knew was that she was softly crooning a lately-learnt ballad which had taken her fancy, and that she felt quietly and sunnily happy, when all at once, without an instant's warning, and unknown to herself; she touched the turning-point of her destiny.
Ethel, who had stopped in her walk, in order to inhale the fragrance of some late-blooming roses, hearing the sound of approaching footsteps on the gravel, turned her head to see who was coming, and a moment later, round a clump of evergreens, appeared the unforgotten face and figure of Everard Lisle, who was on his way to his daily duties at the Chase.
The two were within a dozen yards of each other, and the moment Lisle's eyes fell on Ethel, he came to an abrupt halt, paralysed as it were by sheer amazement. Ethel's heart seemed to stop beating for an instant or two, and then went on with a bound, while a lovely flush suffused her face and throat, and seemed to tingle down to her very fingertips. Everard, on the contrary, had turned almost as pale as a corpse. Ordinarily one of the most self-possessed of men, he had now to draw three or four laboured breaths before a word would come.
After all, it was Ethel who first broke the silence. She advanced a little way and held out her hand with a smile which to Everard seemed little less than heavenly.
"And is it really you, Mr. Lisle?" she said. "I could scarcely believe at first that my eyes were not playing me false. Withington Chase was the place, was it not, to which you told me you had come when--when I saw you last? But I only heard the name once, and that must be my excuse for having forgotten it. In any case, I am very glad to meet you again. It is only three weeks since I left dear St. Oswyth's, and yet when I look back it seems like an age."
By this time Lisle had hold of her hand, which he seemed in no hurry to release.
"Yes, this is my home, Miss Ethel, and has been ever since I left my father's roof. Not the Chase itself, mind you," he smilingly added, "but a much humbler domicile just beyond the park. Sir Gilbert and my father were at the same college somewhere about half a century ago, so when the former found himself

in want of an assistant--a sort of half secretary and half bailiff--he called to mind the fact that the man whose good fortune it had been in years gone by to save his life, and whom he had never quite lost sight of since, had a son, and offered him the post. And now that I have told you so much about myself, allow me to ask, in the name of all that's wonderful, how I happen to find you here?"

"Oh, there's nothing in the least wonderful about that," replied Ethel, who by this time had regained possession of her hand. "I am here as companion, for the time being, to Lady Pell, who is a relative of Sir Gilbert. Of course you have heard that my dear aunts have lost the greater part of their fortune and have been compelled to leave their old home?" Everard nodded. "Well, through Lady Pell, my aunts obtained a tenant for Vale View House in the person of her stepdaughter, and that was how she and they became acquainted. Her companion being away on account of illness, I am filling the position *pro tem* ."

"I hope Lady Pell intends making a long stay at the Chase."

"She came, intending to stay only a couple of days, but, as the result of a letter she received this morning, it seems not unlikely that her visit will be prolonged."

"With all my heart I hope it may," said Everard. There was a fervour in his voice, and a fire in his eyes, which brought back the glow to Ethel's cheeks and recalled, as though they related to an event of yesterday, every word and look of Lisle at that interview on her birthday, when he pleaded his suit with so much earnestness, but pleaded in vain. Well, Everard Lisle was not like some people.

Her heart whispered to her: "He loves you still. You are as dear to him at this moment as you ever were."

She did not speak, but turned away her head and gazed across the park.

"And now I must leave you--for the present," said Everard. "I have my morning's work to attend to, and Sir Gilbert likes punctuality in others if he does not always practise it himself. I often lunch and dine at the Chase. Let us hope that the presence of Lady Pell will not have the effect of depriving me of a privilege which I never valued so highly as I do at this moment."

He smiled, lifted his hat, and went his way.

CHAPTER XXXI.

LUIGI'S ESCAPADE.

Mr. Kinaby's dog-cart, now that the land-steward himself was almost wholly confined to the house, was at the service of Everard Lisle, and he generally made use of it, if the weather happened to be bad, when he was invited to dine at the Chase, thereby saving himself a long wet tramp there and back through the park. To-day the fine forenoon had degenerated into a wet evening, and when Lisle had given his horse and trap into charge of the stable help and, after divesting himself of his wet mackintosh, had made his way to the drawing-room, he found there the Baronet, Lady Pell and Miss Thursby. Sir Gilbert, in his abrupt fashion, at once proceeded to introduce him to the ladies. After bowing to her ladyship, Everard held out his hand to Ethel, saying as he did so: "I have had the pleasure of meeting Miss Thursby on more than one occasion before to-day; in point of fact, we happen to come from the same town, St. Oswyth's."

"And a very charming, old-fashioned town it is," said her ladyship; "and some of the people, whose acquaintance I made there"--with a significant glance at Ethel--"I found to be quite as nice as the place."

At this moment Trant entered the room with the announcement that dinner was served. "That's all very well," said Sir Gilbert testily, "but what has become of my grandson? Where is Mr. Lewis? Send up to his room at once, Trant, and tell him that dinner is waiting." Then turning to Lady Pell, he added: "I hate unpunctuality, especially at meal-times. It would serve the young dog right to make him go without his dinner."

"Is he often behind time?" queried her ladyship.

"No, I can't say that he is. He knows that I wouldn't put up with it."

"Then you can afford, for once in a way, to overlook his remissness. Besides, it would be unfair to blame him before hearing what he may have to say for himself."

"Oh, he'll have some plausible excuse or other, I don't doubt," growled Sir Gilbert. "You would be clever to catch him without one."

Trant reappeared. "Mr. Lewis is not in his room, Sir Gilbert. It seems that he left the house about ten o'clock, and has not been seen since."

Sir Gilbert's eyebrows came together in a frown. Then he shook himself, and forcing a smile, said: "In that case there is no need to wait. Perhaps they have persuaded him to stay and dine at the vicarage, although, when that has been the case before, he has always sent me word." With that he offered his arm to Lady Pell and Everard did the same to Miss Thursby.

When dinner was over there was no sitting out of doors as on the preceding evening. In the drawing-room, the lighted lamps, the drawn curtains and the wood fire, served as so many reminders of the dying year. This evening, out of compliment to her ladyship, Sir Gilbert forewent his usual game of chess. At his request Ethel played and sang for upwards of an hour, during which time it was Lisle's happy privilege to turn over her music and hover round her generally. Between whiles Sir Gilbert and her ladyship, who were seated considerably apart from the young people, conversed in low tones.

Ten o'clock struck all too soon for Everard Lisle. It was his appointed hour for leaving the Chase. When he had taken leave of the ladies, Sir Gilbert quitted the room with him. While the dog-cart was being brought round and he was inducting himself into his mackintosh, the baronet sent a servant to ascertain whether his grandson had yet reached home. No, Mr. Lewis was not in his room, neither had anyone seen him, was the word brought back. "I shall sit up for him, if it be till six o'clock in the morning," said Sir Gilbert grimly to Lisle. With that, he nodded a curt, but not unkindly goodnight, and strode back to the drawing-room.

Sir Gilbert's words were in Everard's mind as he drove through the wind and the rain. What had become of young Clare? Where and by whom had he been detained? Could any harm have befallen him? He did not believe much in the likelihood of his being at the vicarage all these hours; nevertheless, he would drive round there, although it would be more than a couple of miles out of his way, and should Clare chance to be there, he would give him a hint that the sooner he got back to the Chase the better it might be for him.

But the missing delinquent was not at the vicarage. He had left there at his usual hour, and of his after-movements neither Mr. nor Mrs. Merton had any knowledge. "What if he has found his way to the *King's Head* , and is still there?" said Everard to himself as the vicarage door was shut behind him. "In any case, it's a point worth settling;" and with that he turned his horse's head in the direction of Mapleford. Rumours of Luigi's frequent visits to the billiard-room of the hotel in question had come to Lisle's ears, for Mr. Lewis Clare, in virtue of his position as Sir Gilbert's grandson, was a personage of some consequence in the little town, and his comings and goings were not merely noted, but freely commented upon.

Everard's surmise proved to be correct. He found Luigi at the *King's Head* , but not in quite as sober a condition as he might have been. It was the birthday of Miss Jennings, the pretty barmaid, and it had seemed to him that the occasion was one which nothing less than champagne could do justice to. There were several other young men there who were of the same opinion as Mr. Clare--so long as the latter was willing to pay for the wine. The sudden apparition of Lisle turned Luigi cold from head to foot and had the effect of partially sobering him. He did not doubt for a moment that Sir Gilbert had sent for him, and his limbs shook under him as, without a word of farewell to his companions, he rose in obedience to Lisle's beckoning finger and followed him into the open air. "Your grandfather is sitting up for you," said Everard. "The longer you stay here, the

longer you will keep him out of bed. Let me help you into the dog-cart."
"I dare not face him," whimpered Luigi. "I'd almost sooner go and drown myself."
"But you can't stay here all night," urged Lisle. "You have been here far too long already, and I shall not go without taking you with me."
"He'll turn me out neck and crop, I know he will," moaned the other, with a clutch at Lisle's sleeve to enable him to keep his balance.
"Pooh! Don't be a coward. Sir Gilbert's bark, as you ought to know by this time, is far worse than his bite. He will give you a good jacketing, and serve you right, and there will be an end of it."
"Ah!--you don't know him; you think you do, but you don't," said Luigi with the intense gravity of semi-inebriety. "Yes, I'd almost sooner drown myself than face him," he whimpered for the second time.
He was indeed, as Everard could not help reflecting, in no condition to be seen by his grandfather. What was the best thing to do? He stood for a moment or two considering, and then he said: "If you like to stay at my place to-night, I will find you a bed. But in that case, after leaving you there, I must drive to the Chase, inform Sir Gilbert where you are, and make the best excuse I can for your non-appearance."
"Lisle, you're a brick!" ejaculated Luigi, seizing Everard by both arms and making as though he would playfully shake him. "I've never liked you, you know, but to-night you've proved a regular brick.--Yes, that's the card--a shake-down at your place, and you to go and make my excuses to Granddad. Of course you'll know what to say. Suddenly taken ill on my road home--glad to take refuge anywhere--awfully sorry he's been put about--better already and hope to be all right by morning.--You know."
A sharp drive of twenty minutes brought them to Elm Lodge, Mr. Kinaby's house, where, by this time, everybody had retired for the night, for which Everard was not sorry. He let himself and his companion in by means of his latch-key. His intention had been to give up his bed to Luigi, but this the latter would by no means agree to, not through any unselfishness on his part, but because he felt that the trouble of undressing would be too much for him. "All I want and all I'll have is a snooze on a sofa," was his own way of putting it. Accordingly, Everard having provided him with a blanket and pillow, he kicked off his boots and stretched himself out on the couch in the sitting-room. Half a minute later he was fast asleep.
Everard, having turned down the lamp, left him. The dog-cart was waiting at the door, and ten minutes later he drew up at the main entrance to the park. Nixon, the lodge-keeper, was in bed and had to be knocked up. Leaving his horse and trap in the old man's charge, Lisle took a bee-line across the park in the direction of the house. On reaching the terrace he saw that the entire frontage was in darkness, except that the couple of lozenge-shaped openings, high up in the shutters of the study windows showed like two dim patches of yellow light. It was evident that the baronet was keeping his word and had not yet retired.
Going up to one of the windows, Lisle took a coin out of his pocket and tapped

with it on the glass. For a man of his years, Sir Gilbert's hearing was still remarkably acute, and in less than a minute the shutter was unbolted and thrown back, and in his deepest tones came the question: "Who is there?" It was almost on such a night, some quarter of a century before, that Alec Clare had tapped at the same window, and he, Sir Gilbert, had put to him precisely the same question that he was putting now. He shivered as the fact recalled itself to his mind. A chill breath from the tomb seemed for a moment to lift his silvered locks.

"It is I--Everard Lisle," came the clear response.

With fingers that trembled somewhat, Sir Gilbert undid the window-fastenings, and Lisle stepped into the room.

"You have brought me tidings of Lewis?" was the old man's eager query.

"I have, Sir Gilbert. He is at my rooms at Elm Lodge. He is not at all well, and I have persuaded him to stay where he is till morning, in the hope that by then he will have thoroughly recovered."

Sir Gilbert drew himself up to his full height and grasped the young man by one shoulder. "Lisle--um--um, you are trying to keep something from me," he said. "There is something in the background which you do not wish me to know. If it concerns my grandson, I *must* know it, and I look to you to answer my questions with that candour which up to now I have found to be one of your unfailing attributes. Tell me this: did you find my grandson at Elm Lodge on your arrival there after leaving here?"

"No, sir, I did not."

"Where did you find him?"

"I went in search of him and found him at a certain hotel in the town."

"So--so. And the worse for drink, hey?"

"He certainly had imbibed a little more wine than was good for him."

"I thought as much," was Sir Gilbert's stern rejoinder.

"This, perhaps, may be urged in extenuation, sir--that the occasion was a birthday-party--(Mr. Lewis was one among a lot more young men)--that he had had nothing to eat since breakfast, and that the very fact of his being unaccustomed to take much wine was the reason why what he had taken affected him as it did."

"You would make excuses for him, would you? Leave him to do that for himself, if you please. And what is the class of young men whom he chooses for his associates? Nothing better than common riff-raff, I'll be bound." Then all at once his voice broke. "And it is of my grandson--the last of the Clares--that these things are being said!"

Everard hardly knew whether to go or stay. A minute later, Sir Gilbert was himself again. "I am much obliged to you, Lisle," he said, "for the trouble you have taken in this wretched affair. Tell my grandson to come to me in the library at ten o'clock to-morrow. Till then I have no wish to set eyes on him."

When Everard got back to his rooms he found Luigi still sleeping soundly, and so left him for the night. But it was certainly a surprise to him when, on going down next morning between seven and eight o'clock, he found the room empty and his guest gone.

Shortly after daybreak Luigi had woke up with a splitting headache. As soon as he had pulled his wits together and called to mind where he was, he proceeded to empty the carafe of water which Lisle had considerately placed within his reach. Then he sat for a long time with his elbows on his knees and his face buried in his hands. His heart sank within him when he thought of the inevitable interview with his grandfather which could not much longer be delayed, for he had strong doubts as to the amount of credence Sir Gilbert would accord to the story of his sudden illness. That he would be subjected to a severe wigging and have certain penalties of a more or less disagreeable kind imposed on him, he did not doubt; but he anticipated nothing worse than that. He had, however, another cause for disquietude which, as it seemed to him, might not improbably entail results far more dire. He was nearly sure that, in the course of the previous evening, he had made Miss Jennings an offer of his hand and heart, but whether she had accepted or repulsed him, or had merely treated his offer as a foolish joke, he could not for the life of him remember. But what if she had taken his offer seriously and, in the event of his repudiating it, which he would be absolutely bound to do, were to seek out his grandfather and pour her story into his ears I The consequences of her doing so were too terrifying to contemplate.

"Oh, what an idiot I must have been!" he groaned more than once.

Somehow this morning he did not care to face Lisle; so, after a time he let himself out of the house and bent his steps towards the town. He entered the first hairdresser's shop he came to, where he had what is termed a "wash and brush-up," after which he felt considerably refreshed. Next to a chemist's where he called for and drank off at a draught a certain effervescing mixture which was warranted as an infallible "pick-me-up." After that he thought he would take a turn by the river and try to find an appetite for breakfast. Very careful was he not to go near the *King's Head* and Miss Jennings.

By this it was past nine o'clock and time for him to turn his face homeward. He had scarcely gone a dozen yards from the inn when he saw Mr. Kinaby's groom, whom he knew by sight, coming towards him on horseback. On nearing him the man reined up and carrying a finger to his forehead, said: "I've bin lookin' for you all over the town, sir. I've a note for you from Mr. Lisle."

Luigi took the note and tore it open. It was merely a line. "Your grandfather wants to see you in the library at ten o'clock.--E. L."

"All right," said Luigi with a nod to the man. "Tell. Mr. Lisle it shall be attended to."

CHAPTER XXXII.

SIR GILBERT'S DECISION.

Luigi, as he turned the handle of the library door, felt that he would have given something to know what had passed between Lisle and his grandfather overnight. Had the former succeeded in convincing Sir Gilbert that his absence from home was due to a sudden attack of illness, or had he allowed his grandfather to become acquainted with the real facts of the case? His uncertainty on the point was dispelled by Sir Gilbert's first words.

"So, sir, you have recovered sufficiently from your last night's debauch to allow of your coming to see me," he said, taking him in through his contracted lids from head to foot.

Luigi's eyes fell and his knees trembled under him. As he said of himself afterwards, he felt "like a washed-out scarecrow." He tried to moisten his lips, but his tongue was as dry as they. His first thought was: "That scoundrel, Lisle, *did* sell me, after all! Not a bit of use now pretending I was ill."

Clearing his voice, he said: "I am very sorry, sir, that I was not able to get home yesterday in time for dinner. That I took more wine than was good for me I frankly admit. So little am I used to it that a very small quantity tells upon me. I don't know whether you are aware of it, sir, but the occasion was a birthday wine party to drink the health of young Jack Derrick."

"Jack whom did you say?" demanded Sir Gilbert, adding, *sotto voce* : "If the fellow would only stand up and face me like a man and not look so confoundedly cringing and obsequious, I could forgive him almost anything."

"Jack Derrick, sir, son of Colonel Derrick, he who has lately come to reside at Stanbrooke Grange."

Luigi had calculated that his lie was a tolerably safe one. He knew that the Colonel and Sir Gilbert had never met and that, in view of the secluded habits of the latter, there was little likelihood of their doing so. Besides, it was quite true that young Derrick, with whom, however, he was merely on nodding terms, had just come of age, but the rest of his statement was a pure invention. It was the health of Miss Jennings that had been drunk in creaming bumpers.

"Humph!" said Sir Gilbert, as he gave a tug at the lobe of his right ear. Then he took a turn across the room and back again, for he had been standing by the chimney-piece on Luigi's entry. "After all, then," he remarked to himself, "the boy was in better company than I gave him credit for. Still, he deserves a sound wigging and he shall have it." But his frown had lightened perceptibly, a fact which Luigi's furtively glancing eyes did not fail to note.

"Even granting what you say, sir, that is no excuse for allowing yourself to become inebriated as, by your own admission, you were last evening. Be careful not to let it happen again, or you will find that I shall deal with it much more severely. But I have not done with you yet. I have been very much grieved and annoyed to find that on two or three afternoons a week you have taken to frequenting a certain billiard-saloon in the town, and there consorting with a number of young men whose society can be neither creditable nor beneficial to you in any way. I am willing to believe that, in some measure, you have erred through ignorance, through lack of a clear conception of what is due to your position as my grandson. Still, even that excuse can scarcely avail you in the case of Snell, the groom, whom I discharged a few days ago. That you should steal out of the house when you were supposed to be abed and go to the fellow's room and there sit smoking and drinking with him, making him thereby your equal for the time being, seems to me nothing less than disgraceful; indeed, I can scarcely trust myself to say what I there will be no excuse for you think of it. After this warning, however,--none whatever, if you do not keep strictly within the lines of conduct laid down for you. Snell has gone; and as regards the billiard-room, I must ask you to give me your word not to enter it again, nor, indeed, any other, without having obtained my sanction beforehand. Are you prepared to give me the promise I ask?"

"Certainly, sir--most fully and willingly. I give you my word to have no more to do with public billiards after to-day, and I shall be very careful about the class of people I mix with in time to come." Nothing came easier to Luigi than to make promises; the difficulty with him, as with so many of us, lay in the keeping of them. "This is another specimen of Lisle's dirty work," he reflected. "He's been playing the double part of spy and informer. But a day of reckoning will come for him."

"Keep to your promise and you will find yourself no loser by it in the long run," resumed Sir Gilbert. "And now you may go for the present," he said after a minute or two. "But I cannot conceal that I am grievously disappointed in you."

Luigi needed no second bidding. He had "pulled through" the scrape far better than he had expected, and was now inclined to be jubilant. "Grievously disappointed in me, is he?" he said with a short laugh. "What did the old fool expect? A grandson made to pattern, I suppose. Well, Granddad will just have to put up with me and make the best of me as I am."

After a few minutes spent in half-bitter, half-sorrowful rumination, Sir Gilbert said aloud: "I'll go and have a talk with Louisa. She's very clear-headed for one of her sex, and her opinions are nearly always worth listening to."

He found Lady Pell in the morning-room, busy with her crewel work and alone. She had sent Ethel for that after-breakfast ramble which she believed to be so conducive to the girl's health and good looks. Sir Gilbert sat down and proceeded to give her an account of his interview with Luigi. "What to do with him, I know not," he ended by saying. "I am sadly afraid that he will never be a credit to the house of Clare. He seems to have contracted a number of low tastes and reprehensible habits before he and I had ever set eyes on each other, and whether I shall ever succeed in eradicating them seems more than doubtful. It is a sad thing to say, but there are times when I feel almost driven to wish that I had remained ignorant of his existence and he of mine."

"My dear Gilbert, you really should not allow such notions to get into your head. Things are not yet come to that for the poor young man, and remembering that, you ought to regard his shortcomings with the utmost leniency."

"That is what I try to do, Louisa. It is a bitter reflection, but one which often haunts me, that if I had treated this boy's father less hardly, my old age might have been a very different one from what it is to-day."

"You have translated Lewis to an altogether different kind of life from that which he has been used to, and allowances must be made for the fact. Patience and tact will often effect wonders. I would not be in too great a hurry, if I were you. Old habits and ways can't be got rid of in a hurry. If you believe the young man himself is doing his best to second your efforts, why then----"

"But that is just where I'm in doubt."

"Then give him the benefit of the doubt; it will only be generous on your part to do so. I think, if I were you, I would let him travel awhile. Nothing tends more to expand a person's mind--providing," she drily added, "that one has a mind capable of expansion, and in Lewis's case the converse has yet to be proved."

After luncheon he had a further talk with Lady Pell, one result of which was that he asked Luigi for the address of Captain Verinder, and having obtained it, he proceeded to write to that gentleman, asking him, if it would be convenient for him to do so, to call upon the writer between eleven and twelve o'clock on the day but one following. As has already been stated, Sir Gilbert had conceived a distaste for the Captain at their first interview, and he had afterwards been at the pains to snub him most unmercifully. Had he been questioned as to the cause of his dislike, he could only have replied, that it was one of those unreasoning and unreasonable antipathies which nobody cares to formulate in words, even if it were not next to impossible to do so. In point of fact, it was merely an instance the more of "I do not love thee, Doctor Fell."

Now, however, that he had decided to carry out Lady Pell's suggestion, and send Luigi abroad for a time, it seemed to him that the boy's uncle, provided he were willing to undertake the charge, was the proper person into whose hands to entrust him while away from home. He knew nothing whatever to the Captain's detriment, and he told himself that, as a man of sense, he ought not to allow a foolish prejudice to stand in the way of any project which was likely to prove in the slightest degree beneficial to his grandson. Hence his note to the Captain.

It was not without sundry misgivings and in a far from comfortable frame of mind, that next day Captain Verinder journeyed down to Mapleford. A cab conveyed him from the station to the Chase, where he discharged the vehicle, not knowing whether he might be detained half-an-hour, or half-a-day. In any

case, a walk back to the station would do him no harm.
He had evidently been expected, and was at once shown into the room which was already so familiar to him, where he was presently joined by Sir Gilbert, who, for the first time, welcomed him with an outstretched hand.
Augustus Verinder breathed a deep inward sigh of relief.
It is not needful to describe in detail the interview that followed. Sir Gilbert at once entered frankly into the affair, explaining to the Captain exactly why he had sent for him and the task which he was desirous that the latter should undertake. September was still young, and another month of fine weather might almost be depended upon. It was his wish that his grandson should spend that month in foreign travel, chiefly in Switzerland, with, perhaps, a glance at the Italian lakes *en passant* . Would it fall in with Captain Verinder's arrangements to fill the part of Mentor to this latter-day Telemachus during the tour in question? To which the Captain replied, that nothing would afford him greater happiness; and, indeed, his heart leapt for joy at the thought of being able to spend a month on the Continent without being called upon to disburse a shilling of his own.
Various matters having been discussed and settled, Sir Gilbert produced his cheque-book, and after having filled up and signed one of the forms, handed it to the Captain. A glance at it showed the latter that it represented a sum of one hundred and seventy pounds.
"For your expenses," said Sir Gilbert; "but I have included in it twenty pounds for Lewis's outfit, which, seeing that he will be but a month away, ought, I think, to be sufficient."
"Amply sufficient, Sir Gilbert," assented the Captain as he pocketed the cheque.
"I should like Lewis to drop me a line every four or five days, so as to keep me *au courant* with your movements. I am desirous that you should avoid all large towns, such as Paris and Brussels, either in going or returning. It will be best that you should make your way to Bâ*le as speedily as possible and decide on your future course after you reach there."
"Your wishes are my commands, Sir Gilbert."
"How soon will it be convenient for you to start?"
"In thirty-six hours from now I shall be at your disposal."
"Trust you old soldiers for knowing the value of time. And now that we have settled everything so far, you must oblige me by staying to luncheon," said Sir Gilbert with a heartiness that was more assumed than real. Do what he would, he could not like this man. And yet he had nothing valid, nothing tangible to urge against him. "I am a prejudiced old fool," he said to himself, "and the older I get the worse I become."
At luncheon the Captain was fortunate enough to give Lady Pell a distinctly favourable impression of himself, which went to prove that Lady Pell's professed ability to read character at first sight was sometimes at fault. "I agree with you that the man is not *quite* a gentleman," she remarked later to Sir Gilbert; "but in that respect he only resembles the great majority of his sex. In these matters, my

dear cousin, one can't pick and choose. It seems to me that Captain Verinder, as the boy's uncle, is the proper person to entrust him to."

Next morning after breakfast, Luigi said to Lady Pell when no one was by: "Can you spare me five minutes in private, Lady Pell?"

"Certainly, my dear boy," was the cordial response. "Come with me to my sitting-room." There was much about Luigi that she did not like, but it seemed to her that in some respects he was deserving of pity.

"And now----?" she said, looking questioningly at him as she took her usual chair by the window and motioned him to another. The room, which had been specially assigned her, had been the late Lady Clare's boudoir.

Luigi cleared his voice and then, a whimsical smile overspreading his features, said: "Lady Pell, last night I saw the Grey Brother."

Lady Pell pricked up her ears and became at once interested. "Gracious me!" she exclaimed. "You do indeed surprise me. When and where did it happen? You must give me all particulars."

"It was late--between eleven and twelve o'clock--I had stolen out of the house by way of the conservatory on purpose to have a smoke." Here Lady Pell shook a monitory finger at him. "The fact is, I've never been used to the early hours of the Chase, and I can't sleep if I go to bed before midnight. Well, having let myself out, I made my way to the little wood, or spinny, which reaches from the back premises of the Chase nearly as far as the old tower where Martin Rigg, the former keeper, and his daughter have their quarters. It was not the first time I had gone there for a smoke after dark. In the middle of it is a tiny glade, or open space, and there I seated myself on the twisted root of a tree. A young moon was half way up the sky, and the stars were very bright. I had smoked one pipe out and thought I would have another before turning in, but on feeling for my tobacco-pouch, which I had laid down beside me, I could not find it. Slipping off my seat, I stooped to search for it among the grass, found it and stood up again. On turning to resume my seat I found myself confronted by a tall robed and cowled figure, which might have sprung out of the ground for anything I could have told to the contrary. Certainly I had heard no faintest sound of footsteps. That I was considerably flabbergasted, your ladyship will readily believe."

"Such an apparition would be enough to flabbergast anybody, as you term it. But what was it like as regards its features?"

"Its face was nearly hidden by its cowl, and all I can call to mind is that it had a long grizzled beard and two eyes that seemed to look through me."

"Well, and what did you do next?"

"I simply bolted--and I'm not ashamed to confess it."

"Oh!" was her ladyship's sole comment, but to herself she said: "You coward!"

"You won't catch me going there again after dark."

"I suppose not after such a startling experience. But tell me this: did the apparition, if such I may term it, project any shadow of itself in the moonlight?"

Luigi opened his eyes. "Upon my word, I don't know, Lady Pell. I was too confused to notice. But why do you ask?"

"Because I believe it is an understood thing that ghosts have no shadows--what, indeed, are they themselves but shadows? You evidently missed an interesting point there. But why have you chosen to make me your confidant, Lewis?"
"Because after what you said to me the other night when that girl made such a bobbery on the terrace, I thought I would ask your advice before saying a word to anybody else."
"That was very sensible on your part. My advice is, that you keep your singular experience strictly to yourself. The whole affair is inexplicable, and no good can come of talking about it. Your grandfather would be greatly annoyed were he to discover that any such report had emanated from you."

Luigi could scarcely credit his good fortune. That he should not merely be done with Latin declensions and those hateful riding-lessons, but be at liberty to ramble about the Continent for the ensuing month, visiting places he had never seen before, seemed almost too delightful to be true. He could not help saying to himself with a chuckle: "Perhaps if I hadn't drunk Miss J.'s health quite so often the other night, this bit of luck would never have happened to me." It was a relief to him on another account to get away from Mapleford for a time. It would effectually separate him from the aforesaid Miss J., who would be sure to hear of his departure. He trusted that by the time he should return she would have forgotten all about that ridiculous question he had put to her on a certain occasion, her answer to which had quite escaped his memory.

CHAPTER XXXIII.

UNCLE AND NEPHEW.

Luigi had telegraphed to his uncle by which train he should travel, and the Captain met him at the terminus. Sir Gilbert's cheque had already been cashed, and uncle and nephew now proceeded to lay in a small but sufficient supply of travelling necessaries. After that they dined at a French restaurant and finished up the evening at a music-hall.

Next day they crossed to Antwerp, from which place Luigi wrote a few lines to Sir Gilbert from a rough draft furnished him by the Captain.

"My dear Grandfather,--We reached here from Harwich early this morning. We are staying over till to-morrow at my wish, there being many objects of interest in this memorable old city which I have long been desirous of seeing. This forenoon we visited the cathedral and two of the more celebrated churches, in each of which we found much to interest us. The afternoon was devoted to the so-called museum, where is a celebrated collection of paintings, including several by Rubens and other well-known masters of the Dutch school. I need scarcely say that we were highly gratified.

"We start by an early train to-morrow for Bâ*le, which we purpose making our head-quarters. We shall, however, if we find the trains convenient, break our journey for a couple of hours at Cologne in order to visit the Dom, which I feel sure you would not like me to miss seeing."

Within an hour of posting the foregoing letter uncle and nephew were on their way to Brussels, although it was one of the two places specified by Sir Gilbert which he was desirous that his grandson should not visit.

It was not the first time the Captain had been there, and of such an agreeable kind were the recollections he retained of it that he had felt irresistibly tempted to visit it again. The fact was that on the occasion of his previous visit he had left the city richer by twenty-five pounds than he had entered it, that being the amount of his winnings after a couple of nights at the gaming-table. Trifling though such a sum might seem to many people, to the impecunious Captain it represented a very substantial and satisfactory gain. Thus it was scarcely to be wondered at, now he found himself in the neighbourhood and in the possession of ample funds, that a great longing should come over him to tempt fortune in the same way again. He would only risk a small sum, so that if he should prove so unfortunate as to lose it, no great harm would be done, while, if he should be lucky enough to double or treble it, his winnings would help to clear off some of his more pressing liabilities when he should get back to town. It was unfortunate that he was not in a position to prosecute his little adventure alone, but where he went Luigi must of necessity go too--not, as he presently found when he broached the subject, that his nephew needed more than a hint to cause him to exhibit an almost absurd amount of eagerness to follow his worthy relative's example.

Thus it came to pass that about nine o'clock that same evening uncle and nephew, without any further introduction than a few whispered words between the Captain and the man on guard at the door, were at once admitted to the self-styled club or *cercle* (which, in reality, differed scarcely, if at all, from a common gambling haunt), of which the Captain retained such pleasing recollections. It had been agreed that on no account should they risk more than twenty-five pounds between them, out of which the Captain, as being the more experienced of the two, took fifteen for his share, leaving Luigi the remaining ten.

Soon after midnight the Captain perforce stopped playing for lack of funds. His fifteen pounds had vanished to the last franc; but, on the other hand, singular to relate in view of his inexperience, Luigi rose from the table a winner to the extent of fourteen pounds. Captain Verinder at once decided that next morning should see them *en route* for Bâ*le.

But it was not to be. While taking an after-breakfast stroll--he had decided not to start till the midday train--the Captain encountered a man who, a few years before, had been one of his most intimate friends. This person, Tyars by name, was now settled in Brussels and in a good position, and nothing would satisfy him but that Verinder and his nephew must dine and spend the evening at his house, an arrangement to which, after a little demur, the Captain agreed.

As it fell out, however, he was compelled to go alone, Luigi, in the course of the afternoon, being seized with one of the violent sick headaches to which he had been subject at times ever since he could remember. His uncle left him prostrate on a couch in a darkened room.

But for once the usually astute and suspicious Captain had been thoroughly hoodwinked. Scarcely had he disappeared before Luigi sat up, chuckling softly to himself. He was bent on a little adventure of his own in which his uncle should have neither part nor parcel. The demon of gambling had got him in his grip, and Luigi lent a willing ear to his enticements. He had won fourteen pounds last night, why should he not win forty, eighty, a hundred to-night? He could see no reason whatever why he should not.

In the big solid-leather portmanteau which held both his uncle's clothes and his own was stored away a little roll of bank-notes of the value of one hundred pounds, the same being part of the proceeds of Sir Gilbert's cheque. Luigi's intention was to abstract a couple or three five-pound notes and with them, in addition to his overnight winnings, to try his luck at the *cercle* for the second time. He had opened the portmanteau and the roll of notes was in his fingers, when he was startled by the sound of voices, one of which he took to be his uncle's, in the corridor outside. In an instant he had shut down the lid of the portmanteau and crammed, the notes into his pocket. The alarm proved to be a false one, but Luigi, having taken possession of the whole of the notes, saw no reason why he should put any of them back. After all, they were his property and not his uncle's; besides, although he might take them with him to the *cercle* , he was fully determined not to risk more than the sum he had originally fixed on: it was a determination from which nothing should move him. How his uncle would open his eyes in the morning at beholding his nephew's overnight winnings scattered carelessly on the dressing-table!

Captain Verinder opened his eyes very wide indeed when, on entering his nephew's room some time after midnight, he found Luigi pacing it, wild-eyed, haggard, with clenched hands, tumbled hair and rumpled clothes, like a man half distraught. He had come back from the gaming table penniless. In the excitement of play, all his fine resolutions had vanished like chaff before the wind. He had gone on losing madly, recklessly, till not only had the hundred pounds gone, but his previous night's winnings and whatever else he had had in his purse to boot. Well might the Captain when, bit by bit, the truth had been dragged out, sit down and stare at him in blank dismay. No words at his command could have expressed more than a tithe of what he felt.

CHAPTER XXXIV.

A DESPERATE RESOLVE.

It was nine o'clock next morning. Captain Verinder, with his hands clasped behind his back and downcast eyes, was pacing the courtyard of the hotel, which was ornamented with a double row of orange-trees and myrtles in green tubs, and had one end roofed with trellis work festooned with a vine, the leaves of which were now turning brown and golden, and under which were ranged a number of rustic seats interspersed with small marble-topped tables. Presently Luigi, for whom his uncle had been waiting, made his appearance, looking very sallow and cadaverous, while the dark half-circles under his eyes bore mute witness to the sort of night he had spent.

"Don't be afraid that I am about to reproach you for your insensate folly," began his uncle. "Your conscience will do that far more effectually than any words of mine. Besides, I hold myself greatly to blame for bringing you here in the first instance, and it is perhaps no more than just that I should have to put up with the consequences equally with yourself. I have been going into cash matters this morning and find that when our hotel bill has been discharged, we shall have about fifteen pounds left, all told. Now, if you can reveal to me by what miracle of economy two people can contrive to spend a month in Switzerland without exceeding that amount, I shall be much obliged to you."

"Of course it can't be done," said Luigi sulkily. "There's nothing for it but to go back home."

"Oh, indeed. And in that case how, pray, shall we excuse ourselves to Sir Gilbert Clare?"

"Why need he know that we have returned? Why can't we lie quietly by in London till the month has come to an end?"

"For a very simple reason," returned the Captain drily. "Have you forgotten that your grandfather looks to receive a letter from you every few days while you are away? Now, supposing you were to send him a note professedly written from Lausanne, or Geneva, with merely the London postmark on it, what would happen then?"

"I had forgotten all about having to write to the old boy," said Luigi with a smothered imprecation.

"On the other hand," resumed the Captain, "it would be madness to go to him and frankly confess our sins. He would never forgive either of us, and he would regard me, perhaps rightly, as being by far the bigger sinner of the two."

"In that case, what's the best thing to do?"

"Upon my word, I haven't the ghost of an idea. It's a bad lookout all round.

Nowhere can I discern a way out of our quandary. But let's to breakfast with what appetite we may. A hungry stomach is never a good counsellor."

It seemed as if the Captain was destined to encounter people whom he knew. As he was crossing the entrance-hall after breakfast he met a man face to face whom he had not seen for some time. He was Mr. Henriques, the money-lender, who, in days gone by, when Verinder was going gaily down hill but had not yet reached the bottom, had more than once helped him to tide over a temporary difficulty. Both the men now came to a halt and each asked the other what had brought him there. The money-lender was not one of those who have no eyes for a man because he happens to have come down in the world; such men have their uses, as no one knew better than he. More than once since his own collapse Verinder had been enabled to introduce "business" to him, and had not been above accepting a commission for doing so.

"Can you spare me ten minutes?" queried the Captain. "Willingly, if you'll wait till I've breakfasted," replied the other. "I'll join you on the smoking-room balcony in half an hour."

The Captain and Luigi were just in time to catch the midday train. They both looked jubilant, and well they might, for Mr. Henriques had come to their rescue. The Captain had introduced Luigi to him and had frankly explained how they came to be "cornered." (He had always found it advisable to deal frankly with Mr. Henriques.) When the money-lender had satisfied himself, which a few leading questions enabled him to do, that Luigi was really the grandson of Sir Gilbert Clare of Withington Chase, he made no difficulty about advancing him a hundred pounds on the joint note of hand of himself and his uncle. For the time being they were saved, and just then they did not permit any thought of the future to mar their content.

It does not come within the scope of our design to accompany them in their wanderings from place to place. It will be enough to say that they made good use of their time and spent their money with a free hand. Indeed, it was owing to the latter circumstances that they found themselves back in London some days before they were due there, paucity of funds having compelled them to cut short their tour, a fact which they deemed it advisable to keep from the knowledge of Sir Gilbert. Accordingly it was arranged that Luigi should quarter himself for a few days on his uncle, and that the two should then travel down to the Chase as if they had just come straight through from the Continent.

But on reaching the Captain's rooms a very disagreeable surprise awaited them. Mr. Henriques was dead, and the executors on whom devolved the winding up of his affairs wrote, not merely to acquaint Captain Verinder with that melancholy fact, but also to give him notice that the bill at thirty days (the late Mr. H. had declined to have it drawn for a longer period, but had hinted that a

renewal might perhaps be arranged) for one hundred and twenty pounds, principal and interest, bearing the joint signatures of himself and Mr. Lewis Clare, would have to be met in due course, and that, under the circumstances, any renewal of it was out of the question.
Never were two men more dumfoundered. They had eaten their cake and enjoyed it, and now the reckoning must be paid. They were no better off than they had been at Brussels; indeed, they were worse off to the extent of twenty pounds, and, now as then, their predicament was such that, of all people in the world, Sir Gilbert was the last whose ears it must be allowed to reach. It was indeed a sorry home-coming.
In the course of the following day Captain Verinder waited upon the executors, but the only concession he could obtain from them was a week's grace beyond the date when the note would fall due.
"London swarms with money-lenders," said Luigi; "surely, one or other of them would do as Henriques did, and advance us enough money on our joint signatures to pay off this confounded bill."
"Very possibly that might be managed; but what then? We should merely be putting off the evil day for a little while, and the worst of it would be that the longer we succeeded in staving it off, the bigger would be the reckoning when it did come. At present all we have to find is a hundred and twenty pounds, but if we should succeed in negotiating another bill, at the end of two or three months we should have a hundred and fifty to meet, and supposing we were compelled to go on renewing, a little later we should have to face a liability of a couple of hundred pounds; and so it would go up by leaps and bounds in the way of compound interest till some day our good friends the usurers would put the screw on, and the inevitable crash would come. No; we must, if possible, find some better way out of our difficulty than that. I'll sleep on it; perhaps an idea may come to me in the course of the night."
Next morning the Captain seemed in a thoughtful mood, and as Luigi was in no humour for talking, breakfast passed almost in silence. When it had come to an end, and the equipage had been removed, the elder man said: "Draw up that easy chair to the window, and light a weed. I have something to say to you."
As soon as his own meerschaum and Luigi's cigar were well under way, he resumed: "You remember that day about which you spoke to me while we were abroad, when, Mr. Everard Lisle being away on business for your grandfather, the old gentleman called you into his study and got you to write one or two letters for him?"
Luigi nodded.
"Then, you will remember telling me that while you were there a clerk came down from London, bringing with him a parcel of American bonds, for which your grandfather, after having examined and counted them, gave the man a receipt, and that, as soon as the clerk had gone, he asked you to unlock the door of the strong room which opens out of his study, and deposit the bonds in question in a certain drawer marked B. You also said, if I mistake not, that that

was the first time you had set foot inside the strong room."
"And the last," interposed Luigi.
"If I recollect rightly, the bonds in question were endorsed 'Missouri and Eastern Union Preference.'"
"That is so."
"That they are a good sound stock may be taken for granted, otherwise your grandfather would not have invested so largely in them. I see by this morning's newspaper that yesterday they were quoted at from 53 to 53-5/8."
"Yes--what then?" demanded Luigi blankly. He could not imagine what his uncle was driving at.
"Merely this, dear boy--that if we could by any means contrive to annex a few of the bonds in question, a way out of our difficulty would at once be opened for us."
The silence that ensued lasted for some minutes. The Captain wanted what he had said to sink into his nephew's mind. It was a daring suggestion, but, after all, not nearly so audacious as that other suggestion, which had emanated from the same source, that Luigi should personate Sir Gilbert Clare's dead grandson. That suggestion had borne practical fruit, had, in fact, developed into a splendid success. Why should not this one prove equally as successful?
"A very ingenious suggestion indeed, uncle," said Luigi at length; "but how do you propose to carry it into effect? You talk as if I had in my possession a duplicate key of the strong room."
"That is a mere detail," responded the Captain airily, "which I have not yet had time to consider."
"Assuming for the moment that we succeed in obtaining possession of the bonds, and that their loss is discovered, what then?
"Yes, what then? Why should suspicion fall upon you? Should we decide to carry out the affair, it would have to be in such a way as to leave no possible link which would serve to connect you or me with the missing documents. Besides, I think it not unlikely that some long time would elapse before the bonds would be missed. Your grandfather has apparently bought the stock as a permanent investment, and if such be the case, no reason will exist for him to go through the parcel a second time in order to satisfy himself that none of them have been abstracted. Months, nay years, might elapse without the loss being discovered; it is even possible that Sir Gilbert might die in ignorance thereof. It would be singular, would it not, if the bonds should ultimately come to you as his heir? Looked at from that point of view, you would merely be obtaining an advance on your own property."
"Let us suppose once more," persisted Luigi. "The bonds are sold, let us say; their loss is discovered; as a consequence, a hue-and-cry is set afoot and the missing numbers advertised. In that case what is to prevent their being traced back to the first vendor of them after their--hem! abstraction?"
The Captain smiled as he shook the ash out of his meerschaum. "The answer to that is very simple," he said. "I shall know how to put the bonds on the market

through such a channel as will render it an impossibility for them ever to be traced back."

Three days later uncle and nephew, attired in their travelling suits as if fresh from their journey across the Channel, arrived at Withington Chase. Captain Verinder felt it was due to Sir Gilbert that he should personally give him back the young Telemachus who for the past four weeks had been entrusted to his charge.

By this time he and Luigi had settled all the details of their plot, as far as it was possible for them to do so beforehand, and away from the spot.

CHAPTER XXXV.

MATTERS AT THE CHASE.

No great measure of persuasion was needed on the part of Sir Gilbert Clare in order to induce Lady Pell to extend the term of her visit at Withington Chase.

Sooth to lay, age was beginning to tell somewhat upon her ladyship. With advancing years her craving to be continually on the move from place to place began to work less powerfully within her. There were even times when a growing sense of loneliness made itself sadly felt, and when the knowledge that she was both childless and homeless would unseal in her heart a fountain of poignant regrets which would well to her eyes in tears, all the more salt, it may be, in that they were, as a rule, so sternly repressed.

Somehow the Chase seemed more of a home to her than any place she had visited for years. There was a sweet nameless charm about the old mansion which affected her--she could hardly have told how. Even when she had been a month there she felt no desire to pack up her trunks and betake herself elsewhere. This, for her, was an altogether novel experience.

It may be that Lady Pell's liking for the Chase was due in part, if not wholly, to her recollection of a certain happy season she had spent there when in her teens. It had been the scene of the first and, possibly, the only romance her life had known--a poor little futile romance, as events had proved--but perhaps none the less cherished on that account; and it was still the home of the man who had been the ideal of her girlish dreams.

Sir Gilbert, for his part, was well satisfied that his cousin should make the Chase her home for as long as it might suit her convenience to do so. That he would feel her departure as a loss whenever it should take place, he began to realise more clearly the longer she stayed. She was capital company; never otherwise than lively and in good spirits, not a bit in awe of him, and imbued with a sufficiency of the combative element to make her always ready to administer that pinch of contradiction which men like the Baronet need to put them on their mettle.

Without any design or set intention on her part, Ethel had become a great favourite with the old man. As we know, the Baronet had had several sons, but no daughter, and all unwittingly Ethel had slipped into a vacant niche in his heart, of the existence of which he had heretofore been only dimly aware. In Ethel's singing and playing he found something that pleased him exceedingly. And when in some neglected corner she found a heap of old music which had belonged to, and bore the signature of, the first Lady Clare; and when, one evening, without saying anything to him, she ventured to play some of them;

and, when he recognised them--voices from the tomb, as it were, silent for thirty long years--his delight was touching to behold. After that Ethel played and sang to him every evening, when he would sit with closed eyes, an elbow resting on either arm of his big easy-chair, and the fingertips of one hand pressed against those of the other, while an expression of great peace and contentment would gradually steal over his grand old features.

"I can't tell what it is, Louisa, that draws me so to that girl," he remarked one day to Lady Pell. "It's not her good looks, though they are undeniable; and it's not her musical abilities, admirable as they are; it's a charm, a something altogether indefinable and elusive, to which, if I were to try for an hour, I don't think I could give its proper name. Both her eyes and her voice seem to haunt me; it is as if I had seen the one and heard the other in some prior state of existence. At times they affect me in the strangest possible way."

"I don't wonder at your being taken by Ethel Thursby," returned Lady Pell. "She is a dear girl, and I should like to have kept her with me always; but her aunts would only lend her to me for a time. In one sense I shall be quite sorry when Beilby, my ordinary companion, is well enough to resume her duties."

"You must not let her go yet awhile, Louisa. And yet, the longer she stays, the harder it will seem to part from her when the time comes."

"There is some one besides you and me, unless I am very much mistaken, who will find it harder still to part from her when the time comes."

"And who may that be, pray?"

"That very nice secretary of yours, Mr. Everard Lisle."

"Lisle! You don't mean to say----"

"I mean to say that he's over head and ears in love with Ethel Thursby."

"You astonish me. I have remarked nothing."

"Of course not. It was not to be expected. You are only a poor purblind man. Now, *I* have been sure of it for some time; indeed, I began to have my suspicions almost from the first time they met. I confess that I watch the progress of the little comedy, out of a corner of my eye, with a good deal of interest. I like to see a man in earnest, and that's what young Lisle evidently is."

"He's a fine fellow, and I wish--it seems a hard thing to say--that my grandson were more like him."

"Well, well, Gilbert, you must just accept Lewis as he is, and make the best of him. I am afraid it would not be well for us if we could have people manufactured to our own liking. But, when all is said, I am not without hope that your grandson will ultimately prove to be everything that you could desire."

They were still talking when a black-bordered letter, which had just arrived, was brought to Sir Gilbert.

"It is from my daughter-in-law, Mrs. Clare," he said as he examined the postmarks before opening it. "From the mourning envelope, I judge that her venerable relative is dead."

And such, indeed, proved to be the case. Giovanna wrote to say that her grandmother was no more, and that in the course of a few days she hoped to be on her way back to England. She had written twice to Sir Gilbert previously, just a few formal lines couched in studiously respectful terms, her first note containing the announcement of her arrival at Catanzaro, and her second conveying the news that her grandmother still lingered, but that all hope of her recovery had been given up. Brief and simple though the notes were, the composition of them had been anything but a labour of love to Giovanna. She had expended both time and pains over them, and, after all, had been far from satisfied with the result.

Sir Gilbert, however, had Giovanna but known it, was quite satisfied. To him his daughter-in-law's brief formal communications seemed everything that the occasion demanded. He often thought about her, but never unkindly, and he looked forward to her proximate return with a certain amount of pleasure. He had begun to regard her as an agreeable element in the subdued tenour of his existence; and although Lady Pell far more than compensated for her absence, his cousin would not stay at the Chase for ever, indeed, she might take it into her head to start off at any moment, and when her ladyship should be gone Giovanna would step back into the place which for a little while she had unavoidably vacated.

He now gave Mrs. Clare's note to Lady Pell to read.

"I suppose we may expect her back in about a week or ten days," he presently remarked. "It will gratify me to introduce her to you. I think you will be pleased with her."

Lady Pell's sole reply was a little dubious cough. Liberal-minded though she was in many ways--indeed, she prided herself on being so--she was not, as a rule, prepossessed by foreigners. It was an insular prejudice, but one, unfortunately, which she shared in common with numbers of worthy people, who take credit to themselves for their narrow-mindedness, and are proud of boasting that they are "English to the backbone."

"Her mother was an Englishwoman, as I think I have mentioned to you before to-day," remarked Sir Gilbert with a little flash of the eye. "Consequently----"

"Mrs. Clare is only half a foreigner. It is a fact I had forgotten. Yes, that certainly makes a difference, and I at once admit that I am a little curious to meet her. Being the sort of woman you have described to me--still, for all her forty years, or whatever their number may be, so splendidly handsome--you have not, I presume, overlooked the possibility of her one day marrying again."

The Baronet threw a startled glance at his cousin. "No," he exclaimed, "such an idea never entered my mind."

"I can well believe it," rejoined Lady Pell with a little pitying smile. "You men!--you men! But now that I have made you a present of the idea, you cannot fail to perceive the extreme feasibility of it."

"Um-um. But if Mrs. Clare had any thought or intention of marrying again, why need she have waited all these years? Like the rest of us, Louisa, she is not growing younger."

"Possibly she has met no one whom she cared to marry. But, be that as it may, it must at once strike you that the Mrs. Clare of to-day--the daughter-in-law of Sir Gilbert Clare and the mother of the prospective heir of Withington Chase--is a very different personage in the matrimonial market from the Mrs. Clare of six months ago. If she prove anything like the kind of woman I take her to be, you may rely upon it that she will not long be content to remain buried in a little poky neighbourhood such as this. She will want--and very naturally--to see something of the world, and to assume that position in society to which by your own act she has become entitled." Then, perceiving that her words had had more effect than she had intended, she hastened to add: "But these are merely some of my views, and must not be taken for more than they are worth. It may be that I shall find Mrs. Clare a very different kind of person from anything I have imagined her to be."

Sir Gilbert rose stiffly from his chair.

"What you have just told me, Louisa, has put me about a little, and I have no wish to deny it. There is reason in what you say--much reason. For, when all is said, why should not Alec's widow marry again if her inclination tends that way? Only, I hadn't thought of it--that's where it is--I hadn't thought of it."

A happy accident--if that may be termed an accident which was the result of the working out of a series of events altogether outside their own control--had brought Lisle and Ethel together again, but neither of them felt inclined to cavil at having been thus unceremoniously treated. Neither did they evince any disposition to grumble when they found that a day seldom passed without bringing them for a longer or shorter time into the society of each other. Everard was at the Chase nearly every forenoon, and frequently stayed for luncheon, while his invitations to dinner were even more frequent since Lady Pell's arrival than they had been before. The latter fact he owed to his ability as a whist-player, for Sir Gilbert, to his great satisfaction, now found that, with Mrs. Tew to make a fourth, he could count upon a rubber as often as he chose to bring the little party together, which, on an average, was three or four evenings a week. It was a pleasure from which circumstances had long debarred him.

Everard's love for Ethel, which her refusal of him had compelled him to crush down with all the force of his will, but which nothing had availed to kill, under the daily sunshine of her presence sprang up into fresh and vigorous life. To all outward seeming, as he flattered himself, his treatment of her in no wise differed from that which he would have accorded to any other young woman with whom circumstances might have brought him into daily contact; but on that point, as we have seen, he was mistaken, Lady Pell having penetrated his secret almost from the first. He strove to so train both his voice and his eyes that neither of them should betray him, and believed--foolish fellow!--that he had succeeded in the attempt. He had no present intention of risking his fate a second time. Just now it was happiness enough to be enabled to see Ethel and to talk with her day after day, to sit by her at table, to hover round her at the piano, and to be permitted to hold her fingers for a moment within his when the time came for bidding her goodnight. Once again his tongue should bear witness for him--and he would stand or fall by the result: but not yet.

And Ethel--what of her?

She would not have been a woman had she not known that Lisle loved her. If Lady Pell could penetrate his secret, it was scarcely to be expected that she who was alone concerned should be less clear-sighted, lacking though she was both in years and experience.

With Ethel, although she did not know it, it was love that whispered love's secret to her heart. She heard the whisper but failed to recognise the voice. Only a little while before she had been sorely smitten, and not yet had she quite recovered from the blow; although every day that took her farther away from it helped almost imperceptibly to blunt the sharp edge of pain. A consciousness had begun to dawn on her that within her heart, dormant as yet, or only just beginning timidly to unfold, lay the potentialities of a love very different from that which her ignorance had been beguiled into accepting as the "perfect flower of life." Already for her the morn of a new and more beautiful love was beginning to break, before the sweetness and light of which all that was left in her memory of the deposed image of Launce Keymer would fade and crumble into nothingness.

CHAPTER XXXVI.

A DEED OF DARKNESS.

It was late in the afternoon when Captain Verinder and his nephew arrived at Withington Chase. Under the circumstances, Sir Gilbert could not well do otherwise than invite the Captain to dine and sleep there, and when Verinder, although secretly overjoyed, pleaded that his dress clothes were in his portmanteau at the cloakroom of the London terminus, his excuse was at once overruled. "If that is your only objection, sir, you shall be kept in countenance by my grandson and myself. For once in a way we will all wear tweeds at dinner."

Retaining Luigi's hand in his for a few seconds, Sir Gilbert gazed somewhat wistfully into the young man's face. "You have not brought back much of the tan of travel on your cheeks," he said. "How is that, I wonder? Not for years have we had so hot an autumn as the one now drawing to a close."

"My face never either tans or freckles, sir, however hot the weather may be," explained Luigi with a touch of heightened colour. "It is a fact for which I am unable to account."

"Humph! At all events I'm glad to see that your cheeks can take a blush. I am glad, too, judging from your letters, that you seem to have enjoyed yourself while away, although that was by no means the object I had in view in sending you abroad. I trust that your experiences during the last month will not be thrown away upon you, but that they will be productive of benefit to you in more ways than one." With that he turned away, murmuring to himself: "What can be the reason why he never looks me straight in the face? Why do his eyes always flicker and drop when I try to fix them with my own? It is a bad trait, a very bad trait, and it fills me with a vague sense of mistrust. If he would but confront me with Lisle's open unflinching look! That young fellow's eyes are as clear and honest as the day."

It was an immense relief to Luigi to find that his grandfather made no mention of Miss Jennings. His fear had been lest, during his absence, that young person might have sought out Sir Gilbert and have enlightened him as to the absurd offer which he, Luigi, had made her on her birthday night when under the insidious influence of *Veuve Cliequot* . When, therefore, his grandfather turned away without mentioning "Miss J.'s" name he felt that a great danger had passed him by.

But while one weight had been lifted off his mind, another crushed him down with a force from which he found it impossible to free himself. Ever before him loomed the black shadow of the deed to which he had become engaged. Sleeping or waking, it held him with a nightmare grip. He ate his dinner not because he wanted or cared for it, but because not to have done so would have laid him open to question and remark. After dinner came whist, Captain Verinder making up the quartette, *vice* Everard Lisle. Ethel and Luigi, being free to follow their own devices, engaged in a desultory conversation, chiefly anent the latter's recent travel experiences, which before long began to languish and presently died out. Then, with a muttered excuse that he was altogether behindhand with English news, Luigi seized on a batch of illustrated papers and buried himself among them, while Ethel's face brightened perceptibly. She saw before her not merely the prospect of a cosy hour with a favourite author, but an escape from a *tê*te-à*-tê*te* with Mr. Lewis Clare.

Next morning the Captain routed Luigi out of bed at an untimely hour. "I want you to show me Sir Gilbert's study," he said, "and the desk in which he keeps the key of the strong room."

There was no difficulty about doing that, because the study door was never locked overnight, in order that the servants might have access to it betimes, their orders being to have it in readiness for Sir Gilbert by ten o'clock to the minute.

The room was empty when Luigi opened the door and went in, followed by his uncle. "That is the door of the strong room--iron, as you see--and this is the drawer in which the key of it is always kept," said the former.

"And where is the key of the drawer kept?" queried the Captain. "It is one of a bunch grandfather carries about with him and rarely lets out of his own keeping."

Verinder glanced at the door, then he tried the drawer, which, as a matter of course, was locked, and then he stooped and examined the keyhole.

"As far as I can judge," he said, "the lock is of quite an ordinary kind, and you ought not to experience much difficulty in picking it."

"But what will grandfather think when he finds the drawer unlocked?" questioned Luigi.

"Why, merely that he must have omitted to lock it overnight. Of course the key of the strong room will be there just as he left it, and there will be nothing to arouse his suspicions that it has even been touched. He will simply tell himself that he must be more careful in future, and there will be an end of the matter."

It was too early for breakfast, so they left the house and went for a stroll in the grounds.

"I wish, Lewis, my boy," remarked the Captain cheerfully, "you would try not to look quite so glum and down in the mouth. If you had a murder on your mind you could hardly look more wretched than you do. Do, for goodness sake, assume a cheerfulness; even if you can't feel it--though what cause you have for being anything else than cheerful, I cannot for the life of me imagine."

"Oh, I'm not like you; I haven't nerves of cast iron; I wish I had," retorted Luigi. "Be cheerful, indeed! It's all very fine, but how is it possible for me to look other than down in the mouth when I remember the desperate business I'm booked to go through with three nights hence?"

"Desperate business, indeed! What nonsense is this? There's nothing desperate about it, nothing whatever. Here's the affair in a nutshell: you wait in your room till the clock strikes midnight; then you kick off your shoes, steal downstairs in the dark, and make your way to the study. Then you open the slide of your dark lantern and proceed to manipulate your picklocks. After a minute or two the lock yields to your coaxing; you open the drawer and there lies the key you want, ready to your hand. Five minutes later the bonds are yours. By half-past twelve you are not merely back in your own room, but in bed and asleep. *Voilà* tout!* Desperate business, quotha!"

For sole reply Luigi shrugged his shoulders and spread out the palms of his hands with one of those indescribable gestures which an Englishman may perhaps caricature, but cannot even passably imitate.

Although Captain Verinder had had no intimation to that effect, he was quite aware that his visit was expected to come to an end some time between breakfast and luncheon. Accordingly, as soon as the former meal was over, he proceeded to make his adieux. Having said goodbye to Lady Pell and Miss Thursby, he turned to Sir Gilbert, who had already rung the bell and ordered the dog-cart to be brought round, and who now accompanied him as far as the entrance hall, with Luigi bringing up the rear. While waiting they chatted about the weather and other indifferent topics. Presently the dog-cart drove up and Luigi flung wide the door. Then Sir Gilbert, drawing himself up and putting on his most grandiose manner, said, "We shall look to see you again at Withington Chase before very long, Captain Verinder." It was vague and yet sufficiently courteous. Then, as the Captain bowed and murmured his thanks: "I need scarcely tell you how very much obliged I am to you for the care and attention you have lavished on my grandson during the time he has been under your charge, and, as a proof that such is the case, I trust you will do me the favour of accepting this trifling recognition at my hands."

As the Baronet turned back into the house after favouring Verinder with a parting wave of the hand as the latter was being driven off, he muttered to himself: "I can't help it, I really can't, but I do *not* like that man. Of course it's the sheerest prejudice on my part, and, knowing it to be such, I am all the more bound to do my best to get the better of it."

When Captain Verinder opened the envelope which the Baronet had pressed into his hand at parting, he found inside it a cheque for thirty guineas. "A thousand thanks, my dear Sir Gilbert!" he exclaimed with a chuckle. "I don't mind how often you employ me on the same terms. You are obliged to me for the care and attention I have lavished on your grandson, eh? What a pity, in one sense, it is that one dare not enlighten you about the little Brussels episode!"

In accordance with the plan agreed upon between himself and his nephew, the Captain took the first train up to town, but only to return to Mapleford in the course of the forenoon of the following day, bringing with him a set of picklocks, a dark lantern and an old portmanteau. He again took up his quarters at the *Crown and Cushion* hotel, where Luigi called upon him in the course of the afternoon. Then was the purpose for which the portmanteau had been brought from London made manifest, which was to enable Verinder to give his nephew an object-lesson in the art of lock-picking, in which the latter proved himself no inapt pupil.

The day was Saturday, and it was decided that the attempt should be made the following night, because it was an understood thing at the Chase that on Sundays the house should be shut up and every one retire an hour earlier than on week-day nights. Supposing that all should go off successfully, Luigi would conceal the stolen securities in his own room till the morrow, taking the first opportunity that should offer to make his way with them to the *Crown and Cushion* , where his uncle would relieve him of them, and at once hurry off to London, there to negotiate the sale of them through that "safe channel" of which he had previously made mention to his nephew. The Captain did not let Luigi go without once more impressing on him that, if he only carried out to the letter the instructions laid down for him and did not lose his nerve, he ran absolutely no risk of detection. On the other hand, should the scheme, through some blunder on his part, prove abortive, he must be prepared to accept the consequences. In that case, the whole discreditable transaction with Mr. Henriques, and what gave rise to it, would inevitably be brought to Sir Gilbert's notice, with a result which it was impossible to foresee, but which, in any case, must prove nothing short of disastrous.

Never before had Luigi Rispani spent so miserable a Sunday, and yet it came to an end all too soon for him.

At the usual hour everybody retired; indeed, Luigi had crept away some time before without bidding goodnight to anyone. With his ulster wrapped round him--for the autumn nights were chilly--and lighted by a solitary candle, he sat shivering and quaking in his bedroom, waiting for the stroke of midnight. It came, after what seemed an interminable time, a thin tinkle of sound from the old case-clock on the gallery staircase. With the last stroke he stood up, dropped the ulster off his shoulders, and slipped his feet out of his patent shoes. Then he unlocked his portmanteau and took therefrom the bunch of picklocks, the dark lantern, and a travelling flask filled with brandy, into the cup of which he poured a liberal measure of the spirit and drank it off without drawing breath. Then he set light to the wick of the lantern, shut the slide, and put it into one of the pockets of his velvet lounging jacket, and the picklocks into the other. That done, he blew out the candle, crossed to the door, opened it and stood listening intently for fully a couple of minutes. Then he stepped out into the pitch-dark corridor and drew the door to after him. Traversing the corridor with noiseless footsteps, he emerged on the gallery which overlooked the entrance hall. Here he paused to listen again, but darkness and silence had the mansion to themselves. It was the work of a minute to cross the gallery, pass swiftly down the broad old stairs and so into the right-hand corridor on the ground floor, the second door in which was that of Sir Gilbert's study. By this time Luigi's heart was palpitating at such a rate that he was compelled to pause for a few moments with his fingers on the handle of the door till its beatings had slackened. Then he pushed open the door and went in.

Again he waited, scarcely breathing, while one might have counted six slowly. Then, drawing forth his lantern, he pushed the slide halfway back and shot a gleam of light around. All the familiar features of the room were there just as he had seen them last.

Thus far everything had gone so well with him and so exactly as his uncle had predicted it would, that he began to gather courage, and even caught himself smiling at his own exaggerated fears. Well, it was his first attempt in that particular line of business, so that every excuse ought to be made for him, and in all sincerity he hoped it would be his last.

By this he had placed the lantern on his grandfather's desk and had begun to manipulate the picklocks. As the Captain had inferred, the lock was only an ordinary one, and after labouring for about three minutes Luigi succeeded in picking it. His heart gave a great bound as he heard the click of the bolt.

Two seconds later the key of the strong room was in his hand. Taking the lantern in his other hand, he crossed the floor, lifted the metal flap that covered the keyhole, inserted the key, turned it and pulled open the massive iron door. Drawing a deeper breath than common he stepped across the threshold, lifted the lantern above his head and stared around.

The strong room at the Chase had at one time formed part of the room now used by Sir Gilbert as his study. It was his father who had caused the dividing wall to be built, and had turned the smaller chamber into a depository for family papers, leases, deeds, securities and what not. One side of the room was occupied by a row of shelves having a series of cupboards and drawers below them, while two large japanned boxes took up a considerable portion of the floor space; but, even then, there was room enough and to spare to stow away all the archives of the Clare family for generations to come. The room was lighted by a small, barred, oval window high up in the wall.

The drawer in which Luigi had put away the American bonds, on the occasion when his grandfather had claimed his assistance owing to the temporary absence of Everard Lisle, was labelled B, and after his preliminary glance round, he at once made straight for it. Placing his lantern on the nearest shelf, he pulled open the drawer, which was without lock or fastening of any kind.

Yes, there lay the identical bundle of papers which he had placed there several weeks before, and which, in all probability, had never since been touched. The bonds, which were tied together with green tape, must have numbered a score at the least, but it had been decided by Verinder that it would be unadvisable to abstract more than four of them, so that, even should Sir Gilbert have occasion to handle the bundle, he would scarcely discover the loss, unless he should happen to count those that were left. The proceeds of the sale of the four bonds would not only suffice to clear off the note of hand held by the executors of Mr. Henriques, but would, in addition, provide uncle and nephew with a welcome supply of ready money.

Luigi, with the bundle of bonds between his fingers, was stooping over the lantern and examining the knot in the green tape which held them together, when he suddenly became aware that he was no longer alone. He had not heard a sound, and yet, with an indescribable creeping of the flesh and, as it seemed, a stoppage of all the pulses of his being, he felt, he knew, although he could not have told through what channel the knowledge had been conveyed to him, that he was being watched by someone or something from behind. With a gasp that constricted his heart like a vice, he slowly turned his head, to see standing on the threshold, clearly outlined in the semi-darkness, and seeming from the depths of its cowl to be gazing fixedly at him--the figure of the Grey Monk!

A cry of terror broke from his lips, the bundle of bonds dropped from his nerveless fingers, his knees gave way under him, and sinking to the ground, he covered his face with his hands, and so shut out that dread appearance. An instant later he heard the heavy door swing sullenly to, and its bolt shoot into the socket. He was a prisoner in the strong room.

CHAPTER XXXVII.

THE DEFEAT OF ROGUERY.

In the course of the preceding month the apparition of the Grey Monk had been seen on three different occasions after its first appearance to Bessie Ogden, each time by one or another of the domestics at the Chase. Bessie had been scouted and scolded both by Trant and Mrs. Burton, the housekeeper, till at length she was almost ready to believe that she must have been the victim of an optical delusion; and yet, strange to say, it was to no less a person than Trant himself that the Grey Monk next appeared. It was late at night--close upon midnight, in fact--when Trant, who had been some time in bed, but was not yet asleep, suddenly called to mind that he had inadvertently left his bunch of keys downstairs in the servants' hall. On no account was it advisable that he should leave it there till morning; the other servants rose before he did, and there was no telling, with his keys at their command, in what way they might choose to take advantage of his oversight. It would never do to leave such a temptation in their way. Accordingly, he scrambled into a few clothes, thrust his feet into a pair of slippers, and started to go downstairs.

He got as far as the gallery, and then stopped, suddenly frozen to the spot. There, pacing slowly to and fro by the light of a half-moon, which streamed in slantwise through the east window, with bowed head and hands clasped in front of him, was the Grey Monk! Trant's jaw fell, and his eyes seemed to start from their orbits. A moment or two he stared; then he turned and, without a word or a sound, made his way back to his room, shaking in every limb like a huge jelly, and in mortal dread lest a ghostly hand should clutch him from behind.

Next morning he sought an opportunity of unburdening his mind to Sir Gilbert, only to be snapped at and told that he was an old fool for his pains.

"Let me hear of your having whispered a word about this idiotic rubbish, either in the servants' hall or outside the house, and it will be worse for you," said the Baronet, in his most minatory tone. "I'm ashamed of you, Trant, at your time of life."

For all that, Sir Gilbert did not rest till he had told Lady Pell, who in return confided to him his grandson's adventure in the spinny, as related to her by the latter.

"It is most annoying--most disturbing and annoying," said the Baronet, "and I don't at all know what to do in the matter. Perhaps the best thing will be to do nothing, but to keep on ignoring the whole business as I have done from the first. How is it the apparition never troubles me? I only wish it would! It would not escape me, I warrant you, till I had found out something definite about it. Let us hope, however, that we have heard the last of it for a long time to come."

But it was a hope not destined to be fulfilled.

In the course of the following fortnight two more appearances were reported to the Baronet, both coming from members of his own household. In these cases the figure was avouched to have been encountered outside the house and in two widely separated parts of the grounds.

When, on the morning to which we have now come, Mr. Lewis Clare failed to make his appearance at the breakfast table, Sir Gilbert, in something of a huff, sent a servant to his room with an ironical inquiry whether they might expect to see him downstairs by luncheon time. Presently the man came back with the news that Mr. Clare was not in his room and that his bed did not appear to have been slept in. Thereupon the Baronet's eyes met those of Lady Pell. "What fresh folly has he been guilty of? What further disgrace is he going to bring upon himself and me?" were the questions they mutely asked. But to the servant he merely nodded and said, "That will do."

A little later, when her ladyship and Miss Thursby got up from table, he remarked to the former, "I will see you in the course of the morning"; which meant, "As soon as I have any news you shall be told it." Then to himself he added, "I suppose I must employ Lisle to hunt him up again."

He lingered over his breakfast this morning in a way very unusual with him, as if hoping against hope that, from minute to minute, his grandson might make his appearance.

He was leaning back in his chair, a prey to a host of bitter thoughts, when Trant, looking at once mysterious and important, entered the room, carrying in one hand a letter, and in the other a large key.

"If you please, Sir Gilbert," he said, in deprecatory tones, for he knew how ill his master brooked being disturbed when in a brown study, "this letter, addressed to you, with the key of the strong room, has just been found on your study table by the housemaid whose duty it is to dust the room. As the letter is marked 'Immediate,' I thought that perhaps----"

"The key of the strong room lying on my study table, do you say?" broke in Sir Gilbert. "How could it possibly have got there?"

While speaking he had taken both the key and the letter. Having put on his glasses he looked at the address on the letter and shook his head. The writing was wholly strange to him. Wondering greatly, he laid the key on the table in front of him and broke open the envelope. Trant stole out of the room on tiptoe; he seemed to scent a mystery.

"Should Sir Gilbert Clare," began the letter, "feel anxious as to the whereabouts of his self-styled grandson he will find him locked up in the strong room, the key of which accompanies this missive. It will be for the young man to explain to Sir

Gilbert's satisfaction the nature of the business which took him there between twelve and one o'clock this morning.

"Further, it may be as well to open Sir Gilbert Clare's eyes to a fact in respect of which he seems to have been deliberately hoodwinked. Luigi Rispani is *not* his grandson, but merely a nephew of the woman who married John Alexander Clare. The said John Alexander Clare had but one child--a daughter--who died when a few months old. In accepting Luigi Rispani as his grandson Sir Gilbert Clare has allowed himself to be made the victim of a fraud.

"One Who Knows."

For full ten minutes after he had finished reading the note Sir Gilbert sat without moving, his eyes closed and his chin sunk on his breast. So old and worn and white did he look that he might have been taken for one already dead. Many times in his life had he drunk deep of the waters of bitterness, but perhaps never before had they tasted so utterly bitter. For the moment his soul cried out, "I can bear no more! Give me death--give me anything rather than this!" But presently the strong man within him, which was not yet wholly overcome, began to reassert itself, and a voice seemed to say to him, "If what you have just heard be the truth, then is it better that the truth should be known, at whatever cost to yourself and others. Anything is better than that you should remain the unwitting participant in a living lie." He opened his eyes, sighed and sat up. What a change had come over his life in a few short minutes!

Presently he touched the handbell on the table, to which Trant, who had been listening for it, at once responded.

"Present my compliments to Lady Pell, and tell her that I am very desirous of having a word with her here, and as soon as Mr. Lisle arrives request him to come to me." He felt that he must share his burden with someone; it was too weighty to be borne alone.

Lady Pell was quickly on the scene.

"Sit down, Louisa, and oblige me by reading this, which was brought me a few minutes ago," said Sir Gilbert as he handed her the letter.

She took it without a word. When she had read to the end, she turned a scared face on her kinsman.

"This is indeed terrible, if it be true," she said as she gave him back the letter.

"Here is the key of the strong room to confirm it."

At this juncture Everard Lisle entered the room. At sight of Lady Pell he was about to retire, but Sir Gilbert motioned to him to come forward. "Read this, which was found on my study table about half-an-hour ago," he said.

Lisle, standing within a yard of his elbow, did as he was told. He, too, was utterly dumbfoundered and for a few moments knew not what to say. Then a thought struck him. "According to this, sir, Mr. Lewis is still locked up in the strong room."

"Aye--like a rat in a trap," replied the Baronet grimly. "Suppose we go and release him and hear what he has to say for himself. Do you take the key, Lisle. Come, Louisa; I must ask you to keep us company. This seems to me an affair which may necessitate the presence of witnesses."

"Now, be good enough to unlock the door of the strong room," he said to Lisle when they had reached the study.

Everard did as he was told and pulled wide the heavy door.

"Anybody inside?" demanded Sir Gilbert sharply. He was standing just behind Lisle, but his eyes failed to pierce the semi-obscurity of the room.

"Mr. Lewis Clare, sir," replied Everard.

"Ah, it *is* true, then!" He drew in his breath like one suddenly struck in a vital part and caught at Lisle's shoulder. A shiver passed over him from head to foot, but his voice was firm enough when next he spoke.

"You there, come out--come out this instant," he commanded.

Never was there a more abject-looking being than he who responded to the summons, with his blanched face, his dishevelled hair, and his fear-distended eyes. He seemed to crawl rather than walk into the outer room. Sir Gilbert pointed to a chair. "Seat yourself there," he said. The look with which he regarded him was a mixture of pity, contempt and scorn.

Then, in an aside to Lady Pell, he added: "I thank heaven that not a drop of my ancestors' blood runs in this craven's veins. But pray be seated. This may prove to be a lengthy business." As he spoke, he drew a chair forward near his own and they both sat down. Then turning to Everard, he said: "Mr. Lisle, I think I have heard you say that you write shorthand."

"Yes, Sir Gilbert."

"Then station yourself there opposite me. I want you to take notes of the questions I am about to put to this wretched young man and of his answers to the same."

There were so many questions he wanted to ask that for a few moments he seemed at a loss where or how to begin. Luigi, of course, knew nothing about the letter which had reached him so mysteriously with the key of the strong room, and was still unaware that Sir Gilbert had the slightest suspicion of the gross imposition of which he had been made the victim.

For a brief space Sir Gilbert seemed lost in thought, then lifting his head and bending on Luigi from between his contracted lids a look which caused the young fellow to shrink and cower even more abjectly than before, he said: "Luigi Rispani, for that is your name, I know you at last for the vile impostor and cheat that you are. Whether you are aware of it or not, let me tell you this: you have been guilty of that which would inevitably consign you to a felon's cell should I decide to proceed to extremities against you, and, indeed, you deserve nothing less at my hands. But what I may decide to do in the matter will depend in a great measure upon yourself. Answer the questions I am about to put to you truthfully and without prevarication, and I may be induced to deal leniently by you. Lie to me, or strive in any way to throw dust in my eyes, and the moment I discover you in the attempt I will have you given into the custody of the police and will proceed against you with the utmost rigour of the law. What say you, sir? Are you prepared to tell me the absolute and positive truth without a shadow of concealment on your part, or are you not?"

"I *will* tell you the truth, Sir Gilbert, and nothing but the truth; I really will," whined Luigi, who was seated sideways on a chair, huddled up and with one leg crossed under him, his back arched and his head sunk between his shoulders. Every minute or two he was seized with a spasm of nervous trembling, resulting partly from fright and partly from the chill due to his long imprisonment in the strong room.

"So be it," replied Sir Gilbert grimly. "But bear this in mind, that I know more, far more than you think I do." He paused, cleared his voice and then continued. "Luigi Rispani, you are *not* my grandson--that I know already. But tell me this: what relation are you to Captain Verinder, and also to the widow of my late son, John Alexander Clare?"

"Captain Verinder is my great-uncle. Mrs. Clare is my aunt--my father and she were brother and sister."

"How, and with whom did the fraud originate, which led to your imposing yourself on me as my grandson?"

"It was all my great-uncle's doing. It was he who originated the scheme, and it was he who persuaded my aunt and me to join him in carrying it out."

"After all, then, my instinct was not at fault," murmured Sir Gilbert to himself. "It was not prejudice, but Nature's own monition that bade me beware of Verinder."

"You see, Sir Gilbert, this is how it was," went on Luigi, who now seemed eagerly anxious to unbosom himself. "When Mrs. Clare came to London she knew nothing about her husband having been your son. He died in America, and, as it would appear, without having told her anything about his relatives in England. It was Captain Verinder who ferreted out the facts of the case, and everything that followed was due to him. Mrs. Clare's only child had died when it was a few months old, but he persuaded her that if she were to introduce herself to you, bringing a son and heir with her, she would have a far greater claim on your generosity, and might count upon a very different reception at your hands, from any that would be given her as the childless widow she really was. Of myself I can only say that I was weak enough to be overborne by my uncle's persuasions, and--and that I ultimately consented to allow myself to be passed off as your grandson."

Luigi ceased, and for a little while no one spoke. Sir Gilbert, in an absent way, was rubbing his eyeglasses with his pocket-handkerchief, and apparently turning over in his mind what had just been told him. Looking up at length, he said: "You have been frank with me so far, or so I have reason to believe. I hope you will not be less so in answering my next question. Tell me, then, if you please, to what circumstances it was owing that I found you locked up in my strong room."

Luigi hung his head in a way he had not done before, while two spots of vivid red flamed out on his sallow cheeks. Then, flinging up his head with a sort of half-defiant air, he said: "I promised to tell you the truth, Sir Gilbert, and I will. Last night, after waiting till the clock had struck twelve, I came here, picked the lock of your drawer, found the key of the strong room, opened the door and went inside. My intention was to abstract certain American bonds which I knew were there, and pass them over to my uncle for him to dispose of."

"This latter transaction, then, was one in which your uncle was also mixed up?"

"It was his notion entirely, that I should get possession of the bonds. We were both cornered. Nearly all the money you gave us for travelling purposes, had been lost at a Brussels gaming-table. We succeeded in borrowing a hundred pounds on our joint note of hand, which will fall due about a week hence. In order to meet it and so keep the affair from coming to your ears, which it otherwise inevitably would do, my uncle egged me on to abstract four of the bonds in question, the proceeds of the sale of which would have extricated us from our predicament."

"As pretty a piece of villainy as I have heard tell of for many a long day!" remarked Sir Gilbert. "But you were disturbed by someone when in the midst of your nefarious work, otherwise I should not have found you this morning under lock and key."

Luigi nodded, and his eyes, shifting for the first time from Sir Gilbert's face, turned to Lady Pell and then to Lisle, with a look which neither of them could fathom.

"And who was that someone?" demanded Sir Gilbert. "Some member of my household, as a matter of course; still, I fail to understand why--eh, what is that you say? I did not catch your words."

The words uttered at first in little more than a whisper, were now spoken so that all present could hear them.

"It was the Grey Monk who shut me up in the strong room."

CHAPTER XXXVIII.

UNANSWERED QUESTIONS.

Luigi Rispani's quietly spoken words sent a simultaneous thrill through his three listeners.

It may be said to have been the very last answer to his question which Sir Gilbert had expected to receive. Indeed, so disconcerted by it was he, that for a few moments he sat like a man mentally bewildered, who has been asked to accept a statement which his reason refuses to credit, but which he is utterly without the means of refuting. It will be remembered that Lady Pell had already told him of Luigi's strange experience that night in the spinny, besides which, there were all those other occasions of late when the apparition was said to have been seen by different members of the household--a body of testimony to which, when considered in the aggregate, he could no longer refuse to accord a certain amount of credence. There were circumstances, however, connected with this last alleged appearance which put it on an entirely different plane from the others, and which could be explained away by no theory either of optics or of self-created illusions with which Sir Gilbert was acquainted.

"And do you mean deliberately to assert," he said at length, addressing himself to Luigi, "that what you have just told us with regard to this so-called Grey Monk is the positive truth, and not an audacious attempt on your part to smother up the real facts of the case?"

"It is the absolute truth, Sir Gilbert, incredible though it may seem. I had heard no sound, but all at once some instinct told me that I was no longer alone. I turned, and by the light of my lantern saw the figure standing in the shadow a little way back in the other room. Its face was towards me, but so hidden by its cowl, that hardly anything could be seen of it except its long grizzled beard. What followed, I hardly know, only that I heard the door shut and the key turned, and realised that I was a prisoner."

"I presume that neither of you spoke to the other?"

"Not a word passed between us."

For a little while Sir Gilbert remained buried in thought. Then he said: "You may go for the present and remain in your own room till I send for you. In what way I may ultimately determine to deal with you I have not yet made up my mind."

When Luigi--glad enough, one may be sure, to get away--had crept out of the room with the air of a whipt cur, Sir Gilbert turned to Lisle. "You must get through your work without me this morning. I need scarcely tell you that I am very much put about by this business. Preserve the notes you have taken, and when you have an hour to spare you may write them out for me. Perhaps I may never need them, but one cannot tell. Come, Louisa."

They went no farther than the morning-room. Lady Pell could not help seeing how shaken Sir Gilbert was, and at her persuasion he drank a glass of sherry.

"The shocking disclosures of this morning," he began after a few minutes given to silent cogitation, "require, as it seems to me, to be considered from two very opposite points of view. On the one hand, there is the audacious palming off upon me of a supposititious grandson and all the side issues resulting therefrom--as to which I shall have something to say later on. On the other hand, there is this mysterious affair of the Grey Monk, to whose most opportune interference we seem to owe it that Captain Verinder's vile scheme has suffered such a signal collapse. Now there cannot, I think, be the slightest doubt that, let the origin of the previous appearances have been what it may, there was nothing in the least degree supernatural about last night's manifestation. That it was a being of flesh and blood as much as you or I, to my mind admits of no question."

"There I agree with you, Gilbert," remarked Lady Pell. "It was no ghost that locked up Luigi Rispani in the strong room."

"And it was no ghostly hand that wrote the letter which has served so completely to unseal my eyes."

"But who can this mysterious personage be, and where can he have sprung from?"

"And whence and from whom did he obtain the information embodied in his letter to me, which we now know to be absolutely true. Those are questions, Louisa, which there seems little present probability of either you or I being able to answer."

"At any rate," said Lady Pell with a shrug, "it's far from pleasant to know that, after everybody is in bed, the house is perambulated by someone who, to answer some purpose of his own, chooses to disguise himself as the family spectre. What becomes of him in the daytime? Who supplies him with food? He would seem to be able to come and go just as he likes, because he has mostly been seen out of doors in one part of the grounds or another."

Sir Gilbert shook his head. "Mysteries all; more than that we cannot say. But stranger than all to me is the fact that, whoever he may be, he should have a knowledge of certain circumstances in the life of my son which only someone intimately acquainted with him during his brief American career would be at all likely to have. But from beginning to end the affair is altogether beyond my comprehension."

"The allegations conveyed in the letter affect Mrs. Clare most seriously."

"They do indeed. You have heard what Rispani said--that she was a consenting party to the fraud concocted by Verinder. But her every action from the time of her introduction to me affords incontestable proof of the fact. Oh, it is vile--vile I could not have believed it of her. No one could have appeared more open and straightforward than she. I had grown to like her, Louisa--to like her very much. I shall feel the blow for many a day to come--no, not for many, because at the most my remaining days can be but few."

"According to the last note you had from her, Mrs. Clare may be here any day."
"Almost at any hour, unless she should choose to break her journey at London instead of coming direct through to the Chase."
"You will see her when she arrives?"
"It will be no more than just that I should do so. Every opportunity shall be afforded her of refuting the charges which have been brought against her, but that she will succeed in doing so I greatly doubt."
Again for two or three minutes he seemed lost in thought, then he went on: "I cannot deny that, in a certain sense, it is an immense relief to me to find that Rispani is not my grandson. I have felt from the first, not merely that he would fail to be a credit to the family, but that he would be nearly sure to entail positive discredit on it, and that the unsullied name of the Clares would be passed on by him fouled and dishonoured to whomsoever might succeed him. Yes, I can afford to be very thankful that, being such as he is, he is proved to be no grandson of mine. Better, far better, that the direct line should die with me than that it should be continued in one so utterly unworthy of the traditions of his race. But with Alec's widow it is different. Rispani the impostor we have done with; he will go and trouble us no more; but she--she will still remain my daughter-in-law; how vilely soever she may have acted, whatever she may have been guilty of, the tie is one which cannot be severed."
"With regard to Rispani and that unscrupulous uncle of his, I suppose it is not your intention to take proceedings against them?"
"It would only be treating them after their deserts were I to do so. But the affair will be productive of talk and scandal enough without that."
At this juncture there came a tap at the door which was followed by the entrance of Everard Lisle.
"Mr. Luigi Rispani has just left the house, sir," he said. "I thought it right that you should be told as soon as possible. This note, which he sent me by one of the servants, explains his reason for the step."
Sir Gilbert took the note, and having adjusted his glasses, he read aloud as follows:

"Dear Lisle--After what has come to light this morning I find I have not enough courage left to face Sir Gilbert a second time; consequently think it best to take my departure and so save all further bother.
"As I don't suppose anybody will think it worth while to confiscate my few traps, will you be good enough at your convenience to have them forwarded by rail to the address given below.
"With reference to what passed this morning, it seems to me that my wisest plan is to say nothing. *Qui s'excuse* , they say, but, in my case, it would be hopeless to attempt the first, and I have surely done enough of the latter to satisfy anybody.

At any rate, 'them's my sentiments.'
"Yours truly
"L. R."

"What shocking flippancy in one so young!" said Lady Pell.
"Let him go; it is perhaps as well," remarked the Baronet as he gave the note back to Lisle. "His doing so solves what otherwise might have proved a difficulty to me. I think we have already got from him all the information needful for our purpose, but should we require him at any future time, his note will furnish us with a clue to his whereabouts."

Luigi had stolen out of the house almost like a thief in the night--never to cross its threshold again. So many things had happened and in so short a time, and there was mixed up in them such an element of the inexplicable, that he seemed to have lost control of his thoughts, which kept veering about from one point to another unable to fix themselves on anything for more than a few seconds at a time, and tormenting him now with one question and now with another, to which no answer was forthcoming. Who, or what was the Grey Monk? Were it merely a figment of the brain, an illusion of the senses, would it have had the power, not to speak of the will, to shut the door of the strong room upon him and turn the key? And yet to regard it as a being of flesh and blood was to confront himself with one enigma after another and all equally insoluble. Then again, through what channel had Sir Gilbert made the fatal discovery that he, Luigi Rispani, was not his grandson? Evidently no suspicion of the truth had been in his mind only a few hours before. At dinner on Sunday Sir Gilbert had questioned him about his Continental trip, and had seemed satisfied with his answers. The bubble had burst between ten o'clock on Sunday night and half past ten on Monday morning. Whose was the hand that had wrought the mischief?
It was with a sad heart and reluctant feet that Luigi took his way towards the hotel at Mapleford where his uncle was awaiting him. The Captain had scarcely expected him quite so soon, deeming it likely that he would not see his way to leave the Chase till after luncheon. The door of the sitting-room was open and he heard his nephew asking for him below. "Is it success, or failure?" he asked himself, not without a certain tingling at the nerves, while Luigi was coming upstairs. One glance at the latter's face was enough as he halted on the threshold and met his uncle's gaze. Failure complete and unmistakable was written on every line of it. The Captain drew a long breath and set his teeth hard

for a moment or two. "So," he said with a sort of venomous bitterness as Luigi advanced, "you have come to tell me that you have made a mess of the affair! It is just what I have dreaded all along. I was a fool to let you undertake the job. I ought to have carried it through myself."

"I wish with all my heart that you had. What I have come to tell you is that the game's up!"

"What do you mean?" demanded Verinder, his lips fading to a blue-white.

"Just what I say. We're ruined--there's no other word for it. Everything is known to Sir Gilbert."

"Everything is a big word."

"Not bigger than the occasion warrants. But perhaps you would like to hear how it has all come about."

"I should indeed. But before you begin pour yourself out a thimbleful of that brandy on the sideboard. You look as if the blood in your veins had turned to water."

"Small wonder if it has, as you will say yourself by the time I have told you all."

We need not follow Luigi in his narrative, nor record his uncle's comments thereon. There were several points about it which puzzled the Captain, even as they had puzzled his nephew, and for which he could find no adequate explanation. But that in no wise affected the one overwhelming fact, that his edifice of fraud, notwithstanding all the pains he had been at in the building of it, had crumbled to pieces, struck down by some unseen hand, and he was far from certain yet that it might not involve him personally in the catastrophe.

For the first and all-important question which he asked himself was, as to the steps Sir Gilbert Clare might decide upon taking now that the nefarious plot of which he had been made the victim was laid bare from beginning to end. Would he, while the first flame of his resentment still burned fiercely, cause a warrant to be issued for the arrest of one Augustus Verinder? It was a possibility which might well cause even a man who prided himself on his nerve to shake in his shoes, and if the Captain did not exactly do that, he was certainly rendered excessively uncomfortable thereby. His somewhat cynical philosophy notwithstanding, the prospect of two or three years' incarceration in a gaol, with all its concomitant pains and penalties, was no more alluring to him than it is to the majority of people.

But presently a thought came to him from which he did not fail to derive a certain measure of comfort. It would be next to impossible for Sir Gilbert to institute proceedings against him without including his daughter-in-law in the indictment as an accomplice, and one almost equally guilty with himself. Now it seemed to him that the Baronet would think twice before taking so extreme a step, seeing that whatever Giovanna might have been guilty of nothing could alter the fact that she was a member of the Clare family; and that Sir Gilbert would deliberately drag one of his own name through the mire of a prosecution for fraud, seemed, considering the kind of man he was, to be scarcely conceivable.

The Captain had just arrived at this comfortable conclusion when the current of his thoughts was broken by an exclamation from Luigi, who, with his hands deep in his pockets, had been staring disconsolately out of the window for some minutes past.

"If that's not Aunt Giovanna's trunk on the top of a fly which is crawling down the street, I'll eat my hat! Of course it's hers! I can make out her initials on it."

"Then run downstairs; stop the cab and bring your aunt up here," cried the Captain as he started to his feet.

It was indeed Giovanna, back from Italy. She had picked up her maid on her way through London, and on arriving at Mapleford station had hired a cab to convey her to Maylings. But she never got as far as Maylings. The fatal tidings were told her in that room of the *Crown and Cushion* hotel.

She bore the blow very well; but she would feel the effects of it later on far more than at the time. For the present she was simply stunned. She had had much more at stake than either Verinder or her nephew. They had merely lost what had never been theirs to lose. She had forfeited that which, had she not allowed herself to be led away by Verinder's sophistries, would have remained hers through life as an inalienable right--her position as daughter-in-law to the Master of Withington Chase.

But whatever she felt all she said to the Captain was: "I have to thank you for this, Uncle Verinder. If you had let me go to Sir Gilbert, as I wished to do, and tell him the truth--that my child died in infancy--he would not have repulsed me. No, he would have acknowledged me and have made much of me, and at his death I should not have been forgotten. But I listened to you and have lost everything. Oh! I think we are all very rightly punished."

CHAPTER XXXIX.

THE COUNSEL OF EXPERIENCE.

There is no knowing how long Sir Gilbert Clare might have kept on expecting the arrival of his daughter-in-law had it not been for a visit which Mrs. Tew paid him in the course of the day following Luigi's departure from the Chase.

Late in the afternoon of the previous day Mrs. Clare's maid had arrived at Maylings in a cab, bringing with her a note from her mistress, in which the canon's widow was informed that although the writer had returned from Italy it was not her present intention to again take up her abode in the house which Sir Gilbert Clare had so generously placed at her disposal. Would Mrs. Tew, therefore, be at the trouble to hand over to her maid whatever personal belongings she had left behind when she went abroad--a request with which that lady had at once complied. In answer to her questions the maid could tell her nothing, except that the fly in which she and her mistress were being conveyed from the railway station had been met and stopped by Mr. Lewis Clare; that Mrs. Clare had thereupon alighted and had accompanied him into the *Crown and Cushion* hotel (at a window of which she, Lucille, had caught a glimpse of Captain Verinder), and that she was still there, awaiting Lucille's return from Maylings.

From all this it was clear to Sir Gilbert that he need no longer expect the coming of his daughter-in-law. She had been intercepted by Rispani and Verinder, had been told of what had come to light during her absence, and, like her nephew, had preferred an ignominious flight to facing the man she had so bitterly wronged. Evidently she had no plea to urge in extenuation of what she had done. There was nothing for it but to accept her guilt as proved, and to try to forget that any such person had ever intruded her presence upon him.

As we have seen, Lady Pell had long ago penetrated Everard Lisle's love secret, and of late certain signs which, to any eyes less experienced than hers, would have passed unnoted, seemed to indicate that the time had come when he need no longer delay his confession, but might with some measure of confidence ask for that which she felt nearly sure would not be denied him. Many were the opportunities she contrived for throwing the young people together, but day after day went by and the all-important question still remained unasked. At length she began to lose patience with Lisle. "Who would have dreamt that so much timidity lay at the back of that confident bearing and resolute face? Oh, to be a man and afraid of a girl's No! Your laggard courage evidently needs whipping up, my good sir, and mine shall be the hand to do it!"

On the Saturday she said to Sir Gilbert: "I have several times promised myself a visit to the ruins of Dunarvon Castle, but something has always intervened. Now, however, I will put it off no longer, or the last of the fine weather will be gone. You placed the wagonette at my disposal whenever I might choose to avail myself of it, so I shall take Miss Thursby and Mrs. Tew with me, and, as we can't very well dispense with the services of a gentleman on such an occasion, I want you to spare me Mr. Lisle for the whole of Monday."

"Certainly, Louisa. Utilise his services in whatever way may seem best to you."

"I am quite aware that it is not a bit of use asking you to join our little party."

"Not the slightest use, Louisa. As you are aware, I never go anywhere."

"I can't help saying, Gilbert, that it would be better for you in many ways if you did go somewhere. A man in your position, and with your duties, has no business to make a recluse of himself."

"I don't dispute your dictum, only, as it happens, we are not all made after the same pattern. Several years ago the world had become such a tiresome place to me that henceforward I determined to see as little of it as possible. It may have been a weak resolve to come to, but, such as it was, I have kept it, and I am afraid that now I am far too old to change."

Everard Lisle could almost have gone down on his knees to Lady Pell when told of the good fortune in store for him. He had already been to Dunarvon and knew of the lovely woodland walks by which the ruins were surrounded, and that he and Ethel should be able to spend a whole autumn afternoon among them seemed almost too much happiness to be possible. That Lady Pell would afford them ample opportunities for wandering away by their two selves he did not doubt. What if he were to seize the occasion to break the rule of silence he had hitherto imposed on himself, and try for the second time to win where he had failed once already? Well, he would be guided by circumstances. Should a propitious moment offer itself, he would not let it slip, but if not, then would he wait a little longer.

Sir Gilbert in person saw them off. This morning, or so it seemed o her ladyship, he looked more cheerful and in better spirits than she had seen him in since the affair of the strong-room, now a week ago. "He will get over the worst of it in time, as we do with all our troubles," she told herself: "only, he will carry the scar of it to his dying day."

A drive of a dozen miles brought our little party to their destination, whereupon Lady Pell issued her instructions. The first thing to do was to explore the ruins under the conduct of the authorised guide.

After that would come luncheon in a room in the custodian's cottage, which was frequently utilised for that purpose. They had brought their own hamper of good things with them, and their own man to wait upon them. After which it would be time enough to decide how the rest of the day should be spent.

At the end of an hour, having seen all there was to be seen, Lady Pell paid and dismissed the guide; then, in an aside to Mrs. Tew, she said: "I want you to engage Miss Thursby for a few minutes while I have a little private talk with Mr. Lisle."

The canon's widow nodded, and presently the young people found themselves drawn apart, to all appearance in a quite fortuitous way.
"If it won't be troubling you too much, Mr. Lisle," said Lady Pell, "I think I should like to take another peep at that old dungeon about which the guide told us that gruesome legend. Such places have a peculiar but quite absurd fascination for me."
Having taken a second peep into the dungeon, her ladyship led the way up the winding stairs which brought them out on the leads of the keep. "Now that we have got rid of that tiresome guide, one can enjoy the view and be left to find out its most interesting features for oneself."
Lisle did not answer; he was wondering what had become of Ethel and why they couldn't all four be enjoying the view from the keep.
"If I had known that Dunarvon was half as picturesque as it is," said Lady Pell presently, "I would certainly have got Miss Thursby to bring her drawing materials with her. There are charming sketches to be made from half-a-dozen different points of view."
"Would it not be possible to come to Dunarvon on some future day and rectify the omission?" queried Everard with the most innocent air imaginable.
"Come again another day? Impossible!" cried her ladyship. "My time at the Chase is nearly up. A few more days, and Miss Thursby and I will be winging our flight elsewhere. And high time too, in my opinion." She was looking full at Lisle, and he felt himself colouring under her regard.
"Why do you say--'and high time too,' Lady Pell? I--I fail to understand you." It was many a year since his cheeks had burnt as hotly as they did at that moment.
"I should have thought my words were plain enough to be understood by anybody. However, since it seems that nothing else will do, I will deal with you still more plainly." Laying a hand for a moment on his sleeve, she said: "Everard Lisle, you are in love with Ethel Thursby--and small blame to you either! Ah! you needn't start. I've known it all along. Of course you thought, as most of your sex do in such cases, that nobody could see what was the matter with you; whereas to me--not that I set myself up as being cleverer than other people--it was as plain as a pikestaff. Very well. Perceiving what ailed you, I went out of my way to make opportunities for you to be together, and indeed, in a quiet way, did all I could to help you. And with what result, pray? Simply none at all. Week after week has gone by, and here you are, to all seeming, not a bit nearer what you are dying to possess than you were when I arrived at Withington Chase. I am disappointed in you, Everard Lisle."
Her ladyship's somewhat lengthy diatribe had afforded Everard time to recover his self-possession. "Lady Pell," he returned with some emotion, "that in you I have all along had a friend I have felt assured in my own mind, but I must confess I did not think that the feelings with which I regard Miss Thursby had betrayed themselves so plainly on the surface as they seem to have done. However, you have surprised my secret, and I am confident it could not be in better keeping. You deem me dilatory, in that I have so long delayed putting my fortune to the

touch; but there is one circumstance I may be permitted to urge in extenuation of which I feel assured you have no knowledge. Six months ago I proposed to Miss Thursby and was rejected. Can you wonder, then, if I hesitate and seem to shilly-shally before venturing to run the same risk again?"

"That is something which I never so much as suspected," replied her ladyship. "Yes, that certainly puts a somewhat different complexion on the affair. But I would not let myself be too much discouraged by it if I were you, Mr. Lisle."

"I don't think I let it discourage me overmuch," said Everard with a smile. "Only, as I said before, it lies at the back of my apparent hesitation."

"Then take the advice of an old woman who has seen something of the world, and hesitate no longer."

"Ah! then you think I have a chance of success?" exclaimed Lisle with a sudden glow which seemed to irradiate him from head to foot. "You have seen something--you know something?"

"Not quite so fast, my young friend, if you please," said her ladyship in her dryest accents. "I know nothing--absolutely nothing. No whisper in connection with yourself and her has ever passed Miss Thursby's lips to me. As for what I have seen, or may have fancied I have seen, that is a matter of no moment and concerns no one but myself. Still, I say to you as I said before: were I in your place I should hesitate no longer. Are you prepared to seize the first occasion that offers itself?"

"After what has passed between us, I should indeed be a coward not to do so."

"Very well then, the needful opportunity shall be given you after luncheon this afternoon."

CHAPTER XL.

"LOVE TOOK UP THE HARP OF LIFE."

Everard Lisle seemed to tread on air as he walked beside Lady Pell to the custodian's cottage, where they found Mrs. Tew and Ethel awaiting them. Luncheon was ready and they at once sat down to it. They made a very merry little party, Everard in especial being in the gayest of spirits.

"Now, what I should recommend you young people to do," said her ladyship by-and-by, "is to go in search of the Haunted Pool, about which the guide was telling us this morning. He said it was not above a mile away, and, in any case, the woods themselves are most lovely just now. As for Mrs. Tew and I, we shall have a couple of comfortable chairs taken out into the shade of yonder oak, and there have a quiet gossip to ourselves. And don't forget that tea will be ready at five o'clock to the minute."

We may be sure that Lisle and Ethel were by no means loth to carry out her ladyship's behest, and presently they were lost to view among the green shadows of the wood. Lady Pell gazed after them with a well-satisfied smile, but it was with a sigh that the canon's widow followed their retreating figures. "Oh, to be young again and in love!" she said, hardly witting that she spoke aloud.

"And have all the troubled record of our lives to go through again," said her ladyship. "For my part no such desire ever enters my mind. All things considered, I'm pretty well content to be as I am."

Perhaps for the moment she failed to remember that her life had many compensations denied to poor Mrs. Tew.

It was one of those lovely October days which make a golden bridge between summer and winter. The woods were clothed with their richest garments--a kaleidoscope of gorgeous tints, albeit the vesture of decay; The dry leaves rustled under their feet, and little splashes of colour kept dropping round them as they went. Here and there a rabbit peered cautiously at them for a moment, showed a flash of white and was gone. Somewhere out of sight a robin was fluting a monody to the dying year. They walked on for some time in silence; Everard seemed to have left all his gaiety behind him. There was something about his changing moods to-day which Ethel failed to understand. She had known all along that his love had never altered or varied in the slightest, and of late her own heart had whispered its secret to her in accents she could no longer mistake. More than once during the last few weeks she had felt nearly sure Everard was on the point of saying that which, almost unknown to herself, she was secretly longing to hear; but the propitious moment had gone by and he had not spoken, and not improbably it was the vague sense of disappointment that had crept over her at such times which had first served to open her eyes to the truth as regarded herself.

But somehow to-day she had no prevision of what was so imminent. Not even now that she had come with him for a solitary woodland ramble. For that day at least he seemed to have absolved himself from all serious thoughts, from all matters of moment, and to be transformed for the time into the similitude of a laughing, light-hearted school-boy. She could not know--how should she--that it was her presence, that it was the privilege of being able to spend several consecutive hours in her sweet company, which had thus had power to metamorphose him almost beyond his knowledge of himself.

From the summit of the keep he had caught a silvery gleam of water in a hollow no great distance away. It was probably the Haunted Pool, about which the guide had told them, and lay darkling in its forest hollow, with a fringe of bulrushes, and outside that a margin of soft turf that was pleasant to the feet. For all it had the name of being haunted, there was nothing weird or uncanny about the place, but rather an air of sweet solitariness as though of one of Nature's temples, sacred to the shy creatures of the wood, upon which for any human foot to intrude was to break some mystic spell.

For a few moments Lisle and Ethel stood drinking in the silent beauty of the scene. Then said Everard,

"Suppose we rest here awhile, 'the world forgetting, by the world forgot.'" Speaking thus he led the way to the trunk of a tree, blown down in some tempest years before, which had been left unheeded where it had fallen.

And now at length had come the moment so long looked forward to, so long delayed, so long regarded with apprehension, but now at last seized on with a gladness which he himself felt to be closely allied to audacity. For events might yet make a mockery of his gladness and prove it to have no better foundation than a certain oracular utterance on the part of an old lady who believed herself possessed of a gift for seeing farther into a millstone than her neighbours. All this might come to pass of course, and yet he was not at all dismayed. To-day he felt lifted above the common world. For the time he breathed "an ampler ether, a diviner air."

Nevertheless, it was in very commonplace terms that he began what he had to say.

"Do you know, Lady Pell quite startled me as she and I were standing together on the keep before luncheon." He was not looking at Ethel, but leaning forward and punching holes in the turf with the ferrule of his walking-stick.

"I should have thought your nerves proof against anything Lady Pell might have to say to you," answered Ethel smilingly.

"She gave me to understand that her stay at the Chase was drawing to a close, and that in a very little while she and you would be winging your flight elsewhere."

There was a moment's silence, and then Ethel said: "It was a very natural announcement, and I cannot see what there was in it to startle you."

"That is because you look at it from one point of view, and I from another. To you it means fresh faces and other scenes--in short, a change, probably more or less welcome after the quiet and monotony of existence at Withington Chase."

He paused. Ethel was quite aware that he was waiting for her to say: "And from your point of view what does it mean?" By this she needed no one to tell her what his reply would be. Everything had been revealed to her as in a flash, and she marvelled at her blindness. And now the point for her to decide, and that on the instant, was whether she should, or should not, ask him that simple-seeming question, which she felt would but be the precursor to one of infinitely more significance on his part, from answering which there would be no possible escape for her. And in what terms was she prepared to answer it? Her heart-throbs seemed to deafen her and her mind was torn by a conflict of emotions, among which, however, one claimed predominance over the others. She knew and owned to herself that she loved him. Then in the silence a voice spoke. "And from your point of view, Mr. Lisle, what does Lady Pell's announcement mean?" It was as though some force within her had compelled her to put the question in her own despite.

"It means," began Everard, and he paused for an instant as if his breath had suddenly failed him--"it means more, far more than I could tell you in many words." Neither of them had been looking at each other, but Lisle now left off his employment of punching holes in the turf, and drawing himself up, he turned on Ethel a face all aglow with the emotion of the moment.

"When you quit the Chase," he went on, "I shall lose that which to me is the most precious object on earth, and who shall say whether I shall ever find it again? Ethel, on that April day which now seems so long ago that I could fancy it pertained to some prior state of existence, I told you that I loved you, and asked you to become my wife. Your answer was, that you had no love to give me, and that you could never marry me. I took my dismissal and went--indeed, there was nothing else left me to do--not knowing whether I should ever see you again. Then, when, one morning, months afterwards, I came suddenly upon you in one of the garden-paths at the Chase, it seemed as if the gates of Paradise must have opened, and that you had come down its golden stairs to meet me face to face. And the same instant my love for you, which I had locked up in the innermost chamber of my heart as a priceless treasure once more flooded all my being with a rapture of hope. Ethel, that hope has not yet deserted me. If I have not spoken before, it has been because I feared to startle you, because I trembled lest my audacity might be the cause of my losing what I possessed already--your friendship--and yet give me nothing in return. But now the day of timid counsels is over, and at the risk of losing everything I cast silence to the winds. You *must* hear me, you *must* know all, let your sentence be what it may."

He poured forth the words with a fervour with which few who knew him would have credited the ordinarily quiet, self-contained and somewhat self-repressed Everard Lisle. They were both still seated on the trunk of the fallen tree, and he now drew a little closer to Ethel, who, all this time, had been gazing straight

before her with a strangely rapt expression on her face.
"So now again to-day," he went on, "I am going to ask you the self-same question that I asked you on your birthday----"
"Stay I Do not speak another word till you have heard what I have to say."
She had turned and was facing him, the delicate roses of her cheeks somewhat blanched, but her eyes shining clear and full like twin stars of morning. There was that in the way she spoke which compelled attention. Everard was struck dumb. Man though he was, his heart fluttered like a frightened bird. What was he about to be told? That he was too late?--that some rival had been beforehand with him? Where was all his happy confidence now? It seemed to him as if his face had turned grey and old. A shiver went through him from head to foot.
"Come," said Ethel, "let us walk awhile. I have much to tell you."
She rose, and, like an automaton, he did the same. They turned and, side by side, began to pace the turfy margin of the pool. Ethel did not at once break the silence. Many emotions were at work within her, and she wanted to assure herself that she had them well under control before she spoke again.
"Mine is a strange story, Mr. Lisle, as you will at once admit when I have told it you. You know me, and the world knows me, by the name of Ethel Thursby, but that is not my real name. What that is no one knows. Neither does anyone know who were my parents, where I was born, nor, indeed, who I am at all."
Therewith she went on to tell him all those facts in connection with her early history with which the reader is already familiar, beginning with the tragic death of the woman who had passed herself off as her mother on board the *Pandora* , leading up through their adoption of her as their niece by the two Miss Thursbys, to her discovery of the truth as told her in Matthew Thursby's letter on her nineteenth birthday.
It was with growing wonder and interest that Lisle listened to her as, step by step, she unfolded the details of her story.
"I hope you do not for a moment imagine that all this which you have just told me can make a shadow's difference in my love for you," he eagerly began almost before the last words had left her lips.
"But I have still another confession to make," she said, breathing the words, as it were, on the wings of a sigh. "Let me finish, please, before you say anything more."
Then came the confession which the truth that dwelt in her forced from her lips, although it was like tearing her heart to have to make it.
"Mr. Lisle, I have been engaged once already."
"Ah!"--with a swift indrawing of his breath. It was undoubtedly a stab.
"I was young, inexperienced, romantic," resumed Ethel, not allowing herself to notice his exclamation. "He was good-looking and plausible, and he persuaded me into fancying that I loved him, and after a time we became engaged. But, indeed, it was all a foolish fancy, for in my heart I never really cared for him. Fortunately I discovered the sort of man he was before it was too late. He had sought me in the belief that I was an heiress, and when he found I was nothing

of the kind, his only thought was in what way he could most readily break with me. But no such action on his part was called for, for meanwhile it had come to my knowledge that he was already engaged to someone else, to whom he had behaved with a baseness and a heartlessness which seem almost beyond belief. From that moment all was at an end between us. I felt like a prisoner when his fetters are struck off and he is told that he is free. How deep was my thankfulness that my eyes had been mercifully opened in time, I alone can ever know."

Lisle had listened like one devouring her every word, but even before she had come to an end he drew a deep breath of relief. Whomsoever this man might be, she had never really cared for him, her heart had never been touched, he had her own assurance to that effect, and for him, Everard Lisle, that was enough. It was merely one of those lessons of experience which, in one shape or another, we all of us have to learn, only she happily had been spared those bitter consequences which so many of us are called upon to drain to the lees.

If, as a lesson, it served no other purpose, it would at least teach her to discern and appreciate the difference between a spurious love and one that was rooted in the heart's inmost core.

"Since you have chosen to tell me these things," he said, "I can but accept and value them as so many proofs of your confidence, but they weigh with me not so much as the lightest snowflake. They have not moved me by a single hair-breadth from the ground I stood on before, and now, at last, you must listen to what else I have to say. You have no longer any excuse for not doing so. Ethel, answer me once again the question I put to you on your birthday, only this time--this time--let your answer be a different one! Will you be my wife?"

They had come to a halt--why, neither of them could have told--and somehow both her hands found themselves imprisoned in his She did not try to release them, but her face was still averted and the marble of her neck and throat was flushed with tenderest rose.

"Speak, dearest--have you not one word for me?" he pleaded.

Then she turned upon him two darkly shining eyes which seemed the dwelling-place of that great mystery whose other name is love.

"And can you," she said, each syllable punctuated by a heart-throb--"nay, is it even possible, after what I have just told you, that you should still care for one who is nothing more than a waif--who as a wife would come to you parentless, nameless, dowerless? Consider. Take time to think. Do not answer me now, unless----"

"Do not answer you now!" broke in Everard impetuously. "When then should I answer you? Oh, my love--my love--how little you know me! This is my one and only answer."

An instant later she was locked in his arms.

CHAPTER XLI.

SIR GILBERT'S STRANGE EXPERIENCE.

It was considerably past five o'clock before our lovers found themselves back at the cottage, where Lady Pell and Mrs. Tew were awaiting their arrival in order to have tea brought in. When it was over Lady Pell drew Ethel aside.

"Well, my dear, and so he has summoned up courage to speak it last," she said. "I have seen what was coming for a long time, but I certainly thought him somewhat dilatory in bringing matters to a climax. However, all's well that ends well. I congratulate you most heartily. I approve your choice, and so I am sure, will Sir Gilbert when I tell him. Don't say anything now. You and I will have a long talk together in the morning."

Then while the horses were being brought round, she contrived to have a few words with Everard.

"So you have taken an old woman's advice, I find. Of one thing I am quite sure, that you will never have cause to repent having done so. You are a fortunate fellow. You have secured a treasure. Indeed, I'm far from sure that she's not a long way too good for you."

"There I quite agree with you, Lady Pell. Where, indeed, should we find a man worthy of her? But is not that a very good reason why Miss Thursby should have condescended to accept me? We should always try to improve our fellow-creatures where improvement is needed. And that in my case she will find ample scope for her efforts, no one knows better than myself."

He spoke gravely enough, but there was a lurking smile in his eyes which Lady Pell did not fail to note.

"You men have quite a wonderful gift for preaching one doctrine before marriage and its exact opposite after. *Then* you discover that it is yourselves who are perfection and your poor wives who are deficient in this, that or the other quality which you never seemed to take account of before. But it has always been so, and I suppose it always will be."

She was on the point of turning away.

"One moment, Lady Pell," said Everard. "I have not yet told you how deeply grateful I am for the advice you gave me this morning. To that, in a great measure, I owe my present happiness. It gave me just the impulse I needed; it was the spur to urge me forward on the road I ought to go. My sincerest thanks will be yours to the last day of my life."

He was earnest enough now, there could be no mistake on that score.

"Wait till you have been floundering in the quicksands of matrimony for half-a-dozen years and then maybe you will tell a different tale," laughed Lady Pell.

Evening had closed in by the time our party reached the Chase. It was Trant in person, and not one of the footmen, who opened the door for them. He was evidently perturbed; so much so, in fact, that the knot of his white tie had worked itself round under his left ear without his being aware of it. Lady Pell saw at a glance that something was amiss. "What is it, Trant," she asked quickly. "Sir Gilbert----?" Something rose in her throat, but her eyes asked the question her lips refused to finish.

"Sir Gilbert, my lady, is not very well; nothing to be frightened at, if I may take the liberty of saying so," he made haste to add. "If your ladyship will allow me," he went on in a lower voice, "I should like to tell you what I know of the affair before you see Sir Gilbert."

Lady Pell at once led the way to the anteroom. The butler opened the door, bowed her in and followed.

"All morning Sir Gilbert was shut up in his study as usual," began Trant. "At luncheon his appetite was very poor, but he seemed tolerably cheerful. At six o'clock, after I had taken him a glass of Madeira and a biscuit, he went into the hall, put on his soft hat, lighted a cigar and went for a stroll on the terrace, and about half-an-hour later, happening to look through the dining-room window, I saw him going slowly down the steps towards the lower grounds. By this the evening was getting quite dusky. It might have been a quarter of an hour, or twenty minutes later, when I heard the library bell rung sharply. I hurried in and found Sir Gilbert lying back in his easy-chair, looking quite dazed like--in fact, for half a minute or more he stared at me as if he didn't know who I was. 'You rang, sir,' says I. 'Eh?' says he. 'Did I ring, Trant? I don't remember ringing. And I don't remember how I got here. How did I get here, Trant?' shutting his eyes and pressing his hand to his forehead as if trying to bring back something he had forgotten. 'Don't know at all, sir,' says I. 'The bell rang and I answered it.' 'It's very strange, and I can't make it out at all,' says he. 'Be good enough to shut that window, and then bring me a little brandy in a liqueur glass; and, Trant, let me know when the ladies get back from their excursion.'"

Lady Pell had listened with growing impatience to the butler's somewhat long-winded narrative. "Thank you, Trant; I am much obliged to you for telling me this," she said. "You need not trouble to inform Sir Gilbert that I have returned. I will go to him at once. By-the-way, did you hint anything to Sir Gilbert about sending for a doctor?"

"It would have been as much as my place is worth," replied the butler with a solemn shake of the head. "And I shall be much obliged by your ladyship not saying anything about my having spoken to you."

A fire had been lighted in the library, for the autumn evenings were chilly, and Lady Pell found Sir Gilbert seated by it and looking much as usual. There was a small table, with a lamp on it, near his elbow, and the *Times* newspaper was spread open on his knees.

"So you have got back safe and sound," he said in his most cheerful tones as she went forward. "Well, you have had a charming day and I hope you have enjoyed yourselves."

"Oh, most thoroughly. Didn't you find the house a little lonely without us?"

"Indeed I did--both lonely and dull. Dinner, I may tell you, is ordered for an hour later than usual; I felt sure you would come back famished after your long drive."

"And so we have; but you are not yet dressed."

"No--the fact is, I must ask you to excuse me at table to-day, I am slightly out of sorts and don't feel in the mood for company. Perhaps, later on, I may be inclined for a little music. Meanwhile, Trant will not fail to look after me. And now I won't detain you a moment longer."

"Well, I shall come and look you up again as soon as dinner is over."

"Do so. By that time I may possibly have something to tell you."

Lady Pell scarcely waited for dinner to come to an end before she was back in the library. At the door she met Trant bringing out a tray containing the remains of Sir Gilbert's apology for a dinner. "Master seems better, much better, ma'am," he whispered as he passed her. Then she entered, seated herself comfortably near the fire, settled her glasses on her nose, deposited her ball of worsted on the hearthrug at her feet, and gave a preliminary click with her needles.

The Baronet sat gazing into the fire for a little space; then he cleared his voice and said: "Louisa, I have been the subject of a very strange experience to-day."

"Indeed, cousin?" responded her ladyship, in just that tone of sympathetic surprise which indicated that she was fully in touch with him. "But it is not the first strange experience you have had of late."

"No indeed," with a sigh. "But I will tell you all about it. Perhaps you may be able to suggest an explanation where I confess that at present I see none. Feeling somewhat lonely as the day wore on--so used have I become of late to seeing faces round me--and it being still too early to have the lamps lighted, I took a cigar, and having put on my hat and coat, went out for a stroll in the grounds. At first I confined myself to the terrace, but finding the air there rather chilly, after a time I went down the steps and began to pace the sheltered paths of the shrubbery on the lower level. I had finished my cigar--I am a very slow smoker--and in the shrubbery it had grown almost dark before I turned to go indoors. I was crossing that piece of sward on my way to the terrace steps, when I was seized with a sudden giddiness. Everything seemed to go round with me. Stumbling forward a step or two with outstretched hands, my knees gave way under me and I sank, rather than fell, forward on the turf and lost consciousness. When I came in some measure to myself, which must have been after a very few moments, I had a sense of being borne swiftly along in a pair of strong arms. Then, I could tell by the change of atmosphere that I was indoors, and a moment later I felt myself being laid gently down, while the arms that had carried me were withdrawn. And then--perhaps you will scarcely credit it--I seemed to feel a kiss pressed on my forehead--yes, on mine, the forehead of an old man of seventy-four! On the instant I opened my eyes, and there, clearly outlined by the flame of the burning logs on the hearth, I saw bending over me--whom or what think you?"

Thus directly appealed to, Lady Pell simply arched her eyebrows and shook her head as one wholly at a loss for an answer. In the interest excited by her kinsman's narrative her hands, still holding her needles, lay idle on her lap.

"A robed and cowled figure," returned Sir Gilbert, "of whom I could discern little save its long grizzled beard."

"The Grey Monk!" ejaculated her ladyship in a whisper, touched for once with unaccustomed awe.

Sir Gilbert bowed his head in grave assent.

CHAPTER XLII.

SIR GILBERT'S THEORY.

Lady Pell sat looking at her kinsman for a little while in silence, waiting for him to resume his narrative, and it was not till she perceived that he had become oblivious of her presence and was on the point of lapsing into one of his brown studies, that she spoke.

"And what happened after that, cousin?" she asked, "that is to say, after you discovered that you had been brought indoors by the Grey Monk?"

Sir Gilbert, who came to himself with a little start when she began to speak, said: "I have no distinct consciousness of anything that followed till I found Trant standing over me, looking half scared out of his wits, and can only suppose that I must have fainted again. But that, although only for a space of two or three seconds, my eyes beheld a robed and cowled figure, I am as positive as that they behold you at this moment. That it was no hallucination, no piece of visual cheatery, I am firmly convinced."

Some people, in Lady Pell's place, might have said to Sir Gilbert: "Yet, when others professed to have seen the Grey Monk, you treated their assertions with contempt, and would have it that they were the victims of a self-created illusion." But Lady Pell was too wise to venture any such observation. What she said was: "If you have told me this, cousin, with any idea that I might perhaps be able to furnish you with even a hint of some clue to the mystery, I must at once confess that your expectation has been wholly in vain. You yourself cannot possibly be more puzzled than I am."

"I hardly expected to hear you say otherwise," he remarked with a half sigh; and with that he again subsided into silence.

Lady Pell resumed her knitting, only to let her hands fall idle again at the end of a couple of minutes, while wholly unaware that she had done so.

Nothing was heard save the monotonous ticking of the clock on the chimney-piece and the hissing and sputtering of the half-burnt logs on the hearth.

"Louisa," spoke the Baronet suddenly in a voice which brought her ladyship back with a start from the land of visions in which she had been mentally wandering--"Louisa, for the last hour or more a very singular idea has intruded itself persistently upon me; it is one which I have striven in vain to get rid of; indeed, so strongly does it hold me that it has almost assumed the proportions of an absolute conviction. It is--that if the cowl of the Grey Monk, who for weeks past has, so to speak, haunted the Chase, could be plucked back, there would stand revealed the features of none other than my eldest-born--my son so long believed to be dead--my hardly dealt-by Alec!"

"Goodness gracious! Cousin Gilbert, whatever made you get that notion into your head?" Lady Pell was staring at him as if she already detected symptoms of brain disease.
"It came into my mind, Louisa; I didn't put it there, and it refuses to be dislodged. But what if Alec be not really dead? What if the report that he was killed by that explosion was based on some error to which we have not the key? You remember the letter, written in an evidently disguised hand, which was found on my study table together with the key of the strong room?" Lady Pell nodded assent. "Who but Alec would have been in the position to point out the fact that the child--his child--who had died in infancy, was not a boy, but a girl? Who but Alec--my Alec--would have cared to press a kiss on an old man's brow?"
"There is certainly some feasibility in what you say," remarked her ladyship; "but if Alec were still alive he would surely have made the fact known to you long before now."
"You forget that he was a banished man--that it was a condition of the agreement between us that he should never set foot in England till he had my permission to do so. Heaven knows, permission would have been given long ago, because long ago all his early faults and follies were condoned and forgiven, had the faintest suspicion that he was still among the living ever found lodgment in my mind!"
"Even granting your assumption that Alec is still alive (and with all my heart I pray he may be), by what possible motive could he be influenced in coming back to the Chase and allowing himself to be seen by several people under the guise of the family spectre?"
"Ah, now you ask me a question which it is impossible to answer with any degree of certitude. Perhaps it had somehow come to his ears that I had adopted an impostor as my heir. In any case, I care not what may have been the motive which brought him back, if only it were he whose arms I felt about me three short hours ago. I am alone in the world, Louisa, alone and old. I have just been made the victim of a most shameful fraud, and if only, by some miracle, my eldest-born could be restored to me, I should feel that the remnant of my days had indeed been blessed to me far beyond my deserts!"
"Have you thought of any plan yet by which your theory can be tested and the mystery of the Grey Monk elucidated?"
"Not yet--not yet. But I generally lie awake for several hours in the course of the night, and I shall have time to turn the matter over in my mind before morning."
That evening Sir Gilbert did not make his appearance in the drawing-room, but retired at an earlier hour than usual, to fall asleep almost immediately, but only to awake at the end of three hours and remain so till daybreak. During that wakeful period he formulated a certain theory in his mind which he determined to put to the proof immediately after breakfast.
The theory thus worked out by him, briefly stated, was to the following purport:
Some month or more had now gone by since the Grey Monk had so startled Bessie Ogden one evening on the terrace. So far as was known, that was the

apparition's first appearance for upwards of twenty years. Now, it was quite evident to Sir Gilbert that if his son had been haunting the place for several weeks, it could only have been with the knowledge and connivance of one or more members of his household. How otherwise could Alec--supposing always that it were Alec--have been supplied with food and lodging? How else could he have had the run of the house at midnight, as the incident of the strong room proved him to have had? Now, Sir Gilbert's oldest dependent, and indeed the only one left whose memory could go back to so far a period; one, too, whose company had been much sought after by Alec as a youth, was Martin Rigg, the ex-keeper. Martin, who was now over sixty years old, had long been superannuated. Owing to a gunshot wound in his leg, the outcome of a poaching affray, he was a permanent cripple. He and his widowed daughter were now quartered in the old Tower, of which mention was made in the early part of this narrative as being the only remaining portion of the original Chase, the semi-ruinous rooms of which had been specially renovated and fitted up for their occupancy by Sir Gilbert.

Linking one thing with another in his memory, the Baronet, by the time he arose, had come to the conclusion that if anybody was more likely than another to be cognisant of his son's presence at the Chase, that person was Martin Rigg.

He breakfasted in his own room, but in order to relieve the anxiety which he knew Lady Pell would feel on his account, he wrote her a brief note and sent it by Trant, in which he told her that, this morning, he felt quite as well as he usually did, that he had a little special business to transact in the course of the forenoon, but that he would not fail to meet her at luncheon. Then after breakfast, he left the house by the back entrance and took his way through the spinny in the direction of the Tower.

Even at his slow rate of progression, a few minutes' walking brought him to it. Grey and stern as he always remembered it, it loomed before him with no visible sign of life about it. That, however, in no wise disturbed him. He did not doubt that he should find either Martin or his daughter, or, more likely still, both of them at home. Going up to the door, which, though of modern make, was of oak and studded with huge square-headed nails, he rapped loudly at it with the ivory knob of his cane; but to his summons even when repeated, there came no response. Then he tried the handle, but only to find that the door was locked. Thus, at the very outset of the inquiry he had been about to enter upon, he found himself unaccountably baulked.

CHAPTER XLIII.

THE ROOT OF THE MYSTERY.

For a few moments he stood fuming and glaring with angry eyes and bent brows at nothing in particular, while debating with himself what his next step ought to be. Evidently the first thing to do was to ascertain why the Tower was shut up and what had become of Rigg and his daughter. After considering the matter for a little space, he said aloud: "Nixon will be pretty sure to know. I'll go and question him."

Like Rigg, Nixon was another pensioned dependent of the house of Clare, and together with his wife, much younger than himself, filled the post of lodge-keeper at the main entrance to Withington Chase.

Across the park tramped the Baronet, a very unusual thing for him to do. The old lodge-keeper was at home, and it did not take Sir Gilbert long to elicit all that Nixon had to tell. It appeared that Martin Rigg had gone down to Yorkshire to attend the funeral of his only brother, and that his daughter had accompanied him. As to when they might be expected back, Nixon knew nothing.

"Do you happen to know," said Sir Gilbert, "whether Rigg has had anyone staying with him at the Tower of late--a visitor of any kind, I mean?"

Nixon shook his head. "Not to my knowledge, Sir Gilbert."

"And you are sure you heard nothing about any stranger being there?"

"I'm quite certain on that score, Sir Gilbert. And either Martin, or Dulcie would have been sure to speak of it if there had been."

As the Baronet walked back to the Chase he knew not what to think. So powerfully had his imagination been worked upon by the belief, which by this time had grown almost to a conviction, that his son was at the root of the mystery of the Grey Monk, and that, of all men, Rigg was the one to whom he must look to supply him with the key, that his mood was one of bitter disappointment.

After luncheon he told Lady Pell all about his morning's errand and its result.

In her own mind her ladyship had little or no faith in her kinsman's conviction that the Grey Monk was none other than John Alexander Clare, restored to life after some all but miraculous fashion when there was every reason for supposing him to have died twenty long years before. She was not a believer in the improbable, although, if questioned, she would have felt bound to admit that even she had known cases where incidents of the most startling kind had evolved themselves out of lives to all seeming the most commonplace and prosaic.

In the course of the day she took an opportunity of informing Sir Gilbert of the engagement of Ethel Thursby and Everard Lisle. That the news afforded him genuine pleasure could not be doubted. "So I shall not lose my little girl after all!" he said. "That is indeed something worth hearing. She has become very dear to me, Louisa; I may tell you so now; and I should have felt the loss of her more, perhaps, than the occasion would have seemed to warrant, for she has contrived to steal her way into my affections in a quite unaccountable fashion. My old age is the sweeter for her presence. I am very glad that I am not to lose her."

"I shall make it my business to furnish her trousseau."

"And you may rely upon it that she shall not go to her husband without a *cadeau* from me. I suppose she will have no dowry?"

"Not a shilling, so far as I am aware. She is an orphan and was brought up by two maiden aunts who, till a little while ago, were quite comfortably off. Now, however, they have only just enough left to live upon."

"In that case I must see what I can do by way of increasing Lisle's salary. Of course when anything happens to poor Kinaby, Lisle will at once step into his shoes. The furniture which is now at Maylings may as well be transferred to Elm Lodge for the young couple's use. They will make a well-matched pair, Louisa. As you know, I hold Lisle in very high regard, not merely because he happens to be the son of the man who saved my life, but by reason of his own fine qualities. How wide is the difference between him and young Rispani!"

Later in the day he took occasion to congratulate both the young folk, with the old-fashioned courtesy which became him so well, nor did he fail at dinner to drink to their health and happiness in a bumper of the rare old Madeira which was reserved for very special occasions. It was evident to everyone that the Baronet was in high good-humour, and that for the time at least he had succeeded in throwing off the gloom to which late events seemed to have hopelessly condemned him.

It was not till the second day after Sir Gilbert's visit to the Tower that Martin Rigg and his daughter got back home. Within an hour of his return he was summoned to proceed at once to the Chase, where Sir Gilbert received him in his study. Scarcely had he limped slowly into the room before Sir Gilbert, turning quickly upon him with bent brows and an assumption of his most minatory manner, said: "Rigg, how many days ago is it since you last saw my son, Mr. John Alexander Clare?"

That the keeper was utterly taken aback he himself would have been the first to admit. He turned hot and then cold almost as quickly as it takes to write the words. He shifted his weight from one foot to the other and then back again, and so crushed his hard felt hat between his fingers that it was never fit to wear again. For a moment or two his gaze went up to a corner of the ceiling, only to be drawn irresistibly back to the stern face and deep-set eyes of the one man of whom he had ever stood in awe.

"When did I set eyes on Mr. Alec last, sir?" he stammered.
"You heard my question. I said, how many days is it--not years, mind you--since you saw my son last? Now, let me have no prevarication, Rigg. You know that is what I would never put up with either from you or anyone else. I have a right to know the truth in this matter, and I demand to know it. Speak, and dare to tell me a lie at your peril!"
"I have never been in the habit of telling lies, Sir Gilbert, either to you or anybody else," replied the keeper stiffly. "Since you force me to speak, I can't help myself, though I bound myself under a promise not to do so. Sir, I parted from Mr. Alec Clare five days ago, just before I left home to go and bury my brother."
A low cry broke from Sir Gilbert; his figure suddenly lost its rigidity and he sank back in his easy-chair, while his face blanched like that of a man at the point of death. Martin, terrified, made a step forward, but Sir Gilbert, tremblingly held up one hand. "Leave me alone," he murmured, "I shall be better presently." To those of his time of life the shock of sudden joy is oftentimes almost as trying as that of sudden grief.
"Sit down, Rigg," said the Baronet presently, mindful even at such a moment of the man's lameness. Then, as he lay back with closed eyes, little by little the colour ebbed back into his cheeks. It was true, then; his instinct had not led him astray, and his Alec was still in the land of the living! A great fountain of love and gratitude welled up in his heart--of reverent thankfulness and gratitude that it had pleased the Inscrutable Power who sways the destinies of mankind to vouchsafe him this crowning mercy so far beyond his deserts. What happiness to know that his firstborn--he whom, when young, he had so hardly treated that for years his memory of him had been an unending remorse--had been given back to him as it were, indeed, from the tomb, and that a season of reparation might still be granted him! But let us not pry too curiously into all that passed through his mind at this, one of the supreme moments of his life. Let his white hairs and his many sorrows not appeal to us in vain.
After a time he began to question Rigg, eagerly and closely, about all that he knew with reference to Alec. A summary of the information which he elicited piece-meal from the keeper is all that need be given here.
It appeared that "Master Alec," as Martin still, from old habit, persisted in calling him, had been in hiding at the Tower for upwards of a month, in fact, ever since about two days before--quite unintentionally on his part--he so frightened Bessie Ogden on the terrace. The upper room of the old structure, ordinarily used by Martin as a bedroom, had been fitted up with a few extra articles of furniture and given up to his use; while Dulcie, the keeper's daughter, had looked after his meals. More than once Martin had heard him asseverate that he had only returned to the Chase in order to right a great wrong--to send fraud and villainy to the right-about, and that as soon as the task he had set himself was accomplished he should go back to the place from whence he had come. What he had meant thereby Martin did not know. During the day Alec had never

stirred out of the Tower; only after nightfall had he ventured abroad, and then only in the traditional guise of the Grey Monk--a character which in his younger days, when home from school or college, he had assumed more than once out of sheer love of mischief. As to the means by which Alec had been enabled to obtain access to the Chase after the household had retired for the night, that was his own secret, and one which he had never divulged to the keeper.

Extreme was Sir Gilbert's disappointment and chagrin when told that his son had finally quitted the Tower only about forty hour's previously. This had happened during Martin's absence from home, but the latter was already aware that his guest's visit would presently come to an end, and that, although he continued to linger on like one who found it impossible to tear himself away from the home of his boyhood, his task was accomplished and there was nothing more left him to do.

"But if you were away at the time, how do you know that my son left the Tower when you say he did?" demanded the Baronet.

"Because I found this note, sir, waiting for me when I got home," responded the keeper.

Sir Gilbert took the proffered note with an eagerness he made no effort to dissemble.

"Dear Old Martin," it ran, "I am off to-night--Tuesday--and whether we shall ever see each other again is more than I can say. My hearty thanks are due to you and Dulcie for the hospitality you have shown me, and the many kindnesses I have received at your hands. You may be sure that both of you will be often in my thoughts when I am thousands of miles away, and I will not so far wrong you as to think you will forget me. I implicitly trust you to still preserve the same strict secrecy as heretofore with regard to my presence at the Chase. On no account must the faintest whisper of the truth escape the lips of either of you. More on this point I know that I need not write.

"I am especially desirous--in fact, I lay it on you as a charge--that you should keep yourself informed from day to day (which you will have no difficulty in doing) of the state of my dear father's health; and, should any necessity arise for you to do so, I rely upon you to at once telegraph to me, under the name of 'John Alexander,' to the address given you on the other side. That this is most important you will readily understand, and that you will not neglect my wishes in the matter I feel assured.

"And now goodbye till we meet again--if ever we do.

"Your friend,

"A. C."

"Rigg, I should like to keep this, if you have no objection," said the Baronet when h e had read it carefully through.
"No objection whatever, Sir Gilbert; only I should like you to bear in mind that I should have kept my promise to Master Alec, and that nobody would have got a word out of me, if you, sir, hadn't forced me to speak."
"That I quite understand. Under the circumstances no option was left you. But I wish you still to preserve the same secrecy. Not a syllable about this business must pass your lips to anyone else."
"Neither me nor Dulcie is of the gossiping sort. You may trust us for that, sir."
"I am quite sure I may. And now I won't detain you further; but I may tell you this--that, in the long run, you will find yourself no loser by this morning's work."
No sooner had the ex-keeper gone than the Baronet sought Lady Pell in her own room and was closeted with her for nearly a couple of hours. One result of the interview was that he sent a groom to bring back Everard Lisle, who, his morning's work dispatched, had left the Chase some time before.
"Lisle, I want you to start in the course of a few hours for America," he said to Everard when the latter had returned. "You will be the bearer of a note to my long-lost eldest son, John Alexander Clare, who, astounding to relate, I now find, from evidence which it is impossible to dispute, did not meet his death years ago, as, at the time, I was fully led to believe. But I need not enter into particulars just now. It is enough to say that he is still alive. So make your preparations for starting in the morning, and, when you come to dinner this evening, the note I want you to take will be ready for you, and I shall then be in a position to give you my final instructions."
In a matter of such vital importance it did not seem enough to Sir Gilbert to merely entrust his message to the post. A letter might, or might not, reach Alec; but he felt satisfied that Lisle would not rest till he had hunted him down, wherever he might be, and had put his father's message of forgiveness into his hands.
The note Sir Gilbert wrote was a very brief one, and, such as it was, his nervous excitement was so extreme as to render it all but illegible.

"Alec, my son, all is forgiven and forgotten," he wrote. "Come back to me--come back. I want you. It is your father who asks this of you."

CHAPTER XLIV.

BACK AT ST. OSWYTH'S.

Our lovers took a tender farewell of each other.

No other course had been open to Sir Gilbert than to assume that, after leaving the Chase, his son would book himself by an early steamer back to America. Should such prove to be the case, Lisle would be only a few days behind him. Everard calculated that if he were fortunate enough to light on "Mr. John Alexander" immediately after his arrival at Pineapple City, he might count upon being back at the Chase in a day or two under three weeks. He would write to Ethel as soon as he landed at New York, and again on reaching Pineapple City, but he would have to console himself as best he could without any news of, or from, her between the date of his departure and that of his return.

He left Mapleford at an early hour next morning, which was that of Friday. He had already settled in his mind to sail by the *Arbaces* , which was timed to leave Liverpool at noon on Saturday. Thus he had the whole intervening day to himself, and he determined to devote it to a purpose about which he said no word to anyone at the Chase--not even to Ethel.

He had been greatly struck with the story told him by Ethel that afternoon as they wandered together by the margin of the haunted pool, and since then he had thought about it much and often. It was a mystery the solution of which, as it seemed to him, would have to be sought for in the United States. It was from there Ethel had been brought as an infant, and it could scarcely be doubted that she had been born there. Now that he was bound for America on another matter, he had made up his mind, before sailing, to run down to St. Oswyth's, interview the Miss Thursbys, and satisfy himself as to whether there was, or was not, a possibility of eliciting from them sufficient information to enable him to build up a case worth investigating whilst he was in the States.

Ethel had not failed to tell her aunts in her letters about her meeting with Everard Lisle, nor of her surprise at finding that he was in the service of Sir Gilbert Clare, who was none other than first cousin to Lady Pell, and thereafter his name found a mention in nearly all her letters. The sisters were glad that it should be so, and told themselves that it must be pleasant for Ethel to be associated with someone who came from St. Oswyth's, and that the two doubtless found many subjects in common to talk about. Not a suspicion of what was presently to happen ever found lodgment in their minds until Ethel informed them of her actual engagement, subject to their approval. It was a letter full of love and dutiful affection to the aunts, though every word proved that for all time she had given away her heart to Everard Lisle.

The important epistle was delivered at Rose Mount just as the sisters had finished breakfast, and was brought in by Tamsin when she came to clear the table. "From Miss Ethel," said the old woman as she laid it down in front of Miss Matilda, whose turn to enact the part of elder sister it happened to be. Ethel's letters always arrived about breakfast-time and were read aloud by one or other of the sisters, and, somehow, Tamsin generally contrived to be present at the reading--a privilege tacitly accorded her by her mistresses.

Miss Matilda, with characteristic precision, proceeded to slit open the envelope with the tiny pair of scissors which she always carried in a case in her pocket. Tamsin, with dilatory fingers, was removing the breakfast things one by one on to the tray which she had brought in with her.

Miss Matilda read the first few lines aloud, and then paused in a tremor of agitation. A low cry escaped from Miss Jane.

The sisters gazed at each other across the table, the same expression of consternation and distress on the faces of both. "Engaged to Everard Lisle! Oh! who would have thought it?" they exclaimed at the same moment, for not only their thoughts on any given subject, but very often the words by which they gave expression to them, were identical. Then for a minute or more both seemed unable to find another word to say.

"I should have thought," said Miss Matilda at length in her most dignified tone, in which there was yet an unwonted quaver, as she gave a tug at the little knitted shawl which she always wore at breakfast time: "I should have thought that, after the wretched experience Ethel went through so recently, she would have shunned the other sex most assiduously, if not for ever, in any case for a very long time to come."

Miss Matilda took up the letter again and read aloud to the end. Tamsin had transferred the breakfast things to her tray, and had deposited the latter on the sideboard; she now proceeded to draw the cloth off the table and to slowly fold it. Not a word escaped her.

"I am afraid, sister, that we can but bow to the inevitable," said Miss Matilda with a sigh as she folded the letter. "It seems to me that we have no right, even if we had the will, to withhold our approval of the step she has chosen to take."

"My own view exactly," replied Miss Jane with a sorrowful shake of the head. "And yet--oh, dear!--we shall only have the dear girl back at home to lose her permanently after a little while. And I was looking forward---- Oh! I was looking forward to so many things."

And then before more could be said Tamsin's voice broke suddenly in. "And is it not a right and proper thing that Miss Ethel should marry and have a home of her own?" demanded the old woman in tones which had something of an injured ring in them. "Why should she not have a husband to love and cherish her--some good man to whose life she--in her turn--will be a blessing? Ay, and he is a good man, is Mr. Everard Lisle--very different from that other one! If some of us have missed it, is there any reason why we should begrudge it to her? I trow not, indeed--I trow not!"

She and her tray were gone before Miss Matilda had sufficiently recovered from her astonishment to find a word to say.

"Really, the way Tamsin presumes on our good nature and her own length of service is at times most trying. I am afraid that one of these days we shall be under the necessity of giving her notice." It was not the first time Miss Matilda had spoken to the same effect; but no one knew better than she how empty was the threat.

"It seems to me, sister," remarked Miss Jane timidly, "that we have been justly rebuked for our selfishness. We have been thinking more of our own loss than of the dear girl's happiness. That is not as it should be."

Miss Matilda did not answer for a little while. She seemed intent on tearing up the envelope of Ethel's letter into the tiniest of fragments. Then she said gently: "You are right, sister. It *is* the child's happiness that we ought to consider first of all. But"--with a sigh--"we are growing old, and the house will seem very lonely without her."

Then, somehow, tears sprang to the eyes of both, and for a little space they wept silently.

But there were no traces of tears in their eyes when, about four o'clock the same afternoon, just as they had agreed between themselves that if Ethel must marry, there was no one to whom they would sooner entrust her than to Everard Lisle, they were startled by seeing Lisle himself marching up the garden-path and making direct for the front door.

Nor were the sisters less surprised when he informed them of the special purpose which had brought him there. They willingly entered into all the details of the story which Ethel had told him, going over it with him step by step; but in the result he found that he had been unable to add anything of real consequence to that which he knew already.

One thing, however, they were in a position to give him, although he had his doubts as to its value, seeing that it bore date nineteen years back, and that was the address of Kirby Griggs, the lawyer's clerk, who had recognised the portrait of the self-styled Mrs. Montmorenci-Vane as that of his unmarried sister, Martha Griggs. Miss Matilda had found the address after her brother's death in his private memorandum book.

When, after Everard was gone, Tamsin took in the supper tray, she had to set her mouth hard in order to suppress the smile which would otherwise have puckered it. In place of the morning's agitations and tears, the sisters were now complacently discussing the important question of what material Ethel's wedding-dress should be made! "And now to come to the pecuniary part of the affair," said Miss Matilda. "I should not like our dear girl to go to her husband quite empty-handed."

"Certainly not, sister. The same thought has been in my own mind. I do not suppose that Mr. Lisle's position is a specially lucrative one."

"For my part, I should be quite willing to settle on Ethel my half-share of the rental of Vale View House, which, now that Mrs. Loftus has taken it on a seven years' lease, will be a sure source of income for that length of time."

"It would make me very happy to do the same with my half-share. Now that we have grown used to our humbler style of living, we really don't need the rent money. And in future there will be only our two selves, you know, sister."

"No, only our two selves," echoed Miss Matilda, sadly.

That night, when Tamsin went upstairs to her own room, she took out of a drawer her savings bank book and refreshed her memory as to the sum which stood there to her credit, and represented the savings of many laborious years. That sum she made up her mind should be very considerably depleted before she was much older. To what better use could she put the money than in buying a wedding-present for the child who had been, and would ever be, as dear to her rugged, but tender old heart as she could possibly be to the heart of Miss Matilda or Miss Jane!

CHAPTER XLV.

"COME BACK TO ME."

Everard left St. Oswyth's by the six o'clock train on Saturday morning. Four hours later he was in Liverpool. Taking a cab for himself and his portmanteau, he proceeded direct to the shipping office and there booked a berth on board the *Arbaces* for New York. Thence he was driven to the landing-stage, where he found the tender whose duty it was to transfer the passengers and their luggage on board the huge liner anchored out in mid-stream.

On reaching the *Arbaces* Lisle at once made his way to the stateroom which had been allotted him. He knew already that he would have to share it with a fellow-passenger, and when, on entering it, he found there a dressing-case and a small portmanteau, a natural curiosity to ascertain the name of the person who, for the next week or more would be his nightly, if not his daily companion, led him to turn up one of the labels and read what was written thereon. Rarely, perhaps never, in his life had Everard Lisle been more amazed than he was when his eyes took in these words: "John Alexander, Esq. Passenger to New York." By one of those singular coincidences, which are far more common than the generality of people imagine them to be, he and the man of whom he was in pursuit, and on whom he had not expected to set eyes till after a journey of close upon four thousand miles, had crossed each other's path at the outset. Yet, but for the chance of his having read the address label when he did, they would probably have been shipmates for some time before discovering the relation in which each stood to the other, and, in any case, as the *Arbaces* did not call at Queenstown, they would have been compelled in their own despite to make the voyage out and home again.

Lisle had not recovered from his astonishment when the cabin door was opened from without and he saw before him a tall, finely-built man of middle age, with high aquiline features, dark, grave, earnest-looking eyes, a somewhat worn and thoughtful-looking face, and a long flowing beard already flecked with white.

"My cabin chum, I presume," said the stranger in a deep mellow voice, and with an exceedingly pleasant smile. "I hope we shall have a good passage, and that at the end of it our companionship will remain a pleasant recollection in connection with it."

Everard smiled and bowed. "I have taken the liberty of reading the name on your luggage," he said. "Pray excuse the question. I have a special reason for asking it, but are you Mr. John Alexander of Pineapple City in the State of Michigan?"

The other lifted his eyebrows in surprise. "That is certainly my address, and therefore I can only assume that I am the person to whom you refer."

"Then you must be the person whom I was going all the way to Pineapple City in search of I am especially glad that I have met you now and here--for one thing, because my having done so will save me the necessity of a voyage to the States and back. Mr. Alexander, I am the bearer of a letter addressed to you from Sir Gilbert Clare of Withington Chase."

For a moment or two it seemed to Mr. Alexander as if the cabin floor were rising and sinking, as it might have done in a heavy gale. He seated himself on the edge of his berth; his face had faded to an ashen grey.

"A letter from my--from Sir Gilbert Clare for me!" he said, speaking like a man in a dream.

From the case which he carried in his breast pocket, Everard extracted Sir Gilbert's missive and handed it to the other. "I will see you again in the course of a few minutes," he said.

It will be enough to say that neither one nor the other sailed by the *Arbaces* , but caused themselves and their belongings to be transferred back to shore at the last moment.

A few hours later, as they sat together over their coffee and cigars in a private room of the Adelphi Hotel, Liverpool, John Alexander Clare proceeded to give his companion an outline of his history from the time of the explosion of the lake steamer by which he was supposed to have been killed. Of that narrative all that need be given here is such a summary as will enable the reader to follow the sequence of events, the outcome of which was the unpremeditated meeting of himself and Lisle on board the *Arbaces* .

As may perhaps be remembered, Mr. Travis, Alec's business partner, could not reasonably have come to any other conclusion than that the latter had lost his life by the explosion of the *Prairie Belle* , seeing that week after week passed over without bringing any tidings of him; and, indeed, it was not till nearly three months had gone by that one day a tall, emaciated, almost ghastly figure stalked into the office, and for the moment all but made Mr. Travis's hair stand on end when, in hollow tones, it said: "Well, Frank, old fellow, how are you by now?"

It appeared that he had been picked up, clinging to a spar and all but insensible, nearly an hour after the explosion had taken place. His rescuer, a farmer who lived on the margin of the lake, caused Alec to be taken to his house, where he was carefully nursed and tended by the farmer's wife and daughter. He had been terribly bruised and half blinded by the explosion, and for several weeks he wandered in his mind and knew neither where he was, nor what had befallen him.

The farmer and his family belonged to the sect known as Quietists, and as they read no newspapers and held as little communion with the outside world as possible, it followed that Alec's name was omitted from the published list of the survivors of the explosion. Small wonder was it that Travis almost looked upon his partner as on one come back from the grave.

Not till then did Alec learn of the inquiries which had been made about him during his absence. That the man who made them had come specially from

England, Mr. Travis did not doubt, but as he had declined to state the nature of his business, there was nothing more to tell. The fact interested Alec but faintly, and soon passed out of his thoughts. He was a banished man; his wife had deserted him; his child was dead; and to him, after his accident and the illness which resulted from it, his past life gradually assumed the faded proportions of a dream, and not a real experience of his own.

And so one uneventful year after another dragged out its little span, the partners meanwhile prospering in business, and never being other than the best of friends.

At length, through the death of a relative, Mr. Travis succeeded to a considerable property and at once made up his mind to return to England. Alec, who for some years past had been pining for news from home, and who could not but remember that his father was getting well advanced in years, begged of his friend, on his arrival in the old country, to go to Mapleford and make certain inquiries *sub rosa* , and communicate the result to him. This Mr. Travis at once proceeded to do, writing Alec to the effect that his stepmother and his three half-brothers had all been some years dead, that a tablet to his, Alec's memory had been put up in the church where so many of his progenitors were buried, that his son had been adopted by Sir Gilbert as the latter's heir, and that his wife, under the designation of Mrs. Alexander Clare, was residing at the house known as Maylings, within a mile of the Chase.

Alec was astounded. His child had been a girl, and he had still by him, carefully preserved, his wife's heartless letter and the certificate of the infant's death. The result of Mr. Travis's letter was that, three weeks later, Alec landed at Liverpool.

What followed is already known to the reader. Alec's reason for not denouncing Luigi to Sir Gilbert at an earlier date was owing to his wife's absence in Italy, of which he had learnt through certain inquiries made on his account by Martin Rigg. Before taking any positive steps in the affair he was desirous of obtaining some certain evidence as to how far Giovanna was implicated in the fraud, his intention being to seek an interview with her immediately upon her return. Rispani's attempt on the strong room had brought matters to a climax a little sooner than he had anticipated.

He had not failed to hear of Luigi's departure next day from the Chase, but although his mission was accomplished and there no longer existed any reason why he should not return to his far-away home, he stayed on day after day, unable to tear himself from the haunts of his youth and the roof-tree where he had been born. But at length he had made up his mind that the next day should be the final one of his stay, and as the evening shadows closed in he had gone to take his last walk in the grounds and his last look at the old mansion. It was the evening on which Sir Gilbert, finding himself alone indoors owing to the absence of Lady Pell and the others on their expedition to Dunarvon Castle, had gone for a twilight stroll in the shrubbery. From the shelter of a bank of evergreens he had been watched by his son as he passed slowly to and fro on the sward, puffing absently at his cigar and buried deep in thought. Hence it had come to pass that Alec was within a dozen yards of him when, overcome by a sudden dizziness, he stumbled and sank to the ground. His son's strong arms had lifted him and carried him into the library by way of the French window. Then, after depositing him on a couch and pressing a kiss on his forehead, Alec had rung the bell and made a hurried exit by the way he had come.

Next morning he had decided to delay his departure till he should be able to ascertain whether his father was suffering from any after effects of the attack of the previous evening, but the sudden appearance of Sir Gilbert as he emerged from the spinney on his way to the Tower, to all appearance in his usual health, had at once dissipated his fears on that score. It was through an upper window of the Tower that he had seen his father's approach; then had come the latter's unanswered summons at the door, and after that his departure across the park in the direction of the lodge. Alec had rightly surmised that it was a wish to question Martin Rigg that had brought Sir Gilbert to the Tower, but he had of course no knowledge of the motives which had prompted the visit. The same evening, a couple of hours after nightfall, he had emerged from the Tower, and after locking the door and depositing the key in a place where Rigg on his return would know where to look for it, he had crossed the park, no longer wearing the robe and cowl of the Grey Monk, but in his ordinary attire, and after walking to Westwood station, four miles away, had taken the train for London. After a brief stay in town, where nobody recognised him, and where he made no effort to seek out any of his old-time friends or acquaintances, he had journeyed to Liverpool and booked himself as a passenger by the *Arbaces* .

It is not difficult to imagine with what absorbed interest Everard Lisle listened to the narrative of Alec Clare. There still remained one point, and others would doubtless crop up later on, as to which his curiosity was unsatisfied. "Now that you have told me so much, Mr. Clare," he said presently, "perhaps you won't mind enlightening me as to the means by which you were enabled to make your way into and out of the Chase, as it seemed, whenever you chose to do so, without anyone being a bit the wiser."

Alec laughed. "The explanation is a very simple one, or so it will seem when you hear it," he said. "The room which used to be my mother's boudoir, and which has latterly, I believe, been assigned to Lady Pell, has two windows, both of which were originally of the long, narrow, old-fashioned kind, but one of which, at my mother's desire, was modernised into what is called a French window, so that she might have a means of ready access to the garden--for she was somewhat of an invalid--without having to go round by the corridor and the side door. The other window was left untouched and, to all appearance, was not intended to open in any way. But one day, when a lad of ten, I lighted, quite by accident, on a secret spring which, when pressed in a particular way, caused the window to turn bodily on a swivel. Through the aperture thus formed any ordinary sized person could squeeze himself without much difficulty. I kept my discovery to myself, finding it useful on several occasions, when I was a rackety young fellow home for my holidays. To what use I put it of late you will have

guessed already."
Next morning Alec Clare set out on his journey back to Withington Chase. As a rule he was much averse to Sunday travelling, but the present occasion was an altogether exceptional one. He already felt like another man. The ban which had been laid on him more than a score years before had at length been taken off. His father had written, "Come back to me--I want you." The long breach was about to be healed. All was to be forgiven and forgotten. Not as a lonely childless old man would his father henceforth drag out his days. And when he thought of what he himself was going back to, his heart felt full to the point of overflowing with deep thankfulness and that sort of chastened elation which, in the case of those who have seen much tribulation and are imbued with a sense of the unstableness of things mundane, often is all they dare permit themselves to feel.
Everard in the course of the previous afternoon had despatched a telegram to Sir Gilbert, informing him that he had overtaken "Mr. Alexander" before the latter had sailed, and that he, the aforesaid Mr. A., might be looked for at the Chase in the course of the afternoon of the morrow.
He further wrote a brief note to the Baronet informing him that he was called to London by some special private business, and that he had taken the liberty of claiming a couple of days' release from his duties at the Chase.
Everard's telegram arrived at the Chase while Sir Gilbert was at dinner. When he had read it he passed it to Lady Pell, who, as soon as she had taken in the message, gave it back to him with a look that was more expressive than words. Then he got up and left the room. He felt that he could not have spoken without breaking down. An hour later her ladyship went in search of him and found him in his study, seated by the fire with the telegram clasped tightly in his fingers.
"May I come in?" she asked, standing with the handle of the open door in her hand.
"To be sure, Louisa. I am glad you have come. You are the only person who can understand what I feel without my needing to say a word about it. Even now I can scarcely believe that in a few short hours I shall see my boy and hold his hand in mine. Not till death steps in between us, Louisa, shall anything part us again!"
It was Lady Pell who, next afternoon, met Alec at the railway station. Sir Gilbert would not trust himself to go. He was afraid that his emotion would overpower him, and he was nervously shy of making a scene in public. Nor was he at the door to welcome his son when the latter alighted at the Chase, but Lady Pell's instinct told her where to look for him. "Come with me," she said to Alec, and with that she led the way to the study. On reaching it she opened the door and motioned him to enter. Sir Gilbert, his tall, gaunt figure drawn to its fullest height, was standing on the hearthrug, supporting himself with one hand on the chimney-piece, his face turned expectantly towards the door. He was trembling in every limb, and as Alec went quickly forward he put forth his arms and made a faltering step or two to meet him. "Oh, my son--my son!" he cried, his voice breaking into a sob as the last words left his lips.

Lady Pell gently closed the door and left them together.

CHAPTER XLVI.

UNKNITTED THREADS.

Everard Lisle stayed in Liverpool till Monday, on which day he took an early train up to town. His object in going to London was to endeavour by means of the address which Miss Matilda had given him to trace the present whereabouts--if he were still alive--of the man Kirby Griggs. Futile as the hope seemed that, even if he should succeed in finding him, Griggs would be able to supply him with any information that would further in the slightest degree the special purpose he had in view, he yet felt that he could not rest satisfied till he had interviewed him and heard from his own lips all that he had to tell.

The address supplied him was that of a firm of lawyers in Gray's Inn Square, in whose employ Kirby Griggs had been at the date of his interview with Mr. Matthew Thursby.

Fortunately for Everard's purpose, Griggs proved not only to be alive, but still in the service of the same firm--a third-rate clerk on a very limited salary. He was a thin, timid, nervous man, with an anxious, hungry sort of look, as though he rarely had as much to eat as he could have done with. When told the reason which had induced Everard to seek him out, he at once expressed his willingness to give him all the information that lay in his power; but as he was too busy to do so during office hours, he requested Everard to call upon him between seven and eight o'clock the same evening at an address in the suburbs which he gave him.

There Lisle found himself at half-past seven and was at once ushered into the clerk's little parlour, in which sacred apartment--hardly ever entered between one Sunday and another--a fire had this evening been lighted in honour of his visit.

There proved to be no reticence on Griggs' part in discussing in all its bearings that strange episode of twenty years before, in which his sister had played so inexplicable and, ultimately, so tragical a part.

It appeared that she had always been of a romantic and flighty turn of mind, and an insatiable devourer of impossible romances and outrageous love-stories of the very commonest type of penny fiction. She had gone out to the States as maid to a wealthy elderly lady who had died there shortly after her arrival. The next news from Martha had been to the effect that she was on the eve of returning to England by the clipper-ship Pandora, and her brother was requested to meet the vessel on its arrival in dock. Why she had booked herself under the fantastical name of Mrs. Montmorenci-Vane her brother could not imagine, unless it were a name she had picked up in the course of her reading, and had taken a fancy to. Just as little could he understand why, in the presumed state of

her finances, she should have chosen to travel as a saloon passenger. As for whence and from whom his sister had obtained the child which she had passed off on board ship as her own, and what possible object she could have had in view in perpetrating such a hoax--if hoax it could be called--was to Kirby Griggs still as much an enigma as it had been at the time; nothing had occurred in the interim to throw even the faintest ray of light on the affair.
Everard's heart sank within him. It was evident that the lawyer's clerk had nothing of consequence to relate beyond what was known to him already.
After musing awhile, he said: "I presume that nothing was found among your sister's luggage--no letters, or papers, or anything else which, if placed in the hands of anyone who was willing to devote both time and patience to following it up, might ultimately furnish a clue to the mystery we have just been discussing."
"There was nothing--nothing whatever found of the kind you mention," replied Griggs with a shake of the head. Then, after a pause, he gave a little deprecatory cough and added: "As I have no wish to hide anything in connection with the affair, it may perhaps be as well to mention that my sister's boxes contained a quantity of wearing apparel such as seemed, both to me and my wife, far above her station in life, and the only conclusion we could come to was, that it had most likely been a present to her from the lady who had died. After keeping it for three or four years in case any inquiry should be made about it, my wife gradually used it up in the manufacture of garments for our numerous olive branches."
Although Mrs. Griggs made a third at the interview, as yet she had not spoken more than a dozen words, but in the pause that now ensued she suddenly said: "The ring, Kirby--have you forgotten the ring? That might perhaps supply the gentleman with the clue he is looking for."
Griggs started, and his pale face took on an unwonted blush. "I had indeed forgotten the ring," he said, "but that it will in any way help to clear up the affair, I don't for one moment believe." Then turning to Everard, he added: "The ring to which my wife refers is a quite plain hoop of gold, in fact, just like a wedding-ring, except that it is about four times as massive. It was the only article of jewellery found among my sister's luggage, although she was said to have been wearing a gold watch and chain and several dress rings at the time she fell overboard. Unfortunately, about four years ago I was very much pressed for money and was compelled to put the ring in pledge, obtaining on it an advance of thirty shillings. I am sorry to say that I have never since been in a position to redeem it, but it has not been lost, because I have been careful to pay the interest as it fell due."
"As you say," replied Everard, "there is not much likelihood of a ring such as you describe this one as being helping me in any way to discover what I am in search of. Still, I should very much like to see and examine it, and if you will allow me to pay the cost of taking it out of pledge I shall be greatly obliged to you."
"Truth to tell, sir," answered Griggs with a shrug, "I haven't money enough of my

own to spare to enable me to do so. But in any case, nothing can be done in the matter till to-morrow."

So Everard left money for the redemption of the ring and went his way.

At half-past seven the next evening he was again at the house of Kirby Griggs. The ring had been redeemed in the interim. It was what the lawyer's clerk had described it as being, a plain massive hoop of gold, but on the inner side Lisle's keen eyes detected what seemed to him like a faint tracery of some kind, but apparently so worn that without the help of a magnifying glass it was impossible to make out what it was intended to represent. Griggs, who admitted that he had noticed the marks, but without attaching any value to them, volunteered to obtain the loan of a lens from a working watchmaker who lived close by, and accordingly did so. With the aid of the lens and the exercise of some patience, Everard was enabled to make out that what to the naked eye had looked like so many meaningless scratches was in reality an engraved inscription which ran thus: "J. A. C. to G. R. *Pour tout temps* ."

Scarcely had he succeeded in deciphering the inscription before it flashed across him that the words, " *Pour tout temps* " formed the somewhat arrogant motto of the Clares of Withington Chase, as also that the letters J. A. C. were the initials of John Alexander Clare.

By the time he got away from the house, taking the ring with him, it was too late to think of going down to the Chase before next morning. So he wandered about some of the quieter streets till a late hour, turning over and over in his mind his discovery in connection with the ring, but nowhere finding an adequate solution of the singular problem which was thus put before him. From whichever point of view he looked at the matter, it still remained as much a tangle as at first. Out of a dozen questions which he asked himself, there was not one he could answer. He turned into his hotel a little before midnight and went to bed, but sleep came to him only by fits and starts, and all through the dark hours the same series of questions kept ringing their changes in his brain.

After an early breakfast he caught the eight-thirty train for Mapleford. A fly took him and his luggage from the station to Elm Lodge, from whence, a few minutes later, he walked across the park to the Chase.

Sir Gilbert had lingered over breakfast, talking to his son, and in the corridor Everard met him face to face, looking a dozen years younger than when he had seen him last. The change in him was indeed marvellous.

"What! back already?" he said beamingly. "I thought you were going to take a few days' holiday in London. Why didn't you, eh? Why didn't you? But we'll have no work to-day, that's certain. The best thing you can do will be to have the dog-cart out after luncheon and take your sweetheart for a drive--lucky dog that you are, to have won the love of such a girl!" Then his voice took on a deeper tone. "What a happy chance for me was that which brought you and my son together at Liverpool and so gave Alec back to me weeks before I should otherwise have had him! I cannot help feeling as if I somehow owe it all to you. Well, well"--laying a kindly hand on his shoulder--"when your wedding-day is here you will

find that I have not forgotten you." And with a smile and a nod he passed on.
Everard's most pressing object was to secure a private interview with Mr. John Clare--as he was henceforward to be known to the world, although to his father he would never be anything but Alec. Not till he should have recounted to the latter the history of the ring and put it into his hands, would he go in search of Ethel and surprise her by his unexpected return.
Presently he found John alone in the library, hunting up some of the favourite authors of his youth, from whom he felt that he had been too long parted. Sir Gilbert was closeted with one of his tenants in the study.
John Clare greeted Everard with a smile and a cordial grip of the hand. The liking he had conceived for him during the few hours they had spent together in Liverpool had not been, in any degree lessened by what he had heard about him since, both from his father and Lady Pell.
"I thought you were about to give yourself a holiday," he said, "and that we need not look to see you at the Chase for some days to come." He had already had his grizzled beard and heavy moustache carefully trimmed, and certainly he presented a much more civilised appearance than before.
"I was able to finish the business which took me to London in much less time than I expected," replied Everard. "The affair, however, has taken a turn wholly surprising and unexpected--one that seems to bring you, Mr. Clare, into connection with it, although as to the mode in which the connection in question originated I must confess that I am entirely in the dark."
"You excite my curiosity, Lisle. I hope you will not refuse to gratify it."
"Is there any place where we can secure half-an-hour to ourselves without fear of interruption?"
"Perhaps we had better go upstairs to my own room. No one will intrude upon us there."
"May I take the liberty of asking whether you have ever seen this ring before?" said Everard as soon as the two were seated opposite each other in John's dressing-room.
John took the ring and looked at it for a moment or two, as one in doubt. Then all at once a flash of recognition leapt into his eyes and every nerve in his body responded with a thrill. "Yes, I have seen this ring before--many years ago," he said slowly. "Have you any objection to telling me by what strange chance it came into your possession?"
"It was with that purpose I sought this interview. But the story is a long one, and at the beginning will doubtless seem irrelevant to the question you have just put to me."
"You shall tell it in your way. So long as the end of it furnishes me with an answer to my question I shall be satisfied."
"Some nineteen years ago," began Everard presently, "a certain clipper ship named the *Pandora* left New York for London having on board a number of passengers, among them being a certain Mrs. Montmorenci-Vane (that being the name by which she had booked herself), who, although she was dressed as a

lady and wore a quantity of jewellery, had neither the manners nor the appearance of one. With her she had a child, a little girl only a few months old, to attend upon whom during the voyage, her own nursemaid having deserted her in New York--so her story ran--she engaged a woman from among the steerage passengers. Unfortunately, one dark night, Mrs. Montmorenci-Vane fell overboard and was lost.

"Among other passengers on the *Pandora* were two maiden ladies, sisters, of the name of Thursby, who, together with their brother, an elderly bachelor, were returning home after a brief visit to the States. The forlorn condition of the lost woman's infant touched the kind hearts of the sisters, and they made it their business to look after the child's welfare during the remainder of the voyage, naturally expecting that some relations of its mother would be there to meet the ship on its arrival in dock. However, there proved to be no one there to inquire for Mrs. Montmorenci-Vane, but, instead, a lawyer's clerk of the name of Griggs, who had come to meet his sister, the latter having written to inform him that she would take passage by the *Pandora* . Well, in a photograph of the so-called Mrs. Vane the clerk at once recognised his unmarried sister Martha, who had gone out to the States a few months before in the position of lady's-maid. There could be no possible mistake about the photograph. The captain and the whole of the cabin passengers were prepared to affirm that it was a likeness of Mrs. Vane, who had fallen overboard, while Griggs was prepared to swear an affidavit that it was the likeness of his sister. The poor man was terribly puzzled, as well he might be. He could not in the least comprehend why his sister had chosen to call herself Mrs. Vane--whence she had obtained the fine clothes and the jewellery in which she had flaunted on board ship--and, above all, what possible object she could have had in passing off the child of some one else as her own offspring. In the result, he declined to have anything whatever to do with the child, whom he left on the hands of Mr. Matthew Thursby and his sisters to be dealt with in whatever way they might choose.

"What the Miss Thursbys chose to do, was to adopt the child and bring her up as their niece. As such she grew up, never suspecting that the sisters were other than her aunts in reality, and not till her nineteenth birthday, when a letter was put into her hands addressed to her by Mr. Matthew Thursby, who had died many years before, with instructions that it should be read by her on that day--were the facts of her early history, so far as they were known, revealed to her. That the revelation was a great shock to her cannot be doubted, but it made no difference whatever in the relations which had subsisted for so long a time between herself and the sisters. The secret was still kept to themselves, and to this day, the waif of the *Pandora* passes as the niece of the two Miss Thursbys. A little later she became companion, *pro tem* ., to Lady Pell, and accompanied the latter on her visit to Withington Chase. Doubtless you have already met Miss Thursby at luncheon and dinner, and so on, Mr. Clare."

"I have both met and noticed the young lady; indeed, when she and I are at table I find it difficult to take my eyes off her. She affects me in quite a singular way, the like of which I never experienced before. But that is not to the point just now. Pray proceed."

"The next fact needful for me to mention as bearing on my narrative--in what way you will presently understand--is, that Miss Ethel Thursby and I are engaged to be married." He spoke with a heightened colour and an added sparkle in his eyes.

"Ah! is that indeed so? I congratulate you with all my heart, Lisle."

"When, a few days ago," resumed Everard, "Sir Gilbert Clare placed in my hands a letter addressed to you at Pineapple City, with a request that I would at once proceed to America, search you out and give it into your hands, finding myself with a day to spare prior to the sailing of the steamer, I journeyed down to St. Oswyth's, where the Misses Thursby reside, with the object of putting certain questions to them. It seemed to me that there was just a faint chance that, while in the United States, I might be able, as a consequence of the inquiries I intended to set on foot there, to find the clue to the mystery surrounding the birth and parentage of her whom I hope shortly to call my wife; but I was desirous, first of all, to make myself thoroughly acquainted with every feature of the affair that had come under the cognisance of the sisters. As it fell out, however, they had nothing of any consequence to tell me which I did not know already. The only scrap of fresh evidence I brought away with me was the address of the man Griggs, who, in the portrait of Mrs. Vane, had recognised his sister. You know already, why I never got any farther than Liverpool on my way to the States. After parting from you, I went to London and was fortunate enough to find Griggs without difficulty; but, as in the case of the sisters, he had nothing to tell me which would in the least help to further the end I had in view. I was on the point of giving up the whole business in despair, when Mrs. Griggs happened to mention that among the luggage which had been claimed by the lawyer's clerk as his sister's property, there had been found a plain gold ring of very massive make. On expressing my desire to see the ring, I was told that circumstances had compelled Griggs to pledge it. But the following day saw it redeemed and placed in my hands. Perceiving that the inner side bore an inscription of some kind, I procured a lens and by its means was enabled to make out that part of the lettering represented the motto of the Clares of Withington Chase, and another part your own initials. Hence my reason for bringing the ring to you."

"I am glad, Lisle--very glad indeed that you have done so. For the present I will ask you to say nothing to anyone about what has passed between us this morning. You know, of course, that the Mrs. Clare who occupied Maylings for a short time was my wife?"

"She was known to everyone in the neighbourhood as Sir Gilbert's daughter-in-law."

"Can you tell me where to find her? It is requisite that I should see her with as little delay as possible."

"I have no knowledge of Mrs. Clare's movements; but her nephew, Luigi Rispani, left me an address at which a letter or message would at any time find him. It would be no trouble to me to run up to town by the next train, hunt up Rispani, and obtain from him the address of Mrs. Clare, with which he is pretty sure to be acquainted."

"If you will do that for me, Lisle, I shall be infinitely obliged to you."

"I will start at once. There is a train at twelve-thirty. If I have good luck, I ought to be back by seven o'clock."

John Clare held out his hand. "Bring me the address at any cost," he said.

The ring thus strangely recovered had been a present from him to Giovanna Rispani during the period of their brief courtship.

CHAPTER XLVII.

HUSBAND AND WIFE

To John Clare's wife the world of late had become a greatly-changed place. She was alone in London, without a single creature of her own sex whom she could call an acquaintance, much less a friend. She had broken both with her uncle and Luigi. For the latter she had never cared. He had impressed her from the first as being not only morally unscrupulous--that was a defect which she might not have experienced much difficulty in condoning--but as being sly and deceitful into the bargain, and, in short, one of those people who are almost as dangerous to, and as little to be trusted by, those whom they call their friends as by those to whom they owe a grudge which they would gladly wipe off.

Captain Verinder she had learnt to like after a fashion. He was her mother's brother, and that of itself was enough to create a tie between them which, under ordinary circumstances, she would have been one of the last people to ignore. She had liked him for his *bonhomie* , for his persistent good-humour and his half-quizzical, half-cynical way of looking at men and things, and last, but not least, for the frequent doses of flattery he had been in the habit of administering to her, which, even while conscious that it was nothing more than flattery, had possessed the delightful property of raising her in her own estimation, and of causing her to think more highly of herself than she had ever done before.

But this was a state of things which had now come wholly to an end. Giovanna's feelings were very bitter against her uncle. She blamed him and him alone for everything that had happened to her; at his door she laid the entire load of her misfortunes.

It was quite true--and the fact was never lost sight of by her, for she rarely argued crookedly, as Luigi habitually did--that, but for the interest taken by Verinder in her case, in all probability she would never have become aware that she was daughter-in-law to Sir Gilbert Clare. Yet, granting that point to the full, it was impossible for her to forget that it was wholly owing to his influence and persuasions that she had been lured into that career of fraud and double-dealing which, in her case, had ended in irremediable disaster. From her present knowledge of Sir Gilbert Clare she felt convinced that, had she have gone to him at first, as she had proposed to do, and told him the simple truth, far from turning his back upon her, he would have welcomed her as his son's widow, and have settled on her a liberal allowance, which would have been hers to the last day of her life. It made her hate her uncle when she thought of all that she had lost through weakly yielding to the glittering temptation he had so persistently dangled before her. Little by little she had wormed out of Luigi all the particulars of the Brussels episode, and she rightly argued that if Verinder had never introduced his nephew to the gaming-table the series of unfortunate events which resulted therefrom, and culminated in the discovery of Luigi in the strong-room, would never have come to pass. It was clearly the Captain and he alone who was to blame.

He had called upon her twice since their return to town, but her reception of him had been of the coldest; and when, on the occasion of his second visit, his request for a trifling loan of ten pounds was met by a distinct refusal, he perceived that his wisest course would be to keep away from his niece till time should in some measure have softened her rancour against him.

Giovanna had found a temporary home in one of those boardinghouses which abound in the neighbourhood of the west-central squares. But already she had begun to meditate a change. The demands on her purse were too many and, as it seemed to her, too exorbitant. Should she decide to stay in London, she must find cheaper rooms and make up her mind to live more economically in many ways. But just then she could not make up her mind to anything. She was a very lonely and a very miserable woman; indeed, the loneliness of her life sometimes appalled her. There were a number of other boarders in the house, and in the general drawing-room of an evening there was no lack of company of both sexes and of nearly all ages. But Giovanna, who had always been of a reserved and retiring disposition, had an utter distaste for associating with a mixed lot of people, with not one of whom she had anything in common, and, as soon as dinner was over, invariably went upstairs to her own sitting-room on the third floor. In the forenoons, when the weather was fine, she took long, solitary walks, sometimes in the Regents Park, sometimes through the miles of West End shops, but rarely pausing to glance into a window. Invariably dressed in black, and with the upper half of her face closely veiled, but leaving visible the firm and beautiful contours of the mouth and chin, her tall and stately form drew many eyes to it as she slowly threaded her way through the crowd of promenaders, so obviously indifferent to everyone and everything around her. There was about her, or so it seemed, an air of mystery, of romance even, which many of those who turned to gaze after her would have given something to be able to penetrate.

On a certain morning, just as Giovanna was getting ready to go for her usual walk, a message was brought her that there was a gentleman below who was desirous of seeing her. In the belief that it must be either her uncle or Luigi, they being the only visitors she had, she requested the servant to show him upstairs.

A minute later John Clare walked into the room.

Despite the changes which years had wrought in him, Giovanna knew him again the moment she set eyes on him, and the same instant a great fear took possession of her. An inarticulate cry broke from her lips; she shrank away from him with averting hands and terror-fraught eyes, and, when she could go no farther, she crouched trembling in a corner of the room. Her face wore the ghastly hue of death. She had never fainted in her life, and she did not now; but all the fibres of her being were stretched to that point of tension which touches the verge of madness. A little more and her brain would have given way. It was a strange mixture of terror that held her powerless, for, although she had at once recognised that this was no shadowy visitant from the tomb, there was about the affair an undoubted element of the supernatural. That her husband had come in the guise of an avenger one glance at his face had been enough to tell her, and surely it could be nothing less than a miracle which had brought him back to life! To Giovanna miracles were far from being the impossibilities which many of us deem them to be. She had grown up in an atmosphere of superstition, and not all the experience of after-life had quite served to eradicate the noxious weeds thus early implanted within her.

In the look with which John Clare regarded his wife there was an icy sternness such as might well strike with dread the heart of the unhappy woman. At that moment he bore a striking resemblance to his father, as Sir Gilbert had been before years and trouble had broken him down. For some moments he confronted his wife in silence as she cowered before him like some hunted creature driven to bay.

"At last we meet again!" he said, after a time. "You believed that I had died long years ago, but I am here, a living proof to the contrary. From me you have nothing to fear. I come neither to accuse nor to condemn. As you have dealt with the past, so will it deal with you; but certainly it is not for a fallible being such as I to set myself up as your judge."

He spoke slowly and unemotionally, without a trace of passion or the faintest tinge of invective.

"I am here on purpose to ask you certain questions," he resumed, "which I can but trust that you will answer truthfully and to the best of your ability. Will you not be seated?"

She did not answer him in words, but drew herself together as it were, and crossing to the opposite side of the room sat down. By this she had recovered from her fright, and her features had settled into a sort of stony hardness which effectually masked whatever emotions might be at work below.

John too sat down, but there was nearly the entire width of the room between them.

"I want you," he went on, "to carry your mind back to that letter, written by you nearly twenty years ago, in which you told me that our child was dead, that you had come to the conclusion you and I would be happier apart, and that you were on the eve of returning to your friends in Italy. You have not forgotten the letter of which I speak?"

"I have not forgotten it."

"After you had left Barrytown and started on your journey, what happened to you? Did you go direct to New York and at once take ship there?"

"I went direct to New York, but a few hours before the vessel sailed by which I had booked my passage I was seized with a fever and conveyed to a hospital, where I lay for weeks, part of the time out of my mind, and the other part so weak that speech was an impossibility."

"And when you came back to health and strength, it was to find that while you had been in the hospital your maid, a woman of the name of Martha Griggs, had absconded with all your belongings."

It was a bold guess on John Clare's part, but it told.

Giovanna half started to her feet and then sat down again. The mask of apathy fell from her face and a great wonder and curiosity took the place of it. "How did you discover that?" she gasped.

"I have discovered more than that," was John's unmoved reply.

"And the woman--Martha Griggs--is she still living? do you know where to find her?" demanded Giovanna with an eagerness she made no attempt to conceal.

"Martha Griggs was lost overboard on the voyage between New York and London."

"Lost overboard! And my child--what became of her?" She had again risen. Voice, eyes, hands--all asked the question.

On the instant a great light of gladness, the source of which Giovanna was at a loss to comprehend, flamed out of John Clare's eyes.

"So I have surprised your secret, have I?" he said, speaking very slowly.

For a few seconds she stared at him with bewildered eyes; then the truth dawned on her.

"Yes," she replied, "you have surprised my secret, if that is the way you choose to put it. But the child----"

"A child no longer, is alive and well, and at the present moment under her grandfather's roof at Withington Chase."

"At Withington Chase--she! How strange! How wonderful! But I am very glad--oh yes, you may believe me when I tell you that I am very glad! For, whatever you may think, I am not all bad." She crossed quickly to the window and stood there with her back towards him for fully three minutes.

Not till she had resumed her seat did John Clare speak again. "What you wrote me about the child was a lie?" he said presently. It might be taken either as a question or an assertion.

"Yes--a lie," she replied with a little shrug. "It is as well at times to call things by their right names."

"And the certificate you sent me?"

"A forgery. Five dollars was the price I paid for it."

"But what was your object, if I may ask, or what was to be gained by inducing me to believe that the child was dead?"

"After I had made up my mind to leave you and go back to Italy, my one fear was that you would come after me and rob me of the child. To keep you from doing that I invented the story of its death. Myself alone, after the letter I had written you, I knew you would not trouble yourself to come after."

"Never was there a more heartless and cruel fraud perpetrated on anyone!" For the first time his voice vibrated with a suppressed emotion. Not for a little while would he trust himself to say more. Giovanna's only reply was a slight lifting of her brows.

"When you grew better and left the hospital did you make no effort to recover your child?" demanded John as soon as he felt that he could command himself sufficiently to speak again.
"I made every effort a woman in my position could make. You must remember that I had been robbed of money, clothes, everything. I was utterly destitute. Some charitable people interested themselves in my case and the police were communicated with, but nothing came of their inquiries. Then a wild notion took hold of me that the woman, in the belief that I was past recovery, might have made her way to Italy with the child, and that I should find it under my father's roof when I got back to Catanzaro. The same charitable people found me enough money to take me home; but as you know, neither the woman nor my child was there. After that, rather than be called upon to tell and tell again the history of that time, I preferred to give it out that my child was dead. To my father alone was the truth known."
She ceased, and to John Clare it seemed that there was nothing more to be said. He had learnt all that he had come to learn. The missing links had been found; not one was wanting; the chain was complete.
"There is no reason why I should intrude myself any longer upon you," he said as he rose and pushed back his chair. "You have been frankness itself with me, and so far I thank you. I know not what your pecuniary resources are, nor do I seek to know, but I do not forget that you are still my wife and that, as such, a monetary arrangement of some kind will have to be come to with you. I will take my father's opinion in the matter, and in the course of a few days my lawyer shall be instructed to communicate with you."
"And my child--the child of whom I was robbed!" It was like the cry of some animal despoiled of its young made articulate.
She had started to her feet as it broke from her lips, and she now confronted him with heaving bosom and extended hands, her face marble-white and her great black eyes glowing with intense fire.
John had taken up his hat and had reached the door, when her cry caused him to turn.
" *Your* child!" he said with a quiet concentrated scorn that made each word seem a stab. " *My* child, you mean. You long ago forfeited all right to call her yours. What! would you dare to stain her spotlessness with your guilt? Would you, with such a past as yours, dare to claim her for your daughter, and look to her to call you mother? Is it your wish that she should be told the story of your life? Or would you prefer to pose before her as the innocent victim of circumstances which you could not control? No, I will not believe you are quite so depraved as that. As you cannot but know, her way and yours lie wide apart. You did your utmost to rob me of her when she was a child, and now that I have found her she belongs to me alone."
As he went out and shut the door behind him, all the strength seemed to go out of Giovanna's limbs. She sank to the floor and there crouched with clasped hands and bowed head. "He is right--he is right," she moaned. "I am not fit to tie

the latchets of her shoes."

CHAPTER XLVIII.

SIR GILBERT'S GREAT SURPRISE.

On leaving his wife John Clare engaged a hansom and was driven direct to Gray's Inn Square. His object was to find Kirby Griggs and hear again from his lips the story which had already been told him by Everard Lisle. The lawyer's clerk was on the point of going out for his midday meal, so John secured him, and, taking him to a restaurant at which it was possible to engage a private room, he treated him to what Griggs later termed to his wife "a sumptuous repast," and did not let him go till he had drawn from him every scrap of information which bore in any way on the facts he was bent on investigating.

With the aid of the light which his wife's narrative had thrown on the affair, the mystery which had heretofore enshrouded the proceedings and conduct of Martha Griggs was in a great measure dispelled. There could be no doubt that when her mistress was seized with fever and taken to the hospital, the temptation to decamp with the latter's money and luggage had proved too potent for the woman's ill-balanced mind. Having once crossed the narrow boundary which divides honesty from its opposite, it was characteristic of her flighty disposition, surcharged with feminine vanity, that she should masquerade in her mistress's gowns and jewellery and pass herself off under a preposterous name culled from one of her favourite penny romances. What had been her intentions with regard to the disposal of the child after she should have reached England could not even be surmised. Her death, so sudden and unforeseen, had put an end to everything as far as she was concerned.

It would be a difficult matter to analyse John Clare's thoughts and feelings as he journeyed homeward after parting from Kirby Griggs. That which had been no more than a supposition when he left the Chase a few hours before, had now been converted into an indisputable fact. He was going back home to greet his new-found daughter, and that daughter was none other than she who had hitherto been known to the world as Ethel Thursby!

Now did he understand how it happened that from the first he had felt himself so unaccountably drawn towards her. He had read something in her face which had at once puzzled and attracted him; it had been to him like one of those faces which sometimes confront one in dreams, which one seems to know vaguely, but which utterly sets at defiance all one's efforts to endue it with a personality. But surmise and conjecture were at an end. She was his child--his own! He had proved it beyond the possibility of a doubt. So strange, so bewildering, and yet so wonderfully sweet did it seem, that for the time he was as a man walking in a phantasy.

Everard Lisle, on reaching London, had found Luigi Rispani and had obtained from him the address he subsequently gave John Clare, which enabled the latter to go direct to the boarding-house where his wife was staying.
Luigi was in doleful dumps. The bill for one hundred and twenty pounds, which bore the joint signatures of himself and his uncle, had fallen due, and the sum total which the pair of them could scrape together towards meeting it did not amount to much over thirty pounds. To make matters worse for the younger man, for the last few days Captain Verinder had been missing both from his lodgings and his usual haunts, nor did anyone seem to know what had become of him. But pity in such cases is but cold comfort, and he did not content himself with that. Before parting from Luigi he put into his band a cheque for the full amount of the promissory note.

Everard Lisle's capital did not amount to much more than three hundred pounds in all, and was made up of a small legacy bequeathed him by a relative, supplemented by his own savings, for he had no extravagances and was of a thrifty disposition. To finish with this incident, it may be recorded that about a fortnight later John Clare asked Everard to be the bearer of a cheque for a hundred and twenty pounds from him to Luigi Rispani. He had been reading over for the second time the notes of the interview between Luigi and Sir Gilbert, after the former's release from the strong room, as transcribed by Everard from his shorthand memoranda, after which he had gone to his father and made certain representations to him, the outcome of which was the cheque in question.
Great was John Clare's surprise when told that the promissory note had already been met and by whom. He made no attempt to press the cheque on Everard, but quietly put it back into his pocket. He would not spoil the aroma of a fine action by bringing it down to a cash level.
To return.
When Everard got back from London, bringing with him Mrs. Clare's address, he found that in the course of the afternoon Mrs. Forester had driven over from the Shrublands--the house at which Lady Pell had been visiting previous to coming to the Chase--and had insisted upon carrying Lady Pell and Miss Thursby back with her, with the understanding that they were not to return to Withington till the morrow.
Although he had not seen Ethel for a week, not since he had parted from her before setting out on that journey to America which had been stopped short at Liverpool, it was yet a secret relief to him to learn that, at the earliest, they could not meet for another day. And in twenty-four hours much might happen.
Everard Lisle was too clear-sighted not to perceive in what direction, when duly sifted, the evidence bearing on Ethel's parentage, which he had been enabled to bring together, all tended. As yet there was one big gap which required to be

filled up, but it might well be that Mr. John Clare's investigations on the morrow would prove successful in bridging over the hiatus, or, in other words, in forging the last link in a chain of evidence which would then be complete and perfect in every part. Well, and what then? he asked himself. Should the foreshadowed end come to pass, ought he to be anything but glad, jubilant, happy? Certainly he ought to be all that and more, because in that case into his darling's life there would come a happiness greater and richer than her dreams had ever pictured. And yet!--and yet!--There are two sides to every question, and when Everard thought of the other side to this one his heart grew faint within him. "I trust that I shall at least know how to do my duty," he said to himself with proud bitterness.

After his interview with Kirby Griggs, John Clare got back to the Chase in ample time for dinner. On leaving home in the morning he had merely told his father that a pressing matter of business would take him to London for a few hours, and Sir Gilbert had asked no questions. This evening father and son dined alone. A note from Lady Pell had come to hand in the course of the afternoon, stating that she had been persuaded into staying another day at The Shrublands, but that she and Miss Thursby would be back at the Chase without fail on the morrow.

John Clare kept his news to himself till dinner was over, and Trant had finally shut the dining-room door, leaving the two gentlemen over their dessert. John would not tell it before, fearing lest his father's mental excitement on hearing it might take away his appetite for the time, which, in view of all he had gone through of late, was not a desirable thing to do.

"Father, you would hardly guess where I have been to-day," he began, in as indifferent a tone as he could assume as he cracked and began to peel a walnut.

"I am a poor hand at guessing, Alec."

"I have been to London and have had a long interview with my wife."

"So!--Only some very strong motive, I should imagine, would have impelled you to seek such an interview."

"It would have been next to impossible to find a stronger motive--as you shall hear."

He finished peeling his walnut before he resumed.

"As the result of a vile conspiracy you had been led to believe that Luigi Rispani was your grandson. In the anonymous letter written by me, which was the first thing to open your eyes, you were informed that your grandchild was a girl and that she had died in infancy. Only the day before yesterday certain facts were brought to my knowledge which led me to doubt whether my daughter really had died when only a few months old, as I had been induced to believe, and whether, in point of fact, she might not still be living. It was the determination to

get at the truth of the matter which led me to seek an interview with my wife."
He had spoken in studiously quiet tones, but already Sir Gilbert's hands were twitching with nervous excitement.
"Yes, Alec, yes. And the result of your interview?"
"Was to satisfy myself that my long-lost daughter is indeed still alive!"
For a little space Sir Gilbert sat staring straight before him in speechless astonishment. Not all in a moment could his mind take in and assimilate the amazing news which had just been told him.
"Have you fully assured yourself, Alec, of the truth of this?" he said at length. "That woman---- But I do not wish to speak further of her. Only, you know how she imposed upon me; may she not have done the same by you?"
John shook his head. "There is nothing to apprehend on that score. Not the least singular part of the affair is that till to-day she herself neither knew the whereabouts of the child, nor whether it was alive or dead."
"You surprise me more and more." He drew a deep breath. "Oh! Alec, does it, can it mean a daughter for you, and a granddaughter for me?"
"That is what it means, father."
"And where is she? when shall I see her?"
"She will arrive at the Chase in the course of to-morrow."
"Arrive here to-morrow? So soon! Already my heart goes out to meet her. I long to see her, to embrace her."
"She is no stranger to you. You know her already."
"Alec, you trifle with me. I am an old man, and--and----
"Father, I am not trifling with you. On such a subject I would not for the world. What I said just now is the truth. Your granddaughter, under the name of Ethel Thursby, is known and liked by you already."
"Ethel Thursby my granddaughter!"
"There cannot be a shadow of doubt about it."
As before, Sir Gilbert sat in speechless amazement, but this time, if such a thing were possible, his amazement was intensified a hundredfold.
"It is indeed a 'strange eventful history' that I have to narrate to you," resumed John Clare. "Would you rather that I put off telling it you till to-morrow, or----"
"Certainly not. There's no time like the time present. Now that you have told me so much you must tell me all. I shall not sleep a wink to-night unless you do."
Thus adjured, John Clare began the narrative with which the reader is acquainted.

Lady Pell and Ethel did not reach the Chase till after luncheon next day.
Over breakfast father and son agreed that it would be best to entrust her ladyship with the task of breaking to Ethel the news of her surprising change of fortune, whom they would see later on.

"It seems to me," said Sir Gilbert, "that we owe this discovery, in the first place, entirely to the efforts of young Lisle."
"That is undoubtedly so," replied John. "Had he not first moved in the affair, the chances are, nay, it is almost a certainty, that the truth would never have been brought to light."
"We owe him an immense debt of gratitude. In what way can we best contrive to repay at least a part of it?"
"As I understand the affair, he and Ethel are engaged to each other." "True. For the moment the fact had escaped my memory. And yet it was only the other day that I congratulated the pair of them." The two looked at each other for a few moments in silence.
"But the heiress of the House of Clare! One has a right to expect that she should make a very different match." It was Sir Gilbert who spoke.
"Very true. Still, it may be as well to bear in mind that but for Everard Lisle, the House of Clare would never have known that it had an heiress."
"Yes, yes; of course one can't forget that. As I remarked before, the debt is an immense one. But as regards this engagement, what do you advise?"
"Simply that for the present you and I do nothing at all in the affair, but wait and see how matters work themselves out between the young people."
"Um--um. One can pretty well guess the result of that."
"If Lisle is the man I take him to be, when he finds Ethel acknowledged as your granddaughter, one of his first acts will be to offer to release her from her engagement."
"Do you think so? Indeed, I shouldn't wonder if you are right. Lisle's a gentleman through and through, or else I was never more mistaken in my life. But in that case, what about the girl?"
John Clare smiled. "Being of the sex she is, who can foretell what she may choose to do, or not to do? But in any case, it appears to me that you and I must abide by the result, whatever it may be."
"I agree to that. Yes, yes, whatever the dear girl may choose to do shall be fully endorsed by us."
It seemed to John Clare, although he did not say so, that what Ethel would choose to do in such a contingency admitted of very little doubt. He felt intensely grateful to Everard Lisle, and he had already made up his mind that it should be owing to no fault of his if the young folk were not made happy.
Everard was not at the Chase this morning, it being his day for collecting the rents of sundry outlying farms, but he might be expected there in the course of the afternoon.

CHAPTER XLIX.

PAYMENT IN FULL.

It had been one of those softly brilliant days in late October, which sometimes come as if to haunt us with the ghost of the dead and gone summer. The sun had set in a golden haze, and the amber reaches of the upper sky were darkening slowly as the shades of advancing night crept upward from the east, when Ethel and Everard met face to face in the park.

Everard had collected his rents and seen to various other matters, and on his way to the Chase had called at the bank and paid in his day's receipts. At the Chase he had seen neither Sir Gilbert nor John, but as he had nothing special to see the Baronet about, he had contented himself with leaving a note for him on the library table, having reference to one or two matters in which his employer was specially interested. He was ignorant of the return of Lady Pell and Ethel from The Shrublands when he set off to walk across the park home.

Scarcely had Lady Pell had time to take off her bonnet and cloak on her return, before she received a message to the effect that Sir Gilbert would like to see her in the blue parlour at her earliest convenience, and there she presently found both the Baronet and his son.

Then to her in turn was unfolded the extraordinary story which had been told by John to his father the night before, followed by a request that she would take upon herself the office of breaking the news to Ethel before either her father or grandfather should see the girl, which her ladyship willingly agreed to do.

Into the particulars either of that interview, or of the subsequent one between the astounded girl and the two men we need not enter. They must be left to the imagination of those readers who have followed our narrative thus far.

On one point only is it needful to give the details of what passed. It was after Lady Pell had broken her news and Ethel's bewildered faculties had recovered in part from the shock, that the latter said, "You have told me nothing about my mother, Lady Pell. Is she living or dead?"

So wholly unexpected was the question that for a few moments her ladyship was thoroughly nonplussed. Yet the question Ethel had asked was one natural to her sex and age. Whenever she had speculated about her unknown parents, or had indulged in daydreams about them, her silent cry had been, "Mother, where are you? Mother, I want you!" It was not a father whom her heart had gone out in search of. So now, when told that the father from whom she had been separated when an infant in arms, had in some wonderful and as yet unexplained way found her again, the question anent her mother sprang involuntarily to her lips.

"I have told you all that I was commissioned to tell you, my dear, and beyond that my lips are sealed," replied her ladyship with an amount of hesitation quite unusual with her. "Of your mother I can tell you nothing, and if you will take my advice, you will ask no question about her of either your father or your grandfather. You may rely upon it that you will be told all it is requisite for you to know, and beyond that I feel sure that you will not seek to pry."

It is almost needless to state that at the ensuing interview the name of Giovanna Clare was not mentioned. Ethel was still left purposely in the dark as regarded all those points of her history with which her mother was concerned, for since John Clare could not have spoken of his wife to their daughter except in terms of the severest censure, he preferred not to speak of her at all. On one point, however, Ethel was quite clear, for her father had given her distinctly to understand that it was entirely due to Everard Lisle's efforts that they two had been brought together.

The moment the interview was over she had hurried to her room. Her eyes were dim with tears, but they were tears of happiness. She wanted to be alone--she wanted to sit quietly with shut eyes and try to realise the change which had come over her life within the last two hours. So strange and wonderful did it seem, that more than once she asked herself, in all seriousness, whether it was true that she was really awake and not the victim of some inexplicable hallucination.

As she stood before the window, she caught sight of Everard Lisle crossing the park on his way to the Chase. He had left the dog-cart, which had taken him on his rounds, at Elm Lodge, not knowing how long he might be detained by Sir Gilbert.

Ethel's heart seemed to stop beating for a couple of seconds and then went on at express pace. She had not seen her lover for a whole week, and now that they were both back at the Chase what less than a fairy-tale was it that she had to pour into his ear? Hastily putting on her outdoor things she left the house by a side door, and crossing the park to a spot where five huge elms grew within touch of each other, there waited. Close by ran the narrow footpath which led from the Chase to a door in the boundary wall of the park of which Everard Lisle possessed a key, and three minutes' walk beyond which was Elm Lodge. It was by this footpath that he went to and from the Chase, and so saved himself a long detour by way of the main entrance to the park.

Not long had Ethel to wait. Presently she saw Everard in the distance, pacing along with downcast mien and eyes which seemed to see nothing, unless it were some inward pictures conjured up by his own fancy. As a rule his bearing was so resolute and self-assured, he fronted the world so confidently, that Ethel could not help being struck by the change.

Not till Everard was within a few yards of her did Ethel emerge from the umbrage of the trees and go slowly to meet him. He gave a great start the moment his eyes fell on her, and all his face lighted suddenly up as she had foretold it would. Three or four quick strides brought him to her side, and the same instant she was enfolded in his arms and strained close to his heart. Gently disengaging

herself she said--
"Is this the way to treat an unprotected female? You ought really to try to get the better of your primitive instincts. Marriage by capture went out centuries ago. But, oh, Everard, I have so much to tell you!"
She took his arm and together they began to pace slowly to and fro in the shadow of the great trees.
"Do you know, sir, in whose company you are?" she playfully went on presently. "Do you know that she who is now speaking to you is Miss Clare of Withington Chase?"
Everard stopped dead.
"Then what I thought must be true has come true!" he said; and on the instant all the gladness died out of his face, and half his youth seemed to go with it.
But Ethel was not looking at him just then and saw nothing of the change.
"Yes," she resumed, "henceforth my name will be Ethel Thursby Clare. Only an hour ago I was told. I am no longer a waif, a nobody's child. The mystery of my birth is a mystery no longer. I have found a father, a grandfather, a home--though, thanks to my dear aunts, I have never known the want of the last--and I owe them all to you--to you--to you!" As she spoke she faced him suddenly and gazed at him with deep love and devotion in her eyes.
"But do you not see, cannot you comprehend," cried Everard in deep dejection, "how this change in your fortunes affects the whole position of affairs as between you and me? When I sought and won from you a promise to become my wife, I knew you only as Ethel Thursby, a portionless girl no higher in the social scale than myself. To-day I know you as the descendant of an old and honoured family, as the granddaughter of a man both proud and rich, who will naturally be justified in expecting that when Miss Clare marries it will be some person very different from one of his own salaried dependents."
"When you took me for your promised wife, you did so with your eyes open, knowing me to be what I was--a nameless waif--and having no certainty that one day it might not be shown that I was the offspring of beggars, or worse. But did you allow that prospect to deter you in the least? You know well and I know well that you did not; and if it had been proved that I was the descendant of a family of thieves instead of the Clares of Withington, I have such faith in your love for me that I believe you would still have said: I care not whose child you are; you are still my promised wife."
"In believing so you do me no more than justice."
"Then perhaps you will be good enough to explain why the fact that Sir Gilbert Clare is my grandfather should modify or alter in any way the conditions of our engagement."
"We need scarcely trouble ourselves with the why or the wherefore while the indubitable fact remains. The revelations of the last few hours have served to fix a great gulf between you and me. There is no option left me, none, but to release you from your promise, to give it back to you unconditionally."
"Oh, how bitterly proud you are!" cried Ethel, her eyes flashing. "But supposing I

refuse to be released, supposing I refuse to take back my promise, as I most assuredly do--what then?"

"In that case I can but lay it at your feet. When a prisoner's fetters are knocked off he has no option in the matter; he is simply told that he is free. There is one point which neither you nor I should allow ourselves for one moment to forget. You can no longer claim to be your own mistress. Your duty and obedience are due to others. Those others will have views, wishes, prospects in connection with one so dear to them which you cannot afford to disregard."

Ethel shook her head. "Obedience sometimes degenerates into weakness, and wrongs done either to oneself or others are none the less wrongs even if dignified with the name of duty. But I will say no more now, Everard. I see that it would be useless to argue with you. And I must hurry back, for I have long outstayed my time. When we next meet it will be my turn to triumph." Her eyes laughed up at her lover as he stooped and pressed his lips to hers. Then without pausing she flew towards the house.

Merely taking off her hat and jacket, Ethel went direct to the library, where she found both Sir Gilbert and her father, who had been on the point of going to their rooms to dress for dinner. They both welcomed her with a glad smile.

"I sent in search of you half-an-hour ago, but you were nowhere to be found," said the Baronet. "Where have you been hiding yourself? But come up to the fire. I can tell the wind has got round to the east again by the twinge in my left shoulder."

Seating herself on a hassock near the fire, Ethel spread out her hands between her face and the blaze. One of her father's hands lingered for a moment caressingly on her hair.

Although she did not in the least falter in her purpose, her heart was beating much faster than was common, and there was an odd little quaver in her voice when she spoke.

"I have been for a ramble in the park," she said, "and there I met Everard Lisle. Indeed, it was on purpose to meet him that I went, for we had not seen each other since before he set out on that journey which ended so unexpectedly at Liverpool."

"Um--um," murmured the Baronet.

"Then, of course, you had much to say to each other," remarked John Clare. "Doubtless Mr. Lisle was greatly surprised at what you had to tell him."

"I don't think it came upon him altogether as a surprise. Although he did not say so, I fancy he suspected the truth before."

"I have never found Lisle deficient in perspicacity," said Sir Gilbert as if speaking to himself.

"I hope neither of you has forgotten that I am Everard Lisle's promised wife," said Ethel with a little gasp, as her eyes glanced from one to the other and then were again averted.

"That is a fact which neither your grandfather nor I would be at all likely to forget," replied John, gravely.

There was a pause. Presently John reached forward and again laid his hand on her hair. "Darling, you have something more to tell us--I feel sure of it," he said very gently. "Speak. You have nothing to fear."
"Yes, I have something more to tell you. Everard insisted on giving me back my promise and that all should be at an end between us."
The eyes of the two men met across the figure of the crouching girl.
"Doubtless he had some more or less valid reason to urge for insisting that the engagement between you should be broken off." It was her father who spoke.
"Oh, he was quite explicit as to his reasons. I am no longer the nameless, portionless girl to whom he engaged himself, but the granddaughter of Sir Gilbert Clare of Withington Chase; whereas, he is only Sir Gilbert Clare's dependent."
"I felt sure from the first that Lisle had all the instincts of a gentleman," interpolated the Baronet.
"Well, my dear, and what answer did you make this very self-willed young man?" queried John.
"I refused to take back my promise, and told him that whatever might be the alteration in my position and prospects I owed it wholly to him, but that as between him and me nothing whatever was changed."
"He had something to say to that, I have no doubt."
"He persisted in saying that all was at an end between us, and bade me remember that there were others whom I must now consider, and who have a right to expect the duty and obedience which is their due."
The Baronet nodded his head as one in thorough accord with the views thus enunciated.
"Yes--and then?" said John.
"Then I left him and came direct to you"--with a gesture that included both the men.
"You acted very rightly, my dear," remarked her grandfather.
"Both my father and I are fully conscious of our indebtedness to Mr. Lisle," said John. "And you may take my word that neither of us is disposed to undervalue it. But that is not the question before us just now. The points we are anxious to be satisfied upon are, that your happiness is really bound up with your engagement to Mr. Lisle; that you feel inwardly assured not merely that you love him, but of the depth and sincerity of his affection for you, and finally, whether under all the circumstances of the case, it is not desirable that your engagement should remain in abeyance, say for six months, or even for three, with the view of proving at the end of that time whether you really do care for each other as much as you believe you do now."
"Dear father"--she spoke the words with a certain sweet shyness, which thrilled him as with a sense of exquisite music--"put us to whatever test may seem best to you. I have no fear for either Everard or myself. We will submit ourselves to you in every way!
"Is that so?" said John with a smile and a lifting of his eyebrows. "What, then, if I

were to say, I will have no more of this engagement; that it shall come to an end from this hour!"
"That is a question there is no need for me to answer, because I am quite sure you will never say anything of the kind!"
Sir Gilbert chuckled.
"You are no match for the young monkey, that's evident," he remarked. A second later he pulled the bell-rope that was within reach of his hand, and to the servant who came in, he said: "Order dinner to be put back half-an-hour, and then have word sent at once to Elm Lodge that I expect Mr. Lisle to dine here this evening!"
As the man left the room, Sir Gilbert turned to Ethel.
"There shall be no more talk of broken engagements, nor of putting you and your lover to the test. The debt which I and your father owe to Everard Lisle can only be paid in full by giving him our greatest treasure."
Ethel stood up, surprise, doubt, joy, wonder were all expressed in the look she bent on the old man.
"Oh, grandpapa, do you really mean it?" she gasped.
"Most really and truly I mean it!"
With a sudden impulse she seated herself on his knees and flung both her arms round his neck.
"You have made me the happiest girl in England," she murmured brokenly.

CHAPTER L.

THE VEILED STRANGER.

It was only to be expected that Ethel's thoughts should often revert to the conversation with Lady Pell, in the course of which the latter had advised her to ask no questions about her unknown mother at her forthcoming interview with her father and grandfather. It was advice which Ethel had accepted and abided by, but if she had hoped that some mention would be made of that which she so longed to know by one or other of those two who had so many wonderful revelations to make to her, then was she doomed to disappointment. Neither then nor later was the existence of any such person as her mother alluded to in her presence.

It was the only cloud on Ethel's happiness. If her mother were dead, why had she not been frankly told that such was the case? If she were still alive, could it be that all mention of her name had been purposely omitted because she had been guilty of something which must keep her and her daughter for ever apart? But when Ethel asked herself this question, which she did more than once, her thoughts at once reverted to that unknown Mrs. Clare about whom she had heard so much, while staying at the Shrublands, who was said to be the daughter-in-law of Sir Gilbert Clare, and to be an Italian by birth, who had lived for a short time at Maylings, but who seemed to have suddenly left the neighbourhood, for what reason Ethel had never been told, only a few days prior to the arrival of Lady Pell and herself at Withington Chase.

Then came another inevitable question. "Was Mrs. Clare of Maylings my mother?"

She had gathered from various remarks which Lady Pell had let drop from time to time, that Sir Gilbert had had four sons in all, but that only the eldest had lived to arrive at man's estate. If such were the case, and if the late tenant of Maylings were really Sir Gilbert's daughter-in-law, then it seemed to follow as a certainty that she could be the wife of none other than John Alexander Clare--of the man whom she, Ethel, now knew to be her father!

It was a startling conclusion to come to, but, under the circumstances, none other seemed possible.

In accordance with the promise he had made Giovanna, and after consultation with his father, John Clare wrote to a London solicitor empowering him to wait upon Mrs. Clare and propose certain pecuniary arrangements for her acceptance. Return of post brought a reply to the effect that on inquiry at Mrs. Clare's lodgings it had been found that she was temporarily out of town and that the date of her return was uncertain. Evidently till she should have returned nothing further could be done in the matter.

But at this time John Clare's wife was much nearer him that he was aware of. The sudden appearance before her of the husband whom she had long believed to be dead, and the astounding news of which he was the bearer, had combined to produce in Giovanna's mind a feeling of bitter remorse, as regarded certain episodes of the past, to which she had heretofore been a stranger. To know that, as a consequence of her misdeeds, she had forfeited all a mother's rights and privileges, that her daughter would be taught to think of her either as of one dead, or, if as still living, as of one the mere mention of whose name was enough to bring the blush of shame to her cheek, was to drink deeply of the waters of Marah.

Her thoughts did not dwell much upon her husband; she had never greatly cared for him, and she experienced no particular wish, even had such a thing been possible, to be reconciled to him now. It was on the image of her unknown daughter--of her little brown-eyed Netta, stolen from her so long ago and now grown to woman's estate, that her mind perpetually dwelt. Her husband had not deigned to tell her what strange chance had brought him and their daughter together again, no more than he had condescended to enlighten her about the facts of his own history from the time of her desertion of him; but all that mattered nothing. The one fact that her daughter was alive, and, so to speak, within reach of her hand, was all that concerned her. And yet in this world they must never meet!

Yes, an hour's railway journey would have brought them together, and yet were they as widely severed as if a thousand leagues of ocean rolled between them. There was madness in the thought. Day and night it wrought in her brain. She could neither eat nor sleep except by fits and starts at wide-apart intervals. In a week's time she seemed to have aged half-a-dozen years. Her only visitor was Luigi Rispani Sometimes she welcomed his coming and was grateful for his company; at others she wished him away that she might have more leisure to indulge in the long fits of silent brooding to which she was yielding up herself more day by day.

"Luigi *mio* ," she said to him one day, "I want you to go down to Mapleford and make certain inquiries for me."

"Yes, aunt, with pleasure. What is it you wish me to ascertain?"

"I want you to pick up all the information you can about my daughter--where and how my husband found her, with whom she has been living all these years, and the name she has been passing under, together with any other particulars it may be possible to ascertain. If you can, I should like you to see her, so that you may be able to describe her to me. I would give fifty sovereigns this moment for a photograph of her. You have a number of acquaintances in Mapleford, and you ought to be able to bring quite a heap of information back with you. Here are a couple of pounds for your expenses."

Luigi pocketed the money with alacrity and departed. He turned over several plans in his mind for obtaining the information wanted by his aunt, and at length he decided that he would go down by an evening train on the morrow, alight at Westwood, the station this side of Mapleford, where there would be little risk of his being recognised, walk from there to Elm Lodge and seek an interview with Everard Lisle. The latter had already proved, in a way not one man out of a thousand would have done, how well disposed he was towards him, and surely he would scarcely refuse to furnish him with the required information. In any case, although the task was one he by no means relished, he would go to Lisle first of all, and get from him all that he was disposed to give.

But, by a curious chance, the need to do so was spared him. 697 The following afternoon as he was turning out of Tottenham-court Road into Oxford Street, whom should he run against but Miss Jennings, the pretty barmaid, the drinking of whose health on her birthday, not wisely but too often, had been the proximate cause of Luigi's getting into such disgrace with Sir Gilbert, since which occasion neither of them had seen anything of each other. Miss J., who was nothing if not self-possessed, at once stopped, smiled, and held out her hand.

"Why, Mr. Clare, of all people in the world, who would have thought of meeting you?" said the girl.

Luigi noticed with a flutter of gratification that she still addressed him as "Mr. Clare," but the fact was that she did not know him by any other name.

"You see, London is such a little village," he smilingly replied, "that we can't very well help coming across everybody in it that we know. But what brings you, Miss J., so far away from the snuggery of the *King's Head?*"

Then it came out that the girl was about to be married, and had come to spend a short time with some relatives in London prior to that important event.

"Many things have happened down Mapleford way, Mr. Clare," she continued volubly; "more especially at the Chase--even in the little time since you gave us the go-by without saying a word to anybody."

"And what has happened at the Chase?" queried Luigi, with a studied air of indifference.

"Law! haven't you heard? It's in everybody's mouth, how Sir Gilbert's son that was believed to have been killed years ago has come back home from foreign parts, and how since then the old gentleman has discovered his long-lost granddaughter. The young lady had been staying at the Chase for some time before Sir Gilbert discovered that she was his granddaughter. But most likely you know her, for she was there part of the time you were. The name she went by was Miss Ethel Thursby, and---- But I see that you know her," for Luigi had given a violent start.

"Ethel Thursby Sir Gilbert's granddaughter!" he exclaimed. "Are you sure of this, Miss J.?"

"Quite sure. As I said before, everybody is talking of it, but as to how it all came about nobody seems to rightly know. Down at Mapleford you'll hear half-a-dozen versions of the affair in as many hours, but in my opinion they are one and all no better than guess-work, and so long as the few people who know the truth choose to keep their mouths shut, which so far they seem to have done, guess-

work they are likely to remain."
It was not till the afternoon of the following day that aunt and nephew met. Giovanna was intensely interested in all that Luigi had to tell her. She made him describe to her minutely what Ethel was like, and when she found that for a short time they had sojourned together under the same roof, she questioned him again and again about all the details relative to her with which his memory was stored.
Then there came over her an irresistible longing to see her daughter--just for once; just for once to gaze into her eyes, and, if it were possible, to hear her speak. After that, she felt as if she should not greatly care what became of her. She had settled on no plan for the future. Whether she should remain, a lost unit, in the huge wilderness of London, or whether she should go back to Catanzaro, where there still lived some who were related to her, was just now a matter of no moment. She was consumed with a great thirst, and till that should be slaked nothing else mattered.
On the opposite side of the park of Withington Chase to that on which Mapleford is situated, in a pleasantly wooded hollow, nestles the obscure hamlet of Chadswell. Here in an old farmhouse a lady who gave the name of Mrs. Lucas and her nephew engaged apartments. It was an unusual time of year for anyone to seek country lodgings, seeing that November was now well advanced, but that was a matter for those who took the lodgings, and not for those who let them. The hamlet lies about half-a-mile beyond the precincts of the Chase, and such of its inhabitants as are desirous of going to and fro between it and Mapleford on foot are in the habit of utilising a certain ancient right of way across the lower end of the park, which effects a considerable saving of distance, as compared with the high road, between the two places.
Aunt and nephew were of course none other than Giovanna and Luigi. The former had been brought to Chadswell by an inordinate longing to set eyes on her daughter (she could not have taken lodgings in Mapleford or its neighbourhood without running the risk of recognition, which, above all things, she was desirous of avoiding), and the latter had accompanied her at her special request. To Luigi the whole business was insufferably dull and wearisome.
Not till the short November days were closing in did Giovanna set foot outside her lodgings. Then, robed in black and thickly veiled, she made her way to the park, entering it by the stile made use of by the villagers; but instead of keeping to the public footpath, she turned sharply to the left in a straight line for the Hall. At such a season and such an hour there was no one to note her movements, and not till she reached the belt of shrubbery, intersected by numerous walks, which sheltered the house on two of its sides, did she deem it needful to exercise a little more circumspection. Luigi had given her to understand that Ethel was addicted to rambling about the grounds alone (in reality, he had known her too short a time to justify him in making any such statement), and her hope was that she might chance to encounter her while thus engaged.

And encounter her Giovanna did one dusky afternoon after she had been haunting the precincts of the Chase for more than a week. It was not in what was termed the shrubbery, but in the spinney that they met. News had been brought to the Hall that Dulcie Rigg was lying ill at the Tower, and after luncheon Ethel had walked across to inquire after the sick woman and make sure that she had all she needed. It was while on her way back that she came face to face with her mother.

Ethel could not help feeling somewhat startled when thus suddenly confronted by the figure of a tall stranger clothed from head to foot in funereal black. The stranger came to a halt full in front of her, and the path being of the narrowest Ethel could not but do the same. It seemed to her that through the interstices of the veil two eyes of a strangely penetrative quality were eagerly scanning every feature of her face.

"If I mistake not, you are Miss Ethel Clare, till lately known as Miss Ethel Thursby," said the veiled woman in a low rich voice, which yet had in it a tone that thrilled the girl, she knew not why.

"That is my name," replied Ethel with questioning eyes.

"I have come far to see you and speak with you," went on the other. "Not that I wish to detain you more than a very few minutes," she hastened to add. Then she paused, as hesitating what to say next. "My excuse for seeking you out and accosting you," she presently resumed, "must be that many, very many years ago I knew your mother."

"Oh!" came in a low startled cry from Ethel's lips.

"You do not remember your mother?" said the stranger interrogatively.

Ethel shook her head sadly, while tears gathered in her eyes.

"I have heard something of your strange story, of how you and your father have been brought together again after having been separated for so long a time. But tell me this; does your father ever speak to you about your mother? nay, has he ever so much as mentioned her name in your presence?"

Ethel hesitated a moment, then she said proudly, "I am at a loss to know why you, a stranger, should put such questions to me."

The stranger sighed; to the girl it sounded like the sigh of an overwrought heart.

"I do not ask them as one having a right to do so, but simply because I knew and loved your mother when she and I were young together, and because I remember you, an infant, lying in her arms."

"If my father does not speak ta me of her," said Ethel softly, "it is probably because she is dead." Then with a little catch of her breath, she added, "But you, who were her friend, doubtless know far more about her than I can tell you; indeed, I can tell you nothing."

The stranger's bosom was rising and falling as if with some hardly suppressed emotion.

"Yes," she presently said, "I think my friend of long ago must be dead; not that I speak as one who knows; and it must be to spare your feelings that your father never mentions her name. But you will sometimes think of her with kindly

affection, will you not?"
"Yes--yes--that I will not fail to do," said Ethel in a voice which was hardly more than a whisper.
"It is all you *can* do. And now I will detain you no longer. Let me kiss you once; don't refuse me that, and then I will go!
As she spoke she lifted her veil, revealing to Ethel a countenance of noble proportions, but worn and white as that of one newly-risen from a bed of sickness, illumined by two eyes of midnight blackness, out of which there looked at her a soul so anguished and fraught with a sort of dumb despair, that the girl involuntarily recoiled a step. But only for an instant; the next both her hands went out to those of the other and she felt herself drawn forward, close--so close that she could feel the other's heart-beats against her bosom. Then the beautiful pallid face was bent to hers, and soft kisses, a dozen or more, such as those a mother bestows on her sleeping infant, were showered on the lips, the eyes and the brow of the astonished girl, interspersed with half-whispered exclamations in a language strange to Ethel, but which sounded far more soft and musical than her own.
Then suddenly she felt herself released--it was all over in a minute at the most--except that her hands were still imprisoned. For a space of some half-dozen seconds the stranger's eyes seemed to be drinking in her every lineament, as though she would fain fix them for ever in her memory. Then she suddenly lifted the girl's hands to her lips, imprinted on them two passionate kisses and dropped them abruptly.
"Farewell for ever," she said. "Remember me in your prayers."
As the last word left her lips, the veil fell like a shroud over the ivory-white face and anguished eyes, and almost before Ethel realised it she was alone.

It was late when Giovanna got back to her lodgings--so late that Luigi was becoming seriously uneasy about her. It had been raining heavily since seven o'clock, and when she did arrive her garments were saturated. She vouchsafed no explanation, and Luigi knew better than to ask her for any. But he could not help looking at her, for two large hectic spots burnt in her cheeks, and her eyes shone with a strange feverish light in which there was yet a far-away look as though her mind were otherwhere, and she was only half-conscious of the hour and her surroundings.
"Good gracious, aunt, you are wet through!" exclaimed Luigi after watching her for a few moments. "You will catch your death of cold."
She came to herself, as it were, with a start.
"It is nothing, I never take cold," she said. "All the same, I feel rather tired and will say goodnight at once, if you don't mind. I am sorry if I have kept you up."
Then laying a hand affectionately on his shoulder, she added: "I have seen her,

Luigi *mio* , I have talked with her, my arms have held her, my lips have touched hers! I am very, very happy."

Next mornings when she failed to come down at her usual hour, Luigi sent the girl of the house to call her; but she was beyond the reach of any earthly voice. She had died in her sleep peacefully and without a sound.

"Disease of the heart of long standing, accelerated by cerebral excitement," was the verdict of Dr. Mallory.

CHAPTER LI.

SAFE IN PORT.

The marriage of Everard Lisle and Ethel Thursby Clare did not take place till the following April.

Sir Gilbert, his son, his granddaughter and Lady Pell spent the winter in the South of France, where they were joined in February by Everard on his return from Pineapple City, whither he had gone at John Clare's request (for Sir Gilbert strongly objected to his son's going in person) to wind up his affairs, which had been looked after during the past few months by a trusted subordinate, and to dispose of the business.

But it now becomes requisite to go back a little, for many things had happened before Sir Gilbert and the others got back to the Chase.

The first to whom our attention is due are the dear twin-sisters of Rose Mount.

On the morning of the day following that scene at the Chase when Sir Gilbert had unconditionally sanctioned the engagement of his granddaughter to Everard Lisle, Ethel asked her father whether he had any objection to her writing to her "aunts" at Mapleford and informing them of all the wonderful things which had befallen her in the course of the last four-and-twenty hours.

Not only had John Clare no objection to the sisters being informed, but he suggested that instead of Ethel writing to them, Everard Lisle should be sent to them as a special envoy, not only to tell them the news, but to bring them back, *vi et armis* , on a long visit to the Chase.

It was a task which Everard accomplished to the satisfaction of everyone concerned. Of the meeting between Ethel and the sisters, when at length the latter had been persuaded into accepting Sir Gilbert's hospitality, and of the genuine welcome accorded them, we have not space left to speak. It will be enough to say that, a little later, at Sir Gilbert's earnest persuasion, they agreed to leave Rose Mount and St. Oswyth's and make their future home at Maylings (of which they were to become the tenants at a nominal rent), where they would be next door, as one might say, to their "dear girl." That Tamsin should accompany them to their new home was a foregone conclusion; indeed, it would not have seemed like home without her.

John Clare's Christmas present to the sisters, to whom he felt himself so deeply indebted, took the form of a pony and basket carriage. It was a luxury which they had denied themselves ever since the break in their fortunes, but with Vale View House let on a seven years' lease the need for their doing so no longer existed.

In the course of the winter Mrs. Tew was married, the man of her choice being none other than Dr. Mallory, the most popular of the Mapleford *medicos* . As

Lady Pell said, the affair was quite a little romance. It appeared that the canon's widow and the doctor had been in love with each other thirty years before when they were young folk living in quite a different part of the country. As is often the case, something had happened to separate them, and for a quarter of a century or more they had wholly lost touch of each other; so much so that for aught either of them knew the other might be dead. Chance, or accident, one day brought them together, and to their mutual surprise they discovered that the ashes on the altar of their early love which they had believed to be long extinct, still smouldered, and needed nothing but propinquity and favouring circumstances to fan them into a flame which one might pretty safely assume would expire only with life itself.

If the canon's widow believed--which she did firmly--that Dr. Mallory had lived unmarried all these years because he had never got over his early disappointment, it was a charming belief, and certainly the doctor himself would have been the last man to undeceive her.

Little now remains to be done save to furnish the reader with a few brief particulars of the after fortunes of sundry of the characters with one or more episodes of whose life-history the foregoing pages have been concerned.

First, then, as regards the Keymers, father and son.

With Launce Keymer it was the case of the trickster being tricked. Always on the lookout for a woman with money, he met and was introduced to a widow, still young and pretty, whose husband had died two years before, leaving her a fortune of twenty-five thousand pounds. After having obtained a copy of the late Mr. Witley's will from Somerset House, and so satisfied himself as to the genuineness of the bequest, Keymer proposed and was accepted. Not till after his marriage did he discover that nearly the whole of his wife's fortune had been swallowed up in a huge banking failure which had occurred only a few weeks prior to his introduction to her. So extreme was his disgust and disappointment that, after having scraped together every shilling he could lay hands on, he quietly levanted, presumably to the land of the stars and stripes, and his newly married wife saw him no more.

Of Mr. Keymer, senior, it is enough to state that, partly as a consequence of his second wife's extravagance, which he was morally too weak to curb; partly owing to a growing neglect of his business, combined with, or the result of, an increasing fondness for the cup which, whether it cheers or no, does inebriate; and, lastly, because he found himself powerless to compete against the new brewery which a wealthy London syndicate had lately established in St. Oswyth's, he gradually drifted into the bankruptcy court, in the dreary morasses of which we will leave him floundering.

It was scarcely likely that Ethel, in her good fortune, should forget the existence of Miss Hetty Blair, the pretty nursery governess of Dulminster, who once on a time had rendered her such an important service. And when she heard that she was about to be married to a rising young lawyer of a distant town, a very substantial proof of her regard accompanied her wishes for her happiness and welfare.

Of Captain Verinder there is nothing pleasant to report. With such men as he it seems almost inevitable that as they advance in years their failings and vices should become accentuated, and that whatever virtues or good qualities they may originally have been possessed of, should grow "finer by degrees and beautifully less." In point of fact, the Captain began to deteriorate and go down-hill from the date of the collapse of his vile plot. He had built so much on it that its failure thoroughly disheartened him, and afterwards he scarcely seemed to care what became of him. His end was a sad one even for such as he. His body was fished out of the river-ooze down Deptford way. An ugly wound at the back of his head and his turned-out pockets told unequivocally how he had come by his death.

Everything was done that could be done both by John Clare and Everard Lisle in the way of benefiting Luigi Rispani and furnishing him with the opportunity of earning an honourable livelihood, but to no purpose. By means of certain influence which was brought to bear, three different situations were obtained for him, not one of which he kept longer than a month or two. Simply to give him money from time to time was merely helping to demoralise him still further. At length a situation was found for him as drawing-master in a college of his mother's sunny clime, and though he would never reach fame or fortune, aware that he had now only his own endeavours to trust to, he managed to keep his head above water, and earn a very modest livelihood.

Kirby Griggs, to whom, in one sense, John Clare felt that he owed so much, was not forgotten by him. For the man himself he could do nothing, but he succeeded in placing two of his sons with excellent City firms, and, by finding the requisite premium, in having one of his daughters, who had a natural gift that way, apprenticed to one of the best-known milliners at the West End.

In the course of the winter the marble tablet, which had been put up in the church of St. Michael to the memory of John Alexander Clare, was quietly removed.

When at length Sir Gilbert got back to the Chase, it was declared by everybody who saw him that he seemed to have taken a fresh lease of life. And so indeed he had, for when a man's constitution has nothing radically amiss with it, happiness undoubtedly helps to lengthen our days, and Sir Gilbert had now everything to render him happy. The MS. of his County History, so long laid aside, was enthusiastically taken in hand again as soon as his grandson-in-law returned from his honeymoon, and in the course of the following winter was brought to a triumphant conclusion. The title-page records that it is the joint production of "Sir Gilbert Clare, Bart., and Everard Lisle Clare," for before the marriage took place Sir Gilbert insisted upon the young man taking out letters-patent authorising him to add to his own name the surname of the ancient and honourable family of which he was about to become a member.

During the years of his expatriation, John Clare had devoted much of his spare time to experimental physics. It is a study which exercises a potent charm over such of its votaries as venture beyond the threshold of its temple of severe delights, and in the laboratory, which John caused to be fitted up at the Chase, he spent many happy hours in the effort to master those more abstruse secrets, and to arrive at a more correct knowledge of those subtler elements of the material universe, than the conditions of his life had heretofore allowed of his doing.

A few parting words are due to Lady Pell. As soon as the wedding was over she set out to pay a long-deferred round of visits, but by the middle of autumn she was back at the Chase, which henceforward was *de facto* her home. It was not to be expected that her restless proclivities would quite desert her, and occasionally she would start off at an hour's notice, or no notice at all, for some place a couple of hundred miles away, but always to come back with increasing satisfaction, as time went on, to the old roof-tree, under whose shadow, the romance of her life had had its beginning and its end.

Of Ethel and Everard what can be said in conclusion save that theirs was the quiet happiness of well-ordered lives, of duties conscientiously performed, and of unselfish devotion to the well-being of others? In such a soil the sweet flower of content blooms perennially and changes not with the seasons as they come and go.

CPSIA information can be obtained
at www.ICGtesting.com
Printed in the USA
BVHW071541140119
537775BV00006B/301/P

9 780464 763796